PRAISE FOR CH...

POPPING

"A delight to read—don't miss it!" —Heather Graham

"A frothy romantic confection . . . energetic prose and snappy dialogue." —*Publishers Weekly*

MAD ABOUT MADDIE

"A cute, funny story . . . Cheryl Anne Porter makes a great splash with her first single title, contemporary release."
—*Interludes*

"Filled with humor and sexual tension . . . *Mad About Maddie* is a quirky love story that will make readers smile."
—*Writers Club Romance*

"Porter is better known for her historical romance, but readers will be delighted with her humorous take on modern-day romance . . . Guaranteed to have the reader laughing."
—Romancereviewstoday.com

"Readers will be mad about Cheryl Anne Porter's delectably humorous contemporary romance."
—*Reviewers Book Watch*

CAPTIVE ANGEL

"Porter keeps readers on the edge of their seats."
—*Publishers Weekly*

"What a tour de force. *Captive Angel* grips you from the get-go (first page) and never lets go. Cheryl Anne Porter at the top of her form. This is a top-notch romance; not to be missed."

—*Romantic Times*

ST. MARTIN'S PAPERBACKS TITLES
BY CHERYL ANNE PORTER

TO MAKE A MARRIAGE

CHERYL ANNE PORTER

St. Martin's Paperbacks

TO MAKE A MARRIAGE

Copyright © 2004 by Cheryl Anne Porter.

ISBN: 0-312-98281-X

Printed in the United States of America

St. Martin's Paperbacks edition / January 2004

St. Martin's Paperbacks are published by St. Martin's Press, 175 Fifth Avenue, New York, NY 10010.

10 9 8 7 6 5 4 3 2 1

To Donna Pierson, fan and friend extraordinaire.

CHAPTER 1

Wetherington's Point, August 1875
The Midlands, England's heartland

"I am with child." The four words, Victoria knew, damned her. Like hangmen's nooses draped over a gallows, they hung suspended in the air between her and her visibly stunned husband. Tears of shame pricked Victoria's eyes and belied the defiant set of her chin. She—the young Duchess of Moreland, Her Grace Victoria Sofia Redmond Whitfield, a reluctant newlywed wife from Savannah, Georgia—stood ramrod straight in front of the duke, an Englishman little more than a stranger to her.

He—John Spencer Whitfield, the tenth Duke of Moreland—sat enthroned on a sky-blue silk-upholstered chair in the staggeringly grand south parlor on the first floor of his impressive ancestral country estate. He glared at her, as unyielding as if he'd been cut from the same marble that paved the floor. The look on his face plainly told her he would have been happier to learn of an outbreak of cholera in his household than he was with her news. "I should be elated by this . . . revelation," he said, "but of course I am not."

"No, Your Grace, I didn't suppose you would be." When

his granite countenance became too much for her, Victoria shifted her gaze mere inches to his right, to a vase of flowers on the table next to him. She could hardly blame him for being angry, if *angry* was a strong enough word for what he might be feeling. Whatever the emotion was, he had every right to it, she knew that—just as she knew that her news could not have come at a worse moment for them as a couple.

It was so unfair. Just as they were finding some common ground together, a way to be content, if not happy. And then . . . this. Without a doubt, something between them had died with her announcement. She had actually felt it. Had it been hope for their future? Perhaps. Trust? Certainly gone. Respect? Gone, also.

Victoria chanced a quick glance, under cover of her lashes, at her husband. With jet-black hair and smoldering eyes to match, he was certainly handsome and possessed the wonderfully fit physique of a man of athletic pursuits. But beyond his physical attributes—and they were many—he also owned qualities of personality she respected . . . but from afar. He was a man of his word. Responsible. Honest. He was stern and patrician, yes, but that was his heritage and his upbringing. Even so, she wished he would smile more. Laugh more. She was never sure if he was happy, or if such a thing mattered to him.

How was it, then, that she always seemed to want more from him, or of him, than he could or would give her? Confusing her was the realization that she couldn't even say why she hungered for this elusive something from him. She didn't love him. But what did she really know of love? She knew of seduction and betrayal. But not love. She knew also of guilt and remorse, both of which urged her to run to him now and throw her arms around his neck and tell him how very, very sorry she was. But she and he did not have the sort of relationship where such a gesture could heal, much less be wanted. But even had they, he'd hardly welcome that from her at this moment. And maybe never, after this.

Again she tore her gaze from his, casting it over to the French doors, which were thrown open to capture the sweet-scented breeze blowing in from the formal gardens with their neat rows of shrubs and exuberantly blooming flowers. With birds singing their encouragement, with bees and butterflies flitting industriously from one nectar-laden flower to the next, the August afternoon spilled in through the open doors and beckoned to Victoria's senses.

"Are you contemplating fleeing, Victoria?"

Though she started at the deep, rumbling timbre of her husband's voice, she managed to reply evenly. "No, Your Grace. Should I be?"

"That would be most unwise," he said quietly and with complete authority.

Swallowing hard, twisting her lace hanky into knots, Victoria feared she would be burned to a cinder by the blazing contempt directed her way from him. He slowly arched an eyebrow, reminding her of a dark angel. Handsome. Dangerous. Unknowable. Irresistible. "You're certain, then? You are with child?"

To hear her shame spoken aloud by him weighed Victoria down with guilt. Though she felt as if a slab of limestone had fallen on her and was crushing her, she exerted an intense effort of will and found the strength to respond. "Yes, I am. I'm . . . certain I'm with child."

He had every right to ask, *Whose child?* But all he said was: "I see."

The duke, this man to whom she had been quickly wed, following a scandal in Savannah, soberly studied her with those intent black eyes of his, which seemed to bore deep into her secret shame. "How long have you known this, Victoria?"

She knew why he asked. He meant had she known of her delicate condition before their marriage? "I've only just realized it, Your Grace."

"My name is Spencer."

"I recall."

"I am your husband."

"I recall that as well, Your Grace."

He exhaled a breath laden with exasperation. "And so you will call me Spencer when we are alone."

"Yes, Your Gra—I beg your pardon. Spencer." She had trouble thinking of him by his Christian name. He was such a very formal person . . . and a daunting one. Victoria didn't mind admitting that his title, though she also now owned a similar one, intimidated her as well. She half feared he could, by law, have her beheaded or locked away in a tower, should she displease him in any way. And certainly, this bit of news had not pleased him.

"I suppose," he was saying, "I should commend you for telling me so promptly. Not many women would have, under these circumstances. They would have kept their secret as long as possible to make their husbands believe the child was his."

Though her heart knocked against her ribs, Victoria forced the same casual note into her voice that his held. "But the child could very well be yours."

He nodded. "Or it could not."

It was like being in the room with a hungry raptor. Victoria heard herself talking on out of nervousness. "I will admit I contemplated not telling you yet, but in the end, I had no wish to make matters worse by delaying this news. I realized you would have known soon enough, anyway."

"Yes, I suppose I would have done." He cocked his head at a considering angle and roved his gaze over her person.

Victoria had all she could do not to squirm as he blatantly searched for any discernible physical changes that went along with her condition. She could have told him, had he simply asked, they were nonexistent, really. But he hadn't asked. Instead, he chose this silent and probing scrutiny of her. If his intent was to humiliate her, he was succeeding admirably.

"Given the time frame, Victoria, this certainly complicates matters, to put it mildly."

"Yes. Complicated on more than one level, Your Grace."

"How do you mean?"

"I'll be its mother, the poor little creature. It will surely start screaming the moment it realizes that."

She couldn't be certain but she thought she'd almost made him laugh. He quickly rubbed his fingers over his mouth, shifted his position in his chair, and frowned sternly. "Yes, well, you'll have a nanny and a nurse to help you. But surely you know something about babies. You are, after all, a woman."

"Oh, no, sir, that has nothing to do with it. No more than your being male causes you to instantly know all about horses. Truly, I don't know the first thing, except what I've observed."

There was a definite creasing of the skin at the corners of his eyes as he watched her. Was it humor? Did she amuse him? "And what have you observed, Victoria?"

"Mostly that infants are limp little beings who are wet and loud at both ends, Your Grace, and sometimes simultaneously." She grimaced and shook her head at the horror of it all. "Very daunting."

He nodded his agreement. "This entire situation is a bit daunting."

"Yes, Your Grace." Chastened, Victoria lowered her gaze to her shoes, but her thoughts were with the tiny, fragile little life she carried inside her. She was going to have a baby—a helpless mite whose father its mother could not name with any certainty. How could this have happened? But she knew. She saw, in her mind's eye, herself in Savannah, before her marriage, that night in her bedroom when *he'd* come in—*No. It can't be his. It just can't.* But it very well could be, and well she . . . and her husband . . . knew it.

Unexpectedly, emotion welled up inside Victoria, pushing reticence aside and propelling her a step closer to him. "I swear to you, if I could make this not be true, I would do so. I would. But I cannot, and for that I am so very sorry."

He slumped in his chair and rubbed tiredly at his forehead. "Of course there are ways we could . . . *solve* this dilemma, or make it not true, as you said. But we dare not resort to them."

Puzzlement brought a frown to Victoria's face. "What do you mean? I don't understand."

"Yes you do. End the pregnancy. Don't look so naïve or shocked, Victoria. There are ways. But we cannot consider it because the truth is as you said: The child could be mine. And the dangers involved for you are too great. The end result could be you may not be able to have another, should something go wrong, and that would leave me without an heir. And perhaps a wife, as well."

Though he'd spoken as if in great pain emotionally, Victoria stared in horror at her husband as realization swept over her. "You mean an . . . abortion?"

"Yes. Didn't you?"

"No! Never. I meant I wish I could make what happened to me in Savannah not true. That's all. I never wished for an end to my baby." As though physically threatened, she gripped her skirts and moved away from him. "Never. No. I won't do it."

He held a hand out to stop her retreat. "No one is asking you to undergo such a thing, Victoria. I simply expounded on what I thought you to be saying."

She stood her ground, her chin high. "Well, then . . . good. Because I would never consent to such a thing."

His black eyes bored into hers. He didn't have to say it. She knew what he was thinking: She could protest all she wished. Had he insisted, he could have forced her to undergo the hideous procedure. His will, had it been different from hers, would have prevailed. Never in her life had she felt so much like a possession to be treasured or disposed of at the whim of her husband—a man who had taken her to wife and taken her to his bed, as was his right. Despite the heat and the power of her husband's lovemaking, he'd only been performing his duty with her. That was Victoria's belief, and he had never given her reason to believe otherwise. He had offered no protestations of love, no endearments, no statement of want or need.

"How long have you had symptoms?"

"Symptoms?"

"For the love of God, woman. Yes, Victoria. Symptoms. I am trying to ascertain, by the length of time you've had symptoms, exactly whose child this is."

His tone of voice, low and angry, could have been hands wrapped around her throat and squeezing hard. Victoria could produce no more than a whisper. "The child I carry is exactly *mine,* Your Grace."

His dangerously narrowed eyes met her words. "How grand it would be if only that were all that mattered."

There was nothing she could say. This predicament she found herself in was, by society's and the church's dictates, one of her own making, despite the involvement of two men. Victoria lowered her gaze and stared hotly at the lovely rose pattern woven into the thick Aubusson carpet under her feet and thought how unfair it all was.

"Victoria, do me the courtesy of looking at me, please." It was a quiet command she obeyed, one that showed her an impatient glint in her husband's eyes. "I asked you how long you've been experiencing symptoms. And I mean exactly. To the day."

"It's very hard to pin down—"

"Try."

"I—I am trying, Your Grace. Truly, I am. I do not—"

"I will *not* tell you again to address me as Spencer."

Flustered now, Victoria gestured with her hanky. "I'm sorry. I am trying. But, you will forgive me, I find myself hard-pressed, sir, to think of you in intimate terms."

Clearly offended, he looked down his aristocratic nose at her. "I beg your pardon, madam? We could not *be* on more intimate terms."

He meant the bedroom, of course. Victoria felt the flush of embarrassment on her cheeks as she looked away. She wanted so much to tell him that her bed was the only place where he shed more than his clothes, where he allowed her to know anything at all about him. Throughout the course of their days, he behaved as if their nights together had never happened. He treated her like a pretty bird in a gilded cage. She could barely stand it. With that acknowledgment came anger and courage. "Yes, we are intimate," she said, looking into his eyes, "but not in any way that matters. You care nothing for me."

Her husband's grip on his chair's arms visibly tightened. "Do not presume to tell me what or how I feel, Victoria."

"But I speak the truth. You care only for the wealth I brought to your coffers when you married me. That, and my tinge of royal Russian blood with which you mean to enrich your bloodlines."

He slowly sat forward. "And have you, Victoria? Have you enriched my bloodlines with that royal Russian blood? That's exactly what I'm trying to ascertain here. And since you're in a mood for truth, madam, tell me: When did you *really* realize you were with child?"

He was calling her a liar. Outraged, Victoria held her head high. "Only this morning. I have had symptoms for weeks, I admit. But I had no idea what could be the matter with me. Then, earlier, Rosanna brought it to my attention—"

"Who the devil is Rosanna?"

"My lady's maid."

"Yes, of course. Rose. Go on."

It was *Rosanna,* but Victoria chose not to correct him. "As you wish. I had attributed my tiredness and the bouts of illness, as well as my lack of . . ." A furious heat worked its way up her cheeks. One simply did not speak of such things, not even with one's husband—and certainly not in broad daylight and in the parlor.

Spencer waggled a hand at her impatiently. "Yes? Come on, your lack of what?"

"My monthly ills," she blurted, humiliated beyond belief.

But all her husband did was nod. "Ah. And how many have you missed?"

She wanted both to cry and strike out at him for putting her through this awful interrogation. Had he no sensibilities? "I have missed my second one."

"Well, that certainly doesn't clarify anything, does it?" His glare slowly bled into a thoughtful expression as he cocked his head and considered her. "I begin to believe you truly had no idea. What an appalling situation it is that you well-bred young ladies are told nothing of those things that are most important for you to know."

He made it sound as if she were stupid somehow. "I don't know that I agree with your assessment, sir."

He raised an eyebrow. "It is not required that you do."

Arrogant man. Victoria gritted her teeth against the urge to respond in kind. Looking for something about him to hate, she roved her gaze over his face—his undeniably strong and ruggedly handsome face, replete with sculpted masculine planes and hollows that boasted a high forehead and cheekbones, an aquiline nose, stubborn jaw, and generous mouth. To her consternation, she found nothing.

"How many weeks have we been married, Victoria?"

He knew. He just wanted her to have to say. "Nearly eight. Which makes it entirely possible that this baby I carry could be yours."

Although he nodded, he said, "Or it might not be, and nothing but absolute certainty is all that will do."

"I understand that. But how does one decide absolute certainty, Your Grace? Given that we—you and I—look nothing alike, and the baby could resemble me with reddish-brown hair and blue eyes, I don't see how—"

"Oh, but I do." His slashing scimitar of a grin would have made a pirate proud. "Every true Whitfield has the same birthmark."

"Birthmark?" Victoria's expression crimped into one of puzzlement. "But I've never seen . . ." She mentally, furiously, explored what little bit she'd seen of her husband's naked body. Though they'd shared passion, he'd always come to her at night when her room was darkened—

"It's there, Victoria. I have it."

His knowing smirk irritated her further. "I shall take your word for it, sir."

"Would that I could take your word so easily, madam. However, I have a sacred duty to the six hundred years of Whitfields who came before me, as well as to those who will follow me, to protect my title and my holdings through untainted bloodlines. So I must know, and without the first measure of doubt, that the male child who bears my name is indeed my son."

"I could be carrying a female child."

"I am aware of that. If so, we'll . . . try again for a male to inherit the title." He roved his gaze up and down her body in a clearly suggestive way. "And *that* child I will know is mine."

Instant images of tangled covers and passionate moans assailed Victoria. Fighting her body's tingling, tightening response, she raised her chin, determined to ask the one question that meant everything to her. "What will happen should this baby, male or female, I carry now . . . prove not to be yours?"

His expression hardened. "It will not bear my name."

Somewhere, deep in her heart, she'd known he would say that. Still, the shock of hearing the words nearly sent Victoria to the floor. A hand pressed against her mouth to prevent a cry of protest, she stared at the man who would label her child a bastard. He had condemned it, male or female, to a life of being ignored, of being pushed aside, all because of the accident of its conception. And the child, should it be male, would be passed over for the title and the duchy . . . and would come to hate her, his mother, when he was old enough to realize all that had been denied him.

As Victoria's fledgling-mother's heart constricted with pain, she lowered her hand to her side and spoke with quiet passion. "No. You will do no such thing."

He pulled back, clearly surprised. "I beg your pardon. You do not dictate terms to me—"

"In this instance I do, and you will listen to me." Victoria's heart pounded, forcing her to breathe in gasping breaths. "Understand that I will stand here and allow you to heap scorn on me. I have no choice, given my . . . my recent past. I might even deserve it. Certainly, I shamed my family, and I will live with that for the rest of my life. But what I did *not* do was shame you in any way. So you may act as injured as you choose—"

" 'Act as injured'? You think I'm merely acting?" With a tense leonine grace, the duke rose smoothly to his feet and slowly advanced on her. "Perhaps, Victoria, you should consider not saying anything else."

Though she backed up, her hands fisted, she continued with her tirade. "And yet I will. I find I have more to say, and you will hear me out, sir."

When he stopped, his chin lowered, his black eyes sparking fire, Victoria stood her ground, as well. Her husband crossed his arms over his chest. "I see. Then have your say, madam."

"I will." Victoria had never been this afraid—or this determined. "No matter what you might think, I had no idea when I came to your bed on our wedding night that I might be carrying another man's child. None. And I still do not know that it's true. The very likelihood is this child is yours as much as it is mine. And birthmark or no, rest assured, sir, you will not cruelly label this child a bastard because I will swear all day long and to whomever I must that this child is yours, and I will hold you accountable for its future. I have done many things for which I am sorry, but the one thing, *Your Grace,* I will not do is shame my baby by saying I am sorry for having it."

Her husband's lightning-swift movement caught Victoria off guard. Before she could even draw in her next breath, he had her arms pinned in a painful grip and had jerked her to him. "You think hearing you say you're sorry is what I want?"

Victoria's heart thumped so wildly she expected it to jump right out of her chest, but she could not stop her intemperate tongue. "I have no idea what you want because I don't know you in any way that matters. But one thing we both know is how much you knew about me when you married me. You knew I had no claim to innocence—"

"Yes, I knew. And my reasons for marrying you were no more noble than your father's were for marrying you to me. And yes, money exchanged hands. And yes, I now control it and you—"

"Oh, you are sorely mistaken, sir. I have my very large allowance as determined by our marriage contract. And I will do as I please. No man controls me."

"You think not? Whose bed were you in last night? And whose ring is that on your finger?" His grip on her arms tightened as he yanked her even closer to his face. Filling Victoria's vision was the sight of his black and glittering eyes. "Whose name is it you now bear, Victoria?"

"It doesn't matter. If you disown this child I carry now, there will be no others, Your Grace, I swear to you. I will do whatever I have to do to prevent it. I will see to it that no Whitfield heir will come from me—"

"Allow me to grant your wish, madam. When your child is born, if he or she is not a Whitfield, I will be sending both of you back to your father with your divorce papers in your hand. Raising another man's bastard was not a part of our bargain."

"How dare you!" Victoria raged, struggling wildly in his grasp. If she could just gain a free hand, she would slap his face until it bled. But her efforts bore no fruit. Spencer Whitfield easily held her prisoner.

"Be still," he warned, "and listen to me." He waited, glaring daggers at her. With no choice, with her face hot and damp with emotion, she stilled in his embrace, a mockery of a tender prelude to a kiss. "Until this child is born," he said sternly, "I will give you the benefit of my doubt and treat you with the courtesy and respect due you as my duchess. But that is all, and even that I will do from a goodly distance."

Dread washed over Victoria, causing her to forget her physical pain as she envisioned imprisoning towers. "What are you saying? Where are you sending me?"

His smile, so close to her face, to her mouth, was a slash of angry decision. "I'm sending you nowhere. In fact, you will go nowhere. You will, instead, remain here in the country while I reside in London—"

"But you can't leave me alone out here in the Midlands—"

"I assure you I can, and I will."

"But I know no one. I don't know what to do—"

"That much is evident, madam. All your spoiled life, you've had to do nothing except demand. Allow me to assure you that those days of getting your way in everything are gone." With that, he put her away from him.

Victoria caught herself by gripping a chair's curved back. With a hand fisted tightly around her lace hanky, she was aware only of horrible shock as she listened to her husband pronouncing her sentence.

"Between now and the time the child is born, all of Wetherington Point's assets are at your disposal. Too, I shall have a doctor look in on you. He will be instructed to send me reports of your progress. But should you have a need, for whatever reason, to communicate with me, you will do so through my solicitor."

Victoria could barely make sense of all he'd said. She

was a Southern miss and he was a British peer. They had nothing in common, except a marriage neither of them had wanted yet both of them had desperately needed. But what was she to do now? Then, unbidden, something deep inside her turned. She felt her initial horror steadily congealing into an icy disdain that had her raising her chin. "So I'm never to see you again, is that it?"

He raised an eyebrow. "Hardly. But would you care if you did or not?"

"No." She refused even to blink. "Not in the least."

Her husband made a mocking, chuckling sound. "Sorry to disappoint you, but I will return when I am notified it is time for the birthing. And then, my dear, we shall see. We shall see."

Victoria tried very hard to hang on to the cold inside her that stiffened her spine and held her erect. Was this, then, to be her life? A loveless marriage? Alone in a foreign country with a child who could claim no heritage? Suddenly, the years seemed to stretch into eternity—and it was too awful to bear.

"I hate you!" she shouted, startling her husband as much as she did herself. "I do—I hate you, and I'm sorry I married you. I'm also every bit as sorry you were made to marry me. But what's done is done. You can think me the worst person in the world, but I'm not—not in my heart. I am not a wanton. In my innocence, I believed a man's pretty words—"

"That is quite enough." Her husband pointed a warning finger her way. "Believe me, Victoria, I will not listen to—"

"Don't you 'Victoria' me." Lost to reason and caution, she batted his hand away. "You may rest assured that I feel every bit as trapped as you must. Neither one of us wanted this marriage."

"Well said, madam." Her husband again crossed his arms over his chest—and gave Victoria the impression that he waited for her to step over some imaginary line he'd drawn. When she did, he would pounce.

Even realizing that, the words poured forth from her. "You are not the one so far away from home and family and friends. And you are not the one who is sick every day and tired all the time because you are going to have a baby. *I am*. And you are not the one who is scared to death. *I am*." Her fears got the better of her. She took a deep, ragged breath and bleated out a pathetic sob. "I hate it here, and I want to go home to my mother!"

Her hands fisted at her sides, Victoria watched Spencer open his mouth to speak, but then close it. He stood there, staring at her, seeming suddenly to be more at a loss than he was angry. Victoria glared at him, naming him the source of all her problems. Even if her parents did think of him as their savior because he, an impoverished nobleman, had married her, a fallen woman in the eyes of Savannah society, she didn't feel the least bit grateful to him or even think she should.

Finally, the duke spoke . . . slowly, softly: "I wish—fervently so—Victoria, that you *could* be with your mother. Believe me, I do. But that's not possible."

"Why isn't it?" She hiccuped softly, quickly covering her mouth with her hanky, then using it to dab at her tears.

"Because . . ." His voice trailed off as he looked around him, apparently searching for something. He pointed to the chair in which he'd been seated. "Would you like to sit down?"

His solicitousness caught Victoria off guard. Actually, she would have liked nothing better than to sit down, but she refused to accept any kindnesses from him. "No."

Spencer raised his eyebrows. "No? I see. Would you like a drink of water, maybe? Or some tea? Something stronger?"

He was being so nice and polite. Victoria decided she should have screamed at him a long time ago. "No. But please help yourself."

He smiled briefly, uncertainly. "Thank you. I think I will."

This was the oddest exchange, she marveled, given all the

passionate shouting that had just transpired between them. She watched him turn and stalk toward the crystal liquor service set up on an ornate sideboard across the room. Once there, he stood with his back to her, his weight evenly distributed on his strong legs.

Though he'd held her roughly and had threatened divorce; though she had told him she would deny him her bed and an heir, Victoria could do nothing but rove her gaze up and down the solid, muscular length of her husband—

"Victoria," he said suddenly, speaking over his shoulder. She jerked her gaze up guiltily. The sound of crystal tinkling against crystal told her he was pouring himself a drink as he talked. "I'm sorry you feel so alone here. I confess I hadn't really thought about how strange everything must seem to you. Our customs—"

"And your food."

He pivoted to look fully into her face. "Our food?"

"Your cook boils everything."

"I see." He again turned to the sideboard but only long enough to stopper the decanter. When he turned back to her again, he had a brimming glass of whisky in his hand. "You have only to tell Mrs. Pike how you wish your food to be prepared and she will do so. You are, after all, the duchess here."

"I remember." What she didn't know was how long she would be the duchess here. But the weight of the huge sparkling diamond on her left ring finger was a constant reminder. In fact, she was ashamed of how often she stared at it and turned her hand this way and that to see it sparkle. It was so big it was unseemly . . . and beautiful.

"Good." Her husband approached her, holding out a hand to indicate a delicate divan. "Are you sure you won't sit down?"

Somehow it seemed all right to do so now. Besides, her knees felt watery. "I think I will."

As he approached the chair he'd been sitting in a moment

ago, Victoria surged forward and took it first, ignoring him and his stunted snort of protest as she arranged her voluminous skirt of forest-green silk becomingly about her legs and feet. Done with that, she turned innocent eyes up to her husband and watched as he, with a feline grace that she envied, settled himself on that nearby divan. Once he was comfortably seated, she said sweetly, "I believe, sir, that I do feel a thirst coming over me now. Do you suppose there might be some water over there?"

With practiced grace, she charmingly pointed to indicate the bar service at which Spencer had just busied himself. The man's eyes narrowed as he watched her over the rim of his whisky glass.

He took a healthy swig, held it in his mouth a moment, and then swallowed, wincing no doubt at its strength . . . all while staring long and hard at her. "I feel certain there is water there," he drawled at last. "You may feel free to help yourself to some."

If she vacated her seat, he would take it—and reclaim the victory. Victoria inhaled through the thin crevice of her parted lips, all while maintaining eye contact with her husband. She watched him as she would a wriggling water moccasin if she'd found herself in the water with it. "Never mind. I'm not thirsty."

She thought he fought a grin as he inclined his head in acknowledgment. "If you say so. Now, tell me, why do you wish to go to your mother?"

Because I'm pregnant and scared to death and very afraid to be alone here. But she would die first before she would say that again. "I've just . . . never been away from Savannah before. I miss it and everyone there."

"It's only natural that you would. However, and I am sorry for bringing up the unpleasantness again, your family does not wish you to be in Savannah any time soon. But even were that not so, I would not permit you to travel."

"May I ask why not?"

"It would be too dangerous."

"You mean the days on end bumping and rattling in the coaches? The possibility of highwaymen? Staying at the various and atrocious inns along the way? And then the Atlantic crossing on a tossing and churning steamship?"

"Yes, I do. You've made my point admirably."

"But I've only just survived all of that."

He nodded, sipping again at his measure of liquor. "But I was with you. And that was before I knew you were carrying a child who could possibly be my son and heir. A trip such as you've just described would be too dangerous."

"Then you won't allow me to go home?"

"This is your home now, and here you will stay."

Infuriating man. Too bad she didn't have the courage to pick up and hurl at him the small porcelain figurine within her reach on a side table. The satisfying mental picture of her doing exactly that would have to suffice. "Then I'm never to see my home again?"

"I do not like having to repeat myself. I have told you already that you will be staying right here until this child is born. If it should prove not to be a Whitfield, then you will get your wish. You will be returning to your mother for good."

Victoria stared at the arrogant male who was her husband . . . a tall, passionate, and handsome man of broad shoulders, jet-black hair, and eyes equally dark. "But I wish to go home now," she said quietly, stubbornly.

Her duke narrowed his eyes, the shine in them reminding her of the predatory gleam of a leopard. "You may wish all you like, but you do not dictate terms to me, madam. Though it may be a bitter pill for you to swallow, you are my wife, and you will travel only as I see fit. Do we understand each other?"

Victoria locked her gaze with her husband's. "Yes. We do."

CHAPTER 2

England, later in August 1875

An elegant though road-dusty traveling coach bearing the Whitfield coat of arms labored around the rolling green hills of the Midlands area of England. Inside the plush cabin, the Right Honorable—and very hungover—Earl of Roxley, Edward Sparrow, a blastedly cheerful and randy cousin of Spencer's, remarked: "I say, Spence, old man, I quite look forward to seeing your charming wife again."

Seated opposite his cousin and peering out a small, square-cut side window, which was open like the others to allow for airflow through the coach, Spencer absently watched the passing landscape and just as absently replied to his cousin. "That makes one of us, then."

"Oh, come now, certainly it's all the rage to pretend one did not make a love match and that one isn't in love with one's wife, but yours is an especially lovely woman. And I was being honest when I said I look forward to seeing her. She's as witty and charming as she is pleasing to look at. And I do love to hear her talk; that lovely Southern drawl of hers could charm a wild boar—perhaps even you—into purring. So, admit it, you want to see her."

Exasperation had Spencer frowning at Edward, a slender man with thick brown hair and merry, though bloodshot, brown eyes. The younger man held on to the hand strap to steady himself in the gently rocking enclosed cabin and stared back at Spencer, who said: "What makes you think that?"

"Good Lord, dear fellow, we've been on the road from London for nearly two hell-bent days now, destination Wetherington's Point. Are you going to tell me this trip was my idea?"

"Hardly."

Edward's expression crumpled to confused. "Will you at least tell me *why* we are on this trip?"

Spencer fought the urge—only because he knew first-hand the effects of a hangover and could sympathize—to reach over and cuff his cousin. "Had you been sober when we left London, you would know why we are."

"Well, I'm sober now. Frightfully so. Therefore, please tell me why we're in this coach and out in the hellish countryside with that obnoxious sunshine." Edward held a hand up between it and his eyes. "Has it always been that bright?"

Spencer chuckled. "Yes. And it has taken you two days to ask me, Edward."

The earl crimped his lips together. "I occasionally suffer from a singular lack of curiosity. One of my many faults. Now, are you going to enlighten me or not?"

"Certainly. We travel to Wetherington's Point at the request of my overseer."

Edward squinted and frowned. "Your overseer requested my presence at your country house? I find that hard to believe."

"Of course he didn't, dolt. He asked *me* to come. Actions and decisions only I can make in person, that sort of thing."

"Oh, lovely," Edward groaned. "Nothing to do with a peasant uprising involving pitchforks and torches, I hope?"

Spencer shrugged. "Not so far. But they are in a tiff over

some boundaries and fences and escaping cattle. Threats have been made."

"And what exactly am I supposed to do? Help you fight them off?"

"Hardly. You're along, my dear fellow, to get you away from the gaming tables."

"But I was winning."

Spencer shrugged. "For once, but not by very much."

"By enough." Edward leaned forward to tap Spencer on the knee. "You just want to see her, don't you?"

"I do not, and stop saying that."

Undaunted, a smug grin riding his features, Edward sat back. "You want to see her."

"If you say that one more time," Spencer warned, "I will be forced to throttle you." When his cousin only laughed, Spencer added: "You think every man feels the way you do because you do not have a wife of your own and so you look forward to *seeing* every other man's wife."

His brown eyes widening with clearly feigned shock, Edward clamped a hand to his chest, over his heart, and slumped on the narrow leather seat across from Spencer's. "I am wounded, sir, and the various ladies are insulted." He immediately abandoned his pose and sat up, his expression prim. "And I do not look forward to seeing all the wives, mind you. Only the young, pretty, and ignored ones."

Forcing from his mind an image of his own wife, who fit all three categories, Spencer said: "You'll be shot dead by a jealous husband one day."

Edward wrinkled his nose and tossed away Spencer's judgment with a flick of his wrist. "He'll have to catch me first."

"And he will." Though he had remarked in a dry, teasing vein, surprising Spencer was how quickly jealousy and possessiveness had swelled in his heart at simply hearing another man, even his cousin, remark on his wife. He supposed his reaction was only natural, though. No matter her transgressions, Victoria was the Duchess of Moreland. Her title, if nothing else, deserved a show of respect and should not be sullied by scandal. Further scandal.

Dismissing, with effort, thoughts of his wife, Spencer focused on his cousin, a man five years his junior and the oldest son of Spencer's mother's younger brother. Infuriatingly enough, Edward was a man who found all of life to be good and everyone in it wonderful. An awful attitude for a twenty-eight-year-old peer of the realm to have. "How is it, Edward, that your mother has not long since married you off and seen you happily siring her grandchildren?"

Edward ducked his chin and arched an eyebrow. "How do you know for a fact that I have not done so already?"

"You're not going to tell me you've fallen in love?"

"But I have. Every day and every time I see a pretty woman—"

"That is not love. It is lust, dear fellow."

Edward feigned confusion. "Oh. I suppose it is. But to what I was referring earlier was not love and marriage, but the siring of children. My question was: How do you know I have not been off and happily doing just that?"

"No doubt you have." Spencer once again peered out the window to his left. This conversation was damned close to his very real situation with his wife. What had he been thinking to drag Edward along with him to Wetherington's Point? Why was he even—

"Tell me if I'm out of line, Spence, but are you and your new wife estranged?"

With the sound of the horses' jingling tack and their hooves pounding the dusty road serving as a backdrop, Spencer turned to look into his cousin's for-once sincere and concerned eyes. "You are out of line."

Edward sighed. "Then I'm right; you are estranged."

"What we are, or are not, is none of your business, Edward."

"But it is." Edward's expression was deadly serious—and

affectionate. "We share a close kinship, Spencer. You're like a brother to me, so it wounds me to hear the gossip among the ton."

Spencer sat up rigidly. "What are they saying?"

"What else? How you two seemed inseparable when she was introduced at court, but then suddenly she's not been seen at all." Edward leaned forward and spoke conspiratorially. "You can tell me, old man, but you haven't killed her, have you?"

"Don't be a fool. Of course I haven't. But, damn it, Edward, I can't spend every waking minute—"

"You spend no waking minutes with her, and you hide her away." When Spencer narrowed his eyes in warning, Edward added: "I'm telling you only what I hear."

"What else do you hear?"

"How you ignore your fabulously beautiful and wealthy American-heiress wife. Do I really have to tell you how it raises suspicions among those with nothing else to occupy their time except the ruination of others' reputations? You know that set, Spencer. Victoria's sudden absence, following her dazzling debut, and your now being alone in London, not even during the season, is wagging every tongue."

Spencer hit his thigh with his fist. "Damn them. Is nothing sacred? Can a man have no privacy?"

"I'm afraid not—and it's your fault, old man."

Spencer frowned at Edward's grinning expression. "Mine? How the bloody damned devil so?"

"You introduce your charming new wife around; let it be known she has royal Russian blood, causing increased interest in her; make a mad dash of all the balls and dinners; she charms the prince; and then . . . nothing. She disappears, evidently consigned to the country. What else is all of London supposed to think?"

"I don't give a damn what London thinks."

"And me? Do you care what I think?"

Spencer stared at his favorite cousin, wondering if or how

much he should confide in him. Edward was a gadabout, true, but he was loyal and could keep a secret. He was also a good friend. Then Spencer realized that Edward would soon enough see for himself, once they arrived at his country estate, the truth of how strained Spencer's relationship with his wife was.

"Well?" Edward prodded. "My feelings are beginning to be hurt."

Spencer made up his mind and forced himself to speak as dispassionately as possible. "My wife and I are perhaps more than estranged."

Looking instantly stricken, Edward said: "Then it's true. Good heavens, Spencer, I really had no idea—"

"No need for sympathy. All I will tell you is I knew—or thought I knew—what I was getting into when I took Victoria to wife. But I found out it was much worse than I thought. Two weeks ago, the truth came out and we quarreled. I left, saying I would not be back until . . . well, any time soon."

"How awful. May I ask what truth was revealed?"

"You may ask all you want, but I will not answer you."

Edward was undaunted. "As bad as all that? I see. Well, then, I believe I can look forward to a good and bloody battle while at Wetherington's Point. I have always loved a good and bloody battle, whether it be of words, wills, or swords."

Spencer made a sound of self-deprecation. "I think I can promise you two out of three, then."

"Care to say which two?"

Spencer smiled. "No."

Several more miles on the long trip had passed in silence between the two men. Spencer gazed out over the familiar passing landscape . . . green and rolling hills, thousands of forested acres, fertile farmland and quaint villages tucked around almost every turn in the road. Every acre of land, as far as the eye could see, belonged to him and gave him daily headaches. Speaking of headaches, he spared a thought for the occupants of the two less grand vehicles following his, which also belonged to him. The rear wagon held all the necessary baggage for this long trip from London. And the second carriage, the one just behind his coach, carried his valet and secretary, Hornsby and Mr. Milton, respectively. Spencer wondered if they'd killed each other yet.

Suddenly, with Spencer's next breath, gone were thoughts of his bickering staff, because there it was, brought into magnificent view as the coach rounded a bend in the dusty road. Wetherington's Point—the magnificent and stately countryseat of his family's ancestral holdings in the Midlands. Though he loved this land, though it owned a part of his very soul, as did the manor house perched like a crown jewel between two green hills, today he took no joy in seeing its nearness. With disquiet marring his handsome features, Spencer stared out the window at the rapidly approaching manor house.

Just then, the coaches pulled into the graveled drive and slowed, finally stopping smoothly at the impressive front doors of the estate. Footmen appeared to attend to the various duties of welcoming the master and his guest home. *Welcome, indeed.* Spencer knew one person here who would not be happy to see him. And he didn't blame her one damned bit as he'd behaved abominably toward her when last he'd been here. Spencer contemplated making an apology. Should he? Dare he? After all, if the baby was not his . . .

He had no time to finish that thought as he and Edward stepped down from his coach and into the wonderfully warm sunshine. Suddenly, he realized something here was terribly wrong. He looked around. The estate seemed in perfect condition as he had expected. But there was something else. Spencer tensed, realizing that only a funereal quiet, coupled with the sliding gazes of his footmen, greeted him.

Just then, Fredericks, an elderly stick of a wispy-haired man and trusted family retainer for more than forty years, emerged from the house and approached Spencer, stopping in front of him. When he did, the footmen fled, leaving Spencer and Edward alone with Fredericks, who dispensed with the pleasantries and said: "I am afraid I have some rather bad news to impart to you, sir. News best taken with a shot of your finest whisky."

Somehow, some way, Spencer knew it had to do with his wife. "I see. Then let's go inside, shall we?"

Tight-lipped, with fierce emotions roiling just under his skin, Spencer pivoted on his heel and proceeded inside. There, he stalked through the manor, with Edward on his heels and the butler desperately trying to keep up. Spencer closeted them—him, Edward, and the butler—in the familiarity and seclusion of his well-appointed study. He poured himself and the young earl equal measures of whisky and sat down on his worn-leather chair behind his massive desk. Edward discreetly sat down on a chair nearer the fireplace and across the room.

"I assure you, Fredericks," Spencer began, "that I am aware you are merely the messenger here. As such, I assign no blame to you. Now, that said, I want only to know one thing. Where is she?"

Fredericks, an ancient and revered relic whom Spencer had inherited upon his mother's death, stood at rickety attention in front of the carved mahogany desk. But Spencer's question had him abandoning his formal pose. Speaking on a wheezing exhalation, he said: "But how did you know it was regarding the duchess, Your Grace?"

"Oh, who else, Fredericks? She is the only one missing. Now, where is she? What has happened?" Though outwardly he sounded only perturbed at this news, inside Spencer's heart damned near pounded out of his chest with fear. He imagined all sorts of tragedies. A riding accident. A carriage turned over on her. Murder. Drowning in the lake.

"The duchess is . . . no longer with us, Your Grace."

Spencer's eyes rounded; he met Edward's gaze. His cousin shook his head and shrugged his shoulders, as if to say he had no clue, either. Spencer addressed his remarks to his butler. "We have established that, Fredericks. Are you trying *not* to tell me she died and was buried in my absence? I will find it extremely hard to believe that I was not notified in such a case."

"Oh, no, sir. Not at all, sir. Good heavens, no. I never meant to give you that impression. Indeed, I pray daily that the duchess continues to enjoy splendid health, Your Grace."

She will, but only until next I see her, was Spencer's thought. "I did send word to Mr. Dover that I would be arriving today from London. Was that message received by him and did he relay it to you?"

"Yes, Your Grace, he did, indeed. Your overseer is very diligent."

"Then . . . ?"

Fredericks suddenly would not meet Spencer's gaze. "I hope you find everything at Wetherington's Point to your satisfaction?"

"Yes. Quite." He knew the butler meant that the manor house had been thoroughly cleaned from top to bottom, the silver polished, the larder stocked, and the lawns groomed. Spencer cared not one jot for such preparations. "All very nice. Now, out with it, Fredericks. What are you keeping from me? I can tell you are withholding something."

The longtime servant stood there, looking as morose as if he were facing his own beheading. "Perhaps you ought to have more of your whisky, sir."

"I daresay, Spence, old man, this is probably the first time in your life that a *man* has tried to get you drunk."

"Shut up, Edward." Spencer narrowed his eyes in suspicion as he reached for his whisky and tipped it up. He peered over the cut-crystal glass's rim at his butler. Though the man remained as dear and familiar as an old, comfortable shoe,

Spencer felt a growing impatience with him. He lowered his glass. "There, I've drunk all up like a good little boy. Now it's your turn, man. The question before you is a simple one. Where is the duchess?"

The frail butler slumped. "At this exact moment in time, Your Grace, I will have to say that I have no idea."

A rude snort of amused disbelief came from Edward. Spencer's hand tightened around his drink, though he would have preferred it were his cousin's neck. "Fredericks, what the devil do you mean? There *is* something you're not telling me, isn't there?"

Fredericks's Adam's apple bobbed up and down. "I am most sorry, Your Grace, but I find myself in quite the quandary."

Spencer sat forward abruptly in his chair. "Well, by God, man, you are not alone in it, I will say that. Is there some mystery here? What did the duchess do—walk out into the mists and disappear, never to be seen again?"

"I'm afraid that's not far from the truth, Your Grace."

"Oh, this is jolly good entertainment."

"Shut up, Edward. And you, Fredericks, explain your remark."

"As you wish, Your Grace." And yet, amazingly, he said nothing more.

Another snort from Edward, and Spencer snapped. "What I *wish,* Fredericks, is to know where my damned—" He clamped his jaws together so tightly his back teeth ached. Only when he felt more in control did he continue. "That is, the duchess's whereabouts. And, preferably, I'd like to know before I am anywhere near your venerable age."

"I understand, sir. Yet I fear you are not going to like what I have to say with regard to that matter."

"Rest assured that I have yet, in the fifteen minutes or so that I've been home, to like anything at all that you've had to tell me . . . or not tell me, is more like it. So, proceed."

"Yes, Your Grace." Fredericks pulled himself erect. "Her Grace the duchess"—he slid his gaze over to Edward and back to his employer, intoning his words as though he were announcing the death of royalty—"caused her belongings to be packed and left posthaste in a coach."

The butler's words struck Spencer like physical blows, but it was the oddest thing. He felt nothing. Nothing at all. Except cold. Very cold. He sat there, frowning, as he forced his mind around the meaning of his servant's words. *She had her belongings packed and left in a coach?*

Suddenly, the enormity of her actions sank in. She'd left when he'd specifically told her she was to remain here. An onslaught of outrage and insult overrode breeding and years of training in comportment and had Spencer exploding from his chair. The hapless piece of furniture scraped backward with a horrible shrieking sound across the polished wood flooring. He all but spat out his curse: "The very devil, you say! She has packed her belongings and left? *When?* When did this occur?"

"Easy on, Spencer," Edward urged, who had suddenly appeared at his elbow. "Surely there's a simple explanation."

Spencer heard his cousin but had eyes only for Fredericks, who first addressed Edward. "I'm afraid there is not, Lord Roxley."

The elderly retainer, dressed in a suit of black formal clothes too big for him—or perhaps he'd suddenly shrunk inside them—turned his sad gaze his employer's way. "She left almost a week ago, Your Grace."

"A *week* ago, man? A *week*?" Spencer didn't know which stung more: the duchess's fleeing or this glaring lack of loyalty to him on the part of Fredericks, a man who had known Spencer since he was a baby, a man for whom he bore a great deal of affection, and at whom he was now genuinely angry. "You didn't think to do something as simple as dispatch a rider to me with this news?"

"Yes, of course we did, sir. Mrs. Kevins and I—"

"Who the devil is Mrs. Kevins?"

"The new housekeeper the duchess hired in your absence, Your Grace."

Impatient now that he knew this to be an inconsequential domestic detail, Spencer waved it away. "Never mind. Go on."

Accompanying his words with an abbreviated bow, Fredericks said, "Yes, Your Grace. Mrs. Kevins and I wanted very much to apprise you of this development, sir. But it is hardly our place to . . . tattle on the duchess."

"Well, he's got you there, Spence, old man."

Spencer's narrowed eyes ached with the intensity of the humiliation and the anger pressing against the backs of them as he stared at his cousin. "Yes, I can see that." He then addressed Fredericks. "Just out of curiosity, Fredericks, how long would you have waited to notify me—if for no other reason than out of loyalty to me—had I not scheduled this trip at this time?"

The butler again looked everywhere but at Spencer or Edward. "All I can say is your decision to return home at this particular time was fortuitous for all concerned, Your Grace."

"No, you will quickly find it is not all you can say. Damn it, look at me, Fredericks. And you, Edward, may step back." He waited; Edward stepped back; and Fredericks gave Spencer his attention. "Thank you. Now, what do you mean by *fortuitous,* Fredericks? How so?"

"I mean not only did convention prevent us from apprising you, sir, but the duchess left orders."

Spencer ignored Edward's little sick sound of doom and narrowed his eyes. "Orders? What orders? What are you talking about?"

Fredericks pulled himself up to his formal posture. "The duchess forbade us contacting you."

"She . . . forbade? Why in God's name would she—" He didn't finish the question because he already knew the answer: So she could make good her getaway. Feeling a sudden need to sit down, Spencer retrieved his chair and dragged it over to the desk. He then sank down heavily on the padded leather seat and slouched back against its familiar comfort. He closed his eyes and rubbed the taut skin between his eyebrows. *Damn.*

Spencer felt his shoulder being squeezed compassionately. "Are you quite all right, Spence, old man?" Edward asked.

Feeling bleak and empty inside, Spencer opened his eyes. "Never better."

"If I may intrude, Your Grace?"

Spencer indicated with a gesture for the butler, whose brow was furrowed with worry lines, to proceed.

"Thank you, sir. I want . . . well, I just would like to . . . Oh, rot and balderdash, sir, I'm trying to say how sorry I am and that it pains me to see you hurt and I had hoped against hope that the duchess would realize her mistake in leaving and return before you discovered her gone. There, I've said it."

"Oh, jolly well said, Fredericks," Edward cheered.

To Spencer's surprise, he found he could smile, even under these circumstances. "Thank you, Fredericks. You're very kind." Then, his next thought sobered him, but he knew he had to ask it, whether Edward was in the room or not. "When the duchess left . . . was she alone?"

"Hello, what's this?"

"That's enough, Edward."

Obviously perceiving the implication behind Spencer's question, Fredericks's eyes widened and his face colored. "Oh, yes, Your Grace, entirely alone. Well, except for her lady's maid, Rosanna, of course. And Herndon, her driver. And the footmen—"

Spencer had held up a hand to stop him. "I understand, Fredericks. Thank you."

He wondered for how long his wife would be alone. He'd thought at first she'd left to avoid another confrontation with him. After all, she had to have known his overseer had requested his presence here. The nagging thought was no, she didn't have to know. The tenants knew to go directly to Mr. Dover, and the overseer had orders not to involve the duchess but to contact Spencer with any problems or concerns to do with Wetherington's Point. Most likely, the overseer had not crossed paths with Victoria. But even had he, he most likely would not have mentioned to her he had requested Spencer to return at this time.

Spencer had now to accept the possibility that she was not running from his imminent arrival here, or even to her mother, but was instead running to her lover, the other man, perhaps the father of her child. Spencer didn't know the man, or want to know him. But should he ever see him . . . he'd kill him. *If she thinks for one moment that I will allow her to get away with this, she is sorely mistaken. I will follow her and I will find her—* He stopped right there. Follow her where? He sighted on Fredericks, who still stood in front of his desk. "Do you know where the duchess was going? Did she say?"

"Not directly to me. But I heard one of the footmen say they were traveling to Liverpool."

"Liverpool?" Edward's voice was rich with distaste. "Why in God's name would anyone travel to Liverpool?"

Spencer treated Edward's question as rhetorical and focused instead on his butler. "Tell me, Fredericks . . . what occurred here before the duchess's sudden departure? Did something specific happen to precipitate her leaving, is what I'm asking you."

"I believe something might have, yes, sir."

Spencer waited; his butler apparently did, too. Through gritted teeth, Spencer said: "Then out with it, man."

Fredericks's frown lowered his thin, gray eyebrows over his bird's beak of a nose. "Yes, sir. Although I didn't credit it at the time, she did receive a letter late one afternoon."

"A letter?" This, again, was Edward, who made it sound as if he'd never heard of such a thing.

With an abrupt, threatening movement, Spencer turned to his cousin. "Edward, for the love of God, man, quit interrupting. Can you not see the very devil of a time I am having trying to get a coherent narrative out of Fredericks? You do not make it any easier, sir."

Edward sat up stiffly. "My apologies. I will try to refrain from interjecting my continuing startlement with these developments."

Spencer searched Edward's face for signs of sarcasm or defiance and saw neither. "Thank you." He turned to Fredericks. "The letter, man."

"Yes, sir. I mention this particular one because, uh, one heard from Her Grace's lady's maid. . ."

Spencer knew the reason for Fredericks's hesitation this time. He would now be relating gossip. It was not news to Spencer that the servants gossiped among themselves belowstairs. Though he generally condemned it as a ruinous practice, this time he silently thanked God for the gossips; otherwise, he might never have known this detail. "Her lady's maid, eh? That Rose girl?"

"Yes. But it's Rosanna, Your Grace."

"Like I said. What did *one hear* from the girl?"

"She's hardly a girl, sir, being a woman past middle age."

"I could not care less, Fredericks. The letter, if you please."

"Yes, Your Grace. The letter was . . . not from her family and, well, caused a strong reaction in the duchess."

A numbing cold worked its way up Spencer's spine. He'd been right. She was running to the man. *The son of a bitch actually wrote to her here. Have they no shame? They've been plotting this, probably since our very marriage. I've been such a fool.* Feeling ragged and betrayed, Spencer exhaled sharply and asked Fredericks: "And this reaction you spoke of? What was it?"

"She seemed greatly distraught at first. Worried. She hardly ate and paced about as if in turmoil."

"I see." It was small comfort to learn her decision to leave hadn't been an easy one. Spencer thought now of his wife, picturing her pacing and worrying. An image of her, dominated by thick waves of mahogany hair and striking blue eyes, coupled with her succulently desirable body that he did not know anywhere near well enough, assailed his senses— *No. I will not—indeed, I cannot—think of her in that way. I cannot.* He slowly exhaled his breath and resumed his questioning of Fredericks. "How soon after receiving this letter did she leave?"

"If I'm not mistaken, sir, I believe it was two mornings later."

"Two mornings." Well, there it was: two and two neatly put together. She'd received a letter not sent by her family; was greatly upset by it; and soon packed and left, having forbidden his servants to contact him. What else could it mean but a lover's reunion? Like a banked fire threatening to leap once again to flame, Spencer's temper smoldered with the certain knowledge that he'd be a laughingstock when word got out that his wife had flown. People would say this was Whitfield family history repeating itself.

Everyone in London knew that his mother had left his father when Spencer was only three years old. His parents had remained separated, though married, all their lives. And though he loved his mother dearly, and her family as well, and though she'd been a wonderful woman who'd done what she'd had to do under difficult circumstances, Spencer had still suffered from the taunts of other children and then, later, those of casually cruel gossips in the ton.

But he was a grown man now. A titled duke. And while he wanted to say he cared not at all what others said about him, he knew better. He did care—and he cared exactly because of his late father's reputation for being an ineffectual man and husband and a profligate with women and money.

Spencer had worked hard all his adult life to counter that impression of the Whitfields and to recoup the duchy's lost wealth. But events and nature had conspired against him. The damned agricultural depression with its resulting daunting loss of income had forced him, like it had so many others of his peers, to marry a rich American heiress for her money in order to save everything that was dear to him. And, dear God, how much he'd had to compromise to do so. He could only ask himself now . . . was it worth it?

Feeling overwhelmed on several fronts, Spencer forbore a further mental litany of his troubles and told Fredericks: "Thank you. That will be all."

The older man looked surprised. He opened his mouth as if he meant to say more, but then he firmed his lips into a straight line, said, "Yes, sir," bowed deeply, and slowly inched around to walk in a shambling gait to the closed door of the study. The very picture of dejection, Spencer decided.

"That's all?" Edward cried. "Oh, surely not. I hardly think we're to the bottom of this mystery yet, Spencer."

" 'We,' Edward? What 'we' do you mean?"

His cousin's face colored. "Oh. Of course. I see what you mean. Sorry. Didn't mean to make a parlor game of your life unraveling, old man."

"My life is not unraveling."

"But it is. You may be older than me and you certainly outrank me in the scheme of things, my dear cousin, but still . . . I beg to differ. Your life is most definitely unraveling. Even your butler thinks so."

Spencer looked from Edward to Fredericks. No doubt, and as Edward had intimated, Fredericks was disappointed in his duke. Not the usual thing for a butler to make known, however subtly, his opinion of a peer's behavior. But Fredericks was different. He'd adored Spencer from the day thirty years ago when he and his mother had arrived at her family's estate to stay.

From that day forward, Fredericks had championed him

through all the triumphs and travails of boyhood and adolescence. He'd been the one, as well, to comfort Spencer when his mother and then, a few years later, his father had died, leaving Spencer alone and a young duke who'd had to learn fast and hard how to handle himself and his inheritance.

And now this. Frustration took a bite out of Spencer's further eroding mood. He scrubbed a hand over his face, impatient with his own self. *Damn it all to hell. What a huge, bloody disaster.* With a force of will that had seen him through many personal tragedies, Spencer tamped down the hurt he refused to name. This situation must be faced head-on. There could be no shirking of his duties as the duke or to his duchy.

Thinking hard, and weighing his upcoming meetings, obligations, and the problems with the farmers he'd come here to deal with, Spencer called out to Fredericks just as the butler made it to the door. When the man made a wobbling turn in his direction, Spencer said, "Find Mr. Milton for me and have him attend me here. Get word, also, to Mr. Dover that I will see him immediately regarding the tenant farmers."

"You're sending for your overseer and your secretary, man?" Edward's eyes widened with disbelief. "What do you intend to do—have Mr. Milton fire off a scathing letter, which Mr. Dover will deliver to your duchess? I must say, Spencer, I would think you'd first want to fire off a gun."

Spencer stared pointedly at his cousin. "Oh, I do. But with you as my target." With that, Spencer carried on with his butler. "The Earl of Roxley notwithstanding, Fredericks, tell Mr. Milton to bring the tools of his scribe's trade with him when he comes. We have many people to write and meetings to change. And then ask Hornsby to have the footmen carry my traveling trunks to my rooms."

Spencer had further orders for his personal valet, but had no wish to start a domestic war by having them carried to him by the butler. "Tell him I'll be up to direct him when I'm done with Mr. Milton and Mr. Dover."

Fredericks' gaze held Spencer's. A ghost of a smile

played at the corners of the older man's thin-lipped mouth. "Are you leaving us so soon, then, Your Grace?"

Edward cut in. "Yes. Are we leaving so soon, Spencer? Where are we going?"

"*We* are not going anywhere, Edward. *I* am."

"Oh, blast."

Spencer ignored his cousin in favor of answering Fredericks. "Yes, I am leaving as soon as it can be arranged." Fredericks's face split wide in an approving grin. Spencer couldn't let him get away with being so smug. "Do try not to look so happy about being rid of me, will you?"

A twinkling gleam flared in the butler's eyes. "Hardly, sir. It's always a pleasure to have you in residence—and you, as well, Lord Roxley. But will you be traveling back to . . . London, sir?"

"No." Spencer's answering smile was conspiratorial. "Liverpool."

Edward gasped. "Good heavens, you're going after the girl, aren't you?"

Beaming, Fredericks pulled himself up to his full height of an inch or two over five feet and crowed, "Oh, well done, sir. Most excellent."

"Glad you approve. That will be all, Fredericks." He turned to his cousin. "Yes, I'm going after her. Of course I am. She is my wife. And she is possibly carrying my heir."

Edward's eyes rounded and his mouth dropped open. "The hell you say! I am not missing this." Edward chased after the butler. "Fredericks, have them place my bags in the traveling trunks as well. We are going after the duchess."

Spencer pounded a fist on his desk. "Edward, damn it, man, you are not going, and Fredericks will give no such order."

As he watched the butler leave, with Edward on his heels, both of them effectively ignoring him, Spencer suddenly became aware of a growing excitement inside him. He was going after her. This felt good and right. Images filled his mind. Images of the wife he wanted back, damn her. Yes, honor and pride were involved. And yes, he'd pushed her away. Yes, he'd told her he didn't care. But, to his surprise, she'd been all he'd thought about in London. None of his usual haunts or pursuits had held any attraction for him. Only thoughts of her had. So when his overseer had got word to him of this tenant-farmer debacle, he'd jumped at the chance to return here without a loss of face.

And why had he jumped? Spencer finally admitted the truth—because he'd wanted to see his wife, plain and simple. The woman had somehow wormed her way under his skin. He thought now of her fiery temper, her blazing blue eyes, and her indomitable spirit. A smile of admiration found its way to his face. By God, she was magnificent. How could he have thought he didn't care about her? How? The evidence had been right there in front of him all this time. But it had taken her leaving to make him realize it.

His eyes suddenly narrowed as he reminded himself there was every possibility that she'd left him to run to another man. But even if she had, he could not allow her abandonment to stand because the child she carried could possibly be his—and his heir. But if he had any sense, Spencer told himself, he would simply put her aside. A cold-blooded part of his mind assured him her fortune would remain his if he did, especially under these circumstances . . . or, to be fair, the ones he suspected.

Angry again, Spencer picked up his whisky, realized the glass was empty, and set it down again. Staring blankly across the way at a globe of the world, he turned his thoughts to the busy port town on the west coast of England where ships left regularly for America—including Savannah. With any luck, he'd be on one of them before too many days and tides ebbed. With him would be traveling the element of surprise.

CHAPTER 3

Deep in a dark and murky swamp outside Savannah, Georgia Midnight; September 1875

Like a luminous pearl laid out on a length of black velvet for inspection by hot and eager eyes, the silvered moon hung low and refulgent in a charcoal sky. Yet the thick canopy of the swamp's interlaced treetops denied the moon's sun-reflected light, which sought passage through their branches. Down below, the swamp seemed to whisper a warning, saying it would offer no succor to the lone and apprehensive traveler in the small jonboat moving stealthily across the black water's surface and through the misty miasma of its atmosphere.

As if a pact had been made with the swamp itself, the sentient creatures who called this murky place home alternately fell silent and then raised their voices, effectively marking the passage of the foreign one in their midst. The buzzing of thousands of unseen cicadas, clinging to high, woody branches, provided a deep and steady humming vibration that assaulted the ears. And all around, bullfrogs croaked and bull alligators bellowed. From somewhere up ahead of the boat came the surprised squeak and then the stark death-cry of a small, warm-blooded creature that had foolishly ventured too far from safety.

Just then, and off to the right, something thrashed through the undergrowth and slithered into the water . . . something large enough to cause a disturbance that rocked the jonboat being laboriously poled along. And then, there it was, what had joined the narrow craft in the water . . . a big gator. His eyes, shining red in the yellow light shed by the boat's lantern, which hung from a makeshift hook affixed at the apex of the V-shaped hull, watched the intruder pass. Then, slowly, menacingly, the reptile sank under the water's surface without so much as a ripple to betray his intentions.

Overhead, a night bird's mournful dirge told of terrors not yet faced. And all around, the Spanish moss, as if suddenly imbued with a ghostly life of its own, reached down from the spidery tree branches with gossamer-webbed fingers to brush across the face and softly caress the hair of the young woman kneeling in the flimsy, lightweight craft trespassing on these dark waters.

Horrified, certain she'd poled right through some awful spider's huge web and the nasty hairy, creature itself was now somewhere on her, Victoria quickly transferred her long pole to one hand and used her other to pull at her hair. Gasping, mewling in fear, she finally pulled a clump of it away and flung it overboard, staring hard after it, straining, in the lantern's light, to identify it. Finally, her mind recognized it and told her it was nothing more than harmless Spanish moss.

Relieved to the point of weakness, she sat back 'on her heels and tried to untangle the remaining gray tendrils from her long tied-back hair. But the moss came away only in small bits, as though reluctant to give up its hold on her. Frustrated, she gave up the battle. Let it cling to her hair. What difference did it make out here? Soaked with perspiration that was as much the product of her bout of fear as it was the drenching heat, Victoria's every breath was scented with the smoky, bitter smell of the swamp.

Defeat ate at the edges of her determination, telling her that if she had a lick of sense, she'd turn this wobbly boat around right now and go home to the comfort of her bed. Victoria stiffened her spine against such wistful thinking. She had to continue on. She'd come this far and she really had no choice but to be here. None at all. Otherwise, what in the world would she be doing out here, putting herself and her unborn child at possible risk? So there was no sense in complaining about being handed the task of righting a wrong, a wrong only she could right.

Victoria swallowed hard, wishing she didn't care. But she did—and deeply. But that didn't mean she couldn't feel weighed down by the onerous burden that had been placed on her heart. She firmed her lips. Sitting here and letting worry eat a hole in her stomach was getting her nowhere. She needed to move on. Heeding her own advice, Victoria rose again to her knees in the tiny boat. Cutting her gaze left and right, she searched for that submerged gator. It wasn't unheard of for one to come up right under an unwary poler's craft, upset it, and earn itself an easy supper.

She cautiously prodded her long pole along the inky water's bottom, trying to find purchase. "Now, you stay away from here, Mr. Gator, you hear me?" she said softly, nervously. "Go get a nice wild piglet for your meal. My baby and I, even both of us taken together, are too scrawny to fill your belly."

Her speech served the same purpose as did whistling past a graveyard, and well she knew it. When the pole finally met resistance and she pushed off against its hardness, she prayed it was a submerged tree trunk or a big rock—and not the lurking gator. No sense insulting him in his own home by poking him with a sharp stick. Pushing hard despite the protesting muscles in her arms, she again launched her shallow-bottomed and rough-hewn craft forward. Almost effortlessly, it glided through the cypress swamp . . . as if something were pulling it.

Rationally, Victoria knew nothing was, but she couldn't quite convince her overwrought nerves that some shroud-covered skeleton wasn't up ahead, just out of sight, and doing the honors. "Stop that, Victoria," she warned herself, again speaking low and soft. "You keep thinking like that, and you're liable to let go of this pole—and your sanity, as well."

She dipped the pole into the water and moved her lightweight boat along. Disconcertingly, and making her further doubt her own senses, the black night and inky water up ahead kept wanting to merge into one entity. Victoria had to fight the notion that she was poling through the atmosphere, a lost soul on a windless night. No matter how hard she tried to focus her eyes, and no matter how many times she blinked, or paused in her poling to swipe her sleeve across her eyes, her vision remained incapable of separating earth from sky, water from night.

Though she remained alert to the many dangers around her, any one of which could claim a victim in one mere second of inattention and leave nothing behind to be discovered, Victoria tried to calm her fears by telling herself she and her baby were in no danger because she knew these waters like the back of her hand. But even in her own mind, her boast rang hollow. The truth was, she used to know this place . . . but not so much now. The swamp had changed its course, as evidenced by the unfamiliar contours forced upon it by the powerful forces beneath the placid surface.

Victoria swallowed. How well she knew such forces in her own life. A sudden, cold dread born of her mounting troubles swept over her, leaving her chilled despite the night's cloying heat. With desperation tightening her grip on the pole, and feigning a bravery she did not feel, she forced her attention back to the swamp itself. Here lay real terrors.

But she courageously told herself it was a good thing she didn't need directional signs tacked to trees to show her the way on this liquid highway . . . because there weren't any. All she had to guide her was memory and instinct.

Still, she reassured herself, she knew which narrow tributary to pole down, which fork to aim for when an island suddenly appeared in the waterway. She knew because she'd made this journey before, many times, as a child. But those times, she'd been invited, and one or more of the swamp's citizens had been sent to carry her in and out safely, all in the daylight hours. But this time was different. At twenty-two, she was no longer a child; she was alone and it was dark.

And yet, the fact remained: She had no choice but to be here and to do this alone. She could tell no one, not even her family—especially not her family—what was at stake. Not lost on Victoria was the hard irony of her predicament. To do this thing she'd essentially been forced to come here to do could ultimately destroy her, her baby, and others in her family. But not to do it could cost another child her very precious life.

Just as despair threatened to swamp her emotions, Victoria felt a pinprick of pain in her hand as a blood-sucking mosquito stabbed into her flesh. With an agitated cry, she swatted it dead and cursed softly. "Ouch, you blasted thing." Insulted, she brushed the insect carcass off her skin. The lantern's thin light revealed a tiny smear of blood on her hand. Victoria stared at it. "I hope to high heaven that's all of my blood that gets shed tonight."

Hearing the note of bravado in her voice, Victoria dared a tentative smile. Perhaps she was up to this challenge. Perhaps, she was, after all, still a child of this wild place. True, she'd been born and raised on the more civilized fringes of this swamp up at River's End, whose many acres boasted the centerpiece that was her family's home, a beautiful two-story plantation house of tall columns and fifteen rooms. But being a child of privilege and a wealthy Southern daughter hadn't stopped her from running the river and the forest and learning how to avoid the snakes and the quicksand in the swamp, much to her parents' horror. She still knew how to do all that. Once learned, it wasn't something a body forgot.

And knowing those things, she assured herself, helped keep her and her baby safe now. If the coach trip across England and then the passage over the Atlantic hadn't done any apparent harm, then how could poling a jonboat through familiar waters, even at night, and even if it was a swamp, be harmful? No, her baby was fine. Victoria wished she could say the same thing about herself. She wasn't fine. Physically, she was. Healthy as a horse. Strong as an ox. But not in her heart.

Why, she couldn't even tell her own parents she was expecting. Whose child could she say it was? And she certainly hadn't told anyone in Savannah, where people still smiled in a sly way at her and talked to each other behind their hands. Victoria poked her bottom lip out stubbornly as she prodded her long pole into the bottom of the swamp and pushed her boat forward. She'd thought those girls were her friends. Stinging Victoria was the admission that she would have been right in the middle of the gossip sessions if what had happened to her had happened to one of them. But no more. She'd been through so much in the past couple of months that she felt now she would be a more compassionate and loyal friend.

Victoria smiled. She liked the feel of this new person she was becoming. Had moving away from all she'd known and marrying a powerful duke she respected yet feared wrought these changes in her? Against her will, Victoria found her longing thoughts centered on her husband. How could she feel such yearning for his presence? The man wanted nothing from her but her money and an heir. But Victoria could not believe that was all. Too many times, before she'd had to admit her pregnancy to him, she'd seen a glimmer of humor and respect in his eyes and his manner. He'd squired her everywhere, held her arm possessively, danced with her . . . made love to her.

"Oh, stop it, Victoria. These thoughts can only hurt." And they did hurt. Since she'd left England, she'd felt certain at times she could actually hear his voice and feel his touch. She suddenly chuckled as she pictured him again offering her that chair the last time she'd seen him. The poor man hadn't known what to do with a crying, screaming, pregnant woman in the throes of an emotional upset.

Pregnant. Victoria blinked. *Dear Lord, I have a baby on the way.* She still wasn't used to the idea. But she did think she'd made the right decision not to tell her parents. She'd tell them once the child was born, and it was determined who the father was. Shame assailed Victoria that she'd be in this predicament. But it wasn't her fault, she wanted to shout. Yet society said it was. No matter how it happened, the woman was shamed. Victoria shook her head, fighting despair. Then, inside her head, she heard a small voice saying: *You just do what you came here to do, and then you get home right away.*

No, not home. But to England. Her fervent hope was her husband would never know she'd been gone. After all, he'd said he wasn't coming back to Wetherington's Point until she had the baby, which would be some time next year. March, maybe. At any rate, she'd left orders with Fredericks—such a dear little man—not to tattle. So, if everything worked out smoothly, she would be back in England in a matter of weeks with the duke none the wiser. But even if he did find out, it didn't matter because here she was. How many times when she was growing up had her mother accused her of being a child who would rather beg forgiveness than ask permission?

If Spencer discovered her gone, would he forgive her for leaving after he'd told her she could not? She hadn't left out of willfulness. She'd left because of a horrible injustice she had to right. Hopefully. Would he understand? Would he even care? Victoria thought not. After all, her husband could hardly stand to be in the same room with her. And he wanted nothing to do with her or her baby, if it wasn't his.

Victoria firmed her lips with her effort to harden her heart against her earlier warm feelings for her husband. She hadn't thought she'd miss him at all. But now he was all she thought about. Was it possible to betray oneself? she wondered. It seemed so. How could she long for a man who had already rejected her and meant to reject her child, if it wasn't his? Conscience again stung Victoria, telling her she wasn't so naïve that she hadn't expected his reaction or his decision. What else could he do, if the child was not his? She knew all that rationally. But not in her heart. The child was innocent, no matter who its father was, and she would protect it like a mother bear did her cub.

Thus bolstered, Victoria valiantly straightened up and looked around her, getting her bearings and continuing with her careful poling of the small boat. She hoped against hope that her mission tonight would go smoothly and quickly. She had to get back long before daylight stained the sky a light gray. With any luck, she'd get some sleep before the house awakened and she had to get up right along with them. She tried to think where she could hide the clothes she was wearing—an old shirt and a worn pair of pants belonging to Jeff that she'd secretly snatched from the back of her older brother's chest of drawers. She couldn't just tuck them into the laundry and be done with them. She might need them again. Well, she'd think of someplace when the time came.

Knowing how she looked right now got a grin out of Victoria. Jefferson was so much taller and bigger than she was that Victoria had been forced to roll up the pants legs and the shirtsleeves three good, thick turns before she could be sure she wouldn't trip over the one and could use her hands despite the other—

The front of her tiny craft bumped solidly against something in the water. The abrupt stop caused the pole, which Victoria held in both hands and had braced against the riverbed, to jerk crazily, pop loose, and hit her hard in the forehead. Gasping in surprise, she held her breath until the pain subsided. Her only thought was, come the morning, would she have a bruise she couldn't explain?

Rubbing the spot softly, she turned her attention to wondering what she could have hit. Carefully, so as not to lose the all-important pole—her only means of locomotion—she raised it from the shallow but muddy water and laid it lengthwise in the boat. Once it was secure, she crept forward, holding on to the gunwales for balance, until she could peer over the front of the boat where the lantern shed its light.

"Ain't nothin' but some dumb old cypress knees."

Startled by the sound of another human voice, Victoria cried out and pitched over backward into the boat. A close-by bird noisily took wing and just as loudly protested with a stark cry of its own. Blinking, lying on her back, Victoria again clutched at the gunwales and tried to look everywhere at once. But the darkness, outside the lantern's weak circle of light, proved too much. She couldn't see another living soul.

"Up heah. Look up heah, and you'll see me."

Victoria did. She looked up and all around, searching the trees overhead for whoever was hiding from her, yet not finding him. But now that she thought about it, she realized it could only be one person. With that came consternation. "Jubal, is that you?"

From somewhere up above her, a husky chuckle preceded the man saying: "It shore enuff is."

Relief washed in a wave over Victoria. Here was a friend. She let go of the gunwales and, carefully, so as not to rock the boat unduly, hauled herself up onto her elbows. Taking exception to Jubal's continuing to laugh at her, Victoria said: "What in the world is so funny to you, you ornery devil?"

"You look just like a surprised turtle that done found hisself turned over on his back, Miss Victoria."

"I expect I do. And I ought to tell your mother on you," Victoria complained, struggling now to sit up properly. "What would she say upon learning you're out scaring innocent folks on the waterway?"

This, too, tickled him. "You ain't innocent folks. And my mama ain't goin' to say nothin'. She done sent me to fetch you in to her afore you git yourself killed out heah."

Victoria was rankled by this. "I was doing just fine until you scared me. And I suppose she also told you that I'd get my boat stuck right here, too, didn't she?"

"Now, how else I know to be here and waitin'?"

Victoria knew the truth of that. Miss Cicely always seemed to know what went on in the swamp and who was wandering about in it. Folks said she had "the sight," and Victoria believed them. Similar experiences, just like this one, with Jubal waiting right where and when she needed him, had taught her so. Finally sitting upright in the bottom of her boat, Victoria looked all around, but she still couldn't see that stinker anywhere. "You better show yourself, Jubal, before I get to thinking that you're a ghost, and I take my pole to you."

From somewhere up above her came a scoffing sound that adequately expressed Victoria's unseen tormentor's opinion of that. "You cain't hit what you cain't see. And look at you. Why, you ain't goin' to scare no ghost, neither. He could see you got yourself stuck good and hard there between them cypress knees. Otherwise, you'd already be driftin' away on the current. I swan, you ought to know better, Miss Victoria, polin' that there boat so close to this here land. I thought I taught you better than that."

Feeling rightly chastised but not liking it one bit, Victoria responded in kind. "You mean just like my mama taught you to read? You keeping up with your reading, Jubal?" Where the devil was he? Victoria had never seen a being who could just blend in with the plants and trees like Jubal could, if he was of a mind. Most irritating it was, too.

"Cain't," Jubal said, jumping down off a jiggling branch to land heavily on shore and not ten feet away in the lantern's feeble yellow light. His sudden appearance startled another whoop out of Victoria. Jubal—a big, thick-bodied, muscular black man two years older than her—said, "Listen at you. I ain't never knowed you to be such a fraidy cat, Miss Victoria."

"I am not now, and I never have been, a fraidy cat. And don't you change the subject, Jubal. Why can't you go on with your learning?" Victoria was very aware of the absurdity of their carrying on as though they conversed politely in a parlor in broad daylight, instead of in a swamp alive with night-hunting predators all around them. But she had a very good reason for pursuing this with him. "Well?"

"Ain't got nothin' new to read," Jubal complained. "Done read all them old books you give me. Cain't hardly stomach 'em no more 'cause they don't never seem to end no different, no matter how many times I study 'em."

Victoria grinned at his conclusion, but the lantern's light showed her that Jubal's expression was sober. Her heart went out to him. "How are you doing, Jubal? I worry about you, you know."

"You ain't got no cause to worry 'bout some no-account like me."

His words tore at Victoria's heart. She'd known and cared about Jubal since she'd been old enough to be aware of the world around her. But how their lives had changed, his and hers—and neither one of them for the better. "Don't you call yourself a no-account, Jubal, not within my hearing."

"Why not? That's what I am. Didn't yore daddy tell you what happened with me?"

"Yes, he did." And because of what he'd done, he was now a prisoner in the swamp. If he left it, he'd be hunted and, most likely, caught and lynched. Victoria knew that if she succeeded in doing what she'd come here to do, the same fate could await her. Chilling. Absolutely chilling. Yet, what choice did she have? "I don't blame you for what you did, Jubal. Any man, put in your place, would have done the same."

Jubal made a snort of disgust. "Hmph. Most folks don't see it like that, like I'm even a man with feelin's and all."

"I know," Victoria said quietly, sadly. "But I do, Jubal. I know you're a man. A good man." For the first time in her life, she had to admit that she, a white woman, did not know this black man, a former slave of her father's, as she thought she did. "Anyhow, Jubal," she finished lamely, "I'm glad you're here because I'm going to need your help."

"You mean to find yore way back in heah to my mama?"

"Yes, but also in the next few days or weeks. And that's why I asked you about your reading and writing. I'm going to need you to read messages to your mama from me and then write her answers back to me. Can you do that?"

"I shore enuff could if'n I was of a mind to. But what messages? What you talkin' 'bout?"

"You know exactly what I'm talking about, Jubal. Don't pretend you don't."

"What I know is you don't belong to be in this here swamp and messin' in somethin' ain't none of yore business."

"It is my business, Jubal. You know it is."

Jubal shook his head. "Ain't, neither. It's my family's business. Not yours."

"You know that's not true, Jubal." Valuable time was passing, which made Victoria impatient. "Why are you behaving like this?"

He slid his gaze away from hers, finally settling it on his muddy boots. "'Cause I couldn't stomach somethin' happenin' to you. I purely couldn't. You know how I feel 'bout you."

Victoria's heart wrenched as she stared at the top of Jubal's head. Yes, she did know how he felt about her. He'd never acted on it or said more than he just had, but she knew.

"Thank you, Jubal, for being so worried about me." She didn't add that right now in her life he was the only one who seemed to be. But to get them back on an even keel, she assumed a brisk attitude and said, "Now, I guess you better climb on in with me and take me to Miss Cicely before she changes her mind about seeing me."

Jubal surprised her by not complying and staying where he was. Some voice in the back of Victoria's mind told her that he no longer had to do her bidding. He was free to do as he saw fit. And apparently what he saw fit to do was to remain where he was. "Oh, Jubal, what's wrong now?"

He crossed his muscled arms over his broad chest. "You might be in for a good whippin' from my mama if'n I takes you in to her. She purely ain't none too happy 'bout your bein' out here. 'Specially not with you carryin' a baby in yore stomach."

Shock, and the heat that came with it, washed over Victoria, forcing a gasp out of her. "She knows?"

Jubal made a derisive sound. "Listen at you. 'Course she knows."

Victoria wondered how much else Miss Cicely might know, things like whether she was carrying a boy or a girl . . . and who the father was. A renewed sense of urgency, one purely selfish, seized Victoria. She had to get to Miss Cicely and ask her about those things, too. "Jubal, you have to take me to her. I have to see her."

"Maybe if you hadn't gone away from us, things might have turned out differently for me and Jenny."

"Oh, God, Jubal, please." Impatient, undone, Victoria covered her face with her hands; then she used them to gesture at him. "I'm sorry I wasn't here. But I'm here now, and there are things I can do. You know me, Jubal, and you trust me. I'll do everything I can. I swear it." Victoria paused for a breath and changed the subject. "I didn't want to go away, Jubal. I was made to go."

A shake of his head and a grunted denial met her words.

"White folks ain't made to go nowhere. They go wherever they please."

"It must seem that way to you, but it's not always true, Jubal. It certainly wasn't for me." Victoria grinned at the memory. "You should have seen it. Why, my daddy dragged me by my arm all the way to the steamship, and me kicking and screaming."

"Woo-ee, Miss Victoria, I bet you was a sight." Jubal chuckled and then sent her a speculative look. "What you gone do to help us?"

He was coming around. Victoria proceeded cautiously but honestly. "I don't really know, Jubal. And that's why I'm out here now. I want to talk to Miss Cicely, learn what she knows and go from there, I guess. It doesn't sound like much, but I promise you I will do everything I can to make this right."

"I b'lieve you will, I shore do. But what purely give me the worries, Miss Victoria, is this here business you came into the swamp about . . ." He shook his head slowly and fatalistically. "It ain't what you think it is."

Fright and curiosity mixed inside Victoria, causing her to speak sharply. "What are you talking about, Jubal? How is it not what I think it is?"

"I cain't tell you." Jubal stubbornly firmed his lips together, but the lantern's light revealed his chin quivering with emotion. "You cain't do nothin'," he suddenly cried. "Cain't nobody help now."

Victoria felt on the verge of crying right along with him, should he start. "For God's sake, stop saying that, Jubal. Please. We don't know anything for certain yet. There may still be time. Let me try . . . please?"

His stare was assessing, weighing . . . finally, he relaxed, his decision apparently made. Victoria held her breath as he pointed at her and frowned. "What's that getup you got on there?"

It took her a moment to realize his comment could be a

signal that he was going to help her. Victoria grinned and pulled at her pants leg as she spoke. "They're Jefferson's pants and shirt. Aren't I a sight?"

Jubal chuckled and shook his head. "You purely are. Yore daddy would whomp you good if he saw you like this."

"I know. And that's why I'm out here at night—so he won't see me." Victoria sobered. "And that's why I have to hurry."

"Then we'd best be on our way before that big gator following behind your boat gets real hungry and eats us both."

A burst of fear flitted along Victoria's nerve endings. She jerked around and, sure enough, there that big reptile was, submerged but for his eyes. She knew he waited only for her to make one mistake. Just one. And then she was his. Victoria swallowed, thinking the gator wasn't the only one wanting to make a meal, and an example, out of her.

Jubal came forward to free the jonboat from the clutches of the cypress knees. Once he had, he crouched over to step carefully onboard with her. Victoria scooted backward, cramming herself into the craft's narrow, squared-off stern. She made herself as small as she could in an effort to give Jubal the room he needed to stand astraddle in the boat. Thus, he would pole them toward a faint light that suddenly appeared along the way up ahead, even deeper in the swamp.

CHAPTER 4

Hellfire and damnation, Victoria fumed silently some time later. The meeting had not gone well, and she would have to go back. That is, if she could get away again and if Miss Cicely allowed her to come back. Too many ifs, when all she was doing was trying to help. And another thing, Miss Cicely had said she didn't know anything more about the baby Victoria was carrying. She'd said it was too soon for her to see the particulars. Victoria wasn't sure she believed her, but there hadn't been anything she could do to get her to say more.

So here she was now, frustrated in the extreme and her eyes gritty from a lack of sleep. Victoria carefully stood in the jonboat and tied it to the old dock at the very edge of River's End land. For heaven's sake, she fumed, she couldn't just let this matter go. She'd been begged to come here and she had—all the way from England, only to be told this was none of her concern and she was to leave it be.

"Well, I don't think I can leave it be," Victoria said softly to herself. Upsetting her was how Miss Cicely had treated her. Victoria had known and loved that woman all her life. Why, she'd played at her knee and toddled around after her and run to her with all her youthful scrapes and hurts. And yet tonight there had been no happiness and no warmth in

Miss Cicely's eyes for Victoria. She'd as much as told her to forget what she knew and go home where she belonged before she got herself hurt or worse.

Maybe Miss Cicely meant to protect her by warning her away, Victoria considered. That could be. Or maybe something had changed, something that she wouldn't or couldn't tell Victoria. That could be, too. But whatever it was, she was here and she wasn't going away. Victoria blew out the candle that had provided her light in the lantern. The moon was waning but still holding forth in the night sky. With any luck, she could get back inside, wash, and get in bed, all without being detected. Though her heart ached and her mind was in a whirl, the thought of bed sounded heavenly. So did being clean. It was awful how the swamp smell clung to a person.

Before climbing up the rough ladder—nothing more than thick pieces of board nailed across two neighboring pilings—she reached up and petted the family bloodhound. Neville had watched her leave earlier and so had waited right here for her to return. "You've been here this whole time, haven't you? I don't know whether to thank you or be mad at you. Do you realize that if anyone had cared to look out here, you'd have given me away? They'd know how you always wait here if I've taken the boat out."

The dog came to his feet, his tail wagging as Victoria, with the ease of experience, climbed up the makeshift ladder and stood on the dock. She reached out to rub Neville's ears. "Come on, boy, let's go get some sleep."

Before Victoria took her first step, the dog tensed and stared toward the sloping lawn and the imposing but night-shaded big, white house. He lowered his tail and his head . . . and growled.

Victoria stopped cold. Fright had her heart pounding and her limbs weak. Desperately, she looked around, not spying any stealthy movement. But that didn't mean someone wasn't hiding behind a bush. Still, all she saw was the expanse of lawn, silvered by the moon and shadowed by tall trees, no more than black silhouettes against the sky. No one darted around any corners of the house, either, not that she could see. Still, she trusted the dog's sharper instincts more than she did her own.

Victoria squatted down beside Neville, stroked his head, and whispered: "What's out there, boy? What's got you spooked?"

The dog spared her a quick, anxious look, a slurp of his tongue up her cheek, and a worried whine. Then he resumed his vigil. This time he looked more toward his left, to the far end of the house, and raised his long, flopped-over ears alertly. Victoria fully expected him to take off at any moment in full voice and raise the house as he charged after some scalawag who'd come sniffing around on River's End where he had no cause to be.

Yet here the dog was, staying protectively close to her. She assured herself of one thing: She wasn't about to move from this dock until whoever was out there showed his face. And she didn't care if she had to sit here until mid-morning and have her breakfast brought out to her. Her reaction, she knew, was nothing more than pure fright—and Redmond stubbornness. Her chin jutting out to prove it, Victoria vowed that if it were a game of waiting this somebody wanted, she would give it to him.

And so, long moments ticked slowly by. Soon enough, a cramping in her leg muscles had her wincing. Then her foot threatened to go to sleep. She wanted very much to stand up and walk around to get rid of the cramping, but didn't dare. To take her mind off her body's protests, she devised a plan of escape should somebody suddenly rush her. First, Neville would go for him and that would give her time to scream and raise the house and get back in the jonboat and pole back out into the swamp. She doubted that an attacker, if he could get away from Neville, would dare jump in that water to pursue her. If he did, he'd most likely meet a water moccasin or two, or maybe that hungry gator, before he got to her. And if he did get close to her, he'd face a scared woman wielding a sturdy hardwood pole and screaming at the top of her lungs.

Heartened by that brave scenario, and still squatted down by the dog, Victoria shifted her weight to her other foot and rested a knee against the dock. She stroked the hound dog's back, feeling his raised hackles but also feeling more secure for his nearness, his reassuring warmth, and his muscled bulk that came complete with bone-deep loyalty and a set of very sharp teeth. She put her arm around Neville and pulled him closer to her. But the dog suddenly lunged forward, growling low in his throat.

Startled, Victoria released him and stood up, her heart pounding, her hands fisted. In the dark, with only the moon's indistinct light to assist her, she didn't know where to look first, from which direction the danger was coming.

Neville set himself in motion. Victoria instinctively reached for him, but he was already out of her range. Afraid to be alone, she started to go after him. But a small warning voice inside her head told her to stay put. Instantly, she pulled back, a hand over her mouth, and watched Neville to see what he would do. With his head and tail lowered, the dog moved in a menacing manner as he made for the other end of the dock.

"Sister?" came a hissing, masculine whisper close by. "Is that you?"

Victoria started, but shock faded enough to allow reason to take over and remind her that only one person still called her "Sister." "Jefferson?" she called out tentatively, quietly. "Is that you?"

"It sure is. Sister, what in the world are you doing out here?"

Intense relief nearly dropped Victoria in a melting heap on the dock. "You nearly scared the life out of me, big brother."

At the other end of the dock, Jefferson slowly came into view. All Victoria could see of him were his head and shoulders since he stood on the downward slope of the land, nearly to the water's edge. He raised his arms to show her he had a shotgun with him. "You see this gun? I came near to shooting you with it. My God, Sister, do you think I could live with myself if I'd shot you?"

Believing his question didn't really need an answer, Victoria quietly watched as Neville stepped over to Jeff and sniffed at him. Jeff reached up and rubbed the dog's head. "Hey, boy." Then her brother turned to Victoria. "What in the world are you doing out here?"

"I couldn't sleep," Victoria said, adding to herself . . . *not while I was poling the boat and talking to Miss Cicely.*

"So you got dressed up in that rig because you couldn't sleep?"

"Well, I could hardly come out here in my night clothes, now could I? And I didn't want to fuss with putting on a dress."

"Where'd you get those clothes, anyway?"

"Out of your chest of drawers." Victoria realized her mistake the instant the words were out of her mouth and inhaled a hissing breath between her gritted teeth.

"Out of my chest of drawers? When did you do that? I've been in my bedroom until just a few minutes ago. I think I would have noticed if you'd been in there, too, and rummaging around."

"No, not just now, silly. Earlier in the evening when you weren't in there."

"Why didn't you just ask me for them?"

"You wouldn't have given them to me." And he would have had too many questions about why she needed them.

No doubt, Jefferson realized she was hiding something. But all he did was slowly shake his head. "If you don't beat all. I thought you were some river rat who pulled his boat up to the dock, intent on stealing some chickens or equipment. I came out here to scare him off or shoot him."

"Did you hear something out here? I've been out here all this time with Neville," she lied glibly, "and I haven't heard anything."

"No, it wasn't anything I heard. I come out at night regularly to check on the property around the house. All up and down the river lately, most of the plantations have suffered losses. People have awakened to find they're missing tools and livestock and such. I thought we were next."

Victoria listened to her brother talking but knew he was lying every bit as much as she was. He was up to something out here that had nothing to do with river rats. For one thing, if her father were concerned about thievery, he'd hire guards. He certainly wouldn't put his only son on patrol. Still, she made the expected response. "You're right. I do recall Daddy saying something about the robberies."

"I expect you do. It's all he talks about. So I can't fathom why you—knowing that unsavory sorts are about and could be a particular danger to a woman alone—would stray outdoors in the middle of the night."

Victoria raised her chin. "I can take care of myself. I was careful, and I had Neville with me."

"And yet I was able to walk right up on you and came close to shooting you."

"That is the third time you've mentioned shooting me, Jefferson. And don't think I didn't know someone was around. Neville was about to jump on you. He heard you. You're just lucky you identified yourself when you did, or he'd have been on you."

"Neville wouldn't jump me."

"You threaten me and just see if he won't, big brother."

Jefferson sighed, a long-suffering, masculine sound. "All of this could have been avoided, Victoria, if you'd just stay inside where you belong."

Victoria stiffened with offense. "Where I belong?"

"Don't you start with me, Sister. I'm just trying to look out for you, and I'm telling you that you were just lucky this time. You may not be the next time."

Was that a warning? A frisson of fear danced lightly over the hairs on her arms. "I'll take my chances. And here's something for you to think about the next time you go sneaking up on people with a gun in your hands. It could turn out you're not the only one who's armed, and you could get shot just as easily as I could."

A weighted silence billowed into the space between them. Then, Jeff said . . . quietly, evenly: "I probably will before it's all over."

Victoria's heart lurched. She knew only too well, because of the letter she'd received in England, the truth of what he said. Jeff was deeply involved in this awful plot, only she didn't know to what extent. She didn't know, either, which side he was on. Her worst fear was that Jeff would be the villain and would actually harm her. While she was willing to take her chances with her brother, she wasn't willing to place her unborn baby in any more danger than she'd already been forced to do in coming here. But, oh, how it hurt not to be able to trust him.

Jeff tiredly rubbed at his forehead. "You ever going to tell me the real reason, other than you were just homesick, that you ran away and came home?"

Victoria hadn't been expecting that, but she bristled, nevertheless. "I did not run away. I don't run away from anything. And I don't need a reason to come here, Jeff. River's End is my home."

"No, I'm afraid not, Sister. Not anymore."

The hurt cut through her like a knife. Miss Cicely and Jubal had both said the same thing to her. And now Jeff. Did no one want her here? She supposed, though, when she considered her past behavior and the scandal she'd caused in Savannah, she couldn't blame them. Still, with equal measures of stung pride and stubbornness to buoy her up, Victoria retorted in kind. "River's End will always be my home. I was born in that house. My heart is here, and here it remains."

"Maybe so. But it won't ever be your land."

In her agitation, Victoria advanced a step. "Jefferson Caldwell Redmond, what has got into you? You have no call to say something like that to me. I never said, or even thought for one minute, River's End would ever be mine. I know Daddy intends to leave it to you."

"It's good you know that." Jeff's tone had become decidedly cool. "You haven't been home for a few months, Sister. A lot of things have changed."

"Things can't have changed all that much . . . except for you. You've changed. And it hurts me to say it, but not for the better, either." And that was as close as she intended to come in letting him know she suspected him of something.

"I could say the same thing about you. I could also say you are certainly no longer the picture of true Southern womanhood. But then again, you never were." With that, he turned and trudged up the slope of the land.

"Is that supposed to hurt me, Jeff?" Victoria called out, as loudly as she dared, to her brother's back. "Well, it doesn't. In my own heart, I am the woman I want to be. And isn't it just like a man to say what a woman should be?"

Jeff made no comeback to that. Silently, Victoria watched her brother climb up onto the dock and walk toward her. Neville took up a position next to him and padded alongside him. Though each booted footstep of Jeff's made a hollow, somehow threatening, sound on the weathered-wood planking, Victoria held her ground. She wasn't afraid of him. Even though they'd had words, this was Jeff, after all. Her brother.

She glanced down at Neville and suddenly recalled how he had yelped when Jeff had first spoken. That was when it struck her: Neville had been caught off guard by Jefferson being on the right side of the dock because he'd been alerted to something he didn't like off to the left side of it. Did that mean someone was still out there and hiding? Cold dread slipped over Victoria. She started to speak of her concern, but suddenly her brother stood in front of her.

With the shotgun held loosely in the crook of his arm, and even with the barrel pointing down to the dock, he appeared an imposing figure. Rank disapproval rode his features in the form of a frown as he looked her up and down and then met her waiting gaze. "You're not out here because you can't sleep, Sister. You said yourself you took these clothes hours ago. To me, that says you're up to something you shouldn't be."

Victoria stared at her brother, a tall, handsome, light-haired man she loved with all her heart and suspected of atrocious, or at least heartbreakingly neglectful, deeds. "I told you the truth," she said, marveling at how cool her voice sounded. "I couldn't sleep. It's that simple."

"Nothing's that simple."

Victoria held his gaze for a pointed length of time before saying: "I know. Nothing ever is, is it, Jeff?"

Sober of expression, reminding her too much of their father, and apparently intending to ignore her response, Jeff looked past her to the jonboat and again met her gaze. Under his censorious scrutiny, Victoria felt her face burn with guilt. "You stink of swamp," he said, his voice calm and even. "You've been out in that boat, and you went to see Miss Cicely."

Victoria hesitated with her answer, thinking she could of course deny it, but then she decided to take a small chance and see how her brother responded. "Yes, I have, Jeff. I've been out to see Miss Cicely."

Jeff looked away from her and shook his head. When he looked down at her again, his voice was raw with emotion. "You shouldn't have gone out there, Victoria. Don't let Miss Cicely drag you into something you know nothing about."

"I never said she was trying to drag me into anything, Jeff." She hadn't missed that he'd called her "Victoria." He only did that when he was trying to be persuasive or serious with her.

"You don't have to say it. I know Miss Cicely. She doesn't know when to leave well enough alone. Neither do you."

Despite his harsh indictment, Victoria felt an urge to reach out and touch him, to put a comforting hand on his arm. In the end, though, she didn't, but she did take her questioning one step farther. "What is it I should leave alone, Jeff? What are you talking about?"

She prayed he would open up to her and tell her about Jenny and Sofie; prayed he was on the right side of this and would just tell her and let her help before it was too late for them all.

Jeff swung his gaze back to her. The slanting light of the waning moon showed Victoria the hard planes and shadowed angles of his unsmiling face. "Nothing. I just know you. If you've been out to see Miss Cicely in the middle of the night like this, then you meant for it to be a secret. I don't know what you're up to, Sister, but I will say this: You keep on going out there in that swamp and listening to that woman, and she's bound to get you involved in something that will get you hurt or killed."

"How can you talk about her like that, Jeff? We've known and loved her all our lives. Miss Cicely would never do anything that would get us hurt." Victoria's throat felt constricted with emotion. Her dear, sweet, handsome brother. Jeff could very well be a murderer—or a man who had hired a murderer to do his dirty work. Victoria feared she'd be sick right here. She swallowed convulsively and tensed her leg muscles to keep herself standing upright.

"You think she wouldn't? You being out there in that swamp at night to go see her is dangerous. Now, what did Miss Cicely have to say to you? And how did you know she wanted to talk to you?"

"One of the hands gave me a message." She'd ignored his first question and answered his second with a lie. The truth was Miss Cicely hadn't sent for her. She'd gone out there on her own. Another truth was Jeff was interrogating her to see if she knew anything about his secret wrongdoings. If he found out she did, would he shoot her right here on the dock and blame those river rats?

"What hand was that, Sister?"

She shrugged, acting unconcerned. "Oh, I don't know. I'd never met him before. I figured he was new."

"We haven't hired any new hands since you left for England."

"Well, I didn't know that, did I?"

"And you wonder why I'm out here with a gun? Anything could have happened, Sister. What'd he look like?"

Oh, Lord. "Jeff, quit getting all bothered. He was harmless enough. Just some tall, skinny colored boy who said Miss Cicely wanted to see me and for me to come tonight."

Jeff's expression could only be called horrified. "What'd he do? Come right up to the house and ask for you?"

"No, he did not. He saw me outside."

"Outside? When was this? I haven't seen you talking to any colored boys since you've been back."

"Do you watch me every minute, Jeff?"

"No. But it's starting to sound like I'd better."

Victoria's heart nearly tripped over itself. "Oh, for pity's sake, I hardly think that's necessary."

"Well, I do. What did she want, anyhow? Miss Cicely, I mean."

"I know who you mean. And she didn't want anything special. She just heard I was home and wanted to see me."

"Wasn't that sociable of her—and at midnight, too."

Victoria waved a hand in dismissal. "You know how she is. Likes to make everything all mysterious. It was nothing, and here I am, safe and sound."

Jeff shifted his weight to his other leg and looked from

her to the swamp behind her. "All right, but don't go out there again, Sister, you hear me?"

"I do. I hear you." And she had . . . she'd heard him say it.

"I mean it, too."

"I said I heard you. And now, if you don't mind, I'd like to go inside." She had to get away from him and think about this and sort through what she knew and what she suspected. She had no idea how to proceed from here. The trouble just kept getting bigger and bigger—and worse and worse. Victoria started to take a step forward and around Jeff.

He moved to block her way. "You need to do more than just go inside, Sister." Jeff's voice was pleading. "Please. You need to go on home—and I mean to England. Things have changed here. Times are dangerous. I know you and how you get wound up in things. But the hard truth is you are not wanted or needed here."

Victoria blinked back sudden tears. "How can you say these things to me, Jeff? How?"

He was quiet a moment, but then he exhaled, sounding suddenly weary. "I say them for your own good. And I'm sorry, Sister, but that's just the way of it right now. I wish I could say I'm glad you're here, but I'm not. And not for any reason you might think, either."

Victoria took a step toward her brother. "Then tell me what the reason is, Jeff."

"No. I can't. It's better for you if I don't." He roused himself and moved aside, gesturing for her to go. "You just . . . go on inside, now. Get up to the house before anyone else sees you."

Despite her fears for him and of him, Victoria's heart went out to her brother. "Jeff, if there's anything you want to tell me—"

He held up a hand to stop her words. "Go on up to bed, like I told you to do. Please."

Victoria studied his face, seeing lines of worry and grief

drawn across his normally smooth forehead and bracketing either side of his mouth. "All right, big brother, I'll go. But will you come with me?"

He shook his head. "No. But I'll be in directly. I just need to . . . make sure everything is in order out here."

His slight hesitation alerted Victoria. She'd been right in thinking someone else was out there and waiting for Jeff. Almost before she even knew she was going to do it, she'd asked: "Why do you really have that gun with you? Who's out there?"

Frowning, Jeff pulled back. "What are you talking about? Nobody's out there. Leastwise, there'd better not be anybody out there. I'm just going to go make sure, is all. So you go on inside. I'll wait here until you get to the house."

What else could she do? "All right, Jeff. Good night."

"Good night, Sister. Sleep well."

Victoria doubted that she would, but she abruptly brushed by him and hurried down the dock and then started up the spongy lawn, steadily making for the safety of the house. As she trudged up to the back door, a fearful corner of her mind wondered if he suspected she knew what he was involved in and would just shoot her in the back. After all, and as she'd thought a moment ago, he could claim he thought she was a river rat. She could certainly be mistaken for one in the dark and dressed as she was.

By the time she stepped into a deep shadow cast by the house, she had worked herself into a state and just had to know what Jeff was doing. She slipped in between a flowering bush and the solidness of the house's wall behind her. Taking a deep breath for courage, she turned around and looked. She half expected to see her brother sighting down his gun's barrel at her. But what she saw was much worse. Her breath caught before she could exhale it. Jeff was gone. He hadn't waited for her to go safely inside.

The only one about was Neville. The dog sat alertly on

the weathered planking of the dock . . . and looked off to his left. Pressing her lips together, gathering her courage, Victoria quietly moved to the corner of the house and peeked around it. She slid her gaze in the direction Neville indicated. There Jeff was—loping for the far end of the house. What was he doing? Where was he going? She thought of following him, but instantly abandoned that idea. For one thing, she was too tired and had no desire to explain to her brother—again—what the devil she was still doing out here, should he detect her.

And for another thing, she saw no need to go putting herself, and therefore her helpless baby, in further or deliberate danger tonight. Tomorrow would be soon enough to try to figure out what she should do next. Not that she was supposed to do a darned thing. That's what the letter she'd received in England had said. She was to do nothing and wait for instructions. She hadn't received any yet . . . but that didn't mean she wouldn't.

CHAPTER 5

Gracing the plantation home of River's End, the elegant though comfortable morning room had lent itself, for many generations, to Redmond family breakfasts. It did so again this morning. Though the large room faced in the general direction of Savannah, that elegant city remained unseen beyond meandering lowland miles of sandy marshes rimmed by forests of cypress, live oak, and loblolly pine. The room, situated on the ground floor in the northeast corner of the white-pillared and verandah-wrapped house, and furnished with cherished antiques and memories, caught the morning's fresh cross-breeze when its bank of tall windows were thrown open, as they were today.

Commingling with the salty tang of the low-country air were the mouthwatering smells of sausages, bacon, grits, pancakes, eggs, and fruit preserves. Overriding them all was the pervasive aroma of strong coffee. Inside the room, and seated at one end of a long oak table, were the Redmonds.

And holding forth on her daughter's posture and health was the lady of the house. "Victoria, I have called your name three times. Do you hear me? If you don't sit up straight, you are going to fall face-first into your plate."

Blinking, inhaling raggedly, and jerked back to wakefulness by a sudden sound she couldn't quite identify—like that made by someone delicately rapping on a glass with a piece of silverware in order to gain attention—Victoria stiffened her spine and sat up straight.

"Victoria?"

Though her father and brother also stared her way, Victoria quickly focused on her frowning mother, who sat across from her and held a spoon in her hand. She probably had actually tapped her glass with it. Victoria managed a smile, despite the bone-softening lethargy induced by her lack of sleep, and shook her head, trying to make it seem as if she were nothing more than distracted. "I'm sorry, Mama, what did you ask me?"

"I didn't ask you anything, honey. I told you to sit up before you fell into your breakfast. Why are you so tired? What's wrong?"

Victoria swallowed and stared wide-eyed at her mother. "Nothing's wrong, Mama."

"Well, I think we both know better."

"No we do not," Victoria said quickly . . . too quickly.

"We do so." Catherine Redmond used the soft, dulcet tones that matched her still radiant peaches-and-cream, brunette beauty and belied a will of iron where her family was concerned. "Now, though you have denied being in a delicate condition—"

"Mother!" Victoria cried, horrified, her face burning with embarrassment—and the knowledge that her mother was correct.

Right on the heels of her protest came Jeff's. "Mother, please, we're at the breakfast table."

"Catherine, really. Such indelicacy. I am surprised at you." This was Victoria's father, who sat at the head of the table and whose face also was steadily reddening.

Victoria's mother calmly placed a lily-white hand over her demurely covered bosom and looked from one to the other of them. "Well, I am sorry if I have shocked you. But Victoria does have all the symptoms. However, if she denies being with child, then a mother can only suppose that her married daughter is coming down with something dreadful."

"I'm not sick, Mama. And I wish you would not worry yourself over me." Victoria hid a betraying yawn behind her hand. "I'm fine. Really I am."

"I saw that yawn, young lady. And this is your mother you are talking to, so I do not care if you are a fine and grand duchess now. You are, first and foremost, my child."

Victoria shifted uncomfortably on her chair. "I am painfully aware of that, Mama."

Catherine Redmond pursed her lips. "Sarcasm is very unbecoming in a lady of royalty, Victoria."

"I hate to disillusion you, Mama, but given the ones I've met, it seems to be a prized trait. However, I am not actually royalty. My husband is a hereditary duke, not a royal duke. There's a big difference."

Her mother smiled indulgently, as if Victoria were five years old and had just said something precocious. "No there isn't, darling, not in society, where it counts. Now, look here, are you aware you have a bruise on your forehead? It wasn't there yesterday or even last night when you went up to bed. So I do not understand how that could have happened."

"I, uh, hit my head on the . . ." She couldn't think of a single plausible thing and suddenly felt panicky, but then she came up with: "The, uh, headboard on my bed."

"The headboard? How in the world did you come to hit your head on the headboard? Were you thrashing about in a nightmare? And why would you be having nightmares?"

"Catherine, my dear, will you leave the girl alone?"

Grateful in the extreme, Victoria turned to her father. A tall, handsome, gray-haired gentleman whom she loved dearly, he'd abandoned the pile of bills and letters next to his heaped-high plate and turned to his wife, who sat on his left. "She's not a child anymore. She's a grown woman in her own right."

"I am well aware of that, Isaac Redmond. But a mother

doesn't simply turn her worries off because her children have achieved their full growth."

"I wasn't suggesting that you do." Smiling indulgently, he patted his wife's hand. "Just let her alone so she can eat."

Catherine Redmond sat back dramatically. "Well, that's just it, isn't it? She's not eating, and she looks tired. And she says she is not with child. However, I do not see what else it could all mean, unless she is sick with something awful."

"Does she look like she's ill, my love?" Isaac Redmond asked, reaching out to his right for Victoria's hand, though he had his attention on his wife to his left.

Pleasantly surprised, Victoria eagerly took his hand in hers and squeezed affectionately, feeling the warmth and strength in his grip. This was the first overture he'd made to her of this nature since she'd been here. Perhaps he'd forgiven her for the scandal with . . . she hated even to think the dastardly man's name . . . Mr. Loyal Atherton. Loyal, indeed.

"Daddy's right, Mama," Victoria said quickly, pulling her thoughts away from *that* man. "Do I look so awful as all that?"

Just as her mother softened and shook her head no and appeared to be relenting, Jeff said: "Perhaps Sister has swamp fever."

As she barely suppressed a gasp, Victoria's grip reflexively tightened in her father's hand and she snapped her attention to her brother, who sat across from her and on their mother's left. Jefferson regarded her with a challenging glint in his light-colored eyes.

Their mother turned to him and said: "Now, Jefferson, don't you go scaring your sister with talk like that. How could she even get the swamp fever? She'd have to have ventured out into that awful water to be exposed to something like that. And I hardly think, at her age and now that she's a duchess, that she'd—"

A sudden frown, perhaps of dawning suspicion, crossed

Catherine Redmond's face. She turned to Victoria, whose heart was pounding dully in her chest. "Victoria, have you gone out into that swamp?"

Victoria slid her hand out of her father's, hopefully before he had discerned her suddenly moist palm. She lowered her hand to her lap and, under cover of the table, surreptitiously wiped it with her napkin. "Oh, Mama, please, Jefferson is teasing you. I'm not ill, but I will admit to being very tired from the trip here. You know yourself how exhausting it is. And this weather . . ." She prettily fanned herself with a hand. "Why, it's unseasonably warm and humid. I find it has quite taken its toll on my strength."

Though she smiled reassuringly at her mother, Victoria could also see her brother's gaze on her. How dare he raise a suspicion in their mother? Why, he had more to lose than she did, should she choose to open her mouth about his nighttime wanderings—and with a gun, too.

"Be that as it may . . ." Catherine allowed her voice to trail off as she spread jam on a buttermilk biscuit. Done with that task, she roved her gaze over her daughter's face. "I still think you look a bit peaked, so I believe I will send for Dr. Hollis. I want him to take a look at you."

If Dr. Hollis examined her, he'd know soon enough his patient's real condition. Victoria sat straight up in her high-backed hardwood chair. "No, Mama, I don't need a doctor. I'm fine—"

"Now, see? The very fact that you do not want to see Dr. Hollis tells me I ought to send for him."

"She said she doesn't want a doctor, Catherine. For God's sake, leave it be." All heads turned Isaac Redmond's way. Grateful though Victoria was for his intervention, she couldn't fathom her father being so short with her mother. He rarely was—and her mother's face showed her hurt. "I apologize, my love, for speaking so abruptly. You must forgive me." He riffled through the business papers by his plate.

"I blame these. Something is not adding up, and I can't figure exactly what it is."

Catherine Redmond, for once, forgot her petty hurt and put her hand on her husband's. "Oh, Isaac, is it very serious?"

Though he smiled and patted Catherine's hand, Victoria could see the lines of worry bracketing his mouth. Just seeing her father upset had apprehension seizing her stomach. "Nothing to worry yourself with." He looked down the table to Jefferson. "After breakfast, son, I'd like for you to go over these accounts with me, if you would."

"Accounts? Of course." To Victoria's eye, Jefferson looked the way he had when they were children and he'd got caught doing something he shouldn't have been. A sinking feeling assailed her. Surely, no matter what else Jeff was mixed up in, he hadn't involved their father's business interests? "Is the, uh, problem something I'm familiar with?"

"Yes, actually. It's the investments you control." Her father shook his head. "Looks to me like too many things have been shuffled around. I can't find the end of the trail and that concerns me."

"Then, it does me, too, Daddy." Though Jeff sounded sincere, Victoria wondered if he really was.

Catherine Redmond preened like a satisfied hen as she gripped her son's arm and hugged him. "Why, Jefferson Redmond, just listen to you. All grown-up and a captain of industry. A most honorable man."

Victoria caught the fleeting look of pain that crossed her brother's features. Whereas only a moment ago, and like last night, she had been suspicious of him and angry with him, now her heart went out to him. She hated her suspicions. All she knew was he was her brother, and he was hurting and hiding something. But how much of the hurt had he caused himself? And how many people had been hurt, and worse, because of his actions or lack of action?

Victoria suffered a moment of anguish, realizing that Jeff could be next. Or she could be. Hers was not an idle worry. When she'd got back to her room last night, a folded-over, unsigned note of warning had been on her pillow. She'd nearly screamed when she'd seen it, but she'd drawn the only conclusion she could: Whoever had raised old Neville's hackles last night had also sneaked onto River's End land to spy on her and then deliver that note to let her know she was being watched. It had told her to stay out of the swamp if she didn't want Jubal and Miss Cicely dead. It had also warned her again not to tell anyone why she was here and went on to say if she did, that person would be killed, too—and so would she.

Her mother's sudden laugh pulled Victoria out of her thoughts. Catherine had drawn back in her chair to proudly scrutinize her son. But as her gaze swept over his features, her smile bled away and her voice radiated concern. "Why, Jefferson Caldwell Redmond, just look at you. You look downright haggard. I was so focused on Victoria that I almost missed those dark circles under your eyes and how pale you are. I fear you may have the same thing wrong with you that your sister has."

Though his comment was directed to their mother, Jefferson locked gazes with Victoria. "I don't think we have anything wrong between us, do we, Sister?"

Victoria met his level gaze. "No. We're fine."

Their little exchange was evidently not lost on their mother. She looked from her one child to her other. "Did you two have a fuss? Now, don't tell me you did. I do not like it when my children have differences."

Exasperated, Victoria could only stare at her mother. She loved her very much, but the woman was as relentless as an encroaching ivy vine and as keen-eyed as an eagle when it came to her two surviving children. She'd lost three babies to illnesses before their first birthdays. And those heart-wrenching losses, Victoria knew, caused her mother to be ever fearful of her and Jeff's health and happiness. Victoria knew she'd be no different with her own child.

"We're grown up now, Mother," Jeff said. "We don't have squabbles or differences like we did when we were children." Again, he sought Victoria's gaze before continuing. "We deal now with each other as the adults we are and take responsibility for our actions."

"He's right," Victoria said, her gaze again locked with his. "We are very responsible. And just the same as always with each other."

But they weren't. How well she and Jeff both knew it, even if their mother didn't. Her children had grown up and grown apart. And now those differences could tear her family apart.

"All right, if the two of you say nothing is wrong, then nothing is wrong."

Victoria watched her mother nibbling on the biscuit she'd buttered a few moments ago. Her finely arched eyebrows raised, Catherine Redmond stared her daughter's way. "Don't think I haven't noticed that all you're doing is pushing that wonderful food around and not eating it. Now, it's enough that you won't even tell me why you're back home so soon after . . . well, everything. And, of course, I am thrilled to have you here. But now you're going to hurt Annabelle's feelings, if she thinks you no longer like her cooking."

Victoria purposely stuck to the most innocuous of her mother's complaints. "I like Annabelle's cooking just fine. I always have."

Smiling, her perfect eyebrows raised, Catherine Redmond leaned over a fraction toward her daughter. "Then eat more of it, baby. You need to keep your strength up."

Bemused impatience suddenly pushed to the fore of Victoria's emotions. "Mama, you always say that, about keeping my strength up. I have no idea for what, though. After all, I'm not likely to go outside and single-handedly—or even with three grown men helping me—cut down and chop into kindling one of the oaks that line the drive up to River's End, now am I?"

The very picture of injured motherhood, Catherine Redmond raised her chin and again put a hand to her chest, over her heart. "Well, what a fine speech that was for a mother to hear from her ungrateful child."

In the face of her father's and brother's mutinous rumblings and glares her way, and in the interest of peace, which they would not have if Catherine Redmond felt injured and took to her bed, Victoria stopped pushing her scrambled eggs and sausages around on her plate and forked up a big bite, which she popped into her mouth and dutifully chewed and swallowed, thankful only that she wasn't plagued with morning sickness. "See? I eat plenty, Mother."

Catherine Redmond pursed her lips. "You do not eat plenty. A good stiff wind could carry you along to Charleston and right to your aunt Bessie's door, perish the thought. The Lord knows that woman could put a crimp in a body's appetite." With that, Victoria's mother returned her biscuit to her plate and turned her attention to her husband, putting her hand over his to get his attention. "Isaac, don't you think she looks thin, dear?"

He'd gone back to his paperwork, but looked up, obviously confused, when his wife spoke to him. "Who's thin? Bessie? The last time I saw my sister she was pleasingly plump enough—"

"For heaven's sake, Isaac. You never listen to me. Not Bessie. Victoria. Your daughter." Catherine Redmond sat back with much pomp and circumstance and rustling of her skirts as she settled her hands in her lap. "I think it's time you step in, Isaac, and do something before Victoria just withers away."

Filled with dismay, Victoria watched her father look from his wife to Jefferson, then to Victoria herself, and back to his wife. "What exactly would you have me do, Catherine?

Send her to her room? Lock her in a shed and force-feed her through a knothole?"

Looking vexed, Catherine Redmond retorted: "Now you're just being silly."

"For pity's sake, my love, Victoria is a grown woman and knows when she's hungry."

"Grown, certainly. But thinner every day. She's been here a week or more and hasn't taken three good bites yet. Talk to her."

Mouthing some epithet no doubt unsuitable to mixed company, Victoria's father turned to her and commanded: "Victoria, if you love your dear old father, you will eat. And you will do it right now. And while you're at it, stop looking tired. You're worrying your mother." He again settled his gaze on his wife, who exhaled a tsk of exasperation. "There, my dear. I spoke to her. Now, let's hear no more about it, shall we?"

Apparently satisfied with his performance, he again retreated to his paperwork and his coffee. And his wife's opinion of this was: "You are no help, Isaac Wallace Redmond. No help at all."

Biting back a grin, Victoria silently applauded her father's speech. But the truth was, nothing would have suited her more than to go to her room and get back in bed. She could barely keep her eyes open, she was so tired. And, as their mother had commented, Jefferson didn't look any better than she did, maybe worse. Though he'd obviously shaved and changed clothes, Victoria wondered if he'd come back inside in time to get to bed at all. Maybe his meeting with whoever had been out there—

Just then, a noisy clattering of rapid steps all but tumbling down the stairs from the second floor disrupted her thoughts. Victoria and her family, first exchanging "What in the world?" looks among themselves, then turned in the direction of the commotion.

"I never heard such a noise in all my life." This was Isaac

Redmond, who tossed his linen napkin on the table and scooted his chair back. "I'd better go see who that is raising the devil out there."

But he never got the chance because at that instant, a stringy-blond-haired girl of about fifteen years, whom Victoria recognized as the new maid her mother had hired, burst into the breakfast room and stood in the doorway, looking lost in her uniform and agog with excitement.

"Tillie! I declare, child, what a dramatic entrance."

The skinny girl sought Catherine Redmond's attention. "I'm sorry about coming in here like this, Miz Redmond, when you all are dining," she blurted. "And I do remember as how it's Mr. Virgil's butlering duty to tell y'all things, but I couldn't find him and I thought you should know what I've just seen."

Expecting her to proceed, nobody said anything.

Apparently and belatedly struck uncertain of herself, the maid offered a tentative smile and gestured vaguely toward the grand gallery foyer behind her. "I could go look for Mr. Virgil and tell him what-all I seen and then let him tell you, if'n you like."

Wide-eyed with bemusement, Victoria couldn't wait to see what happened next between her mother and this girl, who was the latest beneficiary of her mother's charity. All Victoria knew about Tillie was what she'd been told by her mother. The girl was the eldest daughter of some poor sharecropper family a few miles away and just needed a kind hand up in the world in order to better herself. How this could be achieved by cleaning up after rich people eluded Victoria, but she'd wisely kept that observation to herself.

"That's all right, Tillie," Mrs. Redmond was saying. Her patient tone of voice warred with her tight smile. "You're here now, so tell us what you saw."

"Yes, ma'am." The girl's evident excitement propelled her farther into the room. "I was up there on the second floor and a-carryin' out my cleaning duties when I happened to look out a window. And that's when I seen a fancy carriage just plumb full of right fine-looking gentlemen comin' up the drive. And behind them is a big wagon carrying a piled-up heap of traveling trunks just like the sort her ladyship here had with her when she came home from England."

"Oh, my. England," Catherine Redmond said, covering her mouth with her fingers and staring wide-eyed at her daughter.

"Yes, ma'am. England. Then that uppity—I mean that nice lady's maid, Rosanna, well, she come and looked out the window, too, and she up and said it was the very devil himself come to fetch his own."

Victoria's smile and amusement had died a slow death, the longer the girl had spoken. And now, with the maid at the end of her speech, Victoria's heart was nearly stopped altogether. Her grip tightened reflexively around her fork. This entourage, she knew, could only be that of one person.

"Carriages and traveling trunks, you say?" This was Victoria's father who'd turned around in his chair, an arm over its back, to stare at Tillie.

"Yes, sir, I do," Tillie carried on. "When I seen them all a-comin' up the drive—"

"You mean you *saw* them coming." Catherine Redmond had recovered enough to gently but firmly correct the maid.

"Ain't that what I said, ma'am? 'Cause I did—I seen 'em myself a-comin' right smartly up that big old long drive. They's still a ways off yet. But I hurried down the stairs to tell you I think you got you some mighty important company headed your way right directly. Maybe it's some more real-live royalty. Wouldn't that be grand?"

Intense silence followed her pronouncement. To Victoria, the air in the room seemed to thicken as though molasses had been poured over everything. She didn't need a mirror to tell her that her face was a fine and fancy red about now.

"Thank you, Tillie," the lady of the house said. "Please

find and alert Virgil that we have company coming. And close the doors behind you, if you will."

"Yes, ma'am," the girl replied, as always executing an awkward and abbreviated curtsy Victoria's way before doing as she'd been told.

As soon as the doors closed, Victoria's father, mother, and brother turned, with an accompanying rustle of their clothing across the chair seats, to stare at her.

"Victoria?" her mother questioned, her voice sounding tinny and far away. "Do you know who this could be, by any chance?"

Suddenly too warm, despite the cool breeze coming in through the open windows, Victoria spoke without thinking. "Blast it all! Fredericks must have told. He wasn't supposed to learn I was gone."

"Who is Fredericks and why didn't you want him to know you were gone?"

Victoria stared at her mother as if she'd never seen her before. Then she realized what she'd given away. It was too late now to make up something. After all, the man would soon be standing in front of them. "My husband, Mama. I didn't want him to know I was gone. Fredericks is his butler."

Her mother's mouth gaped open. "Oh, dear sweet Lord, Victoria, your husband didn't know you were gone? What has happened?"

"Nothing, Mama. Nothing has happened." *Not yet.*

"Victoria, I think it's high time you told the truth about your *visit* home." This was her father, no longer sounding like her indulgent champion.

"I agree," Jeff said coolly, his level gaze on his sister. "The scandals continue, don't they, Victoria? One right after the other. Now you've left your husband while still in your honeymoon year."

"I have done no such thing." Spencer had left her first, actually; but this was no time to clear the air on that murky issue, either. Victoria placed her napkin on the table, beside her plate, and stood up, looking from one to the other of her parents. "If you will excuse me?"

"So you can do what? Run away again? I think not," her mother said. Two spots of high color rode her cheeks. "This is the last straw, Victoria Sofia. The very last straw. We have made enough excuses already for you. What you will *not* do is leave us to face that man alone." Victoria opened her mouth to protest, but her mother cut her off with: "Tut-tut. You came back home to River's End with no explanation, daughter. You just showed up on the doorstep with your English maid and your traveling trunks. And we did not press you for reasons because we have missed you so very much and felt so sorrowful for . . . for—"

"Selling me to the highest bidder, like you would a slave?" Victoria supplied cruelly.

Her mother—and father—gasped, but it was her mother who recovered first. "We *never* sold a slave—and we most certainly did not *sell* you. What we *bought* you, though, was respectability. And what we *saved* you from was the lonely life of a spinster. And this is how you thank us? By throwing it in our faces and running away from your husband?" She sat back, glaring at Victoria. "I am completely at my wit's end with you, Victoria. I've a good mind to simply leave you sitting here alone to greet that poor man by yourself. It's what you deserve."

"I'm not afraid to face my husband on my own, Mama." She was, in fact, terrified. "But allow me to remind you that it was not my idea to marry him. And I vow I would have been much happier as a spinster than I was locked away as my husband's prisoner in England."

"Prisoner?" This word was echoed by all three Redmonds.

Victoria looked from one to the other of them. "Yes. Prisoner. I did not run away. I escaped." It wasn't completely a lie.

"Escaped? He had you locked up?" Catherine Redmond

had a shaking hand clasped over her mouth as she turned to her husband. "Oh, dear God, what have we done to our child? Isaac, I thought you knew this man."

"I did, Catherine. And I still do. Don't you see what she's doing? She's trying to muddy the water and take our attention away from her misdeeds. Why, His Grace the Duke of Moreland would never lock a woman up." Victoria's father snapped his attention to her. "Unless he had a very good reason."

Victoria's face stung with burning shame, but she said nothing, not one word. The duke did have a very good reason for locking her up, had he actually chosen to, only she wasn't about to supply it to her parents.

"Do you see, Catherine? She has nothing to say for herself." Her father's expression suddenly crumpled, making him look older, sadder. When he spoke, he sounded defeated. "I swear to you, Victoria, I don't know what to do with you or what even to think anymore. I cannot explain your behavior."

Hurt and shame coursed through Victoria, but she held her head erect. Dignity was all she had at this moment. "You don't have to, Daddy. I am no longer your responsibility."

"No, you are not. And it pains me to say this, but I feel sorry for the man who does bear that burden now. John Spencer Whitfield is a fine, upstanding man with an unblemished reputation."

"Which is more than we can say about you, Sister."

Victoria arrowed her attention her brother's way. "Are you certain, big brother, you wish to enter into this fray with me? Because I would wager you are not so sterling of character as you would have us believe."

Jeff's expression hardened, but he looked away first.

"Victoria!" her mother cried. "That is uncalled for. Jefferson has done nothing."

Her gaze still resting on her brother's profile, Victoria said: "Yes, Mama, that is exactly what I fear. Jefferson has done nothing."

She could see, in her mind, the accusations against him contained in the letter she had received, the one that had set her on this precipitous course for home— No, River's End was no longer her home. Jefferson had been right about that. She had no home. No place she could run to and feel safe. Could anything in life be worse than knowing that?

"Well, Victoria, what do you propose we do? Just sit here eating our eggs?"

"I don't see why not, Mama."

"Oh, you don't? Let me remind you that I did not raise you to—"

A fist being banged on the table—Isaac Redmond's, to be exact—caused the china dishes and silverware to clatter. His quarreling family quickly turned to him at the head of the table. He pointed an accusing finger at Victoria. "Let me remind you, daughter, that your"—his mouth worked as he evidently struggled for an appropriate word—"*situation* was of your own making, not mine or your mother's."

"Believe me, sir, I am aware of that, and I live with the knowledge daily—"

"It is only right that you do." Her father surged to his feet, pressing his palms against the tabletop. Red-faced with anger, he leaned toward Victoria. "What is not right is you have again brought your tangled web of lies to this house. How could you—and after your mother and I went to great expense and discomfort to do the best we could by you under very trying circumstances this past summer? Have you no respect? Now, out with it—the truth. We deserve that much before your husband arrives at our doorstep."

Though she glared at them, Victoria realized she wasn't so sure they did deserve the truth, or that she owed it to them. She tried to convince herself that they said the things they did because they cared and because they were scared for her. But she didn't really believe that. They were embarrassed by her presence here. And their only concern, it seemed to her, was that she would bring more scandal their way. It was horrible, this feeling. She felt certain she could hear the unraveling of the ties that had bound her to her family. The hurt. Dear God, the hurt. Victoria wanted to do nothing more than to run and hide. She wanted to curl up in a secret corner somewhere and not think or do or say. And yet, at this moment, she must do all three.

Stealing over her was a calm and a strength she had never before felt. It washed her in its warmth and helped her compose her expression and her speech. "Forgive me, please, for upsetting you all like this. It truly was not my intention. And I am sorry if my presence here has been a further embarrassment for you. I should have known it would be. But I had thought that River's End would always welcome me. Now I see that I was naïve to think so, after what I did. I won't make this mistake again."

"Victoria, honey—"

"No, Mama, you're going to listen. Not once when I was going through . . . what I was going through did even one of you at this table ever ask me how I was doing or if I was all right. You couldn't see past your own embarrassment to think of me. Not once. Well, let me tell you, it was awful. And it still is." Victoria felt dangerously close to tears. She had to get out of this room and away from these people. "If you will excuse me, I would like merely to be allowed to go make myself presentable for my husband. I do not believe that is so much to ask."

Though her family could not have looked more shocked or miserable, they were nowhere near as surprised as Victoria was to realize she had such dignity inside her. "If you will please simply greet him," she continued, not wanting to give them time to recover their equilibrium and renew their protests, "and show him into the parlor, and entertain him there, I will make every endeavor not to keep you all waiting long."

CHAPTER 6

Followed closely by a heavy dray heaped with traveling trunks, the hired carriage—a fancy landau with matching bays driven by the owner himself, an elderly, cordial man of color who had introduced himself as Mr. Hepplewhite—proceeded along the winding, oak-lined drive up to the impressive house at River's End.

Still at a distance, and like a seductive woman, the white-columned mansion coyly teased the observer with fluttering glimpses of itself around curves in the roadway and through breaks in the seemingly braided branches of the moss-draped oaks. As if encouraged by a soft breeze, the dappled sunlight, like so much bright yellow paint spattered about by a willful child, dotted the lush landscape and danced ahead of the conveyances.

Spencer knew himself well enough to admit that under normal circumstances, he would have been entranced by the exotic beauty of coastal Georgia. The almost painfully green and lush environment fairly spoke to him of languid nights spent with a sultry woman. Indeed, the very warmth of the place encouraged one to slow one's step and lie back and forget one's problems.

Not bloody likely today. Scowling, foul-tempered, and seated across the landau from his secretary and valet,

Spencer couldn't help but compare this scene to the one that fateful day a few weeks back when he'd come home to find his wife gone. On that day, too, he'd been burdened with the carriages, the traveling trunks, Hornsby and Mr. Milton—

And Edward Sparrow, the Right Honorable the Earl of Roxley. Even now, that brigand sat cheerfully mashed up next to Spencer on the carriage's padded leather seat. So far, his blasted cousin had professed a love for every stick, rock, and frog he'd seen in Georgia, but especially he loved her women. Proving this, he'd created a minor stir in Savannah proper by standing in the open carriage, doffing his hat and loudly greeting every comely lady they'd passed as they'd traveled around the many resplendent squares. Spencer counted himself lucky they'd escaped the city without being shot or lynched by a mob of outraged husbands and fathers.

Dismissing that scene from his mind, he concentrated on River's End, the approach to which they now rode through. He found he was able to appreciate the pleasing juxtaposition of the wild beauty that the tame orderliness of the well-manicured grounds seemed only to keep at bay. He noted especially the trailing Spanish moss that draped the oaks with gray beards—but then recalled what, or who, awaited him not too many minutes ahead. With renewed irritation eating at him, he rubbed a finger inside his collar, suddenly detesting this hothouse humidity designed to make breathing damned near impossible unless one were a fish and had gills.

"You're awfully restless, Spence, old man."

Spence, old man, shot his cousin a look. "It's this damned wet and heavy air here. Much like breathing through a damp bath towel, I would suspect."

Edward nodded sagely. "I've had to do that before, and very much against my will. It's not pleasant. But a very good comparison you make."

Spencer cut his gaze his cousin's way but said nothing, lest Edward feel it necessary to enlighten Spencer on the whys and wherefores of his having been forced to breathe through a damp towel. Or not breathe was more like it. No doubt, some lady's husband had come home sooner than expected and found his wife in the bath with Edward. At any rate, Spencer did not wish to be regaled with a tale that was certain to scorch even his far-from-innocent ears.

Though his cousin's shoulder was already pressed against Spencer's, Edward suddenly leaned hard against him and spoke softly. "Do you suppose she'll actually be here, under the circumstances? I mean really. I know we're hoping she is. But do you really suppose she is?"

"If I did not, Edward, do you *suppose* I would be here myself?" Mindful of his secretary and valet only mere feet away, Spencer smiled at his cousin . . . through gritted teeth. "Do not start this line of questioning with me again, Edward, I warn you."

A shared cabin on the Atlantic crossing, as well as many shared bottles of whisky, had provided time and opportunity for Edward to slowly drag out of Spencer every wretched component of his predicament. Spencer now regretted that intimacy because Edward bothered the very devil out of him with his questions and conjectures.

"You see, I was thinking," Edward said, apparently intending to ignore Spencer's warning, "how amusing it would be to find she'd outfoxed us and had never left England. But had only said she meant to travel to Liverpool to throw us off the scent."

"Yes. Very amusing. Only the booking agent very graciously—"

"After you pulled him across the counter by his lapels and shook him."

Spencer ignored this. "At any rate, the booking agent *showed* me the entry where she bought her ticket for passage on a steamship traveling to Savannah."

"That does not mean she actually boarded the ship." Edward had trouble giving up his pet theories. "If she's not here, and I mean at River's End—a name which hardly evokes the grandeur of this place, I must say; look at these magnificent oaks with the wonderfully scary moss—where shall we start our search?"

With each passing second and more intrusive question, Spencer felt less and less inclined to be forthcoming, for all the good it did him. "There is no 'we' in this, Edward. This is my life *you* are dissecting. Besides, that is the fourteenth time, I'll wager, in the past week or more that you have asked me that very question."

Edward appeared appalled. "Really? I say. Then one would think you'd have an answer by now, wouldn't one?"

Spencer caught Mr. Milton and Hornsby staring wide-eyed at him. No doubt, they expected him to pick up and toss his elegantly thin cousin out of the open carriage. Not a bad idea, all in all. Except, upon his return to England, he would have to explain to Edward's dear mother that he had murdered her son. Not a pleasant prospect. She was a kind, gentle woman.

Besides, this time Spencer did have an answer for the Earl of Roxley. "If she's not here"—he no longer worried about keeping his voice down; it was quite impossible to carry on even the most innocuous of conversations in the forced proximity of a carriage this size, and it wasn't as if his two employees weren't aware, to a certain extent, of the reason for their being here—"I shall prevail upon her father for his assistance. He'll know the lay of the land, so to speak, who the right people are, where to look, that sort of thing."

"Oh, jolly good. I'm certain he'll be most happy to help us. However, it seems logical to me that she would be here. A criminal returning to the scene of the crime, as it were."

Spencer frowned mightily. "The woman is my wife and a duchess, Edward. She's hardly a criminal."

Edward tapped Spencer's knee. "No, of course not, old man. Simply a turn of phrase. I meant nothing by it."

After that, Edward was blessedly quiet, which gave Spencer time to wonder if his wife had sought out her former lover once she'd come here. He believed she would have. After all, the letter she'd received had not been from family, according to Fredericks. *The son of a bitch.* He meant the man who had seduced a young girl and then left her on her own to face the consequences and then had the audacity to lure her away again, once she was married. Spencer wondered what the blackguard would do when Victoria told him she carried a baby that could be his. Spencer was willing to bet the wretched man would flee. *Just as I did,* he suddenly realized.

"Do you really think her father will be willing to help?"

"Yes, Edward." After all, Mr. Redmond had been the one, along with his wife, who'd dragged Victoria across the ocean and gone in search of a husband—a very needy but worthy man on foreign soil . . . meaning far, far away from Savannah and all the rumors here. They'd as much as advertised—in a discreet and flattering way, and in the rarefied air of the many balls and suppers held by the ton, of course—for a good, kind, desperate man among the host of impoverished bachelors of the peerage, who would agree to marry their rebellious and compromised daughter for the very high price to be settled upon her. They'd wanted all that and a man who would not mistreat her, either.

Many had pursued her. Victoria Redmond was, after all, as beautiful as she was rich. But the man . . . the fool, the imbecile . . . her parents had chosen—since she'd made it very plain she wanted nothing whatsoever to do with the decision—had been him, Spencer fumed. He'd fit all their criteria, plus he'd been the highest-ranking eligible bachelor to . . . apply for the position.

Looking out the other side of the carriage, away from Edward, Spencer quirked his lips in a self-deprecating manner. There was no other way, delicately or otherwise, to state the proposition than to say he'd applied for the position. It was the truth, yet it certainly wasn't flattering to either one of them. Flattering or not, Spencer didn't think Mr. Redmond would be amused to have his daughter back so soon after the debacle here.

"I think we should go over the other myriad possibilities, Spencer."

Spencer stared into Edward's guileless brown eyes and, very reasonably, said: "And I think I should poke you in the nose for continuing to put it in my business."

Discreet coughing and harrumphing, no doubt meant as a warning to Edward for caution, came from across the narrow aisle from where Spencer and his cousin sat.

Alas, it was lost on Edward. "I'm entirely serious, Spencer. A delving into the range of possibilities we could face in only a few moments' time is called for. Say she's here. What will be your course of action?"

Spencer narrowed his eyes. "I will throw myself into her arms, declare my undying love for her, and beg her to come home with me, whereupon I will throw my duchy and all its wealth at her feet and carry her about on a satin pillow for the rest of her days."

At long last, Edward was insulted. Wordlessly, he turned away, staring out over the cultivated fields, just beyond the lawn, that seemed to stretch on in endless waves. "One would think one would welcome assistance from one's family," he muttered, "even if that family member is of a lesser rank than oneself."

Spencer covered his eyes with a hand and rubbed tiredly at them. *Damn it all to hell.* He flopped his hand into his lap. "All right, Edward, suppose she is here at River's End."

Edward turned excitedly back to Spencer. "No, suppose she isn't, Spencer. Suppose her father, irritated in the extreme to have her show up on his doorstep so soon after her, uh, departure, has already booked passage and left with her to return her to England? Wouldn't that be calamitous?"

"I've thought of that." He hadn't, but he wasn't about to

admit it. He reasoned it out now. "I assume, in that case, should he arrive at Wetherington's Point, he will not be daunted by my absence—"

"Or by Fredericks telling him you've come here to fetch your bride."

Dear God, the possibilities *were* endless. Spencer frowned, thinking about it, putting himself in Mr. Redmond's place. "No. Mr. Redmond doesn't . . . daunt easily in my experience with him. A man who can amass an even greater fortune while being aligned with the losing side of a war would simply leave her at Wetherington's Point with a warning for her to stay put. And then he would return here."

"In which case our trip here will have proved to be pointless."

Spencer eyed Edward meaningfully. "For some of us it already is."

Edward was again oblivious to insult. "Here's something else."

Even Mr. Milton and Hornsby groaned. Spencer almost had, too. "Well, go on, Edward, what is it?"

"Suppose your lovely wife is here and she's come home with a ridiculous story that you abused or neglected her and she's only just escaped being locked up in a tower? If so, we could be riding right into a situation where we'll all be shot on sight."

No one said a word. Spencer wanted very much to tell Edward just how ridiculous his theory was, but found he couldn't. Victoria very well could have done just that.

"Well?" Edward asked.

"Well what?"

"Well, Spencer, what should we do in that case?"

"In a word? Duck."

Edward cuffed his higher-ranking cousin's shoulder. "You're going to get us all killed, man."

Spencer ignored the attack on his person and spoke pointedly. "My dear cousin, I have known the moment in the past several weeks in which that very idea held great appeal for me."

Mr. Milton and Hornsby stared wide-eyed like scared owls at their employer. Spencer merely raised an eyebrow at them. Let them worry. In truth, though, a prick of conscience had assailed Spencer, telling him that the neglected-wife version Edward had just outlined could possibly be proved. But neglectful only in the amount of time he'd spent with her since their wedding. Certainly, the woman, his duchess, had every gown and bauble and indulgence her heart desired. He'd seen to that. Spencer's masculine pride suffered a bit with the realization that even those luxuries had been paid for with Victoria's dowry.

Damn it all, he was tired of riding his own back with that truth. Why couldn't he allow it to count with himself that he had, in exchange for the bailout of his duchy, settled on the young woman a lavish wedding, an honorable six-hundred-year-old title, and instant respectability? That was the bargain brokered with her father, that and his fidelity to the man's daughter, a clause to which he had thus far adhered. He wondered if she could say the same thing since she'd been back in Savannah. Spencer shook his head and exhaled a sigh.

"Are you quite all right, Your Grace?"

Spencer focused on his motherly valet's ruddy and dewlapped face. A concerned expression rode the older man's features. Still, Spencer wanted to shout: *Surely you jest, man. You've experienced every bump in the road and high wave at sea that I have. No, Hornsby, I am not fine. I am, in fact, not certain I will ever be fine again. But thank you for asking.* However, what he actually said was, "Yes, thank you, Hornsby. I'm just tired."

"Spencer, old man, I've thought of something else."

Completely deadpan, Spencer said: "And I feel certain you will tell me what it is, Edward."

"She could not be here at all, you know."

"She'll be here."

As if doing so helped him think out loud, Edward wagged a finger at Spencer. "Not necessarily. She might not have contacted her family in any way since she left England. She might have booked passage to Savannah but, once she arrived here, she then immediately departed for somewhere else . . . with, ahem, someone else. So her family could be none the wiser. If that proves to be so, you will be in the humiliating position of arriving unexpectedly at the Redmonds' front door, your hat in your hand, and bearing the wonderful news that their daughter is missing."

Shocked by this possibility, Spencer stared straight ahead, as good as looking through Hornsby. The horrible thing here was Edward could be absolutely right. That scoundrel who had seduced Victoria could have set it all up, and they were even now elsewhere and together. This realization elevated Spencer's mood to murderous.

"No," he said aloud and with force, needing to hear himself say it. "She's here, I know she is."

No one contradicted him. Spencer again turned his head to look out the side of the carriage opposite from Edward. She had to be here. He could hardly wait to see her, to confront her, and yet he had about convinced himself she was the last person he wanted to see. He indulged himself with a mental image of himself in front of her and smiling and saying, *Why, hello, my dear. How nice to see you. I would be the happiest man on earth right now if you would simply go straight to hell.* And then he would turn around and walk away.

However, that couldn't happen. She was his duchess, and she could be carrying his heir. But he did wonder what his wife would have to say for herself and how she would act. Would she be contrite? Tearful? Angry? Rebellious? Surprised?

Surely, not surprised. She had to have at least feared he would find out she had flown and would then follow her.

Pride and responsibility dictated that he would. But beyond that, Spencer really could not completely deny that he relished the thought of seeing her again. She was, if nothing else, a passionate woman in all ways, but especially in temperament and daring. He respected very much how she had stood up to him on the day she'd told him her news. Very brave of her. And honest. Spencer grinned. Never a dull moment with her, no matter her sins.

But, if the other man was involved at all, Spencer couldn't say, despite weeks of time to do nothing else but think about this situation, how he might behave or what he might do. If it proved to be true that she had run to him and he, Spencer, took her home with him, how could he ever trust her again—or be certain she'd stay? He'd heard it said that the seed of doubt, once planted, never lay fallow, but grew in the heart like a thorny vine until it squeezed out any love it found there. Spencer's mood darkened, bringing a troubled grimace to his face. *Damn it all to hell.*

Though he rocked along in the well-sprung carriage, with the horses' tack jingling pleasantly, and with the sweet scent of exotic flowers filling the air, Spencer sat unmoved by it all. Dear God, he was sick of all this mental wrangling. He simply wanted to collect his wife, worry about the details later, and embark immediately on the return voyage home. But the mere thought of another ocean crossing made Spencer queasy. Given the stormy trip they'd all endured to arrive at this coastal Georgia city, he was loath even to see another steamship, much less board one.

Adding to his discomfort, and doing its part to keep his glower firmly in place, was this seemingly interminable ride out to River's End. They'd already traveled from the raucous and bustling riverfront docks and then through Savannah proper. What a beautiful and orderly city it was, too, laid out around green parklike squares. Still, although they had only disembarked from the steamship and then hopped into this crowded carriage, the day was proving to be one of many upsets. Bearing witness to this was Hornsby, a consummate valet but not a young man anymore, who looked a bit green, and the young and fussy Mr. Milton, who sported an impressive bleached-white coloring.

"If you will forgive me speaking, Your Grace?" Mr. Milton said suddenly, leaning toward Spencer in a respectful imitation of a bow, something hard to execute fully when one was seated.

Spencer eyed the man impatiently, but with considerably more warmth than he would have shown Edward, had his cousin felt inclined to offer another of his outrageous theories. "Please, Mr. Milton. Proceed."

"Thank you, Your Grace. I was thinking that despite the obvious beauty and charms we have encountered here, I feel more as if we've landed on another planet than simply another continent. The people and the language are quite foreign to my eye and my ear. It's all very strange." The properly dressed and sweltering secretary sat back and swatted irritably at some huge, flying, buzzing insect that had rudely landed on his cheek. "Heaven help me, I fear I am being eaten alive by these horrid creatures."

"I expect you'll get used to it over time," Spencer remarked evenly, not possessing the least bit of sympathy for the young man's complaints. Indeed, he'd had nothing but complaints since they'd left Wetherington's Point for Liverpool and points beyond.

Traveling together, it seemed, bred not only familiarity but contempt—at least, on the part of his valet and secretary for each other . . . and Spencer for both of them. He hadn't known the two men shared a mutual hatred—there was no other word for it—until he'd been forced into close company with them for days on end aboard the steamship. Over time, their constant bickering, in combination with the angry seas, had been enough to cause Spencer to seriously consider tossing one or both of them overboard. Of course, he would have thrown Edward over for good measure, as well. Or even himself. Only good breeding, on the one hand, and strong liquor, on the other, had stopped him. And, of course, the thought of Edward's mother.

"Oh, I say," Hornsby drawled, eyeing the bespectacled secretary, "the winged pests do seem especially fond of you, Mr. Milton. They've been buzzing around you since we first stepped on terra firma." The expression on the valet's fleshy, heavily jowled face became faintly superior. "Myself, I have yet to be accosted."

Knowing all too well how this little exchange would play out, Spencer wished he'd not packed his pistol in a far-removed traveling trunk, now that he sorely needed the damned thing.

Sure enough, Mr. Milton's retort to Hornsby was quick in coming. The secretary's smile, which could only be called sour as he focused on his nemesis, revealed plainly enough how close to being accosted Hornsby was—and not by flying insects, either. "I am certain that the reason you have not been bitten, Hornsby, is because you do not smell good to them."

Hornsby was not amused. His glower proved this. "I beg your pardon, sir. How dare you—"

"Tut-tut. Do not interrupt me, my good fellow. First allow me to take exception to what else you said. Meaning, there's not the first thing firma about this terra we find ourselves on. For, despite a few high and dry places, such as this road, I fear it's all fens and bogs and marshes."

"Indeed," Hornsby all but sneered. "A perfect soup for breeding something as hideous as malaria, I'd say." Mr. Milton's horrified intake of breath cheered Hornsby considerably. "Malaria. An Italian term, actually. Two words made into one. *Mal.* And *aria.* Quite literally, 'bad air,' such as that from fens and bogs and marshes."

"Really?" This was the ever-curious Edward Sparrow. "I had no idea, Hornsby."

"Oh, yes, sir, it's quite true. But do you know the symptoms?" He turned to Mr. Milton. "Chief among them are night sweats, a loss of hair, and high fevers. Not very pleasant in the least. And from what I understand, younger persons who are thin and sallow, such as yourself, Mr. Milton, are more prone to it than their older, healthier counterparts."

Mr. Milton pinched his thin lips together and glared at the man mashed up next to him on the narrow seat. "I think you are making the whole thing up, Hornsby. Especially the part about age."

"I say," the outraged valet huffed. "Are you calling me a liar, sir?"

At last exasperated, and fearing they would escalate to an all-out brawl that would tip the landau over—especially if Edward decided to egg them on—Spencer warned: "That will be enough. And I mean for the rest of the day. One more word from either of you and I will bodily and cheerfully toss you both out and under the wheels of the dray following us. Do I make myself clear?"

Like scolded children sitting cramped together, their shoulders hunched, the thin, elegant secretary and the heavyset butler stared wide-eyed and quietly across the aisle at their employer, the duke.

"Good," Spencer added, accepting their contrite demeanors as compliance.

"Excuse me, suh," Mr. Hepplewhite, the driver, called back over his shoulder. "River's End ain't but one mo' turn 'round the bend in the road up heah. I expect we'll be there in a moment or two."

Still eyeing his recalcitrant employees, Spencer said, "Thank you, Mr. Hepplewhite. Not a moment too soon, either."

CHAPTER 7

Because Spencer had reason to believe, given the possibly contentious nature of his visit, that he might not be asked to stay—or would not do so even if he were—at the truly lovely plantation of River's End, he'd asked Mr. Hepplewhite and his son, the burly driver of the dray, to wait and not to unload the trunks. Even now, they were watering their horses and engaging in spirited conversation with several black Redmond employees who were obviously men of their acquaintance.

Once inside, Hornsby and Mr. Milton had been escorted by an elegantly dressed elderly Negro man, who told them he was the butler and introduced himself as Virgil, to a separate parlor near the kitchen. There, they'd been assured, refreshments awaited them.

Spencer hadn't fared as well. He, along with Edward, the elder Redmonds, and their firstborn, a tall, slender, light-haired man named Jefferson, whom Spencer had just met for the first time, were gathered in a more formal and elegant drawing room, also on the first floor. The pleasantries, if they could be called that under these rather strained and unusual circumstances, had been exchanged. And now, the room was quiet . . . preternaturally so, for being occupied by four adults, all of whom spoke the same language, or at least a close approximation of the same language, and all of whom had one very pressing but not-yet-present subject in common.

To Spencer's intense relief, his wife was in residence. And the waiting, now that his quarry was within reach, was, in a word, hell. He cursed the strictures of politeness and convention that saw him and Edward so tamely seated in matching parlor chairs situated across the room from the Redmonds. Spencer's angry inclination was to rage up the stairs, bellowing his wife's name as he charged into every room until he damned well found her and had it out with her. But, alas, that was not to be. This was not his home and he had no idea what, if anything, his wife had told her family her reason was for being here. For all he knew, he was the villain and would be shot dead if he so much as raised his voice.

This concern was readily borne out by the Redmonds' combined and censorious attitude toward him. Their scowls and quietness were oppressive enough even to keep Edward silent. As it was, the stern-faced elder Mr. Redmond stared steadily at Spencer from his perch at the end of the carved mantel mounted above a marble-fronted fireplace that held, instead of firewood, a beautiful array of fresh flowers in a tall vase. Spencer fully expected their beauty to be short-lived, given the pall in the room.

Even the lovely and petite Mrs. Redmond, seated decorously on an upholstered chair close to her husband, sent Spencer unhappy looks. As for the younger Redmond, that tall and dour dandy had seated himself at the opposite end of the fireplace, farther away from his parents than he was from Spencer. What Spencer found most interesting about his hosts and hostess, though, was how they kept glancing—no doubt, they thought surreptitiously—toward the closed doors of the room.

Fed up with silence and subterfuge, Spencer openly allowed his gaze to stray there, too.

"We expect her at any moment now," Mr. Redmond said suddenly, drawing Spencer's attention to him.

Well, that had certainly worked. Spencer nodded regally. "So you've said, Mr. Redmond."

Mrs. Redmond gestured and caught Spencer's attention. "Are you certain I cannot offer you and your cousin some refreshment, Your Grace? Tea, perhaps? Or coffee? We were just enjoying our breakfast when you arrived, so there's still plenty of warm, fresh food available. I could have you a nice plate fixed, if you'd like. Something to fortify you."

Spencer settled his attention on Mrs. Redmond, a softly pretty older version of her daughter. No doubt, he would need fortification before the day was done, but of the sort that came from a whisky bottle. "You're very kind, Mrs. Redmond, but no, thank you."

"I could certainly do with a little something."

Spencer snapped his head to his left, glaring daggers, murder, and lightning bolts his cousin's way.

"Oh," Mrs. Redmond said, sounding disconcerted. "I'll just ring for Virgil."

But Edward had already got the message. For once, he heeded Spencer's warning. "No, don't trouble yourself, Mrs. Redmond. You're very kind. Perhaps another time."

Mollified, Spencer looked again to Mrs. Redmond, who appeared relieved as she settled herself in her chair. "Well, if you're sure. It's just that you've come such a long way. All the way from England."

"Yes, we have," Spencer said, smiling again. "However, they did feed us on the crossing."

Mrs. Redmond laughed . . . a rich, seductive sound that would, no doubt, and God help us all, enchant Edward. "Oh, how well I remember. It's a horribly long and tiring trip, too."

"Very true." The polite small talk raced up the short fuse of Spencer's temper. He hadn't come all this way to sit in a parlor and trade inanities. And well the Redmonds knew it.

Just then, Spencer again caught Catherine Redmond nervously glancing toward the closed door to the room. Enough was enough. If they would not broach the subject, he damned well would. "You did say Victoria is here, did you not, Mrs. Redmond? As you said, I've come a long way, so you can understand my desire to . . . see my wife."

Mrs. Redmond opened her mouth to speak, but before she could utter a single word, the closed doors to the large and airy room opened. All heads turned that way. And there Victoria stood, very much the actress who had been standing in the wings and listening for her cue to make her grand entrance. And grand she was: a vision in a navy blue day dress that captured the color of her eyes. Stunning. Rich mahogany hair piled atop her head. Bewitching figure.

Spencer, along with the other men present, rose to their feet. Utter silence filled the room.

Victoria's gaze sought and found Spencer's. In that instant, he was seized by an unearthly feeling of such magnitude that he felt pinned to the floor, unable to move a muscle or to look away from Victoria. The room, the other people in it with him and her, faded to one feathery-edged blur of sight and sound. Only she and he existed. A sudden, overwhelming feeling of time and energy rushing forward in defiance of the very laws of nature seized Spencer. He felt he was being pushed, flung against his will and without taking a step, right up to Victoria. Like opposing magnetic fields compelled to connect and to collide.

Despite everything she'd done and how she'd humiliated him, Spencer could not look away from her. She seemed no more capable of breaking their locked gazes than he was. This was the most awful and wonderful feeling—

And then it was gone. All was suddenly ordinary motion and action. Spencer exhaled as subtly as was possible for a man who felt he'd just reentered his own body. He frowned, calling himself a practical man who had both feet firmly on the ground. Odd things such as that moment did not happen to him. It was utterly ridiculous. Thus, he was able to convince himself that it hadn't happened at all and nothing was changed. Especially not him. And certainly not Victoria.

She was approaching him now, appearing almost to glide toward him. She stopped in front of him and rested her hand intimately on his sleeve as she raised her face to his. Frowning, wary—Victoria had never before voluntarily touched him—Spencer looked from her hand on his arm to her face. He expected to see guilt in her blue eyes, or maybe a gloating tilt to her expression. But what he actually saw was some jagged, broken emotion that unsettled him and begged him to . . . do what, he had no idea.

"Hello, darling," she finally said, her voice soft and husky.

Spencer came to attention. So, a public scene of tender reunion was to be her game. Very well. He smiled, knowing that only he and she knew she'd never before called him "darling" or any other form of endearment.

"Hello, my dear," he replied glibly. He looked her up and down pointedly, noting her lovely gown. "You're dressed for company. I'm sorry, have I come at an inconvenient time?"

She blinked, looking fearful, and shook her head no. "Company? Who would I be expecting— I mean, no, of course not." She tried a smile but it wouldn't hold. "You're hardly company. I dressed like this for you . . . Spencer."

"You did? For me? How very clever of you, especially since you had no idea I would be arriving today . . . or even at all."

Flicking his gaze to her family, Spencer saw her father and mother and brother exchange anxious glances. But only Spencer saw Victoria's pink little tongue flick out to moisten her lips. So she was nervous, was she? Good. She'd damned well better be.

She quickly recovered and gave his chest a playful pat that had Spencer raising his eyebrows. "Don't be silly. Of course I knew you were coming. I just didn't know . . .

when, exactly. And I find myself wondering what took you so long getting here."

Did she seriously expect him to go along with this charade? "What took me so long? Why, the Atlantic Ocean, mostly. Crossing it, I mean. It's a rather large pond. And we found ourselves on a slow boat."

A snort of amusement from Edward's direction reminded everyone of his presence.

"And you've brought Edward," Victoria announced happily, pulling away from Spencer. No doubt, she was relieved to do so. She turned a dazzling smile on his cousin as she went to grip the young earl's eager hands. "Why, Edward, I do declare, you handsome scamp you, it is wonderful to see you again."

That fool Edward preened and bowed. "Why, thank you, Your Grace—"

"Oh, la. We're family. I'm Victoria to you. And you've been introduced to my family, I am certain?"

"Oh, yes, quite delightful. I must say you're looking radiant, Victoria. It's so good to see you again, too."

He sounded so damned sincere and charming that Spencer could have choked him. Before he could act on that impulse, Mrs. Redmond abruptly stood and cried out. "Victoria! What—? I don't understand. What is the meaning of this?"

Taken aback, Spencer stared from mother to daughter. He watched Victoria release Edward's hands and turn to her mother. "The meaning of what, Mama? I am merely greeting—"

"Not that. You know very well what I mean. *This*. I'm talking about *this*." Clearly vexed, Mrs. Redmond pointed out to the hallway beyond the open doors to the parlor. Mr. Redmond edged over to see for himself, raised his eyebrows, and bleated a surprised curse.

What now? All Spencer could see was the wall and a

large painting of Mrs. Redmond in her younger days. But, in short order, she cleared up the mystery.

"Your traveling bags, Victoria. Duke and Rubin just went by with them and out the front door. And Rosanna followed them, carrying her bags. What are you doing? Where are you going now?"

Her posture stiffening, Victoria raised her chin. "Why, I'm leaving with my husband, Mama."

Her entire family raised protests of one sort or another. Surprised, Spencer looked from his wife to her family and then to Edward, who shrugged, and finally settled his gaze again on Victoria as she continued.

"Isn't that what you and Daddy wanted? Wasn't that what you said to me not more than thirty minutes ago? How River's End is no longer my home? Did I misunderstand?"

"We said nothing of the sort," Isaac Redmond contradicted her. "Certainly your husband and his cousin are more than welcome to stay here. Why, we have already welcomed them into our home and are happy to have them here with us, Victoria, as we are you."

"What your father says is true," her mother seconded. "Even now, rooms are being aired out and made ready."

"I am so sorry, Mama, Daddy. But the rooms won't be needed. We won't be staying."

Though Spencer had no idea what had happened here before he arrived, and who might be at fault, he did intend to support his wife in this. He might have his own devil of a time with her, but she was still the Duchess of Moreland and therefore deserving of his respect. For now and in this matter, at any rate.

Mrs. Redmond held her hands out in supplication. "I don't understand, Victoria. After everything you said at breakfast about"—she cut her gaze over to Spencer—"uh, your life in England, I believe it would be best if you stayed here with us."

So she *had* made him out to be the villain. Spencer angrily firmed his lips together in an effort not to speak precipitously. Let Victoria have her say now. He'd have his when he got her alone.

"I'm sorry, Mama," she was saying, "but I can't stay here." Her voice, to Spencer's surprise, was a hard chip of flint. "It's really very simple. My visit here at home . . ." She stopped, laughed . . . a brittle sound . . . and raised a hand as if to say, *Give me a moment.* "No, I'm sorry, this isn't home anymore, is it?"

Mrs. Redmond pressed a hand against her chest. "Of course it is."

"What I *should* have said," Victoria continued, ignoring her mother's protest to the contrary, "was my time here at River's End, though of short duration, has been very pleasant, and you've all made me feel quite . . . welcome. However, my husband is here now, and I wish to leave with him."

"Oh, Victoria, honey, not like this," her mother cried, pushing her knuckles against her mouth and staring, her heart in her eyes, at her daughter.

Mr. Redmond stepped forward and put his arm around his wife's waist. "Victoria," he said, looking miserable, "this isn't necessary."

Jefferson Redmond came to his feet. "Yes, it is, Daddy. We all know it is. It's way past time Victoria left."

Though Spencer heard Edward's discreet little cough that spoke eloquently of his discomfort in witnessing this domestic scene, Spencer ignored him, glared at Jefferson, and then watched Victoria. For some reason he couldn't name, he admired her at this moment. He really did.

"Why, thank you, Jeff," she said sweetly to her brother. "As always, you're on my side." She turned to her parents. "It breaks my heart, but this is how it has to be." She pivoted to face Spencer. "Isn't it necessary that I go with you?"

"I'm afraid it is," he said without hesitation and thinking how right he'd been to detain the carriages and Mr. Hepplewhite and his son. "It's absolutely necessary that you go with me. And *stay* with me, Victoria."

Spencer saw the uncertainty residing in her eyes. "Yes, of course. Stay with you. That's only as it should be."

He nodded slowly, pointedly. "As long as you understand."

"I do. I understand."

Spencer thought he knew better. He was too smart to delude himself with the notion that she had come to her senses and meant to be an obedient wife from here on out. *Hardly.* He knew full well that he was, at this moment, nothing more to her than a convenient means of escape from whatever the quarrel with her family had been. *Well enough.* He could play that role. He also knew that the moment of her need for him would pass . . . and soon.

This realization did nothing to improve his mood, especially on a morning when he was already dead with weariness. Nevertheless Spencer turned his attention to the elder Redmonds. "If you would be so good as to ring for someone to ask my valet and secretary to make ready to leave? Thank you. And you will, I hope, forgive me for leaving after so short a visit?"

He gave them no time to reply as he turned to his wife. "Victoria?" He held a hand out to her. She came to him and allowed him to take her elbow.

Spencer meant only to turn to Edward to signal him to follow, but Victoria's nearness, her sweet-scented body, the very female warmth of her, caught him off guard. An unexpected jolt of sensual awareness shot through Spencer, leaving him appalled at his body's stiffening response. He breathed in deeply, searching for calm and control, and then exhaled through his mouth, refusing to be affected. When he sought Edward's gaze, he found him smirking. Curse him, he knew. Spencer frowned mightily at him. "Shall we take our leave, Edward?"

Though his mouth twitched with merriment, the Earl of Roxley nodded regally. "Of course. Would you, uh, like me to precede you out of the room?"

Denying the rising heat up his neck to his face, as well as downward and elsewhere, Spencer curled his lip at his cousin. "It won't be necessary."

Edward's gaze momentarily flicked to below Spencer's waist and then again met Spencer's glaring countenance. "I could beg to differ; however, I will not." He then turned to the Redmonds, making his manners. "It was my pleasure to meet you. Perhaps we'll have an opportunity to see each other again."

"You will," Spencer said, surprising them all. "We travel only so far as Savannah at this point." Victoria wrenched in his grasp, but he held her tightly as he told her parents: "We will secure lodging there, and we will let you know where we can be reached."

"There's no need," Mr. Redmond said, holding up a hand to stop Spencer's ready protest to the contrary. "I have just had a new townhouse completed in Savannah proper. It is furnished and staffed and fronts onto Oglethorpe Square. I think you will find it very comfortable there. I would be honored if you would consider it your residence while you are here."

It was a neat solution, and Spencer grabbed it. He nodded his acquiescence to the older man. "As you wish."

"It's not at all what I wish, but it's the best I can do right now." The steely look in his light-colored eyes reminded Spencer that Isaac Redmond was a wily businessman, a self-made baron of international industry, and a man who drove a very hard bargain. He was not to be trifled with. "Victoria knows where it is and can direct you. I'll send a messenger ahead to tell my staff there to ready it for you. You'll find everything you need, including a carriage and horses."

As Spencer gave his attention and his quiet regard to his

father-in-law, a look of understanding and mutual respect passed between them. Spencer smiled. "Thank you. You're very kind."

Mr. Redmond's eyes narrowed slightly. "You be the same to my daughter, Your Grace. Or you'll deal with me."

The implicit warning in the man's words tensed Spencer, but he nodded his understanding and his respect. "I understand, sir."

Following that exchange, with no one protesting or commenting further, and with Edward flanking them, Spencer turned and walked his wife out of her parents' plantation home.

Victoria thought the house in Savannah an absolute jewel. The resplendent three-story, gray-bricked Italianate mansion on Oglethorpe Square boasted iron balconies and railings on its façade. At its back resided an intimate, well-manicured and high-walled garden that ran the width of the back of the house and the length of the property to the alley. A lush growth of trees, magnolia and oak among them, provided welcome shelter from the afternoon sun as she sat alone on a delicately carved wrought-iron, decorative bench.

She allowed her gaze to follow the meandering gravel path that wound its way around the riotously blooming beds of late-summer flowers. At the garden's other end, a securely latched wooden gate opened onto the alley used by the various delivery wagons that plied their trade among the upper crust of Savannah society. One such wagon was making its trundling way past the Redmond home just now. The driver was singing low, probably amusing himself and soothing his horse at the same time.

Though Victoria could only hear the wagon, not see it, she still looked in that direction and smiled. She hadn't realized until now how much she had missed the unique sights, sounds, and smells of Savannah. There wasn't a thing about this gracious city that she didn't love. Well, except the gossips. But she could hardly complain. She'd certainly given them enough to talk about since the days of her not-so-well-behaved childhood onward, although nothing like she had a few months ago. And knowing herself like she did, Victoria sighed, she was nowhere near done giving Savannah's tongues a reason to wag.

They'd do more than wag. Given the reason she'd come home, and the people and lies and misdeeds she might be forced to expose, she only hoped the well-bred, upper-class society didn't lynch her. They very well could, she knew, because the guilty parties whom she suspected were among their ranks. Victoria shook her head. "Lord above, what have I got myself into this time?"

If she received no answer, it was because she already knew what she'd got herself into. And she hated it. Though her body felt refreshed—she'd slept, leaning against her husband's shoulder . . . the familiar scent of him had lulled her senses . . . all the way from River's End and then upstairs most of the day—she still felt weary right to her very soul. What a complication it was that Spencer had come here. She didn't have to wonder why he'd come after her, a woman he'd said he didn't wish to see. Even despite her carrying his possible heir, wounded male pride, turned to anger that she would leave against his specific instructions, would be enough to get him across the Atlantic. But now that he was here, what was she supposed to do with him?

Her woman's heart knew what it would like to do with him, making its point eloquently with some intriguing and sensual images. Chuckling guiltily—well-bred girls were not supposed to enjoy that act in all its varieties—Victoria stared at her shoes, dainty-heeled slippers that matched her navy-blue day dress, and gave in to her purely feminine thoughts that society could not dictate. She would not deny what she felt. The thrill of seeing Spencer again and knowing he had chased her and did want her to come back had made her feel wanted. She hadn't realized how important knowing that was to her until it had happened. Yes, she knew he wanted her back because of the baby and only until she delivered it. Yes, she knew that should it prove not to be a Whitfield, he would send her away. And, yes, she knew she should guard her heart against that day. And she would. But none of those eventualities could lessen, at this moment, the heartwarming thrill she'd experienced just knowing he did care enough, for whatever reason, to come after her.

A sudden, unbidden frisson of desire skittered over Victoria's senses, reminding her that this man wanted her, physically at least, in all the ways a man can want a woman. And she wanted him. His passion for her, and hers for him, had to mean something deeper was there between them, didn't it? But even if it was, dare she give herself over to it? Dare she forget, for even one moment, to guard her heart until the day the baby came? And even if the baby turned out to be his, could she live with him and the knowledge that had the baby not been his, he would have set her aside? Could she love someone like that? Could she trust someone like that?

This wasn't the first time she'd asked herself these questions. The answers to them kept nagging at her, yet she always tried to push them away. But sometimes, like now, they barged through her doubts and shouted to her that the only solution was for her not to allow herself to care for him. Ever. Victoria swallowed the rising emotion clogging her throat. It was already too late. She did care. But how could he have come to mean so much to her already? This wanting to run to him and throw her arms around him and beg him never to put her aside was awful. Had she no pride? How cold and uncaring did he have to be before she cried *enough*?

And yet he wasn't really cold and uncaring. He was, of course, right now, extremely angry with her and mistrusting. But many times he'd been so tender and kind and solicitous of her—admittedly, before they knew about this baby—that she had found herself coming to like and respect him. Again, she saw him, in her mind, squiring her around London as they'd attended balls and she'd been presented at court. His very nearness, the scent of him, the way he wore his clothes, everything about him, had swept her off her feet.

But now, this complicating pregnancy and all the anger and distance and mistrust it had engendered between them had ruined any chance they had to make a marriage together. This was horrible—she could hardly stand to admit it, but she feared she loved her husband. She must never tell him. What would be the gain? None. And yet, seeing him to-day . . . Lord, she had almost forgot how handsome and sensual he was, with his thick black hair and eyes every bit as dark. He simply smoldered with animal vitality. It was the oddest thing to Victoria, that she could want him so much and yet be so afraid of him and so wary, as she must be.

"Whoa! Hold up there!"

Out in the alleyway, the wagon's driver calling out to his team popped Victoria back to the moment and the garden. Happy to be pulled out of the morass of her emotions, she willfully surrendered herself to the moment and the singing birds in the trees. Smiling languidly, lulled by the sunshine's slanting warmth, she breathed in deeply of the richly scented air, redolent with a commingling of sweet-scented flowers and moist earth and the sharper tang of the Savannah River, only several blocks away.

In so many ways, this house . . . she turned her head to stare at its gracious outline . . . felt more welcoming to her than had River's End. Just thinking about the graceful white-columned house where she'd lived most of her life unraveled a thread of sadness inside Victoria. She'd believed she would always be a child of that plantation home. Always. She had so many fond memories of it. But the best, most exciting memories were those of the elaborate dinners and balls—suspended, of course, during the years of the war—her parents had held there, the latter ones in her honor as she'd grown into a young lady. A young lady who had disgraced herself and her family, in short order.

Realizing she'd traveled backward emotionally to troubled times and thoughts, Victoria forced herself to concentrate on today and this new place in which she found herself. This house, with its brick solidness, the new-wood smell inside and the fine wallpapers and the stately furnishings, she liked very much. Or was it more because her family wasn't here to question her every move? That could certainly be a part of it, she acknowledged. Along those lines, she'd have to get word to Jubal that she was no longer at River's End, so he could tell Miss Cicely. Getting information to and from her would certainly be harder now, Victoria realized, since she didn't have access to the swamp. And it wasn't as if Jubal could come here. Although, Victoria had to admit, she wouldn't be surprised if Miss Cicely already knew what had happened this morning at River's End and even knew where Victoria was now.

And Spencer. How to get around him to do those things she needed to do? She couldn't even tell him why she'd come. But even if she could, she wondered, would she? She wasn't certain she could trust him, not with this delicately balanced situation. He didn't know how things worked here, how people thought. This wasn't England where he and his pompous ilk ruled—

"Why, here you are, Victoria."

Startled, gasping, she pressed a hand against her chest, over her pounding heart, as she turned and stared into her husband's face. "Mercy, Your Grace, you nearly frightened the life out of me."

His black eyes studied her. "Not for the first time today, I'd wager."

Guilt had Victoria looking down at her hands in her lap. "And you'd win that wager."

"At any rate, I'm glad I found you out here alone, Victoria. I have some questions for you, as you can well imagine."

"Yes. I can." She intuited the thick vein of anger pulsing

under his almost pleasant tone of voice and feared her frightened-bird's heart would flutter right out of her chest.

"Good."

When he didn't say anything else, Victoria finally raised her gaze to meet his. To her surprise, his attention was not fixed on her. Instead, and standing next to the bench upon which she sat, he'd hooked his thumbs in the waistband of his dark, close-fitting trousers, settled his weight on one leg, and was smiling as he studied the garden. "I looked in the parlor where you told me you'd be. Of course, you were not. I half believed you had again made off without telling me. That seems to be a bad habit of yours, this leading me on merry chases. But then I found your Rose; and she said you'd come outside."

"Rosanna," Victoria corrected. Her emotions a mixture of hesitance and wariness, she added: "And now you've found me. Here I am."

"It's not that simple, Victoria."

"Isn't it, Your Grace?"

"Spencer. And no, it is not. Tell me why you left. And I mean England."

He meant to go directly for her jugular. "I—I told you I wanted to come home to my mother. And that is exactly where you found me. So you see? It *is* that simple."

"If it were that simple, you would not have instructed my servants not to inform me of your leaving."

"I did that only because I hoped to be back before you found out I was gone." The truth just popped out of her mouth, leaving her wide-eyed with guilt.

"Are you telling me you meant to return? That this jaunt of yours is nothing more than a quick trip home to visit your mother?"

"Yes."

His smile became a quick slash across his lips. "You disappoint me, Victoria, with your lies."

"Lies?" Yes, she was lying, but for a good reason. Still,

the audacity of the man bristled her like a porcupine. "I am *not* lying—"

"But you are. The letter you received, Victoria? Who was that from?"

CHAPTER 8

Oh, dear God, he knows about the letter. The shock took the fight and the breath right out of Victoria. She clutched at the wrought-iron edge of the bench seat under her and stared wide-eyed up at him.

"It's all there on your face, Victoria. You did not think I knew about that, nor did you wish for me to know about it. We both know why, too."

"No you don't . . . Spencer. You really don't."

"Then enlighten me."

Though she expected the angry fire in his dark, dark eyes to burn her to a cinder at any second, Victoria raised her chin a proud notch. "I cannot."

She saw a muscle in his jaw working. "Under normal circumstances, Victoria, I would not inquire as to your personal correspondence. However, this situation is not the normal one. That said, the letter you received at Wetherington's Point two days before you left: Who wrote it and what did it say? I cannot put it more plainly than that."

"How do you know so much about this letter, Spencer? I really cannot fathom—"

"For God's sake, Victoria—servants gossip. You know that. You've had them all your life."

He was right. *How stupid of me.* Angry now, more with

herself than the servants, but nevertheless like any timid creature, cornered and frightened, Victoria jumped up, prepared to fight back. "Why did you come after me? Why? You care nothing—"

"This has nothing to do with caring, madam." Spencer glared at her. "This has to do with my heir. You *are* still with child, are you not?"

Embarrassed heat suffused Victoria's face. She purposely kept her voice down because of the proximity of neighbors on both sides. "Yes, I am. I told you the ocean crossing would not harm me or the baby."

"Yes, you did. But you also took a great risk with that undertaking. Tell me why. What—or who—was so important, Victoria, that you would take that risk upon yourself?"

Clutching her hands together, she turned away. "I cannot tell you."

Behind her, Spencer said: "You mean you will not."

"I mean I *cannot*." Gripping her long, full skirt, she pivoted sharply about to face him. "And you're right—I will not."

Disdain capped Spencer's expression and glittered his black eyes. "Answer enough, then, isn't it?"

With her gaze locked with his, Victoria firmed her lips together against the urge to tell him the truth. She yearned for an ally, yearned for Spencer's strong shoulder to rely on. But the letter she'd received in England had been specific: If she enlisted aid, or told anyone why she was here, that person would be killed. And they had spies everywhere. They watched her every move. She knew that much from having found that anonymous note on her pillow last night. Spencer exhaled a dispirited sound and said: "Your silence damns you and condemns us both, Victoria."

Unable to look him in the eye any longer, so guilty did she feel and on so many levels, Victoria looked down and away, staring toward the back gate. "I'm sorry, Spencer, I truly am, but this is how it must be."

When he made no reply, curiosity got the better of Victoria. She looked up at him. Once again he was not focused on her. Instead, a puzzled expression bracketed his eyes and mouth as he concentrated his attention on the back gate.

Fear that they were being watched by interested parties jolted through Victoria. She trained her attention on the gate, and though she saw nothing alarming, wariness still crept over her skin like night falling on a landscape. "What is it, Spencer?"

"I'm not certain," he said, frowning, "but I could swear I saw . . ."

As his voice trailed off, Victoria took up the lead. "Saw what?"

He shook his head and looked down at her. "Nothing. Never mind." He smiled and shifted his weight as if signaling a change in subject. "I find there's such beauty in this city, like I've never seen before. Absolutely astounding."

Victoria stared at him. What was he up to? What had he seen? And why had he so quickly discounted it? However . . . "Yes, there is," she said, politely responding to his comment regarding Savannah's beauty.

Spencer gazed warmly at her, causing her heart to take an irrational leap of joyful awareness. "One would never expect something so . . . delicate and lovely could be found out here in this garden."

His gaze was so intimate, and his stern British demeanor so relaxed, that Victoria had to move away from him and sit down again on the delicately scrollworked bench. "And yet every Savannah house of any presence or reputation has a garden, one peculiar to its owner's tastes."

Spencer's unexpected chuckle treated Victoria to a dazzling display of his white and even teeth. Something inside her quickened. All she could think was she knew how it felt to be kissed by his mouth. But telling herself such thoughts would never do, not when she couldn't trust him, Victoria feigned insult. "Did I say something that amused you, sir?"

"Yes, you always do, Victoria. Now, keep smiling, pretend we are having a polite conversation, and stay here. I saw something in the alley I feel I should investigate. And I don't wish to alert our visitors that we are aware of them."

With that, and leaving her sitting there to process all he'd said, he turned and walked away from her, being careful to avoid the gravel pathway. Victoria stupidly stared after him, but then it struck her: *Spencer! He's unarmed and unaware.* She jumped up and hurried toward him, calling out: "Wait, Spencer." He turned sharply in her direction. She forced a cheerful note into her voice, already laden with urgency. "Allow me to come—"

"No." He punctuated his answer with a cautionary hand held out to stop her—and smiled like death itself. "I will have a simple stroll through the garden . . . my *dear*. Don't trouble yourself. Please . . . go back to the bench and wait there for me."

An eyebrow raised in ominous warning, he waited for her to comply. Frustration ate at Victoria. What should she do? Rush over to him and tell him the truth, thereby signing his death warrant if their visitors in the alley were the men who followed her? Or go back to the bench and hope it wasn't them and Spencer would be fine?

"Victoria . . . the bench."

He was giving her no choice. Heartsick with worry, she hurried back to the bench, sat down and nervously held her lower lip between her teeth as she watched her husband walk away. Maybe, if nothing else, her calling out to Spencer had alerted whoever was out there of his approach, and they would leave in haste.

Victoria's gaze remained riveted on her husband's form. A purely feminine part of her mind, one not impressed by intrigue and lies and danger, remarked that he carried himself with such natural athletic grace. A tall, imposing figure of a man, he was. He'd removed his coat and collar at some point inside and had come out here in his white shirt, open at the strong column of his throat. He'd rolled his shirtsleeves up a few turns, exposing his muscled forearms, which were tanned a light brown.

Popping into Victoria's immediate consciousness now was the remembrance of that bone-melting, staggering shock of a feeling she'd experienced when she'd first walked into the front parlor at River's End this morning and had looked into her husband's eyes. Seeing him had produced a tiny explosion inside her heart and mind that had left her momentarily disoriented. It had been as if her soul had only then recognized him as the man with whom she'd spend the remainder of her life. She'd wondered all day if he'd felt it, too. But there was no way on God's green earth she could ask him, now was there? He'd think her insane. Or bewitched.

Victoria watched Spencer's deliberately meandering stroll through the garden. Every few steps, he stopped to examine a flower or a shrub. A smile came unbidden to Victoria's lips. *What would it have been like,* her wondering mind asked her, *to have met him under other, more innocent, circumstances and have him pursue me for the sole reason that he wished to do so?* Oh, so delicious, the thought.

At that moment, Spencer stopped at the wooden gate at the back of the property. Holding on to the top of it with both hands, he hauled himself up as if he meant to have a quick look up and down the alley. But he couldn't quite get a toehold and pitched backward, almost falling down. Victoria grinned at his curious-little-boy antics.

Apparently deciding on a different tactic, he simply unlatched the gate. Victoria held her breath, praying hard for the alley to be empty of danger. She fisted her hands around her skirt's folds and sat forward, her breaths coming in tight little gasps as Spencer stepped back to allow the gate to swing inward. Victoria feared hordes of awful men would rush him and kill him right in front of her. A mewling cry escaped her . . . Spencer stepped out into the alley and stood in the middle of the rough thoroughfare, his hands planted at his waist, looking first one way and then the other.

When nothing happened, when he simply stood there unharmed moment after moment, Victoria relaxed and breathed deeply—and treated herself to the masculine vision Spencer was. His long and strong muscled legs, and those narrow hips. His trim waist. That broad back and those shoulders. Despite all the tensions between them and her fervent wish not to be affected by her husband, Victoria heaved a sigh of purely feminine appreciation. Heaven help her, John Spencer Whitfield was one powerfully attractive man.

Troubled by the power of her attraction to him, she looked away from him, settling her unfocused gaze instead on a low, green shrub across the way. *Why, oh why, didn't Daddy marry me off to one of those narrow-shouldered, chinless dandies who'd come sniffing around in England?* They would have been much easier, given the pickle she found herself in now, to defend her heart against than Spencer was. Could it be worse? Here she sat, expecting one man's child—if only she knew which man's—while trying to save another man's child—a child he could not acknowledge and maybe did not even want saved.

Victoria's heart sank. Men. How could they be so impossibly heartless? Not for the first time was she aware of how this other awful situation mirrored her own predicament. The timing, of course, was merely coincidence and one thing hadn't anything to do with the other. But, still, it was odd, the lessons life chose to teach one—and at the worst possible moment in a person's life. Wasn't her own burden enough right now for her to bear? Why did she have to take on this one, as well?

Instantly, Victoria felt ashamed for having harbored such selfish thoughts. How could she think only of herself? Guilt had her looking down at her hands folded together in her lap. She carried a tiny life inside her that needed her to be safe and healthy for its sake. She shouldn't be taking risks on another's behalf right now. But she had to. No one else would. Victoria thought of the awful, awful people who had an innocent child held helplessly in their grasp. She feared what they had already done to the child's mother.

Anger hardened Victoria's expression, but she quickly blanked it and forced herself to relax. It couldn't be good for her baby for her to be so upset all the time. Victoria pressed her hand against her still flat abdomen. *We'll be fine, don't you worry.*

Just as she did this, a very close and deafening sound rang out. Jumping and exclaiming with fright, Victoria realized she was on her feet, though she didn't remember standing. In that same instant, she recognized the sound—a gun being fired—and pivoted in the direction of the sound. Out in the alley. "Oh, dear God . . . no."

Spencer. Victoria staggered, grabbing on to the bench for support. She thought first she'd be ill, that she would faint dead away. But from somewhere deep inside her, from a well of strength she hadn't known she possessed, she managed to straighten up and start running, running. "Spencer!"

The gate seemed to get no closer and her legs felt so heavy. The very air surrounding her thickened, became her enemy, slowed her down and dragged her footsteps. Then, from behind her, seemingly coming from out of nowhere, men rushed past her and someone was grabbing her by her arms, telling her something, stopping her, holding her. The men's voices sounded warped, as if they were yelling and speaking through a wall of water.

Perhaps it was the shock, but Victoria felt the sting of tears in her eyes and heard her own voice, like that of a child's, asking: "What's happened? I don't understand."

No one answered her. Then suddenly she realized she had at last made it to the alley—but someone was holding her tightly, trying to force her away. Who? She concentrated on who this person was, fighting his hold on her and looking into his face. Hornsby. Spencer's elderly valet. His stricken expression told its own story. Befuddled, in shock, Victoria shook her head, but the man tightened his hold on her, one arm around her back and his other hand pressed against the back of her head as he forced her cheek to his shoulder. "Don't look, Your Grace. Don't look."

"No! I will look!" Only by sheer dint of will, and pushing and shoving, did Victoria manage to overcome Hornsby's hold on her and look around his considerable bulk. Not more than ten feet away were two men, kneeling on the ground, their backs to her. One was Edward, Spencer's cousin. The other one was her father's man, a big blond man whose name she didn't know. They knelt on either side of a third man, who was down on the ground. Victoria blinked but could make no connections. Then, it hit her. This was what Hornsby didn't want her to see. This was what all the shouting was about.

Spencer lay on his back on the muddy and rutted ground of the well-traveled alleyway . . . and blood stained the front of his white shirt.

"Here, Victoria, drink this." Edward Sparrow, the Right Honorable the Earl of Roxley, handed her a small glass filled with an amber liquid. "This should restore you."

Numb, obedient, Victoria took it and put it to her lips, tipping it up. She swallowed, immediately gagged, and shoved the glass back into his hand. Choking, coughing, she helplessly leaned forward and covered her mouth with her hands.

"There's the girl, now. Effective medicine, isn't it, my dear?" The earl soundly patted her back, which did nothing to help.

Her breath would not come and tears seeped from the corners of her eyes. Since her pregnancy, liquor of any kind, even a taste of it, made her instantly ill, as did cigar smoke. But, finally, her symptoms eased and she thought she might live.

Inhaling deeply, she sat up as Edward squatted down in front of her. Silently, she watched him down the remainder of the whisky he'd first offered her. "There. Much better." He smacked his lips in satisfaction as he admiringly eyed the empty glass. Then he caught her staring at him. "Fine stuff, this." He hefted the shot glass by way of definition. "Found it across the way in the bar service. And you? How are you doing?"

Victoria started to reply and found she could produce nothing more than a raspy croak of sound.

"Easy now. Don't try to talk. Just give yourself a moment. You've had a bit of a shock."

A bit of a shock? She thought about this, but nothing came to mind. Still, she had to admit a shock would explain her feeling so . . . empty, so unaware. But what sort of shock? Frowning, she rubbed her hand under her nose as she stared at Edward. An objective and working part of her brain remarked on her hair being all undone and clinging to her damp face. She brushed it away and over her shoulders. As she did, she examined her surroundings, trying to get her bearings.

She and Edward were in a small but stately library, one that smelled pleasantly of furniture polish and books and a warm, richly scented breeze. The light draperies, hanging from several tall, narrow, open windows around the room, fluttered playfully with each breath of the wind. And yet, this room meant nothing to her. She'd never seen it before. What had happened to her? How had she come to be in here? She wanted to voice these concerns, but only one frustrating word could she manage. "What . . . ?"

Like a sympathetic doctor with a patient who's just come around, Edward smiled and rose effortlessly to his feet. "Good. Your color's coming back. I expect you'll live."

Well, of course she would. She watched Edward cross the room to an ornately carved table and deposit the glass on a silver tray. She frowned, forcing herself to think . . . but all too soon wished she hadn't. Sudden and painful memory rushed back, dragging her emotions along with it. Her eyes widened; she inhaled a ragged breath. This was her father's house in Savannah. His library. She'd been in the garden, sitting there. And then Spencer—

"Spencer!" Gasping, she tried to jump up, but Edward rushed over to her and held her in place with a hand on her shoulder.

"No, my dear duchess, don't try to stand just yet. You gave us all quite the scare, fainting like that. While I and your father's man—nice chap, name of Giddens—managed Spencer, Hornsby carried you in here. Thought he'd have a heart attack with the effort. Not that you're heavy, I'm sure. But this is as far as he could get you. And he is an older man—"

"For God's sake, Edward," Victoria cried, hating how thin and crackly her voice sounded. However, it proved to be sufficient enough to have the startled young earl removing his hand from her shoulder and stepping back. Victoria cleared her throat and coughed. "*Spencer*, Edward. Where is Spencer?"

Edward's response was a chuckle. Disconcerted, Victoria sat back against the maroon velvet-tufted divan on which she found herself. "Why are you laughing?" Her voice sounded so low and hollow. "He's your cousin. I thought you cared for him."

"Oh, but I do. Tremendously. And to answer your question, he is upstairs at the moment."

"At the moment?" She again tried to get up, only to have Edward again force her to remain. "Stop that, Edward. I must go to him."

"No, no, no. Not yet. Hornsby will need more time with him." With that, Edward cheerfully went to pour himself another drink.

Victoria sat there, staring, her gaze blankly following Edward's every move as she puzzled over what he'd told her. Then, it came to her: Spencer's valet would be the one to . . . lay the body out. She blinked against the mental image that wanted to form in her mind of Spencer . . . dead. *No.* A witch's brew of sickening emotion assailed Victoria. She pressed her fingertips to her temples and shook her head against the dawning realization. No, he couldn't be dead. She wouldn't allow it. But she knew what she'd seen in the alley. The evidence spoke for itself.

And now, so did her heart, accusing her of having cared more, so much more, for Spencer than she had realized or would admit. Why else did she think she'd wanted his respect? Why did she think she'd wanted him to care . . . to just *care*? Because his indifference was the opposite of love. Indifference was not caring. It had nearly crushed her, and she knew why: Because she cared—and deeply—for him. If she hadn't, then his behavior toward her wouldn't have mattered. And now? It was too late.

A sudden bone-deep weakness leached the strength from Victoria's bones. Dear God! Her husband. Her *late* husband. Only now did she realize that she could not imagine a life, a world, without Spencer in it. This then was her punishment . . . the knowing, too late, in her mind what her heart had known all along. Victoria swallowed and gritted her teeth as hard as she could, until her jaw ached. *I will not fall apart. I will not.* She inhaled deeply and willed strength into her bones and her heart. What remained for her to do now was to show respect for Spencer and his memory.

Edward, having downed a quick shot at the bar, came toward her. Victoria inhaled a ragged breath and spoke quietly but with authority to the earl. "I wish to go up and help Hornsby with him. It's the least I can do."

Edward shouted a guffawing laugh that startled Victoria terribly. "Oh, I daresay the shock of your doing so would put Hornsby in his grave. No, no, my dear, instead give the old man a few more moments to get your husband bathed and tenderly laid up in bed," Edward blithely, madly, continued. "You can see him then. In the meantime, you and I can have a nice chat in here."

Edward was quite insane, and she had to get out of this library. Making every effort to appear not to be doing so, Victoria cut her gaze around the room. Any sharp or heavy object with which to defend herself would do. Until she found one and had it in her grasp, though, she should humor the man. "All right, Edward," she said, speaking in a placating tone, "I'll wait here with you. Can you . . . can you tell me how he died?"

Edward frowned. "How who died? Oh, of course, you mean—Well, he was shot. Right in the chest. Terrible thing, that. But no more than he deserved."

This was too much, insane or not. "Edward, for God's sake, what are you saying—'no more than he deserved'? How can you say such a thing? *How?*"

The earl's expression pinched with obvious confusion. "How can I not is a better question. The man did try to kill my cousin—your husband, madam—after all. I say he got exactly what he deserved."

The man? "Edward, what man? Are you saying it wasn't Spencer who was—"

"Good God, no! No, of course it wasn't. Oh, I say, Victoria—"

"Edward, please! *Is* Spencer alive?"

"Well, of course he is. Do you think I'd be standing here if—"

Victoria burst into relieved tears and covered her face with her hands. Almost immediately she felt strong and comforting arms going around her. Her intellect told her Edward had squatted in front of her on the floor. Hot, sick, relieved, embarrassed, she sobbed and sobbed.

After a bit, when the emotional storm abated, she became

aware of Edward's cooing and comforting sounds as he smoothed her hair away from her face and patted her back. "You poor thing. I am so sorry, Victoria. No, no, no. Spencer is fine. Why, I'd bet Hornsby's had to tie him to the bed to keep him from coming down here to see about you. And knowing my cousin as I do, he is still roundly cursing whatever ruffian it was who socked him in the jaw and knocked him out."

Victoria pulled back in Edward's embrace and stared at him. "But the blood, Edward," she burbled. "I saw blood. There was . . . blood."

"Yes, there was quite a bit of blood, wasn't there? Ghastly stuff. Here, my dear. Use this. Your nose . . ." Edward pulled a substantial-sized, clean handkerchief from a pocket and handed it to her.

"Oh. Sorry. Thank you." Victoria self-consciously dabbed at her eyes and blew her nose.

Watching her sympathetically, Edward smiled, saying, "You're welcome. Now, about the blood: None of it, happily, was Spencer's."

Victoria eyed him suspiciously. "Are you telling me the truth?"

"I am."

She folded his handkerchief, held on to it, and looked up at him. "Then Spencer is alive and upstairs and not wounded mortally? You swear it?"

"I do, and he isn't. Actually, he's not wounded at all. Only bruised and knocked about a bit. He'll be fine by tomorrow, I expect. And very, very sore."

"Oh, thank God." Intense relief robbed Victoria of bone and muscle. Experiencing a sudden fainting feeling, she sank sideways onto the reclining couch, a hand tucked under her cheek.

Edward tenderly smoothed her hair back from her face. "My dear, are you quite all right?"

"Yes. I just suddenly felt weak. Oh, Edward, I thought he'd been killed, and it was all my fault—"

"Your fault?" His voice sharp, Edward leaned over until he stared intently into her eyes. Under any other circumstances, his posture would have been comical. "How was any of this your fault?"

Victoria froze, knowing she'd said too much. With Edward's face mere inches from hers, she was forced to stare into his brown eyes. "I didn't mean directly. I meant . . . Savannah is my city, and I feel awful that he was . . . welcomed here in such a manner."

"Welcomed? I say, my dear, that's rather a rough welcome-to-town. You will understand, then, if I wish to remain unannounced?"

It was there in the tilt of his head and his arched eyebrows, as he clearly waited for her to explain herself, that he didn't quite believe her. But what could she say? Maybe if she knew more about what had actually happened out in the alley. She clutched at Edward's sleeve. "Please. Tell me what happened. I need to know."

"Very well." He righted himself, but remained squatted in front of her and balanced on the balls of his feet. "Spencer said he stepped out into the alley, stood there a moment, and then went off to his left. Apparently, two men of rough character were lying in wait around some barrels and other refuse behind the next house over."

"Oh, how awful. What were they—common thieves looking for any victim? Could that be it?" She sincerely hoped so.

Edward shrugged. "Possibly. But they certainly had no need to accost him as they did if they meant only to rob him. After all, they were armed, and he wasn't." Edward paused, his expression troubled as he absently smoothed a hand over the divan's soft edge. He appeared to be wrestling with the framing of something he felt reluctant to say. Victoria's heart beat slowly, dully, with apprehension. Finally, the earl settled his gaze on her. "Victoria, I find I am very concerned, and I mean for you. Should I be?"

Choosing to pretend she'd mistaken his meaning, Victoria slowly sat up, with the young earl's steadying assistance. "You're very kind to be concerned. But I'm feeling much better, Edward, thank you. It was just the shock of seeing Spencer . . . lying there. And the blood. And then thinking he was . . . dead."

Edward smiled sympathetically. "I understand. But we must get to the bottom of this. Perhaps if you told me what happened before Spencer stepped into the alley, we can start there."

She nodded. "I shall certainly try. It's really quite straightforward, though. Spencer came outside and we conversed. As we were talking, his attention kept straying to the back gate. I asked him what the matter was, and he said he thought he'd seen something."

"I see." A teasing smile transformed the earl's rather plain features into a very attractive whole that explained his luck with the ladies. "He came outside specifically looking for you, my dear. He finds he has trouble keeping you located."

Victoria smiled self-consciously. "I had told him I would be with Rosanna to supervise the unpacking of my trunks. But she had it well in hand, and clearly did not wish my instruction. So I came outside to catch a breath of fresh air."

"And that's where he found you?"

"Yes, as I've said." Victoria made a show of rearranging her skirt's folds as she also readjusted her opinion of Edward. She'd thought him nothing more than a dandy and a gadabout. But he seemed to know more than he was letting on and he asked very pointed questions, much like a detective would. Clearly, she had best guard her answers. Feeling his waiting stare, she finally asked her own question. "Edward, did Spencer, by chance, tell you what he saw out in the alley that made him think he should investigate?"

"Yes, he told us . . . rather groggily . . . as we were bringing him inside. He said he thought he kept seeing—and it sounds comical, though it isn't—heads bobbing up and down from the other side of the gate. As if they were trying to see over it without being seen themselves, though not very effectively, obviously."

Fright rushed through Victoria. This was no random attack. "Oh, Edward, I wish I had gone with him. I offered, but he wouldn't allow me."

"Well, certainly he wouldn't, my dear. Forgive me, but I hardly think you could have been much help against two men who got the best of Spencer. But did you hear the struggle? Hear anyone's voice? Or shouting?"

"Had I, don't you think I would have raised an alarm myself?"

Edward covered her hand with his. "I didn't mean to insult you, Victoria. I'm merely looking for answers."

Answers she could not allow him to pursue. Victoria clasped his hand with hers, giving it a sincere squeeze. "I know, and no one more than I appreciates your efforts. But I think it makes more sense to look upon this as an awful but random incident, one not likely to recur, don't you?"

"Perhaps. But this deserves looking into as Spencer was very nearly killed. We should report these violent men to the authorities."

Victoria clasped the earl firmly by his shirtsleeves. "No, Edward, do not do that. We cannot bring in the authorities."

If whoever was having her watched saw the police here, they would know or suspect she was telling them the little she knew about the threats, the letters and all the rest—and someone would be killed. Someone she loved.

Edward pulled back to stare at her with surprise-widened brown eyes. "I say, Victoria, what's this? Spencer was very nearly killed! What possible reason could you have for not wanting this incident investigated and the brigands brought to justice?"

Letting go of him, she sat back limply. She could only stare in damning silence at her husband's cousin and keep her secrets and her fears to herself as she thought: *What possible reason, indeed?*

CHAPTER 9

"I am afraid I cannot allow this to pass. You will have to explain yourself, Victoria." Edward's usually cheerful countenance was now sober, emphasizing how long and thin his face really was. "These men need to be found before they strike again at some other innocent person. And I would think you would realize that."

Forced into a corner, Victoria resorted to lies in an effort to keep them all safe. "I realize it only too well, Edward. But not the authorities, please. Think of the scandal an investigation would cause. The police will ask all sorts of questions. How embarrassing to have all of our personal business in *The Morning News*. Why, everyone who is anyone reads it. And then we'd have to stay here overly long for an investigation and then a trial. All of that could take weeks, months. Don't you wish to return to England sometime soon? And even if you don't, think of Spencer. Shouldn't we ask him how he would feel about the unwanted attention of being in the press?"

Edward stared at the carpet and rubbed his chin thoughtfully. "Yes, I see your point. He wouldn't be amused. Perhaps I can conduct an investigation on my own, then, and get to the bottom of this."

Victoria again grabbed the eager earl by his arm. "Edward, no. For God's sake, leave it be. Please. Talk to Spencer first. See what he wants you to do. I would hate for you to anger him over this."

Victoria's very real fear was that Edward should start asking questions in the wrong places and of the wrong people. He could innocently but easily upset the delicate balance that so far existed because Victoria had responded to the letter's dictates and returned immediately to Savannah without telling anyone why. What she needed now was time—unimpeded by Edward's snooping—to see this situation to its end . . . without getting herself or anyone else killed.

Edward scratched absently at his clean-shaven cheek and frowned. "I suppose you're right. This didn't happen to me. It happened to Spencer. His wishes should prevail."

Intense relief coursed through Victoria. She felt certain Spencer would tell his cousin he did not want reporters or police snooping into his reasons for being here . . . or Victoria's. Smiling, exhaling, forcing herself to be a good actress, she said, "Excellent thinking, Edward."

He nodded his agreement. "Yes. Even so, it frightens one to think how differently it could have turned out. It's a good thing the windows were open to catch the breeze, or we inside the house might not have heard a thing and come running so quickly when the gun was fired."

His words recalled the awful memory to her, and Victoria pointed at him. "The gun! You swore to me Spencer wasn't wounded."

His expression earnest, Edward took her by her arms and looked into her eyes. "He wasn't, I swear it."

"Then who was? Whose blood was all over him?"

"I'll tell you. But for you to understand, I'll have to start at the beginning, Victoria. Bear with me." He let go of her and settled on the balls of his feet, resting his forearms atop his knees. "Spencer said he was engaged in a serious bout of fisticuffs when one of the ruffians stepped back, pulled a weapon, and aimed it at him."

Victoria clamped a hand over her mouth, feeling queasy. This attack had been meant as a warning to her. But who knew she had left River's End and was back in Savannah proper? Who knew who could so quickly use that knowledge to hire those awful men and send them around? A face popped into her mind, robbing Victoria of her will. *Dear God. Jefferson. My own brother.*

No. She refused to believe it. She couldn't. Victoria suddenly realized that Edward was asking her something. She blinked, forcing herself to listen to him. "Does this sort of thing happen often in your fair city of Savannah?"

She shook her head. "Not in this part. Perhaps a little more northeast, toward Pirates House or the docks, but not here."

Edward's mouth worked as he apparently digested something she'd said. "Pirates House . . . intriguing name. What is that?"

"A tavern and a meeting house, among other things. A very rough one at times."

"Really?" Edward brightened. "I must go see it for myself."

"I'm certain you will." She waited, her eyebrows raised expectantly.

"Oh, yes. Spencer and the ruffians. I was saying that one of the scofflaws pulled a gun. Spencer says he saw this and quickly grabbed the other fellow, a rather portly gentleman, apparently, and tugged him in front of him. In the end, the blackguard shot his own man."

Victoria shook her head. "Oh, my word, Edward."

He nodded. "So much for honor amongst thieves and all that. But, continuing on. Luckily, since Spencer was right behind the wounded fellow, the bullet did not pass all the way through him. Or if it did, it was at an angle that did not include your husband."

Her husband. Victoria could only stare. Spencer had come within inches of being killed. What had she done by coming here but put their lives, and her unborn child's, in mortal danger?

"It gets a bit murky here," Edward went on, "but the portly wounded ruffian jerked and spun and ended up toppling face-first onto Spencer, who couldn't support his weight and they fell together to the ground. That explains the blood on Spencer. The impact, though, knocked Spencer's breath out of him. Apparently, too, a rather large rock lay embedded in the muddy lane and Spencer managed to hit his head on that. He was a bit dazed—quite understandable, really—but remembers the armed chap struggling to pull his wounded friend off him. Once he'd done that, the blackguard punched Spencer. He has the bruised and swollen jaw and foul humor to prove it, too. But that's the last he remembers before he lost consciousness."

Victoria pressed her hands to her too-hot cheeks. "My word, Edward, he's lucky to be alive. And though I shudder even to think the words, I have to wonder what kept them from shooting him at that point and putting an end to him."

"I've wondered the same thing. Of course, like you, I'm glad they didn't finish him off." He arched an eyebrow, sending her a speculative look. "Victoria, I still find it curious that you believe you are somehow responsible for this attack."

Victoria stared into his accusing eyes and wished she could tell him what she feared and suspected about her brother. But she just couldn't. It would be such a betrayal, and it might not be true at all. "Now, Edward," she said, taking a humoring tack, "I told you I didn't mean it literally. You can't possibly believe I'd wish any harm to Spencer, or take any actions that would bring harm to him."

Edward's smile was apologetic. "Actually, and I'm sorry to say it, Victoria, because I like you very much . . . but I *can* believe it of you. Forgive me, but you stand to benefit tremendously should Spencer die."

Victoria's gasp of shock was genuine. "Edward! Do you

actually believe I somehow masterminded this attack on Spencer?"

"That's what I'm asking you." He spoke so sadly, as if it hurt him more to ask than it did for her to hear him say such a thing.

And well he could ask, even without knowing about the baby. She was the duchess. She would be Spencer's widow. Everything would be hers. But what Edward didn't know— and Victoria hated herself for even thinking—was with Spencer dead, and no one to question her unborn child's paternity, it would be declared the heir. Suddenly she realized she'd been quiet overlong. "When would I have arranged for such an awful thing, Edward?" She heard how drained of emotion her voice sounded. "You're assuming I would know how to go about finding men like those two and dealing with them. I assure you I do not. And for another thing, I didn't even know you were in Savannah until you both showed up at River's End. Since then, I haven't been out of your or Spencer's sight."

Edward's brown eyes warmed with sympathy and kindness, so at odds with what he was saying and with what he was accusing her. "But you were. You said yourself you weren't where you told Spencer you would be. He had to hunt for you, and there you were outside. He, of course, followed you."

Stunned, Victoria could only shake her head. "I did not lure Spencer outside. I can see how it could look that way to you. But I never told him I saw something suspicious in the alley. I didn't send him out there. He went himself. And I have already told you I wanted to go with him. You have only to ask him." She rubbed at her forehead and fought tears. "I am so hurt by your accusations, Edward. You can't believe I'd want Spencer dead. You simply can't."

"I certainly do not want to, Victoria. I like you very much. But Spencer is my cousin, and I have to be sure. You must understand, too, that I, uh, *know*."

Her tears dried up. She pulled back and stared at Edward. It was there in his soft, brown eyes. He knew about her scandal and about the baby. What else could he mean?

Shamed, Victoria lowered her gaze, settling it on her hands in her lap. Spencer had almost been killed. Nothing she did could keep him or Edward safe or uninvolved. She could no longer fight this thing alone. She needed help. So there was only one thing to do: confess. And then enlist their aid. What choice did she have? Just by being here, they were in danger, and they should be aware that they were.

Her mind made up, Victoria said: "I think the attack was meant for me, Edward. If Spencer hadn't come outside when he did, I would have been—"

"Victoria!" Edward clutched her hands in his. "What are you saying? Why would someone wish to harm you?"

Though he ducked his head down low, trying to get her to look at him, Victoria simply couldn't. She swallowed past a painful lump in her throat. This was so terribly difficult. "How much do you know?"

"About what exactly?"

"About . . . me." Shame burned her cheeks and kept her gaze on their joined hands. "And the circumstances of our marriage."

"I know what Spencer has told me."

His reply had Victoria wincing, yet she believed she'd heard a kind and sympathetic note in Edward's voice. She raised her head and was relieved to see the kind slant in his brown eyes. "I see."

Edward shrugged. "Blame the long Atlantic crossing. All that enforced closeness and the ample liquor. If I cannot make someone talk, even if only in self-defense, then no one can."

Victoria's laugh was shaky, emotional. "I'm beginning to see the truth in that." She felt her chin quivering and her eyes filling with tears. "You must think me a wanton, Edward."

He smiled and released her hands. "You dear, sweet

thing. I think no such thing. I think you're the most beautiful and exciting woman I've ever met. With your sweet Southern drawl, I could listen to you talk all day. In fact, I will swear to you now that if my cousin isn't smart enough to keep you by his side forever, I intend fully to sweep you off your feet and carry you and your baby away to my castle where we will live happily ever after."

Victoria smiled gratefully. "You're very kind. And I bet you say that to all the women."

"I do. But with you I mean it. So, lovely lady, can you tell me now what it was that brought you to America?" He mugged a droll expression. "And please don't say a steamship brought you. It's such an old joke."

To her surprise, Victoria found she could chuckle. "You are incorrigible, Edward. Actually, it was a letter."

"Ah, yes. I heard about it when I was with Spencer at Wetherington's Point."

Victoria crinkled her expression into one of apology. "That could not have been pleasant. I am so sorry."

"And you should be. It was awful. I will say that Fredericks did his best for as long as he could not to tell what he knew or what you'd told him not to tell. He's a very loyal old chap. But Spencer can be . . . persuasive."

"Yes, I know. I've had a taste of that myself."

Edward nodded. "My cousin is an imperious ass, isn't he? And please do not tell him I said that."

Again, he'd wrung a laugh from her. "I won't." She inhaled deeply and slowly exhaled, knowing there was no turning back from this point. "The letter, then. I must tell you what it said."

Edward held a hand up to stop her talking. "And I want to hear every word, believe me. There's been tremendous speculation in the past several weeks regarding the content of that letter and its sender. But, my dear sweet Victoria, and on second thought, it's not me you need to tell your story to. It's Spencer."

"I know. He asked me about it out in the garden. But . . . I'm afraid."

"Of Spencer? Nonsense. Imperious ass aside, the man's your husband. And a pussycat where you're concerned."

Victoria seriously doubted that, but Edward gave her no time to gainsay him as, with nimble grace, he came to his feet and held a hand out to her. "Well, Duchess? Do you feel up to seeing your husband now?"

Though she placed her hand in Edward's long-fingered and elegant one, she did not come to her feet. "I don't think I have the strength. Really. I can't face this now. There's so much—"

"There's so much you need to talk about? I agree." His expression sobered. "You must, Victoria. He was nearly killed today. He deserves to know why."

"But I don't *really* know why."

"Of course you do. Come on, off you go. Believe me, I know how Spencer feels about you, even if the humorless jackanapes won't show it. You have no reason to be afraid of him."

Though Edward's revelation regarding Spencer's feelings for her sparked a flare of . . . was it hope? . . . in Victoria's heart, she refused to believe it. She couldn't afford to do so. Too much stood in the way. "I think you overstate your case, Edward. But I do appreciate it—"

"Overstate? Me? Nonsense. It's very simple, really. Why do you think he came after you?"

Victoria sat back. "I don't know. Pride? The baby's possibly being his heir?"

"Certainly those. But he didn't have to come himself, did he? He could have sent his agent. Or hired detectives. Or not have done a thing to find you. But what he did was quickly rearrange his entire life so he could come himself. Now, why would he do that?"

"For the reasons I've already given. His pride. And the possibility this baby represents. Nothing more."

His eyes glinted with humor as Edward shook his head. "Stubborn girl. Why do you think I came along to America with Spencer? Let me tell you: to get the two of you back together."

Embarrassed, too afraid to be hopeful, Victoria demurred. "We are together. We're even in the same house."

"You know what I mean."

"I do." Now she squeezed Edward's hand in an effort to impart her seriousness to him. "I want you to tell me about the Whitfield birthmark."

Confusion, whether genuine or contrived, Victoria could not tell, gathered up Edward's features. "What Whitfield birthmark?"

Victoria narrowed her eyes. "There isn't one, is there?"

Edward laughed out loud. "My dear lady, I assure you that you are in a much better position to find that answer than I am."

"And so I am." With Edward's assistance, Victoria stood. "I'm ready to see Spencer now."

Unsteady on his feet, Spencer stood in the small, airless dressing room adjoining his second-floor bedroom and, with stiff, painful motions, stuffed his shirttail into his britches. His sour expression alone could have doused the same fire and brimstone of hell that more than one person in his life had told him awaited him at the end of his days. He refused to think how close he'd been, only a matter of hours ago, to finding out if they were right. And here he'd thought it sufficient for the day that he'd suffered the humiliation of being set upon by two bullies in an alley and soundly thrashed by them. But apparently he'd been wrong. The crowning moment had been when Edward brought Victoria up to him with no prior warning.

How humiliating. He'd been in bed, dozing, no doubt snoring. And in a nightshirt. With pillows propped behind him. There he'd reclined: his jaw swollen and slack, his knuckles cut and scraped from connecting with teeth, and his entire body bruised and beaten. Spencer rubbed gingerly at his side. One of those bastards had kicked him in his ribs when he was down. So, all in all, what a heroic picture he must have made in bed. His wife had taken one look at him and burst into tears.

After Edward led her to a chair and made her sit, that coward had beat a hasty retreat and closed the door behind him. And then, they'd been alone, he and Victoria. They had simply stared at each other. After enough of that, Spencer recalled, he'd . . . weakly . . . thrown his covers back and, under his own power, accepting no help or support, and telling her to stay put, he'd stalked . . . limped . . . into this very room where he now stood and was losing a battle royal with his own clothing.

Sweating with his pain-producing efforts, Spencer silently cursed everything he could think of, whether it deserved cursing or not. At last, he cursed today and the weather. When would this blasted day be over? Did the sun never set here, was that it? Could it truly be that only this morning he'd rolled off a ship, suffered the long, humid ride out to River's End, argued with his in-laws, retrieved his defiant wife, endured the long ride back to Savannah, and promptly had the hell beat out of him? All of that in one—he pressed his lips together to stop the word but to no avail; it got past him—*fucking* day?

His teeth clenched together in pain, Spencer continued his silent tirade as he closed his pants. *I feel as though I'd been run over by a train and then tossed into a pit of rabid dogs, where I was torn to shreds and finally put back together by a demented three-year-old who used me as his rag doll.* However, Spencer assured himself, he would be damned if he'd have this or any conversation with his wife while in his nightshirt and under the covers of his bed—their bed. No, his bed. She'd made that very clear upon their arrival here by promptly directing the placement of his traveling trunks in this bedroom and hers in another.

Though he had been irate about that, he hadn't felt he had much recourse, beyond an all-out pitched battle with her, but to allow it to happen. For him to raise a fuss about having been denied his wife's bed would have terribly amused Edward and the servants, all of whom seemed to be milling about at that point. And so, under those circumstances, Spencer had wisely conceded her the moment.

However, he would soon disavow her of any notion she might have regarding separate sleeping quarters for the two of them. She would, by damn, sleep with him tonight and every night because only with her in his bed could he be instantly alerted should she try to sneak away for whatever reason, if any, she may have. He suspected she had many. And, as he was damned tired already of chasing her across continents and oceans, her being in his bed was simply a matter of expediency.

He was lying, and his conscience knew it. Closer to the truth, it howled, was he missed the feel of her warm, sweet body next to his at night.

A scowl claimed Spencer's features. *Like bloody hell I do. The woman is nothing but trouble and up to something at every turn.* With that, he pronounced himself as dressed as he intended to get. Defiantly barefooted, Spencer stalked . . . proceeded slowly . . . for the door that led into his bedroom. Poking his aching jaw out pugnaciously, he silently threatened that if Victoria knew what was good for her, she would be sitting exactly where he'd left her while he'd come in here to dress because if she wasn't there, he—

Spencer stopped in his tracks, looking around. He refused to believe this. Absolutely refused. And yet, there he stood in the doorway between the dressing room and his large and airy, very masculine bedroom . . . alone. He stared across the room at the closed bedroom door. He hadn't heard it open and close. What had she done—wafted through the wood like a ghost? He focused now on the chair, an exquisite example of expert craftsmanship, which was empty of its occupant.

Frowning like a thundercloud, Spencer clamped his hands to his waist. "By damn, she has made off again." He couldn't decide if he should be in a rage or simply admit he had no idea how to proceed with his own wife. "I have *never* seen a woman who has less of an idea about how to stay put than *she* does. Enough is enough."

Galvanized by a lightning bolt of temper, he stormed . . . limped . . . across the room, hung a toe on the fringed end of the Persian area rug next to the bed, staggered but caught himself by cursing and clutching at the narrow nightstand table. Righting himself and standing there a moment, simply breathing, he finally and carefully—he was done with any thought of stalking—made his way over to the closed door that opened onto the second-floor hallway. Though his knuckles were grazed and his fingers ached from hitting those bastards who'd attacked him, Spencer jerked open the door to the bedroom, swung it in toward him and—

Collided with Victoria, who let out a loud squawk of surprise. Standing in the hallway, she'd obviously been in the act of turning the doorknob from her side. She held a full glass of very cold water in her hand, which was no longer full. In fact, it was empty. He knew this—and exactly how cold the water was in Georgia—because all of it, every drop, was now spilled down the front of his trousers.

Shocked, clutching desperately at the door's opposing jambs, much like Hercules chained, Spencer stood there, gasping, unable to move.

"Oh, Spencer, I'm so sorry," Victoria cried, stumbling back, her eyes wide with surprise as she looked from his face to his watered-down crotch. She held up the offending glass to him. "We have an icebox."

He nodded. "I daresay I am fully aware of that already, madam."

Her smile faltered. "Yes, I suppose you are. I went to get you a drink. I thought you might like a . . . glass of water."

"Thank you," was his frozen reply. "I think I've had plenty now." He let go of the doorjamb and held, as best he could, his dripping pants away from his skin. "If you will excuse me, I will just go change." Smiling, deadly, he politely indicated the chair he'd expected to find her sitting in a moment ago. "Please. Have a seat."

"Certainly," she said a bit breathlessly, perhaps fearfully, as she quickly sidled past him.

Like a brooding madman, though completely aware of exactly how ridiculous, and possibly obscene, he looked standing there holding the crotch of his wet pants, Spencer turned to watch her go. With her full skirt scurrying behind her and her long mahogany curls swaying to and fro, she hurried to the chair, turned, and sat down with an elegant flourish. Under any other circumstances, he might have found her appearance and her actions adorable. But not this circumstance.

Her spine stiff, her posture perfect, Victoria held the empty glass in both hands in her lap. Then, suddenly, as though holding on to it convicted her of a crime, she plunked it onto a round decorative table, which boasted a green potted plant atop it and was next to her chair. She folded her hands in her lap and looked to him, blue eyes wide and innocent, for approval or perhaps further instructions.

Spencer steadfastly refused to be taken in by her beauty or her obedience. He did not believe her sweet little pose for one moment. To prove it, he let go of his pants long enough to point threateningly at her. "Don't. Move. Do you understand the concept, Victoria, of 'don't move'? Do you really?"

"Yes." Suspiciously cooperative, she settled herself comfortably on her chair. "I won't move."

He remained unconvinced. "Swear it."

Disbelief widened her eyes. "You wish me to swear it?"

"No, I do not *wish* you to swear it. I *require* that you do."

"But I've only just said I would stay—"

"Madam, I chased you across England and an entire ocean because you did not stay where you were told to. And twice, since we've been in this most lovely and gracious home, you have disappeared. And both times, when I found you, I suffered terribly. The first time, I was set upon by ruffians and very nearly killed. And now I have had an iceberg dumped in my pants." He suspected the pained sound she made was to stifle a laugh and was not an expression of pity or remorse. "So, yes, I do, Victoria. I require you to swear it."

She'd clamped a hand over her mouth and now stared bright-eyed at him above it. As he arched an eyebrow in warning, she quickly lowered her hand to her lap and, very seriously, said, "As you wish. I swear—"

"On your mother's grave."

"My mother, not being dead, as you very well know, has no grave."

Spencer actually felt a vein in his forehead swell and throb. "Very well," he said through gritted teeth, which did nothing to alleviate the pain in his jaw, "who is dead that you loved and cherished?"

Victoria poked her bottom lip out and frowned, obviously thinking about it. "My grandmother," she suddenly chirped. "My dear, cherished grandmother is dead. Will she do?"

"Nicely. Swear on her grave."

Victoria exhaled a sigh. "This is so very unnecessary, but if you require it, I swear on my sainted grandmother's grave"—in a very singsong voice—"that I will not move from this chair until you tell me I may do so." She gestured with both hands. "There. I've sworn. Now, go change your pants before you catch your death of cold."

He now had no choice but to trust that she would do as she'd sworn. After all, a man—a woman—was only as good as her word. Spencer determinedly set himself in motion, trying to maintain what dignity he could as he walked stiffly across the room and ignored the cold, soggy feel of the wet fabric that viciously rubbed his thighs and man parts. Given his luck today, the damned underused member and its two close companions would fall off when he stripped out of his clothes. Right now, though, he could honestly say he wouldn't give a tinker's damn if they did. What would it matter? At this rate, he wouldn't be using any of them again, anyway.

Once in his dressing room, Spencer repeated the painful chore of stripping out of his clothes, down to his naked skin. It was with relief, despite his fatalistic thought only moments ago, that he noted he'd lost no vital parts to the cold water. They were a bit shriveled and disgruntled at the moment, but none the worse for having been doused. He rubbed himself dry with his shirt as best he could, tossed it aside, and then carefully reached for suitable replacements out of drawers and off hangers. As quickly as possible, given that he could only move like a creaky-jointed ninety-year-old, he re-dressed and, once again, with his jaw squared, exited the dressing room and stepped into the bedroom.

The chair was empty. He was again alone in the room. This time, the bedroom's door was open to the hallway. He could *not* believe the woman. When he realized a welling and uncontrollable shout of frustration was imminent, Spencer pressed a supporting hand to his sore and swollen jaw. "Son of a *bitch*!"

Making him instantly sorry, and teaching him a resounding lesson, was the shooting pain from chin to ear that had him grimacing.

Far from defeated, Spencer made his way to the door, intent on finding his wife straightaway. The only explanation he would accept for her not being where she'd sworn to stay was the damned house itself was on fire. And he could honestly say he didn't smell any smoke. For another thing, if the house was on fire, why hadn't she alerted him? More and more out of sorts, once he was at the door, he changed his mind about chasing after her. Why should he? Instead, he'd make his point by slamming the damned door off its hinges and thereby announce his displeasure.

He grabbed the door and flung it closed with as much force as he could muster. The door did not come off its hinges, but the resounding bang of sharp noise it made brought some gratification. Spencer stood there a moment, watching the door and listening, thinking that, by God, this would bring them running. But it didn't. Not the first startled cry or sound of hurrying footsteps did he hear. This was outrageous. What if *he'd* been on fire?

Suddenly tired and not giving a damn if he was on fire, Spencer turned to make his way to his bed. Right now all he wanted was the comfort of that soft bed, his supper, a dose of strong medication, and hours upon hours of soothing sleep. At this moment, he didn't care where his wife had gone or what she was doing or even what her game was. If she wished to converse with him, she bloody well knew where he was.

Spencer's stomach growled, reminding him that the supper hour approached and he'd sent Hornsby to bring a tray up to him. Certainly, given his condition, no one here expected him to dress for supper. And it was too damned bad for them if they did. Because, for the rest of this day, he meant to remain in his room with the door solidly, pointedly closed. With his luck, Spencer fumed, the roof would fall in on him. Well, if his jaw and ribs didn't soon stop hurting so badly, he might welcome such a course of relief.

At the bed's side now, and barefooted, Spencer shed his collarless shirt and his britches. He left his clothes pooled on the treacherous rug, the same one that had earlier caught his toe and nearly made him fall—no doubt, to his death, had he. Then, and admitting he was all done in, he gratefully crawled into bed, lay back, and pulled a sheet up and over him to his chest. Only then did he exhale a sigh of contentment and relief . . . and close his eyes.

He had no way of knowing how much time had passed,

but he was more than half asleep when he became aware of
the door to the bedroom being softly opened. Instantly wide
awake, his eyes open, he lay very still, listening, as he stared
up at the high ceiling. The shadows in the room, he noted,
were longer, but not by much. And whoever entered on cat's
paws obviously meant to do so without his knowing it.
Maybe this was Hornsby with that supper tray. Or maybe
this was some kind soul who meant to check on him without
disturbing him. Or kill him without waking him.

Well, aren't I the bloody calm victim? Spencer marveled.
But what the hell was he supposed to do? Scream? Not very
likely, given his ribs, his jaw, and his masculine pride. Fight?
Certainly. But not very effectively, he would imagine. Never
had he felt so helpless. Where the hell was his pistol? Would
he have to resort to sleeping with the damned thing beside
his bed?

Just then, he detected a soft rustling of skirts that relaxed
him and brought a quick grin to his face. He had identified
his visitor. Only one woman who resided in this house
would have a reason to enter his bedroom with him in it.
Wondering what she was about, but still too mentally tired,
as well as physically spent, to deal well with her, even if she
meant to kill him, Spencer decided to close his eyes and
feign sleep. If she intended to explain her behavior or apologize to him for vanishing again, she could jolly well wait
until tomorrow.

No sooner had he closed his eyes than he felt her press up
against the bed. He could hear her soft breathing . . . and
feel her body's warmth. Reason told him she was gazing
down at him. For one second, and despite his ribs, Spencer
considered grabbing her and tossing her onto the bed with
him. He liked the mental image he got of them tussling
about under the covers, until it changed to a more realistic
picture of his diminutive wife screaming and hitting him and
bringing the entire household on the run to witness a woman
finishing him off.

Fatalistic to the very end, Spencer forced himself to lie still. What the devil was she doing? Measuring him for his coffin? He wasn't certain he could stand much more of this mystery. Perhaps he could pretend he was awakening just now—

"Oh, Spencer," she whispered, nearly startling him into giving himself away. Amazingly, he'd managed not to move a muscle. It was just as well. They were all sore. Then, to his utter shock, he felt her hand on his uninjured cheek. His eyelids fluttered. If she noticed, she gave no sign. Her touch was warm, soft, comforting, and a shiver of reaction sent chills over Spencer's body. He fought it, knowing that was exactly the last thing he needed to do at this moment—raise the sheet like a circus tent going up. And still she continued her torture . . . softly caressing his face, her fingers now moving lightly over his bruised and swollen jaw. Sighing softly, she smoothed his hair back from his forehead.

And then, leaning over him—he could tell she did by the shifting of the mattress and also because the sweet scent of her skin suddenly filled his nostrils—she lightly kissed him on his forehead. "I am so sorry," she added, still whispering.

She pulled away, straightening up and . . . Spencer strained to detect any sound . . . apparently moved away from the bed. She had to have tiptoed across the room because he heard no footfalls, only the soft closing of the door behind her.

At last, Spencer sat up, struggling to do so. Frowning, he stared at the same door she'd only just closed. She'd said she was sorry. Sorry for what?

CHAPTER 10

By the next afternoon, it had become abundantly clear to Spencer that if he meant to have a frank discussion with his wife on many subjects, he would need to get her away from the lovely Abercorn Street house that faced Oglethorpe Square with its shading of moss-draped oaks and inviting expanse of green lawn. Since he'd taken breakfast alone in his room and hadn't dressed until late, he had yet to speak with her. She—and that blasted Edward—were receiving callers in the parlor downstairs. Beautifully attired female visitors, so Hornsby had reported, were parading in and out in accordance with Southern protocol.

Hornsby had also, with evident trepidation, told Spencer at breakfast that Her Grace had informed him to tell Spencer he was excused from receiving callers today, given his soreness and his . . . appearance. His ghastly bruised appearance, Spencer knew. Still, the word *overjoyed* best described his reaction. He hated receiving callers and had no desire to meet Savannah's crop of young ladies and their mamas.

Edward was another story. The very busy Hornsby, who made periodic forays downstairs and then hurried upstairs to report the results to his employer, said the Earl of Roxley thought every lady who showed up at the door more beautiful than the last and truly the love of his life. Spencer had scowled at this. The man was making a fool of himself, yet the giggling young ladies and their mamas were said to be enjoying his fawning attentions tremendously. Of course they would. The man was a titled peer of the realm.

Spencer, however, found his cousin not to be the least bit amusing. When Hornsby had become winded and red in the face from traversing the stairs, Mr. Milton had been dispatched downstairs by Spencer . . . on an errand in the library, ostensibly. Mr. Milton had duly reported back to him the appalling story that for every lady who asked after the absent duke, Edward was weaving a different and taller tale. Among some of the ones heard by Spencer's secretary were: the duke, unfortunately, had been stricken with a tropical illness that left him covered with red spots; or the duke had tripped and fallen down the stairs; or the duke had been hit in the head with a falling chandelier. The duke had broken his leg when out in the garden. The duke had been thrown from a horse.

It had been at this point, and outraged, that Spencer had flung back his covers and, with Hornsby's sniffing disapproval over his patient's abandoning the sickroom, had dressed and stolen downstairs. There, pausing in the hallway that ran alongside the front parlor, out of sight and around a corner, he stood, fully prepared to pretend to admire the statuary on a round oak table should anyone pass by or notice him. From this vantage point, he could hear how overjoyed the ladies said they were to see Victoria again so soon and looking so well. He suspected most of the women meant nothing of the sort and very likely were the same ones, he would be willing to wager, whose tongues had wagged without end at the time of Victoria's fall from grace.

And now today, they had come out of rank curiosity, no doubt, regarding Edward, and for fodder to feed the rumor mills. Edward was giving it to them, too, with his exaggerated attentions to them and his ever-changing tales of Spencer's imaginary woes, none of which he would be able to explain at a later date. And wouldn't the ladies have ever so much more to talk about when they got together and compared notes, only to find they'd each been told a different tale? *That damned Edward. He is only making things worse.*

In this whole dismal scenario, though, Spencer had found one ray of sunlight: his wife's comportment. By all reports, and from what he could hear himself, she had remained unfailingly gracious and kind and had told all her childhood friends the same story. She and her husband, the Duke of Moreland—Spencer suspected it amused her to watch these Savannah belles devour themselves with jealousy over her title—were only visiting. She and the duke would not be here very long. And yes, everything was wonderful with her and the duke.

Spencer admitted it: He admired her performance. Had he been her in this polite-society situation, he knew, he would have already bloodied a sugary female viper's lip or two. But he soon tired of listening to the polite chatter and ordered a carriage readied for an outing. Let the brigand behind the attack on him see him out and about—if indeed there was a brigand behind it. The two ruffians could simply have been common thieves, after all, but Spencer seriously doubted it.

Tearing at the very fabric of him was his suspicion that Victoria could be, directly or indirectly, responsible for the attack. While the very assertion, on the surface, seemed as ridiculous as it was horrifying, he firmly believed he would not be wise to discount it. After all, he did not yet know why she had run away from Wetherington's Point. But if she'd come back to be with her lover, who could possibly be a nefarious sort, and then he—an inconvenient husband—had shown up? Well, put that way, it wasn't such a leap, after all, to believe they could quickly come to the conclusion they would be better off with him dead. Such an event would leave Victoria with the title, the duchy, its wealth, and its heir.

A very neat solution, to be sure. But now, the brigand had better beware because Spencer was carrying his gun with him whenever he left the house.

While the carriage was being readied and brought round the back way, so he could escape undetected, Spencer spent his time sorting Mr. Milton and Hornsby out, leaving orders for their afternoon's activities. Then, when the fine black and gleaming carriage, with a sleek team of matching bays, was ready, he escaped outside and directed the driver—a young and cheerful and talkative black man named Zebediah—to make the circuit of some of the squares.

While he did, the young man regaled Spencer with the history of every prominent home they passed and the pedigree of the occupants, as well as the latest gossip regarding them. Zebediah dropped such names as James Oglethorpe, Lachlan McIntosh, William Jay, Button Gwinnett, and John Wesley. And, interspersed with the history lessons, were his protestations of undying love for a girl named Ruby. Normally, Spencer would have put a quick stop to such chatter, but today, finding his driver's charming repartee infectious, as well as informative, he encouraged Zebediah. Any knowledge gained of this unfamiliar place was, after all, power.

The exotic sights, the sounds, the smells, the actual colors of the place, every detail about Savannah enchanted Spencer. The city was so outside his every experience. A towering church of a different denomination resided on every corner, or so it seemed. The city itself, he realized, was nothing at all like London or any other English city he could name. Very unique. And cordial. He'd nearly worn his arm out tipping his hat to the people he passed.

The highlight of the trip, for Spencer, was the circuit around Forsyth Park with its exquisite white fountain. But eventually the heat and the humidity got to him, and he directed Zebediah to take him home. On the ride back, Spencer quietly marveled at the rich mélange of architecture to be found in Savannah. The houses, though generally less grand than what he was used to, were, nevertheless, fascinating in their differing designs. He spotted Italianate, Second Empire, Greek Revival, and Regency, among others.

Returned and recovered now from his outing, after having gone to his bedroom to wash and change clothes, Spencer deemed himself ready to be alone with his wife. He wished he could say it was for amorous purposes, but alas it was not. For one thing, he wasn't certain he could trust her. But even if he could, he feared he was too injured to be an effective performer. Beyond that, he wasn't certain Victoria would welcome his advances. After all, she had clung to that separate-bedroom dictate of hers.

As Spencer slowly descended the curving sweep of stairs from the second floor, he carried on a lively conversation in his head. He could, of course, simply order her to return to his bed. However, here in Savannah, where he didn't feel the lord and master, he was reluctant to impose his will to any degree on her or anyone else. He stopped on the next riser down, holding on to the polished handrail. Staring absently ahead, he wondered if this reluctance was how Victoria felt at Wetherington's Point. It had to be. Everything English had to be as odd to her as everything American was to him, including the food. Given that, hadn't he been the ass to abandon her to it all?

With that uncomfortable accusation following him, Spencer continued down the stairs. He meant to politely wrest his wife away from Edward and whatever callers they might have with them in the parlor. Then, he and Victoria would finally have an all-encompassing discussion, for lack of a better word. Too much was unsaid between them, and Spencer refused to allow the unanswered questions to remain so for even one more afternoon. He knew of course that he might not like, to put it mildly, what he might hear from her regarding her feelings for him, or lack thereof, and her opinion of his behavior in England.

But he had broad shoulders. He could hear criticism of

himself because he knew he had been justified in feeling he'd been made to look the fool. As well, the legal essentials, if nothing else between them, remained the same: If the child she bore was not a Whitfield, then the child could not bear his name. But she had said, in very strong words, she would not agree to that. Then he had told her, in no uncertain terms, she would return, a divorced woman with a bastard child, to Savannah. Now Spencer thought it all so monstrous. And hopeless. He cared too much for her to allow her to leave him.

The admission forced him to pause again and grip the handrail tightly. Standing there, he closed his eyes against the painful truth, but it insisted on whispering in his ear, mocking him. If he cared nothing for Victoria, it said, he would have no qualms about sending her away with her bastard child as he had so self-righteously threatened, now would he?

His heart no more than a lead weight in his chest, Spencer opened his eyes, only to stare absently at the narrow though elegant entryway coming into view at the bottom of the stairs. Thankful that no one was around to catch him just standing there on the stairs, he focused on the polished red-pine wood floor and finally faced the single most important question of all to him. Would six hundred years of Whitfield legacy be undone by the will of his heart? What was he willing to do to make a marriage with Victoria?

He didn't know. Had it really all come down to this? It very well could. Spencer completed his journey down the steps and headed for the parlor. While still around the corner from the room, he stopped, hearing someone just then crossing the foyer. Whoever it was with the masculine tread apparently entered the parlor and closed the double doors behind him. Edward, no doubt. His supposed presence acted as a stop on Spencer's determined mission to confront his wife. Did he really want answers right now, anyway, when he'd only just admitted to himself that he had no idea what he wanted to have happen? In light of that, what did her answers matter when it all came down to this: Could he, would he, send Victoria and her child away?

Certainly, no law said he must. They could remain with him. He did recall telling her—rather callously, now that he thought about it—they would try again for another baby. What had been her answer to that? He frowned, remembering all too well. She had screamed at him, letting him know that this first child, male or female, birthmark or no, would bear his name, or he would have no others from her. So, they were both equally determined to have their way entirely. Which meant, of course, one of them would lose. No room for compromise existed because too much, for both of them, was at stake. Spencer knew only too well that the only way this would turn out happily would be if the child Victoria now carried were his.

Happily? Hardly. They still had to live through six or so months of holding back and denying each other. At the end of that time, how could any tender emotion have a hope of still existing between them, if any ever had? Rubbing absently at his forehead, Spencer muttered an oath for the wretched hopelessness of the predicament. He then put the blame squarely where it belonged—on the third person involved in his marriage. The other man. *The son of a bitch.* He was in this city somewhere. Spencer could feel him, like a dark shadow hovering over him, so much more oppressive now that he was close by.

Spencer had wondered this afternoon, when he'd been in the carriage and tipping his hat to the various men who'd been out and about, if any of them was the man. Why had he never asked what the craven coward's name was? But he knew why. He hadn't wanted that hateful name in his mind. But now he did. He wanted to know who the man was, and he wanted Victoria to be the one to tell him. Outright hatred for this unknown man narrowed Spencer's eyes, especially when he tortured himself with wondering if she loved this other man and wanted to be with him.

Spencer had never asked her that because, like the man's name, he hadn't wanted to know the answer. But now he did. So perhaps that question, rather than all the others, should be the first focus of their discussion. Spencer had to face the possibility that this other man could love Victoria and might not be the cad Spencer believed him to be. What if her parents were the villains here and had torn her away from the man she loved?

The fear that it might be so, the awful wintry bleakness of such a possibility, robbed Spencer of strength and will. He had to sit down. He looked around for a chair, found one, and sat heavily. Swallowing the hard lump of emotion in his throat, he closed his eyes and rubbed his forehead.

It all seemed so ridiculous on the surface. Good Lord, he was a duke. A peer of the realm. And a grown man. He knew how to behave. And yet he didn't. Not in this circumstance. To be around Victoria, day in and day out, to want her as he did, to hear her laugh, to watch her every move . . . Spencer leaned back until his head rested against the wall behind him . . . it would be too much to be in her presence and know her heart belonged to another man. This was the most awful of dilemmas. If he kept Victoria at arm's length until the child was born, and it should prove to be his, then he would have his heir but also a resentful wife whose affection for him, had she had any to begin with, had dwindled. But if he remained in her presence, came to care for her, and the child proved not to be his, could he deny her and the babe? He must, but he wasn't sure he could. And it was that fear, more than anything else, that had him distancing himself from her in England. He had chosen to take the chance of being able to woo her affection back to him, if the child she carried was his, over the possibility of coming to care too much for her, only to turn her away in the end.

He'd thought he had it figured out. But then she'd run back to Georgia, back to this other man. That she might have true feelings for him had not entered Spencer's mind before now. Certainly, her father had not presented that as the situation. And yet, this man had lured her into a compromising situation once—twice, if one counted her running to him the moment she received a letter from him. It had to be from him. That left Spencer with one obvious conclusion: Victoria did have strong feelings for this other man.

"This is absolutely unbelievable," he said softly. "What have I got myself into?" A less judgmental corner of his mind reminded Spencer the situation, as it stood now, was not of his making . . . unless the child was his, of course. He made a chuckling sound of self-deprecation. It always came back to that, didn't it? To the baby and the other man.

But something here did not add up. Spencer's mind had mulled this over more than once. If she'd come back here to be with her lover, what the devil had she been doing out at River's End with her family? Certainly, that locale hadn't offered much hope of a tryst without being discovered—unless she'd been biding her time before she went to him, hoping to make it seem she wasn't here because of him. And now that she was here in Savannah? Well, the man lived in Savannah. Spencer knew that much from Victoria's father. Did she mean to cuckold him right under his nose? She hardly seemed that conniving and cold-blooded. But what else was he supposed to think? Had she taken a separate bedroom from her husband because her lover was in this city?

Spencer thought of all the times he had made love to Victoria. She was a beautiful woman. Her body fired his passion. She was a poem, a woman made for love. Soft, warm, curvaceous. She had given herself freely to him—no, that wasn't true. More out of a sense of wifely duty. That thought did nothing for Spencer's pride, but he'd sensed she hadn't given him all of herself. He had felt her holding back. He'd thought then it was because she was distraught over her scandal and their marrying as virtual strangers. He had sincerely hoped that as time went by and they got to know each other better, outside the bedroom, her reticence would pass.

In fact, he'd hoped, up to that day in the south parlor at Wetherington's Point when she'd announced her condition, they could come to some sort of understanding. An easy affection, maybe. Friendship. He had never hoped for love from her. And didn't intend to give his in return. He had seen, with his parents, the effects of love. His father had been an awful man in many ways, but Spencer's mother had always loved her husband. And it had destroyed her. Spencer had vowed he would not live that—

"Excuse me, Your Lordship—"

Startled, Spencer's eyes popped open almost of their own volition. Standing in front of him and curtsying awkwardly was a lovely black girl in a maid's uniform. "Your Grace," he said to correct her form of address.

"No, sir, I'm Ruby. Grace works in the kitchen."

That threw him. Spencer blinked, could think of nothing to say, but a corner of his mind did remark that here, then, was Zebediah's love.

"I'm sorry to bother you, Your Lordship, but are you feeling poorly?" Ruby asked. "You look a bit peak-ed about the mouth and eyes to me. Maybe you shouldn't be up and about just yet. I could go get that nice Mr. Hornsby for you, if you like."

"No, Ruby, thank you, but that won't be necessary." Spencer stood up as gracefully as he could, given his sore ribs and general bruising. "If you will excuse me?"

"Yessir, Your Lordship." She curtsied again and went on down the narrow entryway and about her business.

Bemused, despite himself and his earlier dire thoughts of his own life's situation, Spencer watched her go and mar-

veled at these Americans and their servants. One never even
saw the domestics in England. Why, they could be fired for
even allowing themselves to be seen by the family. But here,
in his experience so far, the help came and went at will. He'd
seen no fewer than ten at River's End and every bit as many
here in this house. Very odd. But even more surprising to him
was the Americans knew all of their servants' names. Why,
beyond Hornsby and Fredericks and Mr. Milton, who could
hardly be called a domestic, the only maid whose name
Spencer could recall was that Rose girl who was Victoria's
lady's maid. Even her he didn't recall having ever seen.

Eager now to abandon introspection for action, Spencer
rounded the corner and found the parlor doors still closed.
He expected, once he opened the door, to find a gaggle of females in here, all of them tittering away with their heads together as they gossiped and took tea . . . or whatever they
drank here in the afternoon. He listened a moment at the
door. *Damned quiet in there for tittering and tea.* But
wouldn't they be surprised, given all of Edward's dire stories regarding Spencer's fictional travails, to see him walk
into their gathering?

Spencer ordered his features into a semblance of polite
interest as he opened the door and brought a cordial greeting
to his lips.

But the sight that greeted him froze him in place and had
him swallowing his pleasant words of hello. A lancing pain
shot through his heart, causing him to forget his body's
other aches and pains. No tittering females were gathered
here. In fact, only two people who obviously had wanted to
be alone, hence the closed doors, occupied the room. For
one horrible second, Spencer thought the man in the room
with Victoria was Edward. But his reason, and his excellent
eyesight, instantly negated that notion. This man simply
had the same coloring as Edward. In fact, Edward was not
present.

Only Victoria and the man she was allowing to kiss her were in the parlor.

Victoria's scream could only be heard inside her head. Shocked into immobility by the suddenness of Loyal Atherton's outrageous and unforgivable attack on her person, she stood rigidly in his embrace and determinedly kept her teeth gritted. She would be damned before she would allow this boor access to her mouth. She wanted to scratch his eyes out, but her arms were pinned at her sides. She wanted to stomp his booted feet, but he shamelessly had his knee wedged between hers, which threw her off balance. *Horrible man!*

She kept her eyes squeezed tightly shut. She had no wish to see his awful nearness. It was bad enough her every angry breath through her flared nostrils assaulted her senses with his man scent, which made her stomach queasy. She hated him and he violated her by smearing his mouth over hers in a particularly unskilled semblance of a kiss. She wanted nothing more than to fight him with every bit of strength in her body. But experience with him told her such a response would only inflame his lust. So, instead of twisting her head away and jerking about, Victoria remained rigid in his embrace, knowing this kiss could not last forever.

She promised herself that when this monstrous liberty he had taken with her was over, she would slap his silly face right off his skull and scream her lungs out for Spencer, who would then come kill him and good riddance. Just then, Loyal Atherton was ripped away from her with a force that nearly took Victoria with him.

Gasping, staggering, all in one shocked second, she saw—"Spencer!"

Ignoring her, he grabbed the startled, wide-eyed Loyal Atherton by the shoulder, yanked him backward, and jerked him around. Spencer's jaw jutted out; his black eyes glittered . . . and he held the other man by his lapels as he stared murderously into his opponent's eyes.

"This is not what you think!" Victoria cried desperately, her hands held out in supplication. But he ignored her.

"Take your hands off me, sir," Loyal was protesting loudly, his face suffused with high color, his eyebrows lowered. "I will suffer no—"

"That's where you're wrong," Spencer informed him through gritted teeth, his voice no more than a low growl. "You *will* suffer, I promise you that."

As Spencer cocked his arm back and fisted his hand, as Loyal realized what was about to happen and his mouth opened into a perfect circle of surprise and dread, Victoria knew she had to stop Spencer somehow. Only moments before, she'd wished for him to come kill Loyal. And now, here he was and about to do just that. But she hadn't meant it! Though she felt rooted to the spot, she held a hand out to her husband. "Spencer, no! Don't do this! *Please.*"

If he heard her, he gave no indication. He had neither spoken to her nor looked her way. Without a word or another second's hesitation, Spencer—his handsome features distorted by rage and hate, hit Loyal in the jaw so hard that he actually flew backward through the air. "Oh, my God, no!" Victoria cried in dread.

Like a broken doll, Loyal's body struck the heavy mahogany medallion-backed sofa's spine and sent it toppling over with the force of his weight . . . and velocity. On his way down, his booted foot connected with a round decorative table, cluttered with rare and exquisite figurines, and sent that flying and crashing over onto the hardwood floor as well. The figurines shattered.

Horrified, staring at the shattered porcelain pieces, each one lovingly collected by her mother all through Victoria's childhood—it seemed in that instant she could see her mother, much younger than she was now and in successive images, showing her little daughter each new piece and making up a wonderful story about each one—Victoria clamped a hand over her mouth. Her incongruous thought was, *Oh, my word, my mother is going to be beside herself over this.*

Whether Spencer even heard the crash of the sofa, the toppling of the table, and the shattering of the figurines, Victoria could not say. Tiny shards of the delicate porcelain crunched under his footsteps, like so much gravel, as he charged around the upended sofa, intent apparently on jerking Loyal up and pounding the daylights out of him, if he wasn't already dead. And he very well could be, too, because he had yet to move so much as a muscle since Spencer had hit him. Victoria didn't think Spencer cared if Loyal was dead or not. He still meant to make the man, or his dead body, suffer. It was all the same to him.

But not to her. She would not have her husband going to prison or facing a firing squad or a hangman's noose because of the likes of Loyal Atherton. She had to stop him and she would . . . in any way she could.

That meant she had to move quickly since Spencer was unceremoniously hauling Loyal's limp body up by his lapels. Making little mewling sounds of desperation, Victoria despaired of what she could do, how she should intervene. Spencer was lost to reason, that much was obvious. Mere words would not stop him. Maybe she could grab his arm and hold on to him, but he was more than twice her size. She doubted her weight would slow him down in the least. And besides, she didn't want him to miss and hit her instead. Why, she'd wake up in heaven.

Then, she spied it. The iron fireplace poker. No. She didn't want to kill Spencer, just stop him. Oh, dear Lord, he had Loyal up now and was getting ready to hit him again. Panicked, crying out, Victoria grabbed a substantial vase of flowers from off an end table, ran up behind Spencer, reached up, and crashed the vase down on his head.

Spencer made a tortured sound like "Aah" as the vase

broke over his skull. The water baptized him and then cascaded over every surface in its path. Shards of china vase joined the shattered porcelain. And fresh-cut flowers shot about like errant arrows.

Horrified by the effectiveness of her actions, Victoria stumbled backward and watched Spencer fold up like a lady's parasol as he lost his grip on consciousness and Loyal at the same moment.

Both men did a slow and graceful crumple onto the carpet. And just lay there, side by side, on their backs . . . amid the debris of sofa, figurines, water, the vase, and the flowers.

CHAPTER 11

Victoria stood transfixed with shock as she stared at her handiwork. Though her heart pounded blood throughout her body and raced her pulse, though every instinct urged her to think and to do, she found she could not voluntarily move.

In the next instant, the parlor doors were flung open with such force they slammed against the walls behind them. Jumping in surprise, crying out and clutching at her full skirts, Victoria swirled around to see—

An armed mob obviously intent on charging in to the rescue but stopped abruptly in their tracks by the sight greeting them. In their forefront, and wild-eyed, Edward swung about an unnervingly large pistol as he evidently searched for a target. Flanking him on one side was Hornsby, a riding crop in his upraised hand. On Edward's other side, Mr. Milton stood ready to do damage with the large book he held raised over his head. Tillie was there, weaponless but with eyes wide with shock. Another maid Victoria believed was named Ruby sported a heavy silver candlestick in her fist. The cook, a large, florid, and balding man whose name Victoria could not recall, something Swedish, had come armed with a meat cleaver.

Several other assorted servants, black and white, rounded out the mob of would-be defenders of the home front. Their weapons, too, were remarkable. Some had knives. One had a shoe off and held high. Another, a walking cane. And yet another, an iron tool of some sort. However, apparently realizing there was no one left to fight, they advanced no farther into the room than the threshold.

"Victoria! Thank God you're all right," Edward cried, breaking the jagged seconds of silence that had claimed the parlor. His expression as incredulous as that of his companions, he swept his gaze over the ruination in the room. His expression revealed his evident confusion over who he should run to first—her or the downed men. "This is absolutely unbelievable! It looks as if a battle has taken place in here."

As he'd stated the obvious, Victoria saw no need to comment. Though rational thought had eluded her moments ago, she now thought furiously as she formulated and rejected several versions of the truth and what and how much she should say. A bit of luck in her favor, and giving her time, was the positioning of the bodies in relation to the upended divan. The big, heavy piece of furniture lay at an angle— padded cushions toward Edward and his cohorts—and hid all but the odd leg or arm of the two unconscious men. This meant no whole persons were revealed who could be readily identified and fretted over.

Distracting the army, too, were the splattered water, flung flowers, and shards of porcelain dotting the carpet and wood flooring. As well, the tipped-over round table, which had, until only moments ago, proudly displayed the precious figurines, now rolled drunkenly back and forth, back and forth, in an ever-slowing arc. Its motion seemed to entrance the confused congregants.

All except Edward. Obvious concern wrinkled his brow and rounded his eyes. "Victoria, what happened?"

Blinking back a sudden onrush of tears, she cried, "Oh, Edward, it was awful. I wish you'd been here. You shouldn't have left me alone."

"But, my dear, that's just it. You *were* alone when I left not ten minutes ago to make a mad dash for the, uh, necessary room. One can only drink so much tea and lemonade before one must— Oh, bloody hell, what am I going on about? I am terribly sorry for not being present when you so obviously needed me. But, great heavens above, what the devil happened in here?"

What, indeed. "I had a visitor."

Edward raised an eyebrow impossibly high. "A visitor? Forgive the mention of the name in this house, my dear, but who was your visitor? General Sherman, perhaps come back around for another try?"

"Don't be silly. I wish you'd come sooner."

"But we came as soon as we heard loud voices and crashing about," Edward explained. "And as soon as we could gather our weapons." He paused, allowing his continued concern for her to bracket his eyes and mouth. "Are you certain you're quite all right, Victoria? Your color doesn't look good."

She put a hand to her cheek as though she could determine her color by touch. "Yes, I'm fine, thank you."

"As you are the only one left standing, I will agree." Edward indicated—with his gun as a pointer—the scene of battle between him and her. "But what happened to . . . them?"

He still didn't realize, apparently, exactly who "them" were, and Victoria wasn't certain she should enlighten him—not in this mixed company, for certain. But she had other, larger, and more frightening concerns. What if Loyal was dead and Spencer had killed him? The law and morals aside, she could not see herself pointing the finger of guilt at her husband. And what if Spencer was dead and she had killed him? She'd lose her sanity, that was what. Therefore, the two men had to be—must be—simply unconscious. Nothing else would do.

Cognizant of the quiet as Edward and the others awaited her explanation, Victoria waved her hand vaguely at the two men sprawled about in the veritable Greek ruins of the parlor. "They fell."

"They fell?" Edward squawked, sounding like a parrot. He still had not come any farther into the room or lowered the gun he held. Neither had his cohorts with their assorted weapons. They did, however, and behind Edward's back, exchange disbelieving glances with each other.

"Yes," Victoria said, this time more emphatically. "They fell."

Edward stared at her for an awkwardly long time before raising his gaze to the ceiling and studying it. His associates followed suit. Victoria could not stop herself from peering upward, too. She supposed they expected—maybe hoped—to see a gaping hole there. Perhaps they believed the men had fallen through from the floor above. Certainly, such a catastrophe as that could explain this debacle here on the first floor. However, she knew differently. She lowered her gaze and found everyone again staring her way.

Taking a few steps to his left—and followed step for step by his posse—Edward pointed, again with his gun, toward the fallen men. "Who is that?"

He had to mean Loyal, since he knew Spencer. But before Victoria could formulate any type of response, Hornsby worked his way to the front of the crowd where he gained a clearer view of the victims. "Great Scott, it's His Grace!"

He and Mr. Milton, who had gasped loudly at Hornsby's revelation, broke from the herd and ran for their employer. Edward shouted: "Stop right there! I have a gun!"

Amid the general gasps—one of them Victoria's—making the rounds in the room, the two men stopped right there and swung around to face Edward. Hands and weapons—a book, a whip—held high in surrender, they stared wide-eyed and terrified at the armed earl. "There's nothing you can do but hurt him worse with your bumbling about. Leave him be until I can look at him. Come back over here, please." They did. Edward then swung his gaze and his gun to Victoria as he nodded his head in the direction of the downed victims. "There's no blood. I take it he's not mortally wounded?"

He meant Spencer, Victoria knew. "No. I don't think so."

Looking relieved, Edward nodded. "Good. And who is that other man?"

She would have to tell him. Feeling hollow inside and with ravaged nerves drying her mouth, Victoria said: "He's Mr. Loyal Atherton, of the Savannah Athertons. Banking and shipping. His mother is a Conover of South—"

"My dear, I don't mean to interrupt you," Edward said, interrupting her and smiling as he did so, "but perhaps we should save the pedigree and the introduction for when the man is conscious?"

"Oh. Of course."

What Edward didn't know, because they were behind him, but Victoria did because she faced them, was that the cook and maids and butler and assorted other Redmond employees had tensed the moment she'd identified Loyal Atherton. They knew the name and the context, even if Edward and Hornsby and Mr. Milton did not. At this point, the servants . . . slowly, quietly . . . inched backward toward the open doors behind them.

The subtle noises of their retreat caught the British contingency's attention. Edward, along with Hornsby and Mr. Milton, divided their befuddled gazes between the exiting employees and Victoria, who still stood across the room from them, strangely isolated. As though she inhabited an island surrounded by a dragon-filled moat and they dared not approach her and she dared not try to move, either.

"How did this man happen to . . . fall with Spencer?" Edward wanted to know.

Victoria eyed him and then the mob of domestics, who by now had backed up sufficiently to allow Ruby and . . . Sven! That was the cook's name! . . . to each grab a door to the parlor and start pulling it closed after them. "Wait!" Victoria cried. They did. She turned to Spencer's employees.

"Hornsby, Mr. Milton, would you please go with the others? I wish to speak with the earl in private."

The combined prompts of the Duchess of Moreland's request and the Earl of Roxley's gun had them bowing and silently joining the American staff in leaving the room. Once the doors closed behind them all, and in the silence remaining in the parlor, Victoria could hear their dispersing and departing footsteps. Hopefully, no curious ears were pressed to the doors.

This left her alone in the room with Edward, who tucked his gun into the waistband of his trousers. Victoria's gaze locked with his. Though it seemed hours had passed since Spencer had barged in on Loyal kissing her, it had, in reality, been only minutes from that event until this moment.

"It's all right, Victoria, come here." Edward waved her over as he stepped over to his fallen cousin. "When he comes around, I'm sure your face will be the first one he wants to see."

Though Victoria seriously doubted that, given the circumstances that had put him on the floor to begin with, she hurried over to Edward, who surprised her by holding his arms out to her to offer her a quick hug of reassurance. She gladly stepped into his embrace. For her, his warm, slender solidness held the comfort of an old friend. "Oh, Edward, I was so afraid."

He patted her back affectionately. "The evidence in this room says you had every reason to be." With that, he released Victoria and knelt down beside Spencer. Victoria stood behind him and watched as he pressed two fingers to his cousin's neck and held them there. "Pulse good and strong." He raised Spencer's eyelids and checked. "Jolly good." He looked up at Victoria. "Did he hit his head, do you know?"

Victoria's response was the cautious truth. "His head was hit, yes."

Edward raised an eyebrow. "Curious wording, my dear."

But he said nothing else as he raised Spencer's head and probed the back of it. Spencer moaned as if in pain.

Victoria clutched at Edward's shoulder. "You're hurting him!"

"Not terribly so, but hurting him at this moment can't be helped. It's for his own good. Ah, there's yesterday's large lump. Now, just let me see . . ."

Victoria let go of Edward and stood by quietly as he continued his examination of her husband's head. "What I don't understand," the earl said, "is why Spencer and this Atherton chap got into it." When Victoria said nothing, Edward again glanced up at her. Apparently, her solemn expression gave her away. "Ah. I see. Then, is he who I suspect he must be?"

Shame and anger again filled Victoria's heart. "Yes, he is. And he behaved horribly here today."

"It would seem so. There now, all done." Edward gently laid Spencer's head back on the carpet and, a hand resting on his thigh, focused on Victoria. She felt certain her heart would explode with dread and hope before he rendered his verdict. "Good news, my dear. Nothing serious I could detect—"

"Thank heavens!" Victoria clapped her hands together over her heart. "Oh, Edward, that is such wonderful news."

"He'll have a severe headache. Maybe a slight concussion. But for the most part, he'll come around just fine after some bed rest. We might want to have a real doctor look in on him, just to be sure."

Victoria nodded. "I'll get a message straightaway to Dr. Hollis. He's been my family's doctor forever and a day."

"Excellent." Edward turned now to Loyal Atherton and looked him over, saying drolly, "Oh, bad luck. It appears to me as if this one, when he *fell,* hit his jaw on the way down to the floor and oblivion." Edward then looked up at Victoria. "All that aside, and our 'official version' being he fell, tell me what really happened in here, if you would."

With no other choice, really, she launched into her story.

"Loyal bullied his way past the butler, after being told I would receive no more visitors and then burst in here, nearly startling ten years' growth out of me. I told him I had nothing to say to him, that I'm a married woman and he must leave. But he grabbed me and, completely against my will and my wishes, he forced himself on me and kissed me—"

"Unforgivable. And that exact moment was when Spence made his grand entrance?"

Victoria pressed her palms to her too-warm cheeks, reliving it in her mind. "Yes. It was the most awful scene, Edward, the two of them going at it like that. I could not get a word in edgewise to explain to Spencer what he had seen."

"All he saw was another man kissing his wife. So, I daresay the truth would not have sat any better with him than did his leap to a conclusion fueled by his long-held suspicions."

"What long-held suspicions?"

"Oh, surely, Victoria, you know what he suspects—and has done since he arrived at Wetherington's Point and found you gone."

"No, I assure you I do not." Victoria watched as Edward pointed from Loyal to her . . . and back. Realization burst into her consciousness and slackened her jaw. "Spencer thinks I came back here to be with *him*?" Her features now a study in pure distaste, she mimicked Edward by pointing to Loyal Atherton and then herself. "*Him? And me?* Never. Why would he—?"

"Among all the other and obvious reasons, Victoria . . . the letter."

Shame and dismay had her covering her mouth with her hands and staring at Edward. Then, lowering them, she said, "Will this never end? I should have known. He thinks the letter is from Loyal, doesn't he?"

"I hate to sound harsh, my dear, but of course he does, given . . . everything else, and then the way you left England after receiving it and without telling him." Puzzlement suddenly claimed Edward's features. "But hold on. Didn't you tell him last evening about the letter? I thought that's what you went upstairs to do."

"Yes. It was."

"And . . . ?"

"I never got the chance. It's complicated, Edward, but I got called away and then when I came back, he was asleep. And then I hadn't seen him today until he burst in here. Oh, this is all my fault."

"Yes, it is," he said, sounding cheery and friendly, "but don't fret, my dear. Since you did not run away from Spencer at this man's urging, then it's all very fixable. A matter of a simple conversation, really."

Maybe on this one point, Victoria knew, but not on all the others. Conversation alone could not cause a birthmark to be. And then, there was still the letter and the real reason she'd come back to Georgia. Conversation could not solve that crisis, either.

If Edward noticed her prolonged silence, he gave no hint. "Now, tell me, how did this Loyal Atherton dandy get the best of our man Spencer?"

Victoria smoothed her skirts, paying very close attention to the lay of the delicate muslin fabric. "He didn't. I did."

"*You* did?"

"Yes. The vase of flowers." She indicated the broken pieces littering the carpet and floor. "I hit him with it. I was afraid he'd kill Loyal, and I didn't want him to hang for that."

"I see," Edward said. "Very noble of you."

Victoria firmed her lips together primly. "I did it for his own good."

"I don't expect he's going to see it that way. Especially not after the rock he took to the back of his head yesterday. Poor Spence. You have to admit he's had a rough twenty-four hours. I'm not certain he's going to survive this little jaunt to America. Or, if he does, we'll be returning him to England a gibbering idiot in a wheeled chair."

As he moved away from Spencer and scooted over to Loyal, repeating the same examinations he'd performed on his cousin, Victoria sank to her knees at Spencer's side and took one of his large, square-palmed, warm hands in hers and raised it to her cheek. "Oh, Edward, it was awful. I thought I'd killed him. And I was so afraid he'd killed Loyal and would be made to pay with his own life."

"A dastardly thought. But, disaster averted, my dear, as this one will be fine, as well—" Apparently done with his quick examination, Edward pivoted to look at her and caught her nuzzling Spencer's hand. His gaze locked with hers, and he smiled approvingly. "You were prepared to lie for Spence if this other man were a goner, weren't you?"

Suddenly shy, Victoria resettled Spencer's hand at his side. "Yes, I most certainly was. Why do you think I wanted everyone else out of this room except you?"

The earl chuckled. "So we could concoct a plausible story between us?"

She nodded. "Yes. And so you could help me convince Spencer he had to go along with it."

"Not so easily done, I'm afraid, so it's just as well it won't be necessary to lie. But what are we going to do now that Mr. Atherton is so obviously and obnoxiously going to live?" Edward favored Victoria with a conspiratorial leer. "Shall we kill him ourselves?"

"Edward!"

He held both hands up as if in surrender. "Merely jesting. But I do think I'd better have him gone before Spencer comes around fully and finishes the man off. I'll get Giddens to help me get Spence upstairs. He proved helpful yesterday out in the alley. And then he and Zebediah—that chatty black fellow who, by the way, told me he is deeply in love with someone named Ruby—can see to getting Mr. Atherton home, as well as whatever his means of conveyance was for getting here. I will leave it up to you to tell them where that is."

"They know where Loyal lives. But he's not going to forgive this, Edward. Loyal, I mean. I know him. He's going to make further trouble, even if this was his fault. He won't let it go."

Edward raised an eyebrow. "Really? Well, let him try his worst. In the meantime, we'll dig defensive ditches and amass a cache of flower vases. Then, when he attacks, we'll set you on him, my dear. I'll hand you flower vase after flower vase to lob ferociously at him." Victoria tsked and raised her chin. "No, no, now don't dissemble. You do make a rather formidable foe. The evidence is all around us. Rest assured, too, present evidence to the contrary, so does your husband. He will take very good care of you, if you will only allow him to stay conscious long enough to do so."

Spencer woke up to find himself in a bed that seemed familiar to him. His senses told him he was not dressed, except for a nightshirt, and was under the cover of a soft cotton sheet. *Where the—?* A warm breeze wafted across him, bringing to his nose a mélange of scents redolent with sweet flowers, the tang of a river, and the earthy scent of rich, moist earth. Outside somewhere, a cheerfully raised voice, heavy with a Southern accent, called out to someone and then laughed. *Savannah.*

Wanting to look out the open window, he turned his head to the left . . . and made his temple throb hideously. He mouthed an oath and held very still, grimacing. Desperate to get past the pain, he focused on the long gray shadows bleeding down the wall and guessed it was late afternoon.

Spencer put all the clues together. He was in bed, undressed, in the late afternoon, and his head hurt like hell. Was he doomed to spend his life repeating this happenstance over and over? Would he eternally wake up to find it was late afternoon? He slowly turned his head to his right, continuing his harangue. And would he be in bed with his head hurting like a son of a—

"Victoria." Though he was startled by her silent presence,

his voice held nothing of that emotion. Just a croak of a sound that told him his mouth was dry.

Victoria sat primly in a chair pulled up beside his bed. She'd been reading and now quickly closed her book in her lap. She leaned forward, her expression one of relief and concern. "You're awake at last. Would you like some water?"

Spencer thought back to yesterday and the last glass of water she'd brought him and then to how everything in his life was repeating itself. And here he was . . . helplessly lying in bed, completely at her mercy. "No."

Her blue eyes bright with good will, her mahogany curls swinging about her shoulders, she made as if to get up from her chair. "It's no trouble, really."

"Not for *you* it isn't." Spencer smiled, hoping it conveyed the sarcasm he meant it to. "However, I don't wish to have my private parts doused at just this moment, if you don't mind."

"Oh. I see." A bit deflated in expression, she sat back down and stared at him . . . and waited.

"What happened to me, Victoria?" His head pounded with each echoing word that ricocheted around inside his apparently empty head. "I seem to recall everything—who I am, where I am—but that one detail."

"Well, that's good," she said brightly . . . too brightly, perhaps.

Suspicious, Spencer raised an eyebrow, but at great cost to a thumping vein in his forehead. "No, it isn't good. What happened to me?"

"You fell," she said abruptly.

"I fell?" Spencer cried—pain shot through his entire head, wringing a cry from him. The lesson learned was that one must not raise one's voice. "I fell?" he repeated softly. "From where, Victoria? Atop the house?"

"Don't be silly."

"I do not, I assure you, madam, feel the least bit silly."

She sobered. "Your head was hit."

"When I fell?"

"Yes."

"Why did I fall and what hit it?"

She said nothing. Just sniffed and looked around the room, anywhere but at him.

"Victoria?" He waited until she resettled her attention on him. "Every word I utter right now acts as a sharp knife gouging at my brain. Do we understand each other?"

"Yes." Hers was a long-suffering sigh. She put her closed book on the bed, folded her hands primly in her lap and smiled at him.

"And so . . . ?"

She exhaled sharply. "I hit you over the head with a rather substantial vase of flowers—"

"You . . . what?"

"Yes. Downstairs in the front parlor because you were hitting Loyal Atherton—"

"He's the man who was—"

"Kissing me, yes. But what you don't know is I hate the man—"

"Is he who I think he is, Victoria?"

"Yes. I hate him."

"You've said. But it didn't look to me like you do."

Victoria firmed her lips together. "Spencer, I thought you said that talking made your head hurt like someone was stabbing your brain with knives."

"It does."

"Then quit interrupting me, please. It's very rude. You asked me what happened, and I am trying my best to tell you."

Spencer eyed her sardonically. Just like a woman. He was the bruised and battered one lying abed because of her, yet he was supposed to apologize to her. "I'm sorry," he said dutifully.

She inclined her head graciously. "Thank you. Now, where was I?"

He couldn't recall. *Oh, hell. She'll start all over now. Think, man.* "Ah. You were kissing a man you hate."

She bristled at this. "I most certainly was not, sir. He was kissing me, but not very successfully, I don't mind telling you. He took me by surprise and very much against my will, and then you barged in—"

"I do not barge into rooms, madam. I enter."

She raised an eyebrow at him. "I'm sorry. You *entered* and obviously, as anyone would, misunderstood what you were seeing and charged in—do not interrupt me; you *charged* in—and grabbed Loyal and I was afraid you would kill him and hang for it and I couldn't allow that and you wouldn't listen to me, so I had no choice. I had to get you to stop." She paused . . . "I broke that vase of flowers over your head for your own good. Even Edward says so."

"Edward would. But you will forgive me, won't you, if I don't thank you for acting so quickly on my behalf until I have lasted two days in a row in Savannah without ending up in bed and beat to hell?"

Looking hesitant, to Spencer's eye, Victoria picked at something apparently stuck to the bedding and said, "You've been here—I mean in America—for four days now, Spencer."

Confusion reigned. "Four days?" Then, slowly, realization dawned. "Then I've been unconscious . . . how long?"

"Two days. Your . . . *accident* happened two days ago. But you've been in and out of wakefulness, actually, which Dr. Hollis said was a good sign."

"I don't remember any of that, but I'm glad I proved him right."

Victoria smiled—a quick, fleeting thing. "He's rarely wrong. Would you like that water now?"

"No." Spencer tipped his tongue out to wet his lips—

"See there?" Victoria pointed to his mouth. "You are thirsty. I'm getting you a glass of water. And I promise not to toss it on your . . . privates." Before Spencer could protest, she jumped up from her chair and, her red plaid silk skirts flying, she slipped around the foot of the bed to make her way over to a small dresser situated next to the open window.

Spencer painfully turned his head to watch her. Because he knew she couldn't see him, he drank in the sight of her. Her shoulders were slim and narrow, her waist so impossibly tiny for a woman three months gone with child. With her back to him and her body masking her movements, he heard the sound of water being poured into a glass and couldn't resist saying: "You're not putting any poison in that, are you?"

She turned around, apparently not offended, a simple glass of water held in her hand. "No. We're all out just now. Perhaps tomorrow. I'm expecting a delivery." She walked over to the bed, held the glass out to him, seemed to realize how difficult it would be for him to drink lying flat, and pulled the glass back. "Can you sit up? Do you need me to help you? Or I can get Hornsby. He's just downstairs in the kitchen having his supper. I told him I would sit with you until he came back—"

"I can sit up by myself. I'm not an invalid." Flattening his palms against the mattress, Spencer pushed himself up—the room spun sickeningly. Close to passing out, he groaned and flopped back against the pillows, breathing shallowly and breaking out in a cold sweat.

"Spencer! Are you all right?" Victoria thumped the glass down on the nightstand and quickly sat on the side of the bed, leaning toward him and resting her hand on his chest. "Look at you—you're in a sweat. Why, I can feel your heart beating so hard you'd think it'd wear itself out and just stop at any moment, you poor man."

Spencer stared at her. "Please don't say things like that. I fear you can cause them to happen."

The expression on her lovely oval face pulled down at the eyes and mouth, and she stood abruptly, accusingly. "You think me evil. And after all I've done to save your life."

"Save it? By all appearances, madam, you very nearly took it."

That, apparently, was the last straw for her. She stormed around to the end of the bed. Spencer could barely raise his hand to get her to stop. As his weak gesture had no effect, he flopped his hand back down to the bed. Victoria retrieved her book, held it close to her chest and, head held high, the very picture of the injured heroine, said: "I will go now. I never wish to inflict my presence where it is not wanted. And clearly it is not wanted here. Hornsby will be up shortly to attend you, sir. Good day to you."

And with that, she paraded out of the room and, not so very gently, closed the door after her. But then she reopened it immediately and poked her head in. "I forgot to tell you that we're the honored guests two nights from now at River's End for a barbecue. However, because it is such a long drive and my parents would like some time alone with us before their other guests arrive, we will be leaving for there tomorrow and will be staying for as many as three nights. I am hoping, of course, that by tomorrow morning you can be up and around, so we can see if you are strong enough to attend. If not, I will have to break my mother's heart—and she is already upset by the ruination of her figurine collection—and ruin all her plans for the barbecue by telling her you are under the weather, sir. And another thing, they know nothing about this baby or the letter I received or your fight with Loyal Atherton, so please do not bring any of those topics up. Oh, and too, if you will remember, while we are there, we are a loving couple."

Spencer took a moment to assimilate all of that information. He had many questions and he understood everything, except the concept of a barbecue. But he wanted to get back to the "loving couple" statement. "Indeed? A loving couple? Well, then, I will make every endeavor to play my part."

"Thank you." Like a turtle—a particularly fetching turtle—retreating into the safety of its shell, Victoria pulled her head back, obviously getting ready to close the door again.

"Wait." He admitted it: He didn't want her to go. "I assume you will play your part, too, and sleep in the same bed as me while we are there?" It greatly pleased him to see her eyes widen with surprise. "Ah. So you hadn't thought that all the way through to its logical conclusion, I see." She said nothing. "Well, Victoria? Will you play your part as the loving wife?"

"Of course I will," she snapped, her finely arched eyebrows now riding low over her sky-blue eyes. "I did it in London, and I can do it here, too."

"Touché, madam." He tried not to be insulted that she had to pretend to love him. It was irrational, he knew, so he blamed his head injury for its selective yearnings and imperfect memories. "In future, however, please do not accept invitations for me or us without first consulting me or Mr. Milton."

His statement had been calculated to raise her ire and get her back in the room. Indeed, Victoria opened the door more fully and crossed the threshold. "I will *not* consult Mr. Milton. He does not get to say yea or nay to my wishes"— Spencer suppressed a smile at how she suddenly sounded like an imperious duchess—"and I could hardly consult you in this instance, your being unconscious. So I sent a note back with my mother's messenger saying we accepted. They *are* my parents, and I didn't feel you'd say no, even had you been conscious. If you'll remember, we left River's End under rather strained circumstances, and they are trying to make up for that by celebrating our marriage with their friends and colleagues. So this is very important to them, and to me, and I'm hoping I can count on you to behave while we're there."

Her entire speech had been remarkable, and he had enjoyed watching her for every word of it, but that last bit took him by surprise. "My behavior has not been called into question, madam, since I was five years old." He thought a moment. "Twenty-five years old, at any rate. But what would you have done had I not awakened today, Victoria? Dragged me along unconscious?"

"Certainly not. I would have made our excuses." So she would have stayed here with him; this warmed Spencer out of all proportion with her simple words. "However, remember they do not know about your, ah, injuries or the circumstances that caused them. And I think it best that they don't."

"Why? Because you're the one who caused this last one?" He just couldn't resist teasing her, and it surprised him that he couldn't.

That stubborn chin of hers came up a notch. "I did what I had to do under difficult circumstances you helped cause."

"I helped cause, madam?"

"Yes. You attacked Loyal Atherton—"

"He was kissing you."

"We've had this discussion. Now, I was saying my parents have no idea why I am really here—"

"Neither do I."

She looked suddenly guilty. "Oh. That's right. Well, it's neither here nor there at the moment—"

"I think it's here and now, actually. At this moment." Spencer fought waves of dizziness as he tried to sit up—

"No, Spencer, don't try to sit up. You're still too— Oh, for heaven's sake. I swan . . . men." She rushed to his bedside, tossed her book down, and, making a show of her irritation with him, assisted him . . . ineffectually . . . by pulling on his arm, moving pillows around and fluffing them behind him. "I hardly think you're in any shape to hear— Oh, I'm not even supposed to tell you. Or anyone. It's too dangerous."

"Dangerous?" Spencer thought he would pass out from the painful throbbing at his temples. He felt hot and clammy and mad as hell. "Victoria, listen to me. What is dangerous?

You must tell me. Has that Mr. Atherton paid another visit or made threats?"

"No, of course not. But I received another—" She recoiled as if she'd seen a ghost. Closing her eyes momentarily, she put her fingers to her temple. Then she focused on Spencer. "I'm sorry, I have to go. I'll have someone get Hornsby."

She made a sudden move away from the bed, but Spencer grabbed her wrist and captured her startled attention. "You're not going anywhere. What did you receive? Another what? Another letter?"

Tears welled in Victoria's eyes. "I don't know what to do, Spencer. One moment I think I should tell you, and the next I'm too afraid to involve you." She easily pulled her arm out of his weakening grip and turned and fled the room, closing the door behind her.

Alone now, a virtual invalid who could not even reach the glass of water so tantalizingly close to his head; a man who could not seem to conduct one simple conversation with his wife without it ending in a battle of wills or tears or injured feelings or talk of divorce; a man who most likely would, inside of a week, given the frequency and severity of his head injuries, be a drooling idiot or dead, Spencer absolutely gave up. Defeated, he stared up at the ceiling and asked it: "What in hell is going on around here?"

One thing he knew, bright and early tomorrow he would find out.

CHAPTER 12

The next day dawned a beautiful, temperately cool, and blue-skied Friday. By mid-morning, Spencer had deemed it a perfect day for a trip out to a plantation home for a barbecue to be held the next day. He frowned, thinking how foreign those words were to him . . . *plantation, barbecue*. Amused, he could only shake his head. What new and wondrous adventures he was having in America. His hands clasped behind his back, he stood peering out his bedroom's window at the cityscape and beyond to where he knew the Savannah River flowed. Though this very fine Redmond House was no more than several blocks from the water, he found he could not catch a glimpse of the river because of intervening oaks and grand houses and warehouses down at the docks.

Abandoning that view for another, he stretched his body and his gaze acutely to his left to see the street out front. Abercorn, he believed it was named. Already it seemed fairly alive with fashionable carriages and beautifully dressed strollers passing by. He shifted his position again, looking down to the street below. This one ran alongside the Redmond House and was, he believed, East State Street. Yes, that was it. And the square across the way was Oglethorpe Square. Spencer smiled to himself. Not only was his body recovering rapidly—thank God for the Whitfield constitution—but his memory seemed also to be intact.

"Forgive me for interrupting, Your Grace, but should you be up and about? You could give yourself a relapse."

Spencer slowly turned and saw his valet, who acted more like a nanny. The man's heavy jowls gave him an unfortunate resemblance to a sad bulldog. "Thank you for your concern, Hornsby, but I'm feeling much stronger today."

Hornsby held a neat stack of folded white shirts in his arms. "Then we'll definitely be making the trip to River's End, sir?"

"Yes, I'm afraid so. Not looking forward to the carriage ride again with Mr. Milton?"

"No, sir, although one is very happy to be included at a . . . barbecue, Your Grace." The man looked on the verge of shedding tears.

"Oh, come now, Hornsby, it's not as bad as all that."

"I fear it is, sir. From what Mr. Milton has ferreted out from that Ruby girl, a barbecue involves eating copious amounts of roasted pork or beef, or both, outdoors, sir. Some sort of picnic, one can only hope. Evidently it comes with all the *fixin's,* too, whatever those are."

Spencer frowned. "Fixin's? Sounds positively . . . grand. Or pagan."

"Indeed. Furthermore, Mr. Milton, with whom I do not often agree, but I do on this point, seems to think this is something the Church of England would not sanctify."

Spencer bit the inside of his cheek to keep from laughing out loud and thereby horrifying his starchy valet. "I see. Then I suggest we not run home and tell the Archbishop of Canterbury of our attendance. However, I think I can reasonably assert that we will not be sacrificed on a stone altar at the end of the evening, Hornsby. From what I was told, they held that ceremony last month. So we should be safe."

Hornsby's brown eyes widened dangerously. Then he

pivoted about and made for the small dressing room off the bedroom. "I'll see to your wardrobe, sir. And I will also pack your handgun. And plenty of ammunition."

"Thank you, Hornsby." The hell of it was, Spencer couldn't be certain he wouldn't need it. Not because he actually feared being sacrificed, but because an attempt on his life had already been made once. A gut feeling, something he always listened to, told him that the incident in the alley had everything to do with whatever was worrying his wife. And he would not have his wife worried. She was carrying his child. *A* child, at any rate, Spencer instantly corrected himself, frowning at his slip of the tongue. *Whoever's* child it was, worrying on its mother's part could not be good for it, or for the mother.

Concerning Spencer now was his insidiously growing desire to believe the child Victoria carried was his. He wanted to believe this for more than one reason, too. Into his traitorous mind appeared, as if summoned, Victoria's beautiful oval face with her flawless skin, sky-blue eyes, and inviting rosebud of a mouth. Spencer's breath caught, and he blinked, willing away the image of her visage surrounded by the curling cloud of her deeply brunette hair, which she could never seem to completely capture into any certain style. How very beautiful she was—

"Damn it all to hell," Spencer said forcefully, banishing from his consciousness the image of his wife and the desire for her that went with it. He absolutely could not allow his personal wants to influence a decision of such far-reaching consequences for his duchy. And so he wouldn't. Duty and responsibility came first, and he would have to be guided by them, no matter how painful such decisions could be for him.

Thus bolstered for having reaffirmed those points for himself, Spencer concentrated once again on the here and now. Already bathed and dressed and having eaten downstairs, with Edward as company, a breakfast of bacon and sausages and eggs, to which he had added three cups of dark coffee strong enough to curl his hair, wonderful buttermilk biscuits, and something devious called grits, Spencer pronounced himself ready to get out of Hornsby's irritable way.

And as the studious Mr. Milton was downstairs in the library attending to correspondence to England that Spencer had dictated, his orders for his staff were complete. This left him free to pursue other important activities. Uppermost in his mind was confronting his wife and holding a frank discussion of all the questions and concerns he had, several new ones of which she had raised only last evening when he'd awakened to find her seated by his bed. Spencer wondered how often during the time he'd been unconscious she had attended him. Had she done so out of duty and guilt? Perhaps a bit of both. But he wanted to think, though no good could come of such a thought, she'd sat by his bed because she cared and worried about him.

"What the devil?" Spencer muttered. "Enough of this." Angry that his unguarded thoughts always slipped away to her, he deemed it high time he presented himself in her bedroom for a private talk. And there he would stay, he promised himself, until he had the answers he wanted regarding what was going on around here—and he meant from the day she'd left Wetherington's Point onward to this very one.

On a mission now, Spencer left his bedroom and stalked down the hall, thinking what a relief it was to be able again to stalk about and stride purposefully. Damned hard to be in charge of a situation if one was wobbly kneed and forced to hang on to others just to get about. As he knew hers was the next bedroom on his left and down the short hallway from the staircase, Spencer freed his mind to wonder what his wife's bedroom looked like. Would it reflect her? Or like his, since the furnishings here had not been designed with either of them in mind, but rather the elder Redmonds, would it be plush though impersonal? Not that it mattered or that he even cared . . . just a mental exercise to propel him onward. His sensual nature suggested, however, that this moment could be better spent wondering not what the bedroom looked like, but what Victoria looked like in the bed.

The powerful stirrings of desire, never more than the next thought or sight of her away from betraying him, assailed Spencer and fashioned for him a seductive image of Victoria invitingly displayed atop her mattress, waiting for him; the bedding would be soft and full and tangled; she'd have that doe-eyed, just-now-awakening look on her face, her lips full and so in need of being kissed; the thin strap of her filmy nightgown would be sliding off her soft shoulder; her thick and lustrous mahogany curls alluringly arrayed about her, cascading nearly to her waist—

Rigid now as a tree trunk and barely able to catch a deep breath or think a deep thought, Spencer forswore knocking first and excitedly opened the door onto a darkened bedroom and the sounds of coughing and retching. The close, sour smell of the room's air stopped him in his tracks and had him going soft and wrinkling his nose in distaste. Well, one thing he knew: This was definitely his pregnant wife's bedroom. His first thought was to back quietly out of the room and leave her in privacy with her wretched state. And go do what? Walk about and be bored? No, he should see if he could help somehow. Or at least show some concern. After all, her present and appalling condition could very well be his fault entirely.

Courage, man. Leaving the door open behind him to take advantage of the light streaming in from the windows at both ends of the hallway, Spencer strode purposefully into the deeply shadowed room. "Victoria?"

A strangled gasp met his greeting, as it were, only to be followed by her terribly sick-sounding voice calling out: "Go away. Please. Leave me alone."

He knew he should leave her be, but pity and guilt suddenly assailed him. *The poor woman is as sick as a dog, and I've never given one thought to how she is faring.* "I'm sorry, Victoria, but I'm staying."

"Oh, God," she groaned. "What do you want?"

What, indeed. "I, uh, came to see how you are this morning."

"Well, sir, I am sick. Very sick."

Irritated at the darkness in the room because it hindered him in readily seeing her, Spencer called out: "Where the devil are you?"

"Go away! I don't want you to see me like this! Please."

Manners dictated that he should honor her wish. But, as the saying went . . . in for a penny, in for a pound. Far from going away, Spencer listened, trying to locate her by her sniffling and shuffling about. Was she actually hiding from him? Would he have to search under the bed? "I have every right to ascertain your well-being, madam. I am your husband—"

"*So?*" This was yelled at what Spencer suspected was the top of her vocal range.

The sound gave him a sharp pain behind his left eye and made both of his ears hurt. Blinking, realizing his eyes watered as well, he waited for his eyesight to adjust to the semi-darkness. Aha. Just ahead of him and to his right was the bed. Directly across the way were the windows, which had to be closed, as the draperies were drawn against the day and no breeze stirred the fabric. "I've decided to stay, Victoria, and tend to you."

"Tend to me? You? I think not, sir. If you wish to help, go get Rosanna for me."

"I have no intention of doing that. I would have to ask every female in the house if she was this Rosanna creature because I have no idea what the girl looks like—"

"She's not a girl," his wife shrieked. "How many times must I tell you she is a gray-haired woman past middle age? There aren't that many of them here, Spencer. Find her."

He'd always heard that women in a delicate condition sometimes suffered sudden foul moods. This seemed to be one of them. Still, he had no intention of searching for her maid. Instead, he made his way over to the curtains. "I will not. But where is the woman when her mistress is in this much distress? Such neglect. Does she fancy being fired in a foreign country?"

"Don't you dare." Her voice was low and threatening enough to stand the hairs up on Spencer's arms. "I sent her away with the . . . the other basin. She gave me this clean one and a cold rag before she left. I told her not to come back because she gets sick when I do."

"Then why, in God's name, would you want me to go get her now? Damned useless wench, I'd say."

"She most certainly is not. For the love of God, Spencer, go away. Forget Rosanna, too. Just leave me here to die."

"I'm sorry but I cannot do that. You could be carrying my heir, madam. And I begin to think you are, because, as sick as you are, and drawing on the stories I've heard from the Whitfield women, the first people in the world Whitfield men make deathly ill of us are our mothers. Brace yourself, Victoria, I'm going to open the curtains and windows."

"No!" Hers was the wail of a lost soul.

But Spencer did just as he'd threatened—he flung the draperies back and raised the windows up in their casements. Blessedly clean and fresh air and wondrous sunlight filled the room. Spencer leaned over, bracing himself on the sill and breathing in deeply of great draughts of Savannah's finest air. But Victoria's sudden cry, apparently against the light, startled Spencer so badly he nearly fell out the window and onto the hard ground two floors below. To save himself, he reared back . . . and hit the back of his neck on the raised window. The impact sent him to his knees. He saw stars and thought he would pass out.

Victoria's gasp preceded: "Spencer? Are you all right?"

As the world spun sickeningly, Spencer nearly bit through his bottom lip to keep from spouting every obnoxiously foul combination of curse words he knew. "No, Victoria, I am not all right. I have not been all right since the day

I arrived at Wetherington's Point nearly a month ago to find you inexplicably gone. Since that day, I have been on a merry chase for answers, which lead only to more questions and dead ends and could, in reality, end in my actual death. Does that answer your question, madam?"

A moment of silence ensued. Then, "You spoke harshly to me," she burbled, right before she began to cry.

Spencer cursed softly but in earnest as he dropped to all fours—if he tried to stand up, something told him, he'd join his wife in retching—and crawled across the carpet toward the sound of Victoria's pathetic sobs. He found her seated on the floor with her back pressed against her disheveled bed's wooden side rail and her head leaned back against the mattress and bedding. A large porcelain basin, such as one would find in a chamber set, reposed between her long and lovely legs, which were splayed straight out in front of her.

Spencer put a tentative hand on her arm. "Victoria?"

Clad in her nightgown, which was hiked up to her thighs, she held a damp cloth in her hand and rolled her head slowly to stare bleakly at him. Her pathetically tear-streaked face could not hide the ravages of her morning's illness. "Do not touch me. I shall bite you, if you do."

Believing her completely, Spencer snatched his hand back. "Fair enough." As he roved his gaze over her face, he felt an intense sympathy swell his heart. "You poor creature, look at you. I had no idea."

Fresh tears rolled down her cheeks. She wiped at them with her damp cloth. "Nor did I want you to know. I had no wish for you to see me like this. These hideous dry heaves are the worst."

He nodded his understanding. "I've experienced them before myself. Obviously, not from the same cause. Too much strong drink, in my case."

Spencer eased himself into position next to her, mimicking her pose. Legs straight out in front of him, back against the side rail, head resting against the bedding. He would have liked nothing better than to take her in his arms and hold her, comfort her, but she had given ample warning that should he touch her, she would bite him. Even worse, he knew if he held her like this, tenderly, intimately, he might never let her go. *Damned awkward situation!*

"If I recall, Victoria," he said quickly, conversationally, "you weren't like this—I mean this sick—when we were first married or even all the time we were in London." Then, he remembered they'd had separate bedrooms there, too, and he hadn't seen her very many times in the morning. Wondering if he'd been as unaware and unattentive then as he had been up to now, he added, "Were you?"

"No. I wasn't anywhere near this sick then. An occasional queasiness. It's only been this bad in the past few weeks."

"I see. I'd say I'm sorry . . . if I thought I was responsible."

Hurt and shame sparked in her eyes. She said nothing, but stared at him and then looked away. Raising the cloth she held and pressing it to her forehead, she again laid her head back against the bedding and closed her eyes.

What an unmitigated ass I am. Why did I say such a thing as that—and especially at this moment? He hadn't meant to add insult to injury; he'd spoken without thinking. *From now on, man . . . think. Look at her, for God's sake.* In fact, he could not look away from the delicate sweep of her eyelashes against her pale skin and the intense vulnerability of her slender white throat with the steadily beating pulse at its base. The sight tore at his heart, and made a mockery of his earlier erotic thoughts of her.

Certainly, she wore the thin nightgown with the falling strap he had envisioned in his hallway fantasy. And her wonderful mahogany-colored hair did hang about her shoulders, but in damp strings. The poor woman was all but unrecognizable as the beautiful woman he had wed. Right now, she looked more like a cholera victim . . . weak, pale, thin, dark circles under her eyes . . . than she did an object of desire. And yet, he felt no revulsion, only tender regard and concern—and guilt for being such a dolt.

"I'm sorry, Victoria," Spencer blurted, almost before he knew he would. But he meant it sincerely, he realized. He felt a warm flush rise up his neck and cheeks. He didn't apologize often or easily, but found he needed to say more. "I said a tactless and uncalled-for thing. I hope you can forgive me."

Victoria moved the damp cloth away from her forehead as she opened her eyes and turned her head his way. "Are you apologizing to me, Spencer?"

The way she said it. As if it were a momentous event she could not believe. Self-conscious pride had Spencer shifting his position and frowning at her. "I believe that is the idea when one says one is sorry."

His reward was the ghost of a smile she sent him. "Then I forgive you."

Surprising him was how good her forgiveness made him feel. "Good. Has a doctor, uh, seen you, Victoria? Forgive my indelicacy, but I mean . . . is everything going along as it should?"

She nodded. "Of course, your doctor in England checked in on me. And then when Dr. Hollis was here to see about you, I swore him to secrecy on my behalf and told him of my condition. He examined me and said everything appeared normal. Even the sickness."

Intense relief washed over Spencer. "Jolly good, then. Glad to hear it." Then he saw them sitting there on the floor, like two sulking children sent to their room for misbehaving. It was suddenly funny, and Spencer betrayed his thought by chuckling.

"Why are you laughing? Is it the way I look?" She quickly and worriedly smoothed her hair back from her face.

"No, no, not the way you look. And you look pathetic, by the way."

"Why, thank you, kind sir." A mock gracious note of Southern gentility tinged her voice, as did a smile at the corners of her mouth. "And you? How are you feeling since losing your battle with the raised window?"

"I am relieved merely not to be paralyzed, madam. But am I correct in saying you appear to be recovering from your morning's bout? Are you feeling stronger yet?"

She nodded. "Better. It's passing. And that frightens me."

A jab of concern had Spencer shifting his shoulders until he'd turned more to her. "Really? How?"

"A bit ago I was too sick to die. However, now that I'm feeling better, I fear I shall pass over at any moment."

Spencer chuckled. "Try not to, if you would, please. No doubt, I'd be charged with your murder and hanged for it."

"How sentimental you are. You warm my heart, sir."

Spencer could only grin and hide how he truly felt. Looking at her, seeing her inner strength and beauty shining through despite her bout of illness, he wished she truly meant what she'd said . . . that he warmed her heart. Fanciful thinking, that's what it was. Nothing between them had changed. All the problems and concerns and questions remained. Spencer cleared his throat as if that would suppress his yearnings for her. "My intent, in coming in here this morning, Victoria, was to question you"—she raised an eyebrow at that, and Spencer quickly reworded—"or, rather, discuss with you those topics between us that need discussing and clarifying. But obviously you are not up to such a discussion at the moment."

"No, I am not. But allow me time to bathe and dress and see how I feel then." Her blue eyes peered intently into his. "And you're right: We must talk, and we need to do so before we leave for River's End."

The urgency in her voice tensed Spencer's muscles.

"I'm not going to like what you have to tell me, am I, Victoria?"

She shook her head. "No."

As it turned out, Victoria felt much refreshed following her bath, with Rosanna's help, and a light breakfast brought up to her by Tillie. With her hair piled atop her head and pinned there to keep its weight off her neck during the heat of the day, and donning one of her lighter, looser day dresses of pink linen, Victoria felt capable of convening a war council, as it were. Tillie had carried Victoria's handwritten notes around to Spencer and Edward in which she'd asked them to meet her in the parlor at eleven-thirty.

It was that time now, but Victoria had yet to leave her bedroom. She needed privacy for a moment, so she'd sent Rosanna and Tillie off to attend to the packing for their approaching departure for River's End. Once she was alone, Victoria picked up one of her jewelry boxes and removed a false bottom. In the small compartment was the folded-over letter she had received at Wetherington's Point. With it were the others she'd received since she'd been back in Georgia, one at River's End and two here.

These she put in her skirt's pocket as she exited the now cleaned and aired-out bedroom. As she passed by and spoke to different ones of the servants busily going about their duties, she still worried about showing the correspondence to the two men. How well she knew she'd been warned not to involve anyone. But what else was she supposed to do? Spencer had nearly been killed once already. The attack on him in the alley had been no random assault by common thieves. Her last note had confirmed that. He had to be told so he could protect himself. And Edward, intelligent, inquisitive, would be a tremendous ally. Another set of eyes and ears—and fists.

Victoria achieved the landing to the sweep of curving stairs that led to the first floor and the parlor . . . the same parlor where Spencer had fought with Loyal Atherton. Holding on to the handrail, she started down, thinking and worrying about how quiet Loyal was. Not one word from him. She'd half expected him to challenge Spencer to an illegal duel. But nothing . . . so far. Well, if the horrid man knew what was good for him, he'd stay away.

Victoria stepped off the last riser and walked briskly up the short, narrow hallway, heading resolutely for the corner around which were the double doors of the parlor's entrance. An appreciative part of her mind noted with pleasure how warm and elegant, yet comfortable, the house and its furnishings were. Her parents would be happy here. She knew they meant to move here to take advantage of the social life in Savannah proper and for her father to be closer to the banks, City Hall, and Factor's Row, where the cotton exchange and the warehouses were. He had a hand in every business in Savannah, it seemed, just as her mother did in the social activities. And River's End? It would be Jefferson's.

Victoria did not resent this as she used to do, even though she and Jeff had come to words over it out on the dock several nights ago. How long ago had that been? So much had happened since then. Had it really been less than a week? Yes, it had. Victoria made a sound of disbelief. Hard to believe. But, truly, it seemed right and fitting that a Redmond should carry on at the plantation. And she, after all, was no longer a Redmond. She was a Whitfield.

A Whitfield? When did I change my allegiance? This startling question popped into Victoria's mind at the exact second she opened a door into the parlor and found herself faced with John Spencer Whitfield and his cousin, Edward Sparrow. The men gallantly rose to their feet as she stood there, staring, her hand still on the door's knob. Her gaze sought and found Spencer's. Quite unexpectedly, and as if it were independent of her will, her heart skipped a happy beat and raced her pulse. Oh, how awful. She was doomed if she should fall in love with—

"Victoria?" Spencer said, striding purposefully toward her with that leonine grace of his she so admired. "Are you quite all right? You look as if you've had a surprise or a shock."

Victoria snapped her attention to her husband . . . a Whitfield . . . and forced a smile as she closed the door behind her. "I've just had both—a surprise and a shock—but never mind. It's neither here nor there."

"Nothing good comes of your saying it's neither here nor there." Though concern lowered his eyebrows over his black and glittering eyes, he took her elbow and guided her into the parlor. "May I say you look lovely, my dear?"

Victoria blinked, staring up at her husband as a part of her mind remarked on his high, smooth forehead and the delicious prominence of his cheekbones. She barely came to his shoulder and felt so protected when he was nearby. What was she going to do when he put her aside if this baby was not his? She must guard her heart better. She must.

But look at him . . . he certainly wasn't helping. Why did he have to be dressed so daringly as he had been earlier in close-fitting, buff-colored riding britches, black and highly polished Hessians, and a neatly ironed white shirt, open at the throat? He stirred her feminine senses, and they seemed to need no provocation in that area since she'd been pregnant. He was all she thought about if she didn't keep her mind actively busy on other subjects and concerns. She would have thought that would be easy, given that those concerns were literally life or death for the very people in this room.

"Victoria? You seem so distracted."

"I'm sorry. But I am. I was. Did you just say I look lovely, Spencer?"

"I did. Very lovely and very . . . recovered over your state this morning. One would never suspect." His devilish grin made jelly out of her knees. "Why? Am I not supposed to remark on my wife's radiance?"

"Radiance? No. I mean yes. Of course. You just never have before. I had no idea I could lay claim to being radiant."

He quirked his full and sensual lips. Was he suppressing a smile? "No? Then I am remiss. And look, we have Edward here with us."

"Victoria," Edward said formally, accompanying his greeting with a bow. Though Spencer was attired for riding, Edward was attired formally and looked as if he meant to call on the queen herself. Starched and polished he was. Hair neatly cut and combed. Every detail in place.

"Why, Edward," Victoria teased, "which young lady's head are you trying to turn this morning?"

As Spencer handed her around to the same medallion-backed sofa he had knocked Loyal Atherton over a few days ago, he said, "Your note asking for this meeting caught him on the way out the front door, Victoria. I believe he meant to call on a certain Miss Lucinda Barrett."

Surprised, and staring at Edward, whose face colored, Victoria had to sit down. Of course, the sofa had long since been righted and repositioned. The small, round table was once again next to it, but now it sported a lone vase of fresh flowers. No figurines. "Lucinda Barrett? Why, where in the world did you meet her, Edward?"

"Is she not suitable?" Edward wanted to know, a frown creasing his forehead and pulling his mouth down.

"My word, she's eminently suitable, and one of my dear friends— Oh, of course, you met her when she and her sweet mother paid a call the same day . . ." Victoria swallowed back her next words and cut her gaze over to her husband. She'd nearly said *on the same day Loyal Atherton paid a call.*

"Yes," Edward quickly said, neatly covering her near-gaffe.

But Spencer seemed oblivious to their tension as he settled himself next to Victoria on the sofa. The Earl of Roxley raised his eyebrows at Victoria, signaling his relief, and then favored her with his smiling, eager attention. "As my cousin has so kindly informed you, Miss Barrett has invited me to make a call this morning."

"Oh, my stars, Edward, I didn't know. You go right ahead. I don't want to keep you—"

"No, no, I feel this is more important. Family, as it were. Besides, I've already sent word asking if I may call later before we depart for River's End. If not, then I will see her tomorrow, certainly, at the, uh, barbecue?"

"Why, of course you will. I'm certain Mama has invited the Barretts, as well as the Carpenters and the Sales and the McIntoshes and the Cliftons. All very prominent and all dear friends and relatives you met the other day. You should have your pick of any number of young ladies to get acquainted with."

Edward grinned boyishly, the smile lighting his brown eyes.

"Have a seat, Edward, before you faint from excitement," Spencer said drolly. He surprised Victoria by placing his arm along the sofa's serpentine spine, essentially around her shoulders, had she been sitting back. But, of course, she sat properly forward on the cushion.

His smile gone now, a belligerent expression having taken its place, Edward retorted: "I've never fainted, sir." But when Spencer merely raised an eyebrow, he abruptly sat down and gave Victoria his undivided attention.

So did Spencer. Feeling suddenly too warm and overwhelmed by all she had to say and to reveal, Victoria felt uncertain how to start . . . and decided to start there. "I know I asked for this meeting, and I feel it's essential we have it before we leave for River's End. But I'm not certain how to begin, really. There's so much to say. So much I don't know myself but only suspect, so I don't know if I should mention everything or just start with—"

"Allow me to start, then," Spencer said. "I have a question for you, Victoria, regarding something that needs settling."

CHAPTER 13

What could Victoria do except smile and say, "And what is that?"

"Three nights ago, the second time you left my room, after dousing me with the cold water and I went to change my clothes, where did you go and why?"

Edward's sharp bark of laughter forestalled Victoria's answering. "She doused you with cold water?"

"Shut up, Edward." Spencer's glare could have cut diamonds. "It's not amusing, and I was speaking to my wife."

His question and his petulant tone took Victoria by surprise. Obviously, he had been brooding about this, but she'd expected his first question to be about the letter or Loyal Atherton. "I'm sorry, but I was—"

Edward continued to make strangled, choking noises, and Victoria feared the cousins could come to blows right here in this parlor. *What is it about this room and men?* She quickly said: "Why did I leave, you mean, after swearing on my grandmother's grave that I would not?"

"Yes. Exactly. Your poor grandmother."

"My grandmother was never poor a day in her life. And to answer your question, I was called away by Rosanna."

"Ah, the infamous and never-present lady's maid."

"She is always present. Except when you're about. At any

rate, it was an unfortunate squabble with Tillie over the placement of my belongings."

"I beg your pardon? Tillie?"

"Yes, Tillie. She's a maid at River's End, and one of my mother's many charity cases. A skinny blond girl with stringy hair and the mannerisms and curiosity of a cat. A sharecropper's daughter Mama's taught to read and write and has given employment. I have no idea why my mother does these things. At any rate, and for some reason I cannot fathom, she—Tillie—begged Mama to allow her to come here to bolster our army of servants. I don't know why Mama agreed because she knows Tillie and Rosanna do not get along."

Victoria knew Spencer had not a hair's worth of interest in a discussion of maids and whom they did or did not like. But he had listened to her admittedly prattling speech with what she realized was growing and amused interest. What had brought about this sudden change in him, this warmth and solicitousness with regard to her? Had he really meant it earlier when he said he was coming to believe the baby she carried was truly his? While this cheered her on one front, it did not on another. She would like to be liked, and wanted, for herself.

As if he'd suddenly remembered he was supposed to be irate with her, Spencer narrowed his eyes and brought a frown to his strong, handsome features. "I take it this disagreement between your maids was important enough for you to abandon your solemn vow to me not to leave your chair?"

"If I hadn't gone, it would have escalated to hair-pulling and scratching and shrieking. I didn't think your hurting head would appreciate such a serenade at that point."

"And you would have been right. But you didn't come back." His expectant and challenging expression said he knew she had and waited to see if she would own up to having done so.

Victoria raised her chin. "I did, but you were already asleep. And now I have a question of curiosity for Edward."

"For Edward?"

"For me?"

Victoria nodded first at Spencer and then his cousin. "Yes. You. You seem to have medical training. Am I right?"

"Medical training?" This was Spencer, sounding alarmed. "What has he done?" He pointed at his cousin. "We've talked about this before, Edward."

Looking supremely guilty, especially with the tops of his ears turning a nice red, Edward cried, "I've done nothing—"

"I don't know what you two are talking about," Victoria cut in, "but I'm referring to here in the parlor with you and . . . Loyal Atherton. When you were both unconscious, Edward knew exactly what to do and what to check for. I was very impressed."

"Thank you, Victoria." Edward sent Spencer a smug look. "She was impressed with me, Spence, old man."

"She wouldn't be if she knew where you received your alleged training." He turned to Victoria. "My esteemed cousin has had no formal training. The peers are not to have professions, you see. However, Edward has spent a shameful amount of time and money at gaming tables and boxing matches and illegal duels, the scoundrel. Always the second or the man in the corner. He's also famous for his, uh, 'medical examinations' of other men's wives, if you will forgive me for being so indelicate."

"Oh, dear. Oh, my." Flames of embarrassment raced like wildfire across Victoria's flushed skin.

"Exactly, my dear. Why do you think I brought him with me to America? It was to keep him from getting killed."

"No it wasn't," Edward countered. "You took me with you to Wetherington's Point to keep me from getting killed in London. But you did not want me, in the worst way, to come here with you to Georgia."

Spencer gave a regal nod of his head. "I stand corrected. You're right. You did invite yourself along on this trip."

"There, you see?" Edward said, his expression triumphant.

"You worry about him, don't you?" Victoria's heart was alight with warmth and respect as she smiled at her husband. "And you care about him."

Perhaps it was masculine pride that had Spencer scowling. Victoria realized she could see right through this façade now to the man underneath. "No, I do not. I care about his mother. A lovely woman. I watch over him for her sake. Despite his being a grown man and an earl, he is her adored only child."

Edward guffawed. "And you, as well, are an adored only child, my dear cousin." He turned to Victoria. "Has your husband told you about his treks out to the horse-breeding barn when he was but a little chap? Quite the interested and wide-eyed party, he was, too, from all the stories—"

"That will be enough, Edward." Looking sorely discomfited, Spencer abruptly sat forward on the divan. "I say we should get on with this discussion and stick to the point or points." He turned to Victoria. "We cede the floor to you, my dear. Start at the beginning, if you would."

Caught off guard, having been engrossed in the brotherlike banter between the two men, Victoria shot her husband a quick look. So, here it was, the conversation they so desperately needed to have. And yet, it remained the conversation she so desperately did not want to have, fearing as she did his response to everything she had to tell him. "Start at the beginning?" she repeated.

"Yes. The letter. Tell me about the letter."

His heart in his throat, Spencer watched Victoria. She tucked a stray strand of glistening dark hair behind her ear and twisted her hands together in her lap. She had yet to utter a word or to look directly at him since he'd asked her about the letter. Whatever she needed to reveal, he could see, was difficult for her to say. What she couldn't know, though, was how damned hard it was for him to sit here at her side and await her response. But he knew enough not to hurry her or chide her in any way. Should he do so, given the ample evidence he had of her excitable emotions of late, she could just as easily scream at him and jump up and run out in tears— and never tell him about the letter.

Into the quiet that had descended on the three of them . . . Spencer exchanged a glance with Edward and saw his cousin's expression to be every bit as sober and apprehensive as his own must be . . . Victoria suddenly spoke. "I suppose the best way to begin is for you to read the letter for yourselves."

"Then I take it you have it with you? Here. Today."

"Yes. I always have it with me. I find myself reading and rereading it, sometimes several times a day. I suppose I simply don't want it to be true. And I keep hoping I've misread it or made too much of it. But I can't see how I could. It's very straightforward." With that, she worked a hand into a pocket of her skirt. She pulled out, to his utter shock, not one letter, but perhaps as many as three or four others and sorted through them, apparently looking for the correct one.

Spencer prided himself on his cool control, but it failed him at this moment. His voice, high and loud, revealed the depth of his concern. "Victoria, what are all these letters? I had no idea."

"I know. It's been very frightening for me, but I couldn't tell you. I just couldn't."

"Why couldn't you tell me?"

She exhaled slowly, deeply. "Because I feared for your life, if I did. But then you were attacked, and I realized I had no choice but to tell you. And Edward, as well. We're all at risk." She again bent her head to her task, shuffling the letters over and under each other, glancing at each, until . . . "Ah. Here it is. The first one. The one that started it all."

Without ceremony, she handed over the letter. Spencer held it, staring at it. A single sheet of common, ordinary writing paper. But this sheet of paper had already changed his life and hers and their life together forever and in ways he suspected they had yet to realize. He half expected the damned thing to burn his fingers or suddenly disintegrate into ashes as if it had been burned. And to simply hand over such a prized and fought-over treasure, as it were, with no due pomp and circumstance was, ironically, startling. Staring at it, he turned the folded sheet of paper over and over in his hands.

"Aren't you going to read it, Spencer?" Victoria's question had him staring her way. She sat so close to him he could feel the heat from her body. She smiled. "I expected you would rush to do so." Of course, he had expected he would, too, so he couldn't really explain his sudden reticence. "If nothing else," she added quietly, "I supposed you would look first at the signature."

With the letter of contention now in his possession and the emotion of the thing tightening his chest, Spencer stared at his wife. "I'm not certain I want to see it, Victoria."

Had that hollow voice really been his? It must have been because she smiled a sad, understanding smile and reached over to squeeze his hand. The intimate gesture took Spencer's breath away and made it hard to capture his next one. Looking directly into his eyes and holding his gaze locked with hers, Victoria said: "It's not from Loyal Atherton. And it's not a love letter. Far from it."

She knew his fears. Spencer searched her blue eyes and saw only their intrinsic clarity and sincerity and a melting warmth that surprised him. His heart turned over helplessly.

Fearing a shameful display of undone emotions, he sniffed gruffly and frowned and cleared his throat. "I never thought it was."

Though she raised her eyebrows in surprise, and though Edward gave a wordless cry of disbelief from his side of the room where he sat, Victoria evidently chose to take Spencer at his word. "Good. I'm glad you didn't."

Once she let go of his hand and sat back, giving him room, Spencer wordlessly opened the letter. He glanced at the signature, didn't recognize it as anyone he knew, and then read the first line to himself:

If you are reading this, Victoria, then I am dead.

The shock of the words had Spencer jumping to his feet and brandishing the letter at his wife. "Good *God,* Victoria! This is absolutely monstrous! Is this someone's idea of a joke?"

Wide-eyed, startled, she shook her head no and opened her mouth to speak—

"What is it? What does it say?" Edward, too, had come to his feet and was obviously upset as he looked from Spencer to Victoria and back to his cousin. "Tell me!" he demanded. "Read it aloud."

"I don't think I can," Spencer cried. He turned to his wife. "Why didn't you tell me? I would have helped you. I would have done anything—"

"You can't, Spencer. You couldn't. Read it!" She pointed to the letter he held. "Read it, and you'll know why. I'm taking a great chance right now by just showing it to you. In fact, with the windows open and the servants about, we should keep our voices down. Edward, if you would, please carry your chair over here. I don't want anyone to overhear our conversation."

"As serious as all that? Very well." Turning, he easily picked up his chair and brought it closer to the sofa. Once he'd set it down, he said, quietly: "Now, will someone please tell me what the letter says?"

Spencer held it out to Victoria. "Here. You said you read it all the time. So surely the words have lost some of their horror for you."

"They haven't, but I'll read it," she all but whispered, "and then you tell me if the horror will ever leave you." She held her hand out for the letter. "Give it to me. And please don't stop me or say anything until I am done. I'm not certain I can get through it, if you do."

"As you wish." He handed her the letter and sat down as she had requested, but he sat heavily, as though his legs had simply collapsed.

She waited, also, until Edward sat. Only then did she begin to read:

" 'If you are reading this, Victoria, then I am dead.' " Edward's gasp of shock had Victoria looking at him. Spencer ached for her obvious hurt. He wanted, with every fiber in his being, to slide across the sofa's cushions and take her in his embrace and shield her from her own reading of the monstrous letter she held in her hand. But he didn't dare. He feared she would shatter like a crisp autumn leaf if he touched her. He feared also, that he would, too.

" 'I am being made to write this letter,' " Victoria read on. " 'As I do, a gun is being held to my head. They are watching every word I write. And when I am done, they will kill me because I know too much. But I am not afraid. I am sorry only that I will never see you again. I love you like a sister, Victoria. And I love Jefferson. You never knew it, but he was my lover and is the father of my daughter. I named her Sofie, after you, and she's only five years old. But Jefferson would never acknowledge her, and he's put us aside now as if we don't even matter to him. But they have Sofie now, and they say you must come back to Savannah. They won't tell me why, only that you must. Do not hesitate. And do not tell anyone why you are here. If you do, they will know, and they will kill Sofie—and you and whoever you tell. But if you come home and do everything they say and they get everything they want, then they will take her, unharmed, to my mother.

" 'It breaks my heart to tell you this next thing, but Jefferson knows all about this, and he won't do anything to stop them. Don't trust him, Victoria. Don't tell him why you're here. It's all up to you. My baby's life is in your hands. You must come. When you do, they will get in touch with you. Do everything they say—or they'll kill Sofie! Please tell my mother and my brother that I love them. Love, Jenny.' "

With no emotion on her face, Victoria raised her head from the letter and slowly lowered it to her lap. She said nothing. She didn't move. She just stared straight ahead. As she had continued to read, as the full extent of the horror had unfolded, and as the words she read warred with the sweet melody of her soft, Southern voice, Spencer had found himself dreading her coming to the end of the letter.

He knew it was irrational, but he'd felt Jenny's death could actually be staved off if Victoria did not finish reading her words. Maybe Victoria thought so, too, and that was why she made a point daily of reading them over and over to herself, as she'd said she did. Maybe she thought the strength of her attention to Jenny's words would keep her alive. But, clearly, Jenny was not. He'd seen no date on the letter, but judging by when Victoria had received it and how much time it would have taken to make its way to her in England, and factoring in how much time had elapsed between then and now, Spencer concluded Jenny had been killed as long as two months ago. About the same time he and Victoria had married.

"I know this sounds ridiculous," Edward said solemnly, breaking the silence in the room, "but I half feared I'd hear the report of a gun being fired when you completed your reading of the letter, Victoria."

She nodded. "I feel the same way every time I read it."

So they all felt it. Spencer lowered his gaze to the rug under his feet. He found he could not look another human being in the face. That he, that they all, could belong to a species capable of such heinous deeds was too mortifying, too shameful. He had never in his life felt so sick at heart. So hopeless. He swallowed convulsively. Once he felt more in control, he asked: "Who is Jenny, Victoria? Obviously, she's a close friend of some sort?"

A new, sadder emotion capped Victoria's expression. "Not so obvious. Or so easy. As she said, we loved each other like sisters. In fact, we grew up together. I saw her every day of my life until . . . the war. But this letter is the first I've heard from her since then."

"How awful for you to lose contact like that with someone so close to you."

Victoria's smile was one of pity and shame. "Yes. Awful. But for all the right reasons, I suppose."

Did she mean the war? "Were you on opposite sides in the conflict? I read that so many families in the North and the South found themselves in that awful circumstance."

"Yes. Opposite sides, but in different ways."

"Victoria, you're being very mysterious."

"I'm sorry. I don't mean to be. I'll try to explain. You see, my father owned slaves. In fact, he inherited them from his father. All of our slaves had been with our family for generations and knew no other life. You have to understand that when my father inherited, the plantation was the only business. Daddy was not wealthy as he is now. River's End was all he had, and he felt the responsibility not only for his family but also for the slaves."

"Admirable."

"Yes. But no less troublesome to him. He hated the concept of owning people. Not everyone thought of their slaves as people. But it was how we were raised."

"I see. Not a very popular stance, I imagine."

"No. If our leanings had become public knowledge, we

could have been burned out and killed. It was awful for my father. He knew if he went under, that he would have to sell the slaves into God knows what kind of awful life. He did the best by them that he could, but he still hated it. I think his not wanting that awful dependence on the wretched hardship of others is what drove him to find other ways to be successful."

"That explains the shipping and railroads and other investments."

"Yes. The moment he was no longer dependent on the income from the crops he grew, he wanted to free our slaves. In fact, he did, but very quietly. Any of them who wanted to go were given their papers and allowed to leave. Some did, but they mostly came back scared and hungry and begging for work. And Daddy gave it to them. Others were too afraid to go. Where could they go? What could they do? No one would hire them. And River's End was the only home they knew. It's a terrible truth that they have nowhere to go and such a hard time on their own because we've given them no other choices, really."

"An awful system. But a pervasive one, it seems. I mean across your country and in others, too. Even mine."

Victoria nodded. "I know. It's not easy to live with a thing like that on your conscience. Mama was just as determined as Daddy, too. She made certain I could read and write, the same as Jefferson. She taught us herself. And right along with us, she secretly saw to it that as many of our slaves were taught to read and write—"

"I say! And even during a time when this was against the law?" This was Edward cutting in, sounding proud of Catherine Redmond.

"Yes. Laws have never stopped Mama from doing what she thought was right. And education was right."

Spencer added: "No doubt many owners feared education because with it comes realization and ambition."

Victoria faced him now. "You are very right. But you'd be

surprised at how many owners did feel the same way, only privately. However, no matter how much I try to make it sound . . . acceptable, it isn't. My arguments, even to myself, sound like excuses."

"Victoria," Spencer said, thoughtfully, "where is all this leading? What are you trying to tell us?"

"Oh, Spencer, can't you see? Jenny is a former slave. So are her mother and brother. Sofie is a mulatto child." Victoria squeezed her eyes shut and took a shuddering breath. "That poor sweet little girl. I never even knew she existed."

"Oh, my word," Edward said quietly. "That's why . . . your brother put Jenny aside, isn't it? He can't acknowledge her in any way. Or his own daughter."

"He can't, and he won't—for their safety as much as his," Victoria corrected. "And right now that little girl is being used as a pawn against my brother for some reason. I have no evidence of that, but it's the only reason I can accept for why he isn't doing everything in his power to free her from whoever has her."

This was the most awful, heart-wrenching story Spencer had ever heard. Feeling suddenly too hot despite the open windows in the room, hearing but not listening to the happy, industrious sounds wafting in with the air from out in the street and the fashionable square across the way, he sat forward and rested his elbows atop his knees . . . and finally faced himself. *What must Victoria think when she reads that letter every day?* He meant apart from the tragedy of Jenny's death, Victoria's fear for the little girl Sofie, and her brother's obvious involvement.

What must she think of *him*, her own husband—a man so ready and willing to put her aside as this Jenny had been? And for essentially the same reason. A child. An innocent child.

Spencer truly had never thought of it in this way. Always before he'd considered only his heritage, his name, his land, his pride—his, his, his. *For God's sake, man, think of some-*

one but yourself for once. He swore to himself right then that he would. He would do everything within his power to get this little Sofie safely back to her grandmother. The woman had to be beside herself with grief and worry. And Jenny's brother as well. Spencer wondered where the two lived and how they were holding up. Good Lord, did they even know?

Spencer thought of the child Victoria carried. Not once, earlier on . . . before he came to care for her, before his decision had become so hard to live with . . . had he wondered about or considered what would become of Victoria and the baby if he turned them out. He supposed he had always assumed she would simply return here to her wealthy family and all her friends. And do what? Face their scorn and pity and gossip? What would it do to the child to face such heartlessness from the people around him?

Spencer suddenly saw himself as a little boy slowly becoming aware of the world around him and of what was said about him and his mother living apart from his father. For how many years, though he had loved her tremendously, had he been ashamed and blamed his mother and been cool toward her? How many? They had only reconciled a few years before her death. And now, here he was, prepared to consign Victoria and her child to the same hateful and regretted existence he himself had lived. How could he do it? How?

"Spencer? Are you all right?" Victoria spoke in a low, quiet voice, the comforting sort one would use with the bereaved at a funeral.

Spencer turned his head to look at his wife. She was comforting him? He couldn't believe it. Why didn't she hate him? "How have you lived with this for so long? How have you stood it?"

Looking bereft, she exhaled and seemed to turn her focus inward. "I don't think about myself. I think about Sofie and her fear. I wonder where she is and who is taking care of her, if anyone is. I wonder how she's being treated and if she's afraid. She has to be. She can't understand what's happened to her. I think about those things, and I just want to die." Suddenly, Victoria's expression sharpened and she turned to him. "Oh, Spencer, you must believe me when I say I wrestled with this when I got the letter. I had no desire to endanger our—my—child in any way, but what else could I do but come here?"

He hadn't missed her changing *our* to *my*. It was so damned complicated. "There was nothing else you could do. You did exactly what you had to, and I could not be more proud of you. Or more ashamed of myself."

She pulled back. Confusion clouded her expression. "Ashamed of yourself? But why? What have you done to be ashamed of?"

"Plenty." The depth of his emotions propelled Spencer into action without further thought. He went down on one knee on the carpet and in front of his wife. He had startled her, he could see, and he didn't care if he looked ridiculous to Edward, but he took the letter and the other notes from her, put them next to her on the sofa and then held both of her hands. He looked into her surprised and deeply blue eyes. "Can you forgive me, Victoria? Can you ever? I've been a horse's ass—and a pompous one, at that—to you since our marriage—"

"Here, here," came from Edward, who softly clapped his hands together. "Bravo, old man. About time you owned up to it."

"Shut up, Edward," Spencer warned. His wife's tearful little bleat of a laugh incongruously lifted Spencer's spirit. She couldn't laugh at him and Edward if she didn't forgive him, he reasoned—and hoped.

He sought her gaze for confirmation of this and saw warmth and welcoming and . . . dare he hope it? . . . love reflected in blue eyes fringed round with long and thick dark lashes. Overcome with his own emotions in the face of hers, Spencer feigned further irritation with Edward and forgetfulness of his subject. "Now, what was I saying before I was so rudely interrupted?"

Once again, Edward butted in. "You were saying you were a horse's ass, I do believe, Spence, old man. A pompous one."

Spencer smiled into Victoria's eyes. "If you will excuse me, I must go strangle the life out of my cousin." He made as if to pull his hands from hers.

She held tight. "Think of your aunt, Spencer. Remember, she loves him."

"Damn. A terrible complication. But maybe we can still get rid of him." Without letting go of Victoria's hands, he turned more fully to his cousin. "Edward, you are herewith excused to go make your call on that poor young woman who's awaiting your silly presence this morning."

Edward crossed his arms over his chest. "A jolly good try, Spencer. But I'm going nowhere. I wouldn't miss your being down on bended knee like this for all the lovely women in Savannah."

Spencer stared at Edward's clearly amused face and then returned his gaze to his wife. "Do you see what I must contend with?"

Her smile was radiant. They were both, Spencer knew, saying so many things with their eyes and their joined hands that they really could not yet say to each other, despite the moment. "Yes, I can, you poor man. However—"

"You're calling him a poor man for having to put up with me? May I remind you, Victoria, that I am still in the room and can hear you?"

This time it was Victoria who looked past Spencer to Edward and said, while smiling, "Shut up, Edward. I was about to speak in your defense, actually." The moment seemed to overtake her as her expression turned solemn. "I was going to say we need you alive to help us with this. Remember, this letter is only the first one. I have received others. And now that I've told you two, if these awful men find out in any way, it is Sofie who will pay, as will we unless we can stop them somehow."

Edward made a sound of distress. "You're absolutely right, Victoria: This is most dire. Forgive my frivolity. Most inappropriate of me."

Once again, she smiled. "Not in the least, Edward. We must keep our heads and go about our daily lives, despite this awful burden. And I hope that laughter will be a part of our days. Indeed, with the barbecue and the crush of people there to wish Spencer and me well, we will have to put forward a cheery attitude and, all three of us, behave as if nothing is the matter."

"Well spoken," Spencer said, giving Victoria's hands a last affectionate squeeze before pulling his away from hers and rising effortlessly to his feet. Further declarations between them could wait for a more private and appropriate moment. Catching him completely off guard was a sudden dizziness that forced him to tense his muscles and stand very still, a hand to his temple, until he regained his equilibrium.

"Spencer? What's wrong?" Sharp concern put an edge in Victoria's voice as she surged to her feet and put a bolstering arm around his waist. With her other hand, she held on to his arm.

As well, Edward had rushed to his other side and supported him from there. "Steady on, cousin. Why don't you sit down?"

Spencer blinked until the room righted itself and he felt better. "No. I'm fine, really. Just a reminder that I'm not yet completely recovered."

"Well, of course you're not," Victoria cried. "Will you please sit down, as Edward suggested?"

Because it was easier, and not because he felt as if he

needed to do so, Spencer turned and—with his wife's and his cousin's help—sat down . . . again, a little too heavily for his pride's sake. Victoria and Edward hovered over him like concerned parents. "I am really quite all right. And I would be obliged if you would take your seats, as well."

With their actions performed in concert, as if of one mind, they parted and quickly flitted to their respective places. They looked so young and comical doing so, like scolded children, that Spencer felt bad for being short with them. He smiled despite himself and exhaled his amusement. "All right, then. Let's see what we know, shall we?" He turned to his wife. "Please don't be insulted by my next question, Victoria, but I feel we must ask those that come to mind, no matter how seemingly trivial or illogical."

She sat up straight and folded her hands together in her lap, signaling her readiness to answer. "I understand and shall not be insulted."

"Good. Now, the handwriting in the letter. I assume you recognized it as truly being Jenny's? I mean, you have seen her handwriting before, correct?"

"Oh, yes. Many times. It's hers. Had I believed the letter to be a forgery, Spencer, I . . . well, I like to think I would have turned to you for help."

Although he doubted seriously that she would have, given his treatment of her at Wetherington's Point, he smiled sincerely and hoped his expression revealed the depth of his feelings for her. "I like to think so, as well."

"How precious," Edward said with studied, probably feigned, boredom. "Before we get all moony-eyed and gushy, I have a question I would like to ask."

Exhaling a purposely dramatic sigh, Spencer tore his gaze away from his wife's beautiful oval face and turned to his cousin. "You have the floor, Edward. Ask away."

Edward inclined his head in acknowledgment. "Thank you, kind sir. Victoria, in the letter, your friend Jenny says you are to do everything these dastardly devils tell you to do. What have you been instructed to do so far?"

Lending the act a fluttering butterfly quality, she raised a hand to her chest and held it against her skin, just below her throat. "That's the odd thing, Edward. I haven't been instructed to do a thing. I don't even know how I'm involved or what these awful people think I can do. I don't even know why they need me, except I'm a Redmond—was—and Jefferson is Sofie's father and involved somehow and won't help her. Do you see? It's so confusing."

"Yes, it is. So, in these other notes . . ." He pointed to the ones next to her on the sofa. "No demand for ransom? Anything like that?"

"No. Nothing. I wish there were. Doing something—anything!—is better than simply waiting and worrying. The only thing I know for certain is I am being watched."

A lance of fear stabbed at Spencer's heart and had him leaning intently toward her, his hand braced against the cushion between them. "Those men in the alley. Do you think that's what they were doing out there?"

"I do. That, and these notes I've received say as much." Victoria pointed to them there between him and her. "One at River's End, and two here. I don't recognize the handwriting, but it's the same in all three. They're clearly from the men who have Sofie."

"You said 'clearly'? How so?"

"They recount for me my day's activities and then mention Sofie, as if to remind me of what's at stake. But even that is not as frightening to me as how they are delivered."

"How *are* they delivered?" Spencer felt a murderous anger well up inside him that his wife would be threatened and frightened by these cowards who preyed on innocent women and children. Well, now that he knew about this, he'd find them . . . and he'd deal with them, just as he had Loyal Atherton, only more seriously. Suddenly, that man and his romantic mooning after Victoria, despite accosting her for a kiss, seemed so inconsequential now as to be ridiculous.

"I can't really say they're delivered," Victoria answered. "It's more accurate to say they're placed. They're placed on my pillow."

In the flight of a second's passing, Spencer pictured, in his mind, an evil, shadowy villain sidling into Victoria's bedroom and laying a note on her pillow. The sudden realization of her absolute vulnerability nearly stopped his heart completely. "Good God! Right on your pillow?"

"Why, the audacity of the act!" Edward cried. "They're purposely trying to terrify you."

Victoria nodded somberly. "And they are succeeding."

Spencer shook a no-nonsense finger at his wife. "From this moment forward, Victoria, you are not to be alone for one moment of the day or the night, do you understand?"

"I do, and I shall be relieved not to be." She peered at him from under the sweep of her fringe of eyelashes.

Her expression brought to Spencer's mind images of them sleeping together—at long last. He cleared his throat. "Yes. Well. Here's something that may have already occurred to you, Victoria, but it needs to be said for the benefit of all of us."

She gestured for him to proceed. "Then please say it."

"Unless we are talking about a very skilled sneak, and given that a stranger could not wander through River's End, or here at this house, without being noticed and challenged, I can only conclude—"

"That a servant or other sort of employee is involved," Edward finished for him. His expression suddenly changed to disbelief. "Good Lord, one hates to think of such betrayal after one has housed, fed, clothed, and employed a person."

"It could be much worse than a trusted servant, Edward," Victoria said quietly. "Given everything we've said here, and what Jenny said in her letter, I can only conclude that a member of my family is also involved."

"You mean your brother." Spencer spoke the words to spare her having to say them.

Nodding, looking as if her heart were breaking, Victoria stared at him with rounded and baleful blue eyes. "Yes."

CHAPTER 14

They arrived at River's End late that afternoon on the wings of a sudden and fearsome thunderstorm that seemed evilly intent on chasing them out of Savannah and into the surrounding jungle of the sandy, swampy lowlands. An ill wind, the storm's precursor, circled around the horses' hooves and the carriages' wheels, frightening the animals and the occupants alike as it rose up in great swirls, like so many taunting spirits, threatening to tear away bowler hats and bonnets alike. The pines and the oaks and the cypress trees swayed hypnotically back and forth as branches and needles and leaves crackled with a secret language all their own.

What had first been white and scudding clouds quickly became black and gray bruises on the darkening sky, as though the rolling grumbles of thunder had struck them with fists and they bled warm rain upon the earth and the two struggling landaus. A shard of lightning crackling overhead in horizontal patterns reminded Victoria of the blood veins in an old person's hands.

The soaked drivers, Zebediah and his brother, Otis, knew to direct the horses around to the side of the plantation home to the covered port where the passengers could alight safely from the landaus and proceed directly into the house itself. Welcoming Victoria, her husband, and their entourage into the small receiving room were the elderly, dignified butler named Virgil and two young, wide-eyed maids. The scene was a chaotic symphony of rain pounding on the roof, frightened horses neighing, anxious drivers calling out to the animals to calm them, the acrid scent of the lightning, the smell of the rich earth, and the happy cries of relief and greeting from the Redmonds to their arriving family.

Victoria's mother, father, and brother stayed in the background, more toward the hallway behind them than in the actual fray of the arrival. Capes and coats and hats and bonnets, all of them dripping with rain, were shed and handed over to the servants, who also greeted the party of six cheerfully and with relief. "Welcome home, Miz Victoria," Virgil said, bowing creakily and speaking slowly as he always had. "We shore enough thought we'd lose you to this here devil storm. I prayed and prayed and now I can thank the Lord you done made it through."

Smiling, happy to see the old man, and more happy than she would admit to be back at River's End, Victoria patted his arm affectionately and then, at his insistent urging, handed him her long and dripping cape. "Oh, Virgil, that water is dripping all over you and will ruin your nice suit of clothes."

"Don't pay that no never-mind. I'll dry out, shore enough, Miz Victoria."

"If you insist. But it's good to be here, and I thank you for your prayers." She smiled after him as he moved to Spencer, bowed formally, and held out his hand for his cape.

"Oh, my stars, look at y'all," Catherine Redmond fussed worriedly in the background. Victoria turned, pointedly looking past her brother—she found it so hard to understand him or forgive him—to see her parents standing next to each other. Her mother craned her neck to look everyone over. Not an easy thing to do with the cramped, square room being so crowded. After all, the three River's End servants, Victoria, Spencer, Hornsby, Mr. Milton, Rosanna, and Tillie were all wedged into it. "Why are you so wet? Didn't Zebediah and Otis put the hoods up on the landaus for you?"

On the way here, Victoria had told Spencer her mother would fuss about these very things. She now exchanged a look with her husband before answering her mother. "Of course they did, Mama. It's just that the storm came up so quickly. We were one minute in sunshine and the next in a terrifying downpour. Fortunately, Rosanna and Hornsby had packed well and were prepared with our capes at the first sign of bad weather. Still, in our rush to get the hoods up on the landaus and our capes unpacked and actually on us all, we were soaked."

"You poor things, I can believe it. You're the very embodiment of drowned rats. This weather, I swan, I never saw the like. I told your father you'd all be struck dead by lightning before you ever got here."

"We thought so ourselves a few times," Victoria assured her. She'd feared this next meeting would be awkward, given how she had left angry less than a week ago with Spencer and Edward in tow. But so far, thanks in large part to her mother's chattering and fussing over them, so good.

"Now, where's that nice young Earl of Roxley? Why isn't he with you? I have a room already made up for him. And more than one female heart will be broken if he doesn't attend the barbecue tomorrow afternoon."

Before Victoria could answer, she felt Spencer take her elbow. Smiling down at her, but looking resolute, he threaded her safely through the crush of people and over to her family. As he walked, the other people parted, just as when he talked, everyone else quieted. The mark of a leader, Victoria knew. People treated her father the same way.

When they stood in front of the elder Redmonds and Jefferson, who had yet to say a word, Spencer said: "My cousin will be along, Mrs. Redmond. He had a social call to pay before he left Savannah, but I'm certain this weather has delayed him. I am, of course, assuming the Earl of Roxley has the sense to stay in out of the rain. But he may not have and could arrive momentarily, to no one's surprise. Just as we have, come to think of it."

Murmurs of laughter greeted his words, and then they all stood there, quietly, awkwardly, Victoria and Spencer facing her equally uncomfortable family. Victoria's expression and her mood fell. Now that she faced them, she couldn't find the right words and didn't know what to say, what to do. Her father's expression showed a certain amount of proud reticence tinged with a yearning. Jeff's expression, oddly, mirrored his father's. And her mother looked wide-eyed with tears rushing to them.

Though her heart pounded with apprehension, Victoria could hear behind her the nervous shuffling of feet and a few sniffles and a low cough. The poor servants and Mr. Milton. How awful this must be for them, too.

Into the tension-filled silence, Spencer said, in that wonderfully melodic and formal voice of his: "Forgive me my lack of manners. Perhaps you have not met my wife? Mr. and Mrs. Redmond, may I introduce you to the Tenth Duchess of Moreland, among her many other and lesser titles, more than half of which I feel certain she herself is not aware and could not therefore recite? Nevertheless, I present to you Her Grace Victoria Sofia Redmond Whitfield. You may know her as your only daughter. And you, sir"—he turned to Jefferson—"have the equal pleasure of knowing her as your younger sister."

For a moment, stunned silence held sway between Victoria and her family. But then, as one, they burst into laughter, and the tension was broken. Victoria surged forward to be enfolded in their embrace. As they kissed each other and hugged and cried, Victoria knew in that wonderful, noisy, rain-dripping, shining moment that she loved, with all her heart, John Spencer Whitfield, the Tenth Duke of Moreland, among his many other and lesser titles, all of which she felt certain he was aware and could recite.

Suitably dried off and his suit of clothing changed, Spencer stood in the billiard room on the first floor. He held a fine whisky in one hand and a finely crafted cue stick in his other. A very mellow cigar was clamped between his teeth as he squinted through its smoke to watch Jefferson Redmond, across the table from him, consider his next shot from all angles.

"The women tossed you out, did they, Your Grace?" Isaac Redmond asked cheerfully. A crystal glass of whisky in his hand and a cigar held between two fingers of his other hand, he sat in a big brown leather chair to Spencer's right.

Spencer shifted his grip on his whisky so he could also hold the cigar with the same hand. He exhaled the smoke and said: "Most certainly they did, Mr. Redmond. I barely had time to dry off and change my clothes before I was summarily dismissed."

"I'm not surprised. Not much feminine company out here for Catherine, so she's sorely missed her time with our Victoria."

Spencer barely bit back a correction. She was his Victoria now. He knew it was foolish to think such a thing. She was, of course, still this man's daughter. But a powerful sense of possessiveness over her had seized Spencer earlier in Savannah, given all the danger she was in. Once he had his responses under control, Spencer politely said: "I can fully understand how Mrs. Redmond feels. Anyone who knows Victoria would rue every moment spent away from her."

"Glad to hear you say that."

A note in the older man's voice implied he was, instead, surprised to hear Spencer say that. Spencer very coolly looked from his father-in-law to his brother-in-law across the billiard table from him. Jefferson raised his eyebrows and gave a subtle shake of his head. Spencer could not interpret the younger man's meaning. Commiseration? Warning? Arrogance? He redirected his attention to Mr. Redmond, bluntly asking: "What else would you expect me to say, Mr. Redmond?"

Isaac Redmond sent Spencer a look . . . perhaps of mild disbelief . . . as he secured his cigar in an ashtray on a table to his right and also set his whisky down. With great nonchalance, the older man reached down to fondle the ears of the big rawboned hound dog named Neville, who had flopped at his feet. Earlier, the dog had sniffed at Spencer's pants leg and then raised his intelligent eyes to look him over. Spencer had immediately squatted down and held out a hand to the dog. The keen hunter had politely sniffed at Spencer, and then grinned and wagged his tail.

Evidently, the dog's reaction was a huge social triumph, or so Isaac Redmond had told him. It seemed Neville didn't like too many people, but he certainly seemed to like him, and that was good. Spencer was further told the dog liked Victoria best of all. Privately, Spencer had assured himself he knew exactly how the dog felt. He liked Victoria best of all, too.

His expression friendly but not reaching his eyes, Mr. Redmond sat back in his chair, retrieved his drink, and took a sip. "I don't know exactly what I expected you to say, Your Grace. I just know what Victoria said the day you and your entourage came riding up the drive to River's End."

"And what was that?" Guilt assailed Spencer. He could only imagine what she'd said.

"My daughter said you had no idea she was gone. She also said she was surprised to find you cared enough about her to come after her."

"I see." What else could he say?

Mr. Redmond carefully set his whisky glass down again, making his actions seem those of a man who believed he would need both hands free for a physical confrontation. "And I still do not know, Your Grace, why she came home after only two months of married life in England. Not really, I mean."

"What reason did she give you for her . . . visit here?"

"My daughter said she was homesick."

"Which you don't believe."

"I do. Who wouldn't miss a place as beautiful as our great state of Georgia? And who wouldn't want to spend all her life in Savannah, in particular? However, there's more to this story. A father knows these things about his children. You'll know what I mean one day when you're a father, Your Grace."

"Indeed, I shall." Spencer's heart gave a wrenching thump as he thought of the baby Victoria carried even now. Under normal circumstances, this would have been the perfect moment to break the wonderful news of an impending birth. However, his and Victoria's were a far cry from the normal circumstances.

"Am I to take it then, sir," Mr. Redmond persisted, "that you are not going to tell me, either, why my daughter is here?"

Spencer grew weary of this relentless questioning. Time for someone else besides him to be discomfited. Though he addressed Victoria's father, Spencer locked onto Jefferson Redmond's gaze across the width of the billiard table that squatted between them. "I assure you, Mr. Redmond, that your daughter's return to River's End had nothing to do with me. Or my treatment—or mistreatment—of her, which I believe is the implication here."

Isaac Redmond sat forward and slapped his own leg. "I knew it! So you didn't have her locked away in a tower somewhere, a prisoner against her will?"

Jefferson Redmond, and his steadily reddening face, was forgotten. Spencer shot his father-in-law a stunned look. "What the devil? Locked away in a tower? A prisoner? Victoria said that?"

"As much as. She implied she had no freedom of movement."

Again, what could Spencer say? "I see."

"I told her I had a hard time believing that, given your reputation and my own dealings with you."

"Thank you for your trust in me, Mr. Redmond."

"However," the older man said, giving pointed emphasis to the word, "I assured her mother that should a man mistreat my daughter, Your Grace, I'd have no qualms with regard to taking him to hand."

Spencer bowed slightly in acknowledgment of the warning in Isaac Redmond's voice. "We understand each other, Mr. Redmond. I can assure you that Victoria has no reason to fear me. And I assure you I feel the very same way you do with regard to her being mistreated." Spencer again arrowed a glance the way of her brother. "Should a man—any man, for any reason—threaten or harm my wife, he will answer to me. And it will be the last thing he remembers doing before he leaves this mortal coil."

"Well said, sir." This was from Isaac Redmond. Spencer looked his way and saw the man had visibly relaxed in his chair.

But Victoria's brother's response was the exact opposite. He stood taller; tiny white lines bracketed his mouth. Too late, Spencer wondered if, in his haste to allay the father's concerns, he had not alerted the son's suspicions. Had he given too much away? Did Jefferson now understand that Spencer knew Victoria's true reason for coming home? Did he suspect Spencer knew of Jefferson's complicity in the abominable plot against his child? Spencer quickly replayed in his mind what he had said and could not find anything any loving husband would not have said under the same circumstances. He feared, however, he could not say as much for his challenging looks or the intonation in his voice.

"Jefferson, my boy, do you intend today to take that shot? You've considered it from every angle except from under the table."

Jefferson set himself in motion around the table. "Sorry, Daddy. I had trouble concentrating with all the talk distracting me."

Isaac Redmond raised a hand in acknowledgment. "Point taken, son."

A silence, more companionable than antagonistic, settled over the men, leaving Spencer free now to contemplate how Victoria might be faring upstairs with her mother. The women were apparently still chattering away in the large and airy and richly decorated bedroom Mrs. Redmond had assigned him and Victoria. The suite of rooms boasted a sitting room and shared dressing room. Mrs. Redmond had been excitedly knocking on the door almost before he and Victoria—she in the dressing room with her lady's maid, and he in the bedroom with Hornsby—had time to dry off and change.

He worried about Victoria. She had to be tired. She needed her rest but could hardly say why without giving a reason. For his part, and fortunately, the ride and the cooling air and the activity of getting the hoods up had cleared his head and his headache. As he watched Jefferson finally take his shot—successfully—and walk around the table to consider his next move, Spencer allowed his mind to stray upstairs to his wife. He pictured the two women getting in the way of that . . . what was her name? Rose Ann, wasn't it? At any rate, his plump, proper, and gray-haired employee from Wetherington's Point. He'd finally seen the woman in the course of packing up and leaving the house in Savannah. Not a young girl, at all.

Thinking of Savannah had Spencer directing his attention to the bank of tall, narrow windows directly across from where he stood. Outside he saw this end of the long and winding, oak-lined drive that led to the front door of River's End. Worry on another level pushed its way to the forefront of Spencer's thoughts. He leaned over to his left to the small table positioned there, where he set his emptied drink. The cigar followed suit, being placed in an ash-tray. He straightened up and considered the weather outside.

The rain had lessened in intensity in the last hour from an all-out deluge to a nice, steady patter. The window he peered out of was open, as was one off to Spencer's left. This arrangement provided a cross-ventilation current to draw the cigar smoke out and keep the air in the room fresh. Twilight was about to descend, he realized with a start. Where had the time gone? Interestingly enough, though the rain still fell, the sky was remarkably light. As if the sun were not going to go down without a fight. It was just as well that the day held, Spencer decided.

Edward and his escort, a large blond fellow by the name of Gibson or Gibbons or something like that, had not arrived yet. Spencer deemed it too early to be concerned and tried to convince himself that Edward had probably accepted an invitation to stay over in Savannah or had gone back to the Redmond House to wait out the storm, which may not have abated yet at that location. In either instance, Edward would be here tomorrow, all-hail-fellow-well-met and full of sauce and vinegar. At least, he had better be.

His eyes narrowed, Spencer watched Jefferson Redmond—his opponent, he feared, in more ways than one—take his next shot and make it, too. Lucky bastard. For now. Still, "A difficult shot. Well done, Jefferson."

Jefferson slowly straightened up and looked into Spencer's eyes with blue ones so like Victoria's. Spencer had time only to read a hesitance there, an uncertainty. "Thank you, Your Grace."

"You can call me Spencer, you know. I am your brother-in-law."

"I know . . . Your Grace."

Spencer arched an eyebrow at the young man who had to be younger even than Edward. So this was how it was going to be.

Given the kidnappings and the murder and the threats and the blackmailing undercurrents that Spencer now knew marked his wife's return to Savannah, he could not help but worry about Edward's well-being. Not because he loved him, but because the boy's mother did and would have Spencer drawn and quartered should something happen to her precious son. Not in any hurry to test that medieval death sentence, Spencer again assured himself he would kill his cousin himself, should he be so careless as to get himself, well, killed. Hearing himself, Spencer pronounced his worrying ridiculous. Of course, Edward was healthy and merely delayed by the weather.

Still, Spencer was glad the billiard room was located at the front of the large house and faced the oak-lined approach. This way, he could occasionally and surreptitiously glance outside to see if any riders approached.

Upstairs, Victoria pronounced herself content merely to listen without comment, except for the occasional murmur or nod of assent, to her mother's worries about the weather and how it might affect tomorrow afternoon's barbecue. Catherine said over and over how excited she was about the coming social gathering of all of Savannah's finest citizens. Why, there had not been a decent party in all of Savannah since the July Fourth celebration—or maybe there had been one, right before Victoria had shown up, traveling trunks, English maid, and all, on the front porch.

She makes me sound like an unwanted distant cousin come to take endless advantage of her hospitality, Victoria thought with wry amusement.

She reclined gratefully, tiredly, atop a fainting couch in the sitting room that complemented the guest bedroom she and Spencer had been assigned by her mother, much to Victoria's surprise. She'd assumed they would be in her bedroom, but of course she now realized her narrow bed would never do for two people, especially not when one of them was as broad shouldered and as tall as Spencer. And she had to admit, she felt very pampered, indeed, to be put in this bedroom, the most elegant one after that of her parents.

Why, not too long ago, she'd barely been allowed to step one foot in this room, and now here she was, a guest in it. The notion of being a guest in her childhood home was a strange one to her but not unpleasantly so, she found, since Spencer was coupled with that designation.

In the background, behind her mother, Victoria could hear Rosanna in the bedroom itself as she opened and closed drawers, putting away Victoria's belongings. She believed Hornsby was in there, also, taking care of Spencer's things. He had to think this arrangement barbaric, given how separately husbands and wives of the peerage lived. Indeed, how separately she and Spencer had lived. To make matters worse, he and Rosanna despised each other, based solely, Victoria believed, on her and Spencer not getting on previously. Even now, their truce—hers and Spencer's—was a delicate one. She hoped the cease-fire held with her maid and his valet, as well.

As her mother went through the guest list and benignly gossiped about every prominent household in Savannah, Victoria schooled her features into an interested expression but found her thoughts wandering downstairs to her husband. He'd said such wonderful things to her this afternoon in the parlor of the house in Savannah. Or had tried to, at any rate. That darned Edward, the scamp, kept interrupting.

She'd hoped Spencer would say more intimate things to her on the ride out to River's End, but the weather had interrupted that. Well, darn if it wasn't one thing or another contriving to keep her and her husband apart. Victoria heard her own warm thoughts about the man. Only yesterday she would not have indulged these. But so much had changed and kept changing with each passing day . . . or hour, even.

At any rate, she hoped Spencer felt stronger now than he had earlier in Savannah. The poor man shouldn't have to endure a bout of billiards and drinks and cigar smoking with her father and Jefferson. *Oh, dear, the scent of cigar smoke.* It would make her so ill to smell it on him later. She hadn't told him the effect it had on her. But even had she, what could he do? Ask her father not to smoke his afternoon cigar? Not without having to explain why. He'd had no choice, either, about the billiards. Why, being a big, strong man, she thought fondly, he'd rather pass out face-first on the table than say he couldn't participate in such a manly pursuit because he'd been attacked twice in as many days, once by rough men and once by his tiny wife, and had been knocked unconscious and lost two days in bed.

Before she could feel too sorry for him, Victoria reminded herself that at least he would recover from his symptoms much quicker than she would hers. Worse, right now her mother's delicate perfume was making Victoria queasy. What a twist that scents she had always enjoyed now sometimes made her ill. Victoria raised her hanky to her mouth, and swallowed thickly.

She did not dare get sick in front of her mother. How would she explain that? Oh, when *did* these symptoms disappear? Or did they at all? She wished so much she could ask her mother, but how could she without revealing her secret? The truth was she couldn't say a thing before she knew what her and her baby's fate would be. The nature of that decision would determine whether or not her announcement would be a joyous occasion or one fraught with more heartache for her family. Right now, with her mother so excited and her color high and her eyes sparkling, Victoria was loath to ruin her happy spirits.

Suddenly serious, her mother sat back on the delicate silk-covered chair positioned opposite Victoria's. "Honey, are you feeling ill? Your color has gone suddenly pale."

Pale, indeed. What Catherine Redmond couldn't see but Victoria could, given that her mother's back was to the opened door that led from the dressing room into the bedroom, was Rosanna. She had obviously heard Victoria's mother's comment and had bustled over to the doorway, her eyes wide with concern. Victoria warned her off by fluttering her hanky in the air, a gesture which also served to wave away Victoria's mother's concerns. Rosanna nodded and sharply turned around to re-enter the bedroom. Victoria heaved a sigh of relief . . . and felt her stomach turn over. Why did this have to happen now? She hadn't been sick before in the afternoons, not even on the tossing and turning Atlantic Ocean crossing.

"Maybe you're just tired from the drive out here."

Victoria jumped on this explanation. "Yes, Mama. It was appalling and tiring. We were all just drenched, and the wind about took my bonnet."

"You poor thing. Oh, I hope you're not going to take sick, not after all my planning for tomorrow." Her mother leaned in toward Victoria, innocently giving her a solid whiff of her lavender perfume, and felt her daughter's forehead. "Well, you're not feverish, thank the Lord."

Victoria fought a gag. *Oh, dear Lord, no, I can't be ill, not now, not with Mama in here.* But the truth was . . . she was going to be ill. Her breathing quickened and she broke out in a sweat.

"Victoria, what on earth—?"

Victoria swung her legs over the side of the couch and sat forward. "I'm sorry, Mama, but I think I'm going to be sick!"

"Sick? Why on earth would you be sick?"

"I don't know," she groaned, clamping a hand over her mouth.

"Rosanna!" Catherine Redmond cried. "Come here! Something is wrong with Victoria!"

Victoria jumped up quickly, intent on making a run for the nearest basin. But the second she stood, instead of being ill, she smacked into an invisible brick wall. Her muscles suddenly relaxed; blood drained from her head . . . and she felt herself losing her grip on consciousness. The next thing she knew, the carpet came up to meet her and—

Downstairs in the billiard room, behind closed doors, Spencer leaned over the table, about to make the shot that would end the game successfully in his favor. But before he could shoot, he heard a steady, somehow frantic-sounding drumming on the stairs, like that of running footsteps. Accompanying this was a keening, feminine cry. Instantly alert, Spencer straightened up and looked to his hosts.

"What's that noise?" Jefferson said, looking as if he feared he'd heard a ghost instead of seen one.

"I'll tell you what it is." Looking thoroughly put out, Isaac Redmond jumped up from his chair—or meant to. He had forgotten about the sleeping dog, which he stepped on and made howl. The animal's bellowing and skittering away from him upended the older man, knocking him back into his chair. "Damn it all to hell! I'm sorry, Neville, come here, boy." The dog wouldn't, and this irritated the elder Mr. Redmond further. "If that is that girl Tillie again, running down the stairs like I've told her a hundred times not to do, I'll fire her—"

"Isaac! Isaac Redmond! Oh, dear God, come quickly! Spencer! Heaven help us! Something's terribly wrong! Isaac! Victoria has fainted and fallen to the floor! Help! Come quick!"

"That's your mother!" Isaac Redmond cried, staring at Jefferson. In the next instant, he gripped the leather chair's arms and made ready to pull himself up. "See what's the matter, Jefferson. Don't simply stand there like a fool!"

Spencer was already in motion. His heart in his throat, his pulse racing, he had needed to hear nothing past *Victoria has fainted and fallen to the floor*. He shoved his cue stick into Jefferson's startled hands, barked out a gruff "Here!" and loped for the closed door. Just as he reached for the doorknob, the door was thrown open from the other side by Catherine Redmond, who charged into the room. In that same instant, Neville raced out and down the hallway, bellowing as if he'd been scalded. Other voices from various parts of the house were raised in confused alarm. The sound of running feet converged on the billiard room.

But none of this mattered to Spencer because the door had caught him squarely and vertically in the middle of his forehead and almost knocked him senseless. Losing his balance, he staggered back against a decorative sideboard that held the liquor service . . . and managed to upset that for his hosts. Crashing crystal and shattering glasses combined with the sudden strong smell of good Kentucky bourbon and the loud report of a silver tray hitting the hardwood floor.

But these sounds were secondary noise to Spencer over his own cry of pain, as he had, when he fell backward, jarred his kidneys against the edge of the hardwood furniture. And now, holding his forehead with both hands, he cursed roundly: "Son of a *bitch*! Will I make it through even one blasted day in this godforsaken swamp of a miserable city without someone trying to kill me? Damn! Damn the blue-blazing hell—"

Spencer bit back the rest of his tirade in order to keep from further insulting his hosts and their city and from killing, with his language alone, his horrified and apologetic mother-in-law.

"Oh, my word, Spencer, you poor man, I am so sorry. Here, let me see." She reached up, almost on tiptoes, trying to feel his forehead—which was already swelling . . . he could feel it . . . with a lump. "I should have knocked first, but Victoria— Oh, my word, now you're bleeding! Sit down, Spencer. Wait here." Catherine Redmond whipped around to the congregated servants. "Virgil, send Zebediah after Dr. Hollis. Tell him there's been an accident."

But Spencer had no intention of sitting and waiting for anyone or of arguing the point. He pulled a handkerchief out of a pocket and pressed it to his forehead as he raced out the door and around the wide-eyed staff, all of whom quickly cleared a path for him. Spencer heard running feet behind him, right on his heels. In the next instant his shirtsleeve was grabbed and he was nearly pulled off balance.

Not happy, he turned to face Jefferson Redmond, a man who matched Spencer's height but not his breadth. "You're covered in blood, Spencer. You can't go up there like this. You'll scare her to death."

Spencer's glare for his brother-in-law was a practiced, icy one that served as a warning. "How can I scare her if she's fainted dead away? And I suggest, sir, that you unhand me."

Jefferson immediately complied. "Fine, but we're going with you."

"Suit yourselves." With that and the Redmonds on his heels, Spencer charged down the hall to the staircase and took the first riser. As he did, the dog Neville flew past him and up the stairs in a bullet-quick flash with his long toenails scratching at the polished wood of the stairs. Though momentarily startled, Spencer followed on the dog's heels, taking the wide yet curving stairs two, three at a time. The hound quickly outdistanced him and disappeared around the landing. *Of course he can go faster. He has four legs, the bloody cur,* was Spencer's uncharitable thought.

Just then, on a wide part of the stairs, Jefferson Redmond also pushed past Spencer and sprang as nimbly up the remaining ones as had the dog. Spencer did not even waste breath on cursing the younger man. But in another two stairs, Isaac Redmond's polite "Pardon me, sir" as he hared by had Spencer narrowing his eyes at the white-haired man's back. The last straw came when Mrs. Redmond nudged him with her hip and, skirts held high in both hands, tore up the steps like a woman half her age. "What the *hell*? Are the Redmonds descended from a herd of deer?"

"Language, Your Grace," she chirped, not slowing down.

"Excuse me, madam, but I've suffered a head injury! I

think I am allowed to curse!" Spencer called after her bouncing bottom. As slowly as he *apparently* was going, he felt certain that by the time he achieved the top of the stairs, Victoria would have already delivered the baby and it would itself be grown and married and the parent of three small children of its own.

Spencer renewed his efforts and his speed—or tried to. With one hand pressing the increasingly blood-soaked handkerchief to his forehead, he found his balance was off and he was forced to grip the banister and pull himself along. *How many bloody stairs are there?* Finally, he achieved the landing and its one-hundred-and-eighty-degree turn . . . and stood there, staring disconsolately at the next flight up. "Son of a bitch."

But, ever the trouper, he firmed his lips and his resolve, exhaled mightily, and attacked each tread with renewed vigor. He kept thinking—fearing—he would pass out, but he didn't. Actually, he didn't see how he could. With all the exerting he was doing, he was thoroughly pumping blood to his head—and right out through the gaping hole in his forehead. So, though he might remain conscious, he could drop dead at any moment.

Just then, as his hope flagged, he achieved the second floor. Full of pride for his accomplishment, he stood there . . . simply breathing, his hand on the newel cap. And that was when the piercing female scream, coming from somewhere down the hall, jerked him upright and chilled his blood.

"Oh, my God, Victoria!" Catherine Redmond screamed. "Oh no, my baby!"

CHAPTER 15

Victoria returned to consciousness with no recollection of where she was. She couldn't seem to focus her attention on any one thing, except the filmy canopy hung above the amply stuffed feather mattress on the incredibly comfortable bed that hugged her to its bosom. The room was low-lit and smoky from the kerosene lamps. Yet, she thought she smelled the clean, tangy scent of damp air, like one encountered following a rainstorm. A window must be open. Restlessly, she moved her limbs and fussed: "Where am I? What happened?"

A rush of voices met her words. "Oh, she's come to again." "Thank God." "I was so scared, Isaac." "I know, my dear."

Immediately, a large, warm hand enfolded one of Victoria's and a masculine voice said, softly, "You're fine, Victoria. You fainted, and now you're in bed. At River's End."

She turned toward the voice and saw Spencer seated beside the bed. Her cotton-stuffed brain and unfocused gaze told her only that he didn't look quite right. There was something wrong or different about him, but her mind would go no farther in trying to decide what exactly the matter was. Her gaze traveled past him, and she saw he was flanked by her entire family and Rosanna and Hornsby and Mr. Milton.

Not quite fully aware, she mumbled, "What is everyone doing in here?"

"We're concerned for you, sweetheart," her mother explained. And judging by the sympathetically frowning family and servants surrounding her mother, Victoria judged she must be right. "You gave us all quite the scare," Catherine Redmond continued. "You fainted but apparently came to after I ran to get everyone. Then you tried to stand on your own too quickly, according to Rosanna, and before she could assist you. Then, when I came back up here, I was in time to see you faint again. I was so frightened, I screamed and doubly scared everyone."

"An excellent and concise rendering of the sequence of events, Mrs. Redmond," Spencer said. "Thank you."

Victoria's shocked gaze was now pinned on her husband. "Spencer. Good Lord, you're bleeding. And it's all over your shirt."

"Oh, damn." Grimacing, he pressed a folded white cloth to his forehead. "I thought it had stopped. Sorry."

She looked him over for other signs of violence. "What happened?"

He smiled. "It was nothing." He glanced at Victoria's mother before saying, "I merely lost an argument with a quickly opened door."

"You poor man."

"Hardly. I feel certain that the infamous hardheadedness of the Whitfields will see me through. How are you feeling?"

"I don't know." Victoria pulled her hand from his and distractedly rubbed her forehead. "All I remember is I was talking to my mother—"

"Now, baby, don't try to remember everything at once." Her mother rushed forward and around Spencer to lean over Victoria and kiss her cheek. "How are you, sweetheart?" She smoothed Victoria's hair, so like her own, back from her face. "I just wish I knew what in the world is wrong with you. Something has to be, honey. You haven't been yourself since you've been home, and I want to know why. I sent for Dr. Hollis to see to you and Spencer, and I am going to tell that man to give you a thorough going-over."

In Victoria's still weakened state, her mother's sympathy and concern quivered her chin as she burbled tearfully: "Oh, Mama, it's been the most awful time. I don't know what to do. You see, I'm going to have a—"

"Nap. She's going to have a nap now. So, if you will excuse us, please." Speaking loudly—or so it seemed to Victoria's heightened senses—Spencer surged to his feet. Smiling yet firm in his manner, he gently drew a surprised Catherine Redmond away from Victoria. "I think it best if we allow her time to rest, don't you? And if you don't mind, I would like to be alone with her for now and until Dr. Hollis arrives."

A murmur of protests and shuffling of feet ensued. Victoria shifted her gaze from her frowning, muttering family to her husband, who raised a hand to silence them. "She is, after all, my wife. And so my wishes for her must take precedence over yours. I would ask, also, that you have our supper trays brought up to us as I think it best we dine here. Too, if you would be so kind as to ask my cousin to come up, should he arrive. Or at least have someone inform me of his safe arrival."

His outright dismissal of them silenced any arguments. One by one, her family came over and kissed her or squeezed her hand, said sweet but inane things to her and then filed out. As her father was the last of the procession to leave, he closed the door behind him. Though she loved them all, Victoria was glad Spencer had made them leave. So many people. She hadn't been able to concentrate. But now that she was alone with her husband, she gave him her undivided attention.

He sat again on the chair beside the bed. His handsome features radiated concern. "What did happen, Victoria? Why did you faint?"

She had to think about it. "I'm not sure . . . oh, yes: I

jumped up from the couch to find a basin because my mother's perfume made me ill."

"Her perfume?"

"Yes. Certain smells. Perfumes and cigar smoke, mostly. I cannot tolerate them. Liquor, the taste of it, also makes me ill."

"I had no idea." He pulled guiltily at his ruined shirt. "I've been smoking. Is the scent on me bothersome to you?"

"No. Not yet, at any rate. However, the blood is, Spencer. We are going to kill you yet."

"I had wondered if that was the intention. However, to be on the safe side—with the smell of cigar smoke on me, I mean—I will keep my distance." She really wished he wouldn't, but how could she say that? "How are you feeling now, Victoria? Any stronger? Would you like a glass of water?" He grinned devilishly. "I promise not to fling it on you."

Victoria stared at her grinning, teasing husband. Who was this man? Could he really be the same stern and distant duke she'd married? Why was he doing this, revealing a warmer side of himself? It wasn't fair, and she wouldn't allow it. When she spoke, she injected a more neutral tone and topic into the conversation. "Thank you, no. No water. But . . . you. I can't get over your poor head. At least the bleeding has again stopped." She critically scrutinized his wound. "It doesn't look so bad. I doubt you'll need stitches."

"Do you, indeed? I wonder, then, why your mother feels a need to send for Dr. Hollis with you here to render medical opinions."

She ignored his further teasing. "Oh, dear. Dr. Hollis."

"Exactly. Can we trust him to, uh, keep our secret?"

"Yes. You may not remember, but he examined me in Savannah and promised he would say nothing. Unless I had a complication, as he put it, and my family needed to be told for my health's sake."

"Oh, I do remember that now." The teasing lights returned to his black eyes. "Will you tell him I don't need stitches?"

Victoria picked at a pulled thread in the muslin sheet. "No, of course not." When Spencer laughed gently, she met his gaze. "You seem different, Spencer."

"I do?" He raised his eyebrows. "Different how?"

"You're . . . nicer. To me, I mean. To everyone, really."

He arched an eyebrow. "And you sound positively suspicious about that."

"I'm sorry. You're just not . . . yourself."

"Credit these damned head injuries. It's a wonder I can even remember my name or my titles with a brain like scrambled eggs. But now the worst has happened: I have become . . . nice."

His laugh—a rich, melodic sound—further captivated Victoria's woman's heart and had her dangerously encouraging him. "You should laugh more. I like that, too."

"You do? Then I truly have become a pleasant chap." He leaned forward in his chair, his elbows resting on his knees. He again took her hand in his, as if this were the usual thing between them, and intimately rubbed his thumb over her fingers. Watching him, feeling his warm touch, and the response her body had to it, Victoria found breathing difficult.

"All this talk of *me* being different," Spencer said, smiling seductively, his black eyes gleaming. "What's got into *you*, Victoria? Are you trying to seduce me?"

Shocked, she tried to pull her hand free, but he held on. "I hardly think—"

"Please don't. We've done too much thinking already, don't you think?" His laugh was apparently for his own wording, but Victoria was too apprehensive and too enthralled to respond in kind.

Her eyes were so rounded she felt certain she must look like a hoot owl. She had to get him off this subject. Simply had to. If she didn't, and before she knew it, she would be under his spell and would give in to what her body urged her to do. Embarrassed for herself, Victoria shifted her legs under the sheet and swallowed and sniffed. "But we have to think, Spencer. There's too much wrong between us not to."

The teasing lights in his eyes slowly died. "Of course."

Though she hated losing this precious moment between them, though she wanted to give in to him, Victoria knew she could not. To be thrust aside later with a broken heart would kill her. "I almost told my mother about . . . the baby, Spencer. I'm sorry."

"Yes. That." He let go of her hand and sat back. His powerful legs spread, his knees apart, he crossed his arms over his chest. His frown produced faint lines across his forehead and puckered his wound slightly. "Of course, I couldn't allow you to tell her. And we know all the reasons why."

Well, she'd certainly succeeded in putting him off, hadn't she? Here they were again—back to the distance and the hesitation and the hard, hard truth between them. As she returned his steady gaze, as the silence stretched out between them, something inside Victoria, at that exact moment, cried out, saying it could take no more. Not one moment more of this struggle, this yearning for him and, at the same time, fearing the consequences in six months. She must do something—and do it now.

Suddenly flooding Victoria's consciousness was the instantaneous knowledge of what she had to do. "Spencer, I've made a decision regarding myself and my baby."

Spencer's features stretched with surprise and raised his eyebrows. "You have? When did you do this?"

"I've been thinking about it all along, only at the back of my mind until now."

"I see. Go on."

Now that she'd begun, it felt like jumping off a cliff. So final. No way back. And no way not to jump. "When the baby is born, no matter whose it should prove to be, I wish to . . ."

She looked down, fighting tears, hating how hard this was, this facing one's past and paying the price of it. Even worse was having her painfully vulnerable child pay along with her. Inhaling a bolstering breath, preparing her heart for what she had to say, Victoria met Spencer's waiting, wary gaze. "What I'm trying to say is I wish to be on my own. Only, I will not be returning to Georgia."

"I see." Though he'd retreated behind his granite duke's façade, he had to be recalling, Victoria figured, that day in the parlor at Wetherington's Point when he'd told her he would send her back here to her father. "Where would you go?"

"I don't know exactly. But I'd stay in England."

If it was possible, he appeared uncertain, even hurt. "Where in England, Victoria?"

"I don't know, Spencer. Somewhere. I don't yet know all the details."

"How will you live?"

"I have my allowance."

He smiled rather bleakly. "I don't know what to say, Victoria, except you've thought this through, haven't you, with no regard to me, or even the possibility of a change of heart?"

"I feel I must be prepared when the day comes."

"Admirable, but not necessary."

"How can you say it's not necessary?" Victoria's heart burned like a lump of coal. She struggled to a sitting position atop the mattress and pushed her hair back over her shoulders. "I know this is hard to hear—"

Spencer had come to his feet. He stood . . . so tall and handsome . . . and silently beside the bed. His mouth no more than a thin, rigid line, he stared down at her. "We have no need to have this discussion, Victoria."

"But we do. I can't go on like this, Spencer. I can't be around you all these months and see you like this and come to"—she bit back the words *care about*—"rely on you, only to have you send me away—"

"Victoria, please. One battle at a time. Right now, we're tired—bloody tired, some of us—and facing monstrous enemies. Let's live through this first, and then we'll worry about eventualities six months in the future."

Could he be more pompous and infuriating? Angry, Victoria tugged the top sheet off her and swung her legs over the side of the bed. Unaided, a hand out to stop him from helping her, she stood. Steadying herself by holding on to the overstuffed but firm mattress, she faced her husband.

"This cannot wait six months, Spencer. It will not magically correct itself. With only silence and mistrust between us, what do we do from there? Will we know how to proceed together? How will we make a marriage? On what will we base it?"

He cocked his head at a wary angle. "What exactly, are you saying, Victoria?"

The moment was here. But the words absolutely would not come. Some yearning part of her heart would not allow them past her lips. As if possessed of their own volition, her teeth clenched, holding the oh-so-final words in. Victoria swallowed, felt on the verge of tears again.

"Victoria?"

With a supreme effort of will, she blurted: "I want to be the one to make the break. I'm asking you for a divorce."

At that exact second, with the words still ringing in the air, before Spencer could reply or do anything but stare in shock at her, the door from the hallway opened. He pivoted about, no doubt ready to send flying whoever had dared to interrupt them. Of like mind, and almost shouting with disbelief, Victoria moved away from the bed until she could see around her husband.

There stood the jovial Dr. Hollis with his medical bag. Victoria's mother was behind him, peering curiously around his shoulder. "Yoo-hoo, you two," she sang out. "We are in luck. Dr. Hollis was nearby. And here he is, ready to see his patients."

It was two hours later, and night had fallen. The rain had stopped, leaving the air fresh and cool. Downstairs, as Victoria was very aware, her family and Dr. Hollis were dining together in the formal dining room. Wonderful aromas floated up the stairs, along with snippets of conversation or a muted laugh. Upstairs, in the elegantly appointed sitting room that formed part of the suite assigned to the Duke and Duchess of Moreland, Hornsby had wheeled in, on a white-cloth-covered cart that could double as a small dining table, the requested private supper for the suite's occupants.

Hornsby and Rosanna had then worked together—for once and quietly—to arrange a suitable and pleasing setting for their employers. A tiny vase with a single red rose was set in the middle of the cart and between the place settings. Covers were whisked off warmed plates and placed on the cart's middle shelf, which was hidden from view by the long drape of the tablecloth. Linen napkins were snapped open and readied for use. A bottle of wine was decanted, and the heavy silverware was correctly positioned. Finally, two nicely padded chairs had been pulled from an intimate grouping in the room and placed one at either side of the charming, polished wood cart.

Once these preparations were concluded, Rosanna and Hornsby went downstairs for their evening meal. And that left the Whitfields alone in each other's presence for the first time since Dr. Hollis had opened the bedroom door earlier. Though they were dining together, one word had yet to pass between them. Monks who had taken vows of silence could probably carry on a far livelier conversation amongst themselves than she and her husband seemed capable of having, Victoria groused but not with too much conviction. Meaning, she wasn't certain she wished to hear Spencer's thoughts right now.

And so, the only sounds in the room were those made by a meal in progress. Silver cutlery clattering against a dinner plate. Water or wine being poured into the appropriate glass. Victoria kept her gaze on her plate, which was heaped high with many of her favorites. Annabelle had outdone herself.

The cook had prepared a roast of beef, glazed ham, buttered potatoes, squash fried with onions, green beans flavored with strips of bacon, buttermilk biscuits, peach preserves, and apple pie. Wonderful.

However, the dinner cart was hardly big enough to avoid seeing Spencer, even if Victoria did not look directly at her husband. After all, he sat no more than a very few feet away from her, facing her. She could smell the clean scent of him. He'd of course bathed and changed his clothes. Gone was the bloody shirt, replaced by a crisply ironed white one, open at the throat. Earlier he had stalked back into the sitting room wearing the buff riding pants she loved to see him in, his finely honed thigh muscles working with each step he took in his highly polished Hessians. His black hair had still been damp and a lock had fallen provocatively across his forehead.

It wasn't the only thing that crossed his forehead. As it turned out, she'd been wrong. He had needed stitches, Rosanna had reported. Five of them. And now, a thin white bandage of gauze was wrapped, Indian style, around his head, doing nothing to detract from his dark and dangerous good looks. Victoria was not immune. He was the most handsome and desirable of men.

Certainly, she knew what it was like to have this man kiss her, to have his hands roving over her body and pleasing her. She knew what it was like to have him move down her naked body, kissing and nipping and sampling as he went. She knew the power of his lovemaking and what it meant to lose herself, if not her mind, in the hypnotic rhythm of his thrusts—

A loud clattering sound jolted Victoria back to the moment and had her gasping. Her gaze locked with Spencer's. His frankly staring black eyes and raised eyebrows told her the offending sound had come from her side of the table. She cast her frantic gaze downward, searching—and saw, to her horror, what had happened. She'd become lost in her sensual reverie and apparently her nerveless fingers had dropped her fork onto the rim of her dinner plate. Certain she was red up to her hairline, she fumbled for the incriminating piece of heavy silverware and finally secured it in her grip.

"Victoria?"

Her gaze locked with his. "I'm fine. Really. Just a momentary thing. Please. Go on with your meal."

He didn't look as reassured as she'd tried to make him. "Are you certain?"

She nodded furiously, feeling the heat of her blush deepen. What she wouldn't give right now for her fan to cool her face. As she had no idea where it was, she plopped her fork on the tablecloth, plucked her napkin off her lap, and folded it into a thick square, which she used to cool her face. "I'm fine. Really."

"Do you feel ill?"

"Far from it, Your Grace." When he raised an eyebrow to an impossible height, Victoria instantly realized why and corrected herself. "I mean 'Spencer.' "

He did not acknowledge her correction but asked: "Why did you drop your fork?"

"I'm sure I couldn't say." She was sure she *wouldn't* say, that much she knew.

When she could no longer sustain eye contact with him, she set about the business of unfurling her napkin and very precisely placing it across her lap. Only now, her clothing felt twisted for some reason. Exasperated, and fumbling under her husband's watchful eyes, she, as ladylike as possible, twisted and turned in her chair, adjusting the lay of her long and clinging skirts. She wished now she'd fussed more with Rosanna when she'd insisted Victoria dress comfortably in her nightclothes—a white linen lawn gown and wrapper, both frilled and laced. Light and heavenly, yes, but not very formidable covering. What she needed was a full suit of armor.

"What *are* you doing, Victoria? What is the matter?"

She sat suddenly still and met his dark eyes. "I am making myself more comfortable."

"And are you now?"

Clearly, he was perturbed. His voice was that of a reproving parent forced to dine with an especially irritating child. How dare he? Victoria snatched up her water glass, downed the contents, and thumped the glass back down on the dinner cart. Forcing herself to meet his steady gaze, she raised her napkin to delicately wipe at her lips. For some reason, this amused her husband, if one could judge by the grin—smirk?—toying with his lips. "I beg your pardon, sir, but what is so funny?"

He grinned outright now. "I do apologize, madam, but I have just never before seen a lady wipe her mouth with the corner of a tablecloth."

"The—?" She snapped her gaze down to her lap. Sure enough, she had crumpled in her fisted hands not her blasted napkin but the tag end of the table covering. Completely vexed, but not about to be bested, Victoria primly straightened the rumpled cloth and smoothed it over her knees until it hung free between her and the cart as it was supposed to do. As she did, she explained, straight-faced: "It's quite the usual thing in America, you know. I'm surprised you have not observed this custom before in your travels to this continent."

"Apparently, and before now, I have moved in the wrong circles to see such . . . table customs."

Pompous man. Curse the luck, now she could not find her napkin. As nonchalantly as possible, and tucking her hair behind her ears as she did, Victoria looked to either side of her chair. No napkin. Not on the floor. Not stuck between the chair and herself. Where had it gone?

"I believe you will find it behind you," Spencer said, pointing to her left.

Victoria sat rigidly still. "I don't know what you're talking about."

"Of course you do. Your napkin. Somehow, in all your twisting about, it's got behind you. Would you like for me to retrieve it for you?"

"No."

"As you wish." He picked up the water pitcher and, his expression innocent, said: "As you've downed yours, would you care for more water?"

"No, thank you." *Damnable man.* Victoria feared she would have to literally kill her husband to get him to go back to eating and ignoring her as he had been doing for the past ten minutes since they'd convened for supper.

As if he'd read her thoughts, Spencer replaced the water pitcher without comment and continued with his meal. Victoria subtly exhaled her relief and picked up her fork. Stabbing a bite of ham with more force than was necessary . . . a sudden memory assailed her: When she'd been a little girl and angry and had done this same thing, her father had always told her such force wasn't required as the animal was already dead . . . she poked the polite-sized tidbit into her mouth and chewed defiantly as she glared at her remaining meal.

"Because the child you carry could be my heir," Spencer said without warning, "there's not going to be a divorce. Or even a separation."

Victoria had to choke down the ham she'd been in the process of swallowing. Her heart thumping and knocking about in her chest, she watched her husband calmly pouring himself a second serving of wine. His black-eyed devil's gaze briefly met hers and then returned to his task.

"May I have more water, please?"

"Of course." So very accommodating, Spencer set the wine bottle down, grasped the water pitcher by its handle, and refilled her glass. Done with his task, he picked up his fork and continued eating.

Taken aback, Victoria stared, without the least bit of sympathy, at his gauze-wrapped head. That was it? Really? He could simply say there was not going to be a divorce or a separation? After being the one who had first brought it up back in England all those weeks ago and allowing it to hang, like a guillotine blade, over her head? How many nights had she cried herself to sleep worrying about this? Well, he just did not get his way all the time, now did he? Or the last word, either.

"Oh, yes, there most certainly is going to be a divorce," she announced boldly into the quiet between them.

Spencer abruptly raised his head and watched her as he chewed his mouthful, swallowed and reached a hand down to his lap, ostensibly for his napkin—but came up, apparently unknown to him, with the other end of the tablecloth, which he used to wipe his mouth. Only a momentary flaring of her eyes escaped Victoria's rigid control. She absolutely had her back teeth clamped together to keep from laughing out loud. But, alas, a strangled guffaw got away. She quickly raised her fist to her mouth and coughed to cover the laugh.

"Is something wrong, Victoria?" Spencer said, so coolly British and civilly. "Your face is red."

His would be, too, if she told him what he'd just done. But she simply could not do it to the man. He'd already taken three blows to the head, two nearly coma-inducing and one requiring stitches, on her behalf in less than a week. Why add outright embarrassment to the awful list of punishments he would be made to endure? Finally, Victoria was able to open her mouth without shrieking with glee and, exhaling sharply, said: "No. Nothing is wrong."

"Good." Still oblivious, he smoothed the tablecloth back down onto his lap and again went back to his meal.

Victoria sat there, stunned. Had he already forgot her challenge to what he'd said? No, she suspected, he hadn't forgot. He'd simply chosen to ignore it and her. But wait . . . hadn't she had the last word on the subject, as it stood now? Yes, she believed she had. Good. Now she could spend her time thinking about more pleasant things. Like the buttered potatoes on her plate and this entire meal. It was, along with every other one she'd had since she'd been home, wonderful. She vowed that before she left for England—to live on her own, mind you—she would hire, at an exorbitant rate if necessary, a Southern cook. Perhaps that Sven fellow from the house in Savannah. Would her mother be furious if she stole him from her?

Good Lord, a Swedish cook in the South. She frowned, thinking: *Maybe he's from southern Sweden—*

"No, Victoria. There is *not* going to be a divorce."

That did it. Angry now, this time she purposely clattered her fork onto her nearly empty plate. Bracing her wrists against the table's edge and to either side of her dinner plate, she leaned toward her husband and said: "Why ever not?"

"I have already said. The child you bear could be my heir."

"And I have already said that makes no difference to how I feel. But even so, a divorce would not change the child's status, would it?"

"No. But there will be no divorce. And I do not have to give further reasons, madam."

"Maybe not in England you don't, sir. But right outside that very window over there is an ancient oak tree dripping with Spanish moss that says you are in my country now and yes, you do have to give a reason."

He shrugged. "Very well. Because it is too costly and would require an act of Parliament to make it so."

"You're in Parliament. See that it gets done. It should be easy enough for you."

"Not so easy as you'd think, madam. I have political enemies who would take great glee in holding my feet to the fire—"

"They're not the only ones who would—"

"—over just such an issue as this. And I will not give them the satisfaction or subject my family to such a scandal—"

"What family? Do you mean Edward's esteemed mother? Or Edward himself? If Edward is your concern, sir, put that fear to rest. In fact, I think he'd be glad if you were to divorce me—"

"You will have to explain your remark, Victoria, because I don't—"

"Gladly. Edward has already told me he would be happy to whisk me and my baby off to his castle, should you be so unwise as to set me aside—"

"He *what*?" Spencer's outburst seemed to have the power to lift him bodily to his feet, where he stood rigidly at attention. "The devil, you say! Edward said that?" Spencer's face was very red and his voice had gone up considerably higher than his normal pitch.

Horrified at what she had revealed, horrified at Spencer's reaction, and terrified she would not be able to calm him, Victoria hurriedly scooted her chair back and stood. "He didn't mean it, Spencer. Surely you know him—"

"Oh, yes, madam, I do know him—and much better than you do. I will take the backstabbing little womanizing jackanapes apart limb by limb—"

A knocking on the door to the hallway and its opening with a squeak had cut off Spencer's harangue. "Hallo, in the sitting room! We're coming in!"

That voice. That British voice. Victoria's heart plunged to her feet. But Spencer, triumphant, arched an eyebrow. Though she really didn't have to look to know who was there, she turned with her husband to see Edward, with perfectly horrible timing, standing blithely unaware in the doorway and grinning. With him was Neville, who sat unconcernedly down and panted gently and watched without comment.

"Ah, there you are," Edward trilled. "The two lovebirds— Good heavens, Spencer! You're bandaged like a perfect savage. What in the world has happened to you now?"

"Not nearly as much as is about to happen to you, my dear cousin." Spencer stalked toward a clearly startled Edward . . . with Victoria now hanging, ineffectually, on to his arm and crying out sharply for him to stop.

CHAPTER 16

"Stop, Spencer! I mean it, or I'll sic Neville on you! I will. I'll do it."

Spencer sighted on the loose-jointed, rawboned dog. The animal had come to his feet and looked on, though not as benignly as Spencer would have liked. Cutting through his anger at Edward were Isaac Redmond's words earlier about how the dog liked Victoria best of all. And already the hunter had heard its name and his and *sic* in the same sentence.

Halfway to the door and Edward, who had not exhibited the sense to flee but who still stood in the doorway, Spencer stopped. Gently but firmly, he disengaged his wife's sharp fingernails from his arm and held her by her comely shoulders. As he stared down into her face, in one instant he shed his anger at Edward, though he'd not let that one know it. Replacing it was Spencer's concern for Victoria's well-being. After all, she'd experienced the same awful and eventful day, with a few exceptions, that he'd lived through. This constant upheaval could not be good for her in such a delicate condition. But, beyond that, he just did not like to see her upset.

So, when he spoke to her, his voice was more cajoling and reassuring than probably it was good for her to hear. "Shh, before you upset yourself and bring your entire overwrought family up here. I am not really going to kill Edward."

"I say! Imagine my relief, Spence, old man."

Spence, old man, never lost eye contact with his wife. "Shut up, Edward, before you make a liar out of me."

Victoria's bottom lip poked out mutinously. "Or hit him. You're not to kill him or to hit him."

"Why all this sudden concern for Edward? Give me one good reason why I shouldn't soundly thrash him."

When Victoria offered nothing, only frowned as if in thought, Edward cleared his throat and said, "Uh, Victoria? Dear?"

Spencer spared his cousin a triumphant smirk, but it was short-lived in the face of Victoria's blurted response.

"Because I like him and he's a nice man and he's not as big as you are, so that would be unfair, and he is my friend."

"Aha, Spencer. There you have it."

Again, Edward was ignored as Spencer released his wife and soberly informed her: "That was as many as four. I asked only for one."

She pursed her lips and looked up at him from under the cover of her dark dusting of eyelashes. Spencer's breath caught. She made the most enchanting of pictures. The ways in which he yearned to express himself to her, the words he wanted to use to describe her, were normally so sickeningly romantic to him that it further surprised him to realize he now, and finally, understood the Romantic poets and why they chose such sugary wording. He couldn't help himself. The frothy descriptions flowed into his consciousness . . . her porcelain skin; that little upturned nose; those wide and striking blue eyes; the pink Cupid's bow of a mouth; and the veritable riot of shining mahogany hair—

Why was she staring at him like that? Spencer snapped out of his reverie, only to realize he had forgotten what he'd been about to say. "I'm sorry. What was I saying?"

"You weren't saying anything. I was."

She was so exquisitely alive. And dressed like this in her nightclothes—alarm stiffened Spencer's knees. "Good Lord, Edward, my wife is in her nightclothes and here you are, practically in the bedroom with us, man."

Again, Victoria grabbed his arm and pulled his attention down to her. "It's all right, Spencer, he's seen me like this before."

The most incredible and stunned silence filled the sitting room and seemed to thicken with each passing second.

"Oh, I say, Victoria," Edward said, sounding droll and like death itself. "We could have done without that."

As usual, Spencer ignored Edward and stood there, offended, his jaw firmed, his pulse beating a threatening tattoo. "You will have to explain your remark, madam."

Looking very guilty, she said: "It's all very innocent, Spencer."

"I will be the judge of that. Proceed."

She narrowed her eyes at him. "Very well. On those nights when you were unconscious, and when I couldn't sleep for worrying, I would go sit by your bed. And Edward would sometimes come in to check on you, too, when I was there. He would sit with me and reassure me. He was a great comfort."

She'd sat by his bed on those nights when he'd been unconscious. Spencer forgot everything else she'd said. How . . . heartwarming, really. Half afraid his heart was in his eyes, he admitted he was losing badly. He never seemed to remember, until she stood right next to him or in front of him, that the top of her head came barely to his shoulder. Somehow, she always seemed more formidable than her height warranted.

"Spencer?"

He gave himself a mental shake and said, rather too loudly, "Yes. I'm sure he was. A great comfort to you."

He then arrowed a not-quite-jealous-because-he-really-did-trust-him glare his cousin's way, only to see the insolent young man had leaned a shoulder against the doorjamb and crossed his arms over his chest. He stood there, in his nonchalant pose, grinning and waggling his eyebrows.

The incorrigible cad said, "So you see, Spencer, I am a great comfort to your wife in your times of, uh, incapacity, which by the looks of you, are occurring with ever greater frequency. By the by, you really must tell me, at some point, what happened to you to warrant that bandage—"

"I ran into a door."

Edward arched an eyebrow in disbelief. "If you say so, old man. However, and more to the point, you are not to hit or to kill me. Those are your wife's very words. And I heartily second them. Don't I, Neville?"

Spencer ignored both the dog's answering woof and Edward as he addressed his wife. "I find I cannot promise, madam, that at some point in the very near future I will not have to hit Edward."

"Oh, I say," Edward the Interrupter sang out from his position by the open door. "I won't stand for it. It's not fair. I've only just arrived, at great peril to my person, given the damnable conditions of the road, if one can call it that just now, and have yet to have my supper. As I don't fancy having the stuffing knocked out of me on an empty stomach, I must ask you why you feel you must thrash me. What offense could I have possibly committed in my absence?"

Victoria surged forward. Her voice rang with apology. "I'm so sorry, Edward. It's my fault. I didn't mean to say anything."

Edward studied her. "Say? About what, exactly, my dear?"

"You were so kind to me and warmed my heart with your declaration when you said you would whisk me off to your castle, should Spencer be so . . . stupid as to set me aside once the baby is born, if it's not a Whitfield."

"O-oh, lovely." The sickly gray pallor that leached the color from Edward's face did Spencer's heart a world of good. "Now, how—in the name of *God*—did that little gem happen to come up, pray tell?"

Crossing his arms over his chest and relaxing a knee, Spencer spoke before his wife could. "Very naturally, I would say, in our conversation. You see, Victoria's asked me for a divorce, Edward—"

"Surely not! Has it really come to that, then?" Edward's troubled gaze darted between him and Victoria.

"Apparently it has."

"I do not believe the pair of you." Suddenly, Edward was the scolding parent. Spencer exchanged a look of surprise with Victoria. "Stop that and pay attention to me. The two of you—nay, the *three* of us—don't have enough problems right now and right under our very noses that you two can't even have a civil meal together—a meal I have not yet had, I remind you—without threatening divorce? Good God, you could be having a child together."

"We are fully aware of that, Edward. But Victoria has a solution for that, as well. She has decided she will reside somewhere in England. But she doesn't know where. Perhaps you would like to offer her a room in that castle of yours?"

"I will do no such thing. For one thing, I haven't got a castle. And for another, you would literally die, Spencer, before you would allow this woman to get away from you. And you—" Visibly angry now, Edward indicated Victoria, who Spencer saw was nervously kneading her skirts' fabric with her white-knuckled fists. "Don't you have any idea at all how much this man"—he indicated Spencer—"loves you?"

That night, covered only by a thin cotton bedsheet, Victoria lay alone in the big bed in the guest bedroom intended for her and Spencer. After the exhausting day she'd had, she knew she ought to be fast asleep. And she had been, for hours, it seemed. But now she was awake. She didn't remember actually waking up. Instead, only slowly had she realized her eyes were open and she was awake. She didn't think anything sinister was afoot to have pulled her out of sleep because, earlier, Neville had curled up on the rug beside the bed, announcing his intention to sleep here tonight. So, if anything at all were amiss, Victoria knew Neville would not only alert but would also defend her.

Victoria's confident smile suddenly abandoned her. Neville *was* still here with her, wasn't he? On her stomach, and feeling the hard little mound in her belly that was her growing baby, Victoria crabbed across the bed until she could see over the mattress's edge. Confounding her efforts were her own hair, which cascaded over her shoulders to obscure her view, and the veil-like mosquito netting, which she had become tangled in. Making fussy sounds, she tossed her head to swing her hair over one shoulder, fought the netting into submission and, with the moonlight streaming in through the open windows to bathe the room in silvery shadows, she looked for Neville.

And there he was. Victoria exhaled her relief. The bloodhound lay stretched out on his side. He raised his head; his glittering eyes stared back at her. Grinning, Victoria snapped her fingers and patted the mattress. "Come here, boy," she whispered, wanting to rub the dog's silky ears and smooth his head. "Did I wake you?"

Neville thumped his tail against the floor but laid his head back down, ignoring her. Victoria chuckled, calling herself notoriously ineffective with males of any breed.

Sighing, righting herself on the bed and fluffing her pillows, she lay down, turned on her side and curled up into a little ball. Her head lay on one pillow, but the other one—the one Spencer should have his head on—she held tightly in her arms. Wide awake now, blinking to adjust her vision because of the gauzy film of the mosquito netting that completely surrounded the bed, she stared absently across the room at the partially raised windows.

This was so frustrating. Why was she so wide awake?

When she'd been a little girl, she'd slept her deepest on nights like this . . . with the wind soughing through the oaks' branches, causing them to creak like a comfortable old rocking chair; with the leaves rustling and the cicadas buzzing steadily. Sometimes she would hear other comforting sounds. A horse's neigh. An owl in a tree somewhere far off, faintly asking whoo-whoo. Even the sounds of the swamp . . . bullfrogs or alligators bellowing, the gentle lapping of the water against the dock . . . could lull her to sweet oblivion.

But not tonight. Tonight the natural music of River's End carried no charm for her. No sooner had Edward blurted that about Spencer loving her—which he most certainly did not—Spencer had, without a word, stalked right by her and Edward and Neville and stomped down the stairs to ask to be put into another bedroom. He'd cited his injury and her . . . *illness* as reasons they should sleep separately. So much for his saying she should not be alone day or night because of the danger she faced. But, of course she wasn't really alone, not with Neville here.

At any rate, the whole thing had upset her mother and, the next thing Victoria had known, here she had come upstairs again with poor Dr. Hollis in tow. The man wanted no part of Victoria's lies to her family regarding her delicate condition, but he'd reluctantly gone along, calling her fainting spells a case of the vapors. Her mother had not been reassured. She had fussed and fluttered around Victoria until she'd thought she'd cry or scream or jump out the very window she now faced, had her father not intervened and dragged his wife away.

It was all just so silly, Victoria decided. It really was. Especially after the way Spencer had gone down on one knee in front of her in Savannah and begged her forgiveness for acting like such an ass toward her. A pompous ass, she believed he'd said. And here he was, on the very same day, again acting like one. But Victoria's conscience would not let her off so easily, reminding her she had asked the man for a divorce—a man with fresh stitches in his forehead and two lumps on the back of his head, all having something to do with her. What had her father always told Jefferson? You never hit a man when he's down? Yes, that was it. She had hit a man when he was down. She ought to be ashamed of herself.

Victoria sat up. She ought to go apologize to her husband right now, oughtn't she? She furiously kicked her legs until the bedsheet lay discarded at the end of the big bed. She sat there a moment, testing her will for this act . . . in the middle of the night. Could this wait until morning? No. Mama had told her, upon her marriage, that a couple should never go to bed angry at each other. She and Spencer had done exactly that. Maybe she still had time to set the situation to rights if she got up now and went to him.

Oh, I don't think he'll appreciate being awakened, not after the day he's had. Victoria absently stared at a mantel clock across the room and above the fireplace. She chewed on her bottom lip as she procrastinated. *What time is it?* She couldn't see the clock's hands from where she sat but, slowly, a sly-fox feminine smile claimed her lips . . . *I could see it if I got out of bed and went over there and looked, couldn't I?* And if she did that, well, she would already be out of bed and could easily be on her way to Spencer's room. She knew which one it was. Much earlier, she'd sent the discreet and ever-reliable Rosanna to see.

So, why was she still sitting here? Victoria asked herself. What more did she need to know? Her decision made, she excitedly wriggled over to the side of the mattress, gathered the mosquito netting up and slipped under it as she slid off the bed. By the time her feet touched the floor, Neville had again raised his head. The dog studied her with unnerving intelligence. "Well?" Victoria asked him. "Are you going with me, boy?"

Neville exhaled a breath that, to Victoria's ears, sounded

like resignation. She smiled. Looking hugely sad, as he always did, the bloodhound pulled himself to his feet and, with a slow wag of his tail, like a clock's pendulum marking time, narrowed his eyes at her. "Good. But we must be quiet. Shhh."

As if protesting this *we*, Neville perked up his long floppy ears as much as was possible for him to do. Victoria tsked. "Oh, all right, I'm the one who's noisy. Go on now, take me to Spencer." The dog didn't move; he just stared up at her. "For heaven's sake, you may as well go. You're already awake. And what else do you have to do? Now, come on, help me find my slippers and wrapper."

Her slippers and wrapper were, of course, where she'd left them: the slippers beside the bed, the wrapper draped across the foot of the bed. Victoria wriggled her feet into the slippers as she also pulled on her wrapper, tugging her hair out from under it with a swift brushing motion of her arm. "There, Neville. We are as ready as we'll ever be." The dog drooped his ears to their lowest point. "Oh, stop that. You always see the bad in things."

She softened her words by quickly hugging the big dog to her, laying her cheek atop his head, feeling his silky warmth and the strength in his body. Neville responded with happy wriggling and sloppy kisses—and a woof of pleasure. Victoria straightened up, putting a finger to her lips. "Shh, remember? We don't want to wake anyone. Well, except Spencer, of course."

With that, and with no other reasons presenting themselves to stop her, Victoria, with Neville by her side, padded softly across the room and over to the closed door that led out into the hallway. She eased the door open and poked her head out, looking both ways. Dark and empty. Thankfully, the window at the end of the hall was draped with thin sheers that allowed in available moonlight to keep her from having to grope about in the pitch-black of the house's interior.

Satisfied she would not be detected, Victoria eased out of

her bedroom, waited for Neville to clear the threshold, closed the door after them, and then quickly, giddily, skittered down the middle of the long runner of carpet that covered the red-pine wood flooring. Neville padded along at her side.

In no time at all, they were outside the closed door to Spencer's bedroom. Her fisted hands pressed to her mouth, Victoria faced the door, took a breath for courage, and said a bolstering prayer. Then, with Neville all but pressed against her legs, she gripped the doorknob and slowly turned it until she met resistance. Holding the knob turned as far as it would go, she eased the door inward, thankful that its hinges were well oiled and noiseless, and entered the room. Again she waited for Neville and then closed this door behind them. Her back against the door, Victoria stood there, blinking, helping her eyes to adjust to the gray gloom.

Because she'd lived most of her life in this very house, she knew this bedroom was similar in design and furnishings to the one she'd just left. With every sense on alert, and shivering with excitement, Victoria sighted on the oversized mosquito-netted bed, which reposed in the middle of the room. The misshapen coverings told her that Spencer was there. Well, of course he was. Where else would he be? Practically on tiptoes, Victoria set herself in motion, each cautious step taking her closer and closer to her sleeping husband. Neville took each step with her, staying by her side.

In only a moment, it seemed, she and her dog stood beside the bed. As she listened to Spencer's deep and regular breathing, Victoria spared a glance for the bloodhound as he settled himself, Sphinx-like, on the oval rug beside the bed. Apparently, he felt his part in this mission was complete. Victoria stared at her sleeping husband, or at the back of his head, really, as he lay on his side, his face away from her. Poor man. He'd been through so much. Victoria made her way around to the other side of the four-poster bed, where she silently fumbled for the opening in the filmy netting, found it, tugged it aside, and leaned in toward her husband. She stopped, stared, and silently nagged. *Just like a man. He's taken the bandage from around his head. I swan, I don't know why we even call doctors to these men.*

But seeing his stitches melted her heart. She forgave him and, smiling indulgently, gently shook his shoulder. "Spencer? Are you awake?"

Feeling the touch on his shoulder, and because he'd been expecting trouble since they'd been here, Spencer exploded into wakefulness and acted on pure instinct. In less than a second, he had his loaded gun out from under his pillow with one hand and the intruder next to his bed with the other. The gasping interloper . . . small, lightweight . . . he hauled up tightly by the shirtfront onto the bed and rolled them both atop the mattress until he was astraddle the villain. He pressed his pistol's bore tight against his victim's forehead. "Don't even move," he warned—

But the snarling growl that met Spencer's threat startled him into jerking his attention to his right—only to see the muscled and suddenly vicious bloodhound, Neville, coming seemingly out of nowhere and, covered in the mosquito netting though not hampered in the least by it, leaping onto the bed. The bloodhound's bared teeth, slobbering jowls, and outraged snarls propelled the charging animal toward Spencer, who bellowed in fear and protest but still heard someone cry: "No, Neville! No!"

A crazily calm corner of Spencer's mind remarked how like Victoria that voice sounded. In the same instant, the dog's solid body collided with Spencer, knocking the gun out of his hand as they went hurtling through space and even more mosquito netting—only to land hard on the floor and roll over and over. When they stopped, Spencer found himself cocooned with Neville and on the bottom, on his back, with the dog atop him . . . and viciously snapping at him.

Luckily, the two of them, now thoroughly tangled in the mosquito netting, were not really able to effectively hurt the other, he realized.

Spencer's concern, though, was that Neville didn't know this. Suddenly, he became aware that a third person, or entity, had, at some point, joined the fray. Straddling Spencer's legs, this newcomer to the battle tugged at the entangled dog and shouted: "Neville, stop it! Get off, boy! Off! Do you hear me? Stop it!"

It was Victoria—again. But where exactly was the intruder? Had he seen his chance and run off? Just as Victoria seemed to be making some headway with the dog, as she furiously tried to unravel the hound from Spencer, the door to the bedroom burst open and disgorged an evident crowd of people all speaking at once.

"What's going on in here?" "I've got a gun on you!" "Good Lord, Isaac, be careful with that thing!" "Look at the bed—it's torn apart!" "Quiet, Mr. Milton. Hello, over there, whoever you are, don't you move. Someone light the blasted lamp." "What did you hear, Jefferson? What woke you up?" "I heard a big thump and then Victoria crying out." "I say, Mr. Redmond, can I get by you to go see what is wrong?" "No, hold up, Edward. We can't see a blasted thing and don't know what's going on yet. Could be dangerous." "I daresay it is, but fair enough, sir. Hornsby, old soul, what on earth do you intend doing with that chamber pot?"

"Daddy, help me!" Victoria cried, sounding peeved and desperate. "It's Neville—he's attacked Spencer!"

A moment of stunned silence followed this. "Neville?" Mr. Redmond called out, clearly puzzled. Neville responded with a yowl of appeal.

"Victoria," Spencer hissed, "please leave the dog be. Try to calm him. Right now, you're making him struggle and his toenails are gouging and scratching me. Remember, too, madam, I sleep in the nude. Need I say more?"

Victoria gasped and sat back, blessedly leaving the dog alone. "Oh, my word."

"Would someone please light a lamp? Can't see a blamed thing. Y'all wait here until we can see. Don't want you falling all over them and making matters worse. Victoria, are you injured?"

"No, Daddy. I'm fine. But Spencer and Neville aren't."

Several gasps and murmurs greeted this, but her father called out: "What's wrong with Spencer and Neville?"

Spencer raised an eyebrow at Victoria, defying her to describe this. "You just have to see it, Daddy."

"Go light that lamp," Isaac Redmond directed someone in one breath, and in the next, addressed his daughter: "Why did Neville attack Spencer? That doesn't seem like him."

"He thought Spencer meant to hurt me."

"Hurt you? Why, I'll shoot the man who harms my daughter."

"Oh, I say, Mr. Redmond, I hardly think my cousin would harm—"

"Unhand me, sir! I've every right to blast him to kingdom come, should he even think about it."

"No one's trying to hurt me," Victoria shrieked, provoking the dog into struggling again, which in turn made Spencer bellow and Victoria cry out, even louder. "If you don't get over here this instant and untangle Neville from Spencer, then he just might tear my husband's throat out and leave our baby without a father! Now, *hurry*!"

"Baby?"

"Father?"

"I don't think my cousin wanted that known just yet."

"Why not?"

"What baby?"

"Sister is going to have a baby? Why, I can hardly realize it."

"Oh, my word, my baby is going to have a baby." Mrs.

Redmond started sobbing. "I knew it, Isaac. I told you she was expecting."

"Now, now, my dear, don't cry, it's all right." Then, more stridently: "Why has no one lit that lamp?"

"Isaac, we have to send for Dr. Hollis. She could be hurt. Where's Virgil? Virgil, are you in here?"

"Virgil's not here, Mother," Jefferson said. "Now, leave poor Dr. Hollis alone. He was here only a matter of hours ago and looked at her—twice. I'm sure Sister is fine. You're going to kill the old man if you keep him running out here at all hours."

While all of this transpired on one side of the bed, on the other side and during the same concurrent seconds, Spencer gave up the struggle. He slumped in defeat and from exhaustion. Fortunately, Neville was of a like mind. The net-wrapped dog lay on his belly atop Spencer's chest, panting and whining.

For her part, and perhaps realizing, despite her best efforts to untangle them, that Spencer and Neville were too mummified in the netting to separate without the aid of an experienced Egyptologist, Victoria sagged to the floor and sat, in profile, next to Spencer's head. Given that she faced the same way he did and they were on the side of the bed closest to the windows and the moonlight, he could see how dejected she looked.

"I am so sorry," she whispered urgently, under cover of the noisy but ineffective commotion of the others present in the room. "What a complication, Spencer. I've put us in an awful position."

Spencer stared at her. He felt the hard floor under him, the weight of the dog atop him, and the pressure of the twisted yards upon yards of mosquito netting holding him in place. "Some of us already are in an awful position, Victoria."

She put a comforting hand on his shoulder. "You poor man. I meant my silly blurting about the baby, of course.

Now they know, and my mother will make a big to-do about it at the barbecue. And then, later on, when this child doesn't have the birthmark—"

"It doesn't matter."

This stopped her. With her head cocked at a puzzled angle, she stared intently at him—but then suddenly carried on. "You are very forgiving. Thank you. But of course it matters, Spencer. I hadn't meant to tell them until you and I . . . knew the truth. But now, my hasty words change everything. This is so awful. I wasn't prepared to have to admit to them right now that I don't know who—"

"No, Victoria. You misunderstand me." Every instinct born of being a peer screamed at Spencer not to correct her misunderstanding, to allow it to stand. But he held Victoria's gaze . . . and a sudden calm came over him, a lifting of his spirits, a certainty that what he was about to say was the right thing to do. But it would also be the most wrong thing he had ever done. And he didn't care. He simply did not care. How simple it all really was, in the end.

Evident bafflement brought mercurial changes to Victoria's expression as her gaze searched his face. "How did I misunderstand? What do you mean?"

All he had to do was say nothing . . . and nothing would change. If he remained silent, he would uphold his responsibility to all those blue-blooded Whitfields and to society. But if he spoke, if he proceeded with this madness of the heart, then his entire life would change and everything he had ever believed would be a lie. But if he said nothing now, then the remainder of *his* life would be a lie. He was at a crossroads. Spencer inhaled, opened his mouth to speak . . . and then closed it.

"Spencer?" Victoria cocked her head at a questioning angle. When she did, a long lustrous lock of her hair fell forward over her shoulder, entrancing Spencer. "Are you all right?"

He chuckled. "I have never been more all right or worse off, Victoria, than I am at this very moment. And I don't even mean physically, tangled up here with this dog."

As though she weren't even aware of her own actions, Victoria slowly and purposefully smoothed her hair back from her face. She behaved as though he were a madman she didn't dare look away from because he would suddenly attack her if she did. "I have no idea anymore what you mean, Spencer."

"I mean, Victoria, that I—" Sudden irritation seized him. "Could you please move this bit of netting from my face? Yes, that one. Over the sutures. Carefully. Thank you." She did . . . and waited. Spencer screwed up his courage and rushed the words out. If he didn't say them now, he never would. "I said it doesn't matter that they know because I suddenly realize I love you, and I will not live without you. So, who the baby's father is doesn't matter. You see, you are my wife, the baby is ours, and I will dare anyone to say differently. There. I've said it."

CHAPTER 17

Spencer didn't know what he expected her to say or do, but he certainly hadn't factored in the possibility that she would stare at him with owl-rounded eyes and a general air of disbelief. "No, I'm sorry, but you do not get to just say that. You don't. You've, you've"—she waved a hand around and over him as she talked—"taken too many hits to your head. You don't know what you're saying. Spencer, you have a responsibility to your duchy, to six hundred years of Whitfields—"

"Darling, shut up." He'd said it with the utmost affection and respect for her. "I just said I love you, woman, and the baby is mine. I am the present duke, so what I say goes in this generation. I daresay this baby won't be the first questionable Whitfield to inherit, but that is neither here nor there. I have said it doesn't matter, and *that* is what matters."

"Do you have a headache, Spencer?" She pressed her palm to his forehead. "You could be feverish—"

"No, no, no." He shook his head to dislodge her hand. "I am fine. Of sound mind and body, discounting the attached canine, of course. Victoria, did you not *hear* what I said? I said I love you and—"

"You are a pompous ass, do you know that?" Her voice, too, was tinged with affection and respect.

"I do. But under these insanely ridiculous circumstances,

I think I am entitled, madam. After all, I have just determined the course of my duchy, the rest of my life and yours, hopefully, all while wrapped like a sausage with a panting dog who has been eating, I do believe, and if you will excuse me, excrement."

Victoria sniffed, and her voice sounded emotional. "Do you know something, Spencer?" She leaned over him, angling away from the dog, and tenderly kissed his mouth, very lightly. "I love you, too. I do. And I will probably never love you more than I do at this moment. What you just said was an amazing thing. Simply amazing."

Now Spencer didn't trust himself to speak. Not lost on him, either, was the irony that it had taken being hit over the head three times, attacked by a foul-breathed dog, and tied up like a mummy to hold him in place long enough to make him admit what his heart had known all along . . . he loved his wife. He shuddered to think what could have happened to him in the next few days had he not admitted it now. He might have been lynched or beheaded, the way it was going.

But still, the realization was too new . . . too raw, somehow. He needed more time with it, time to grow into his understanding of what he'd just said. And so, he resorted to a more immediate concern. "I take it you were the intruder in the room, Victoria. Did I hurt you? I tossed you around quite a bit."

"I'm not hurt. But you did scare me."

"I am certain I did. Why *did* you come in here?"

She looked everywhere but at him. "Well, it hardly seems important now, given what you've just said, and what I've said, but I told myself I wanted to apologize to you."

"Apologize? For what?"

She worried her fingers and stared at them. "It's not important. And it wasn't really my true reason for coming in here, anyway."

Spencer arched an eyebrow. "I see. Then what was?"

The moonshine backlit her mahogany hair, giving her a halo of vulnerability. "I wanted to sleep with you."

Though Spencer's heart gave a happy leap at her unexpected words, he could only stare at her, which was just as well given that he remained trussed up with the dog. "You wanted to sleep with me?"

"Yes. Just sleep." Her words tumbled out of her as though she feared her courage would fail her. "I know you have a headache, so I wasn't going to ask for more—"

"Victoria—"

"No, let me finish. I . . . I miss your body next to mine. You used to sleep with me sometimes in England after we"—her voice dropped to an embarrassed whisper—"made love. I liked that. The sleeping together. And the . . . other, of course. But I didn't want you to be angry with me because of what Edward said about your loving me. I didn't expect it. I certainly had no right to—"

"Victoria." Spencer's heart swelled with love for her. She'd missed him. She'd wanted his nearness. She'd come in here simply to be with him. So moved was Spencer that at first he could say nothing more than what he already had. Then, he gathered his courage. Why was saying he loved his wife the hardest thing of all for him to say? Why was admitting he needed her so difficult? And yet, it was. He didn't trust easily and this love was the most awful and intense sort of trust to extend to another person. But even knowing that, he still wanted to do exactly that.

And so, he said: "When this debacle between Neville and me is over, I would like very much to sleep with you, too, for the remainder of the night. And every night thereafter. Forever. That is, if I do not die first from this dog's breath. Good Lord."

Victoria's solution was to pet the animal. "Poor Neville. He didn't mean any real harm."

"Oh, poor Neville meant great harm, Victoria. But I don't blame him. If I believed someone meant you harm, I would react in exactly the same way he did. Although I would hope I would do so with better breath. And armed with more than my teeth."

In the next second, he realized the room had quieted and was suddenly lighter. Apparently, the accursed kerosene lamp had finally been lit by someone. He exchanged a look with Victoria and Neville, and then looked toward the foot of the bed with a degree of confidence for whom he would see. And he was right. There, clumped at the bed's foot and apparently stunned into further inaction by the sight that greeted them were Edward, the elder Redmonds, Jefferson Redmond, Hornsby, and Mr. Milton. All in their nightclothes; Mr. Redmond armed with a shotgun; Hornsby with a chamber pot.

"Great Scott!" Mr. Redmond cried. "What the devil happened here?"

"Never mind that," Mrs. Redmond fussed, rushing to her daughter's side. "Pardon me, Your Grace." She held up her trailing nightclothes as she stepped over him, cocooned there on the floor with the dog, to get to her daughter.

"Of course. Please. Don't mind me."

"Thank you." Leaning over Victoria, Mrs. Redmond put an arm around Victoria's shoulders. "Oh, honey, are you all right? Why didn't you tell me you were going to have a baby, sweetheart?"

Victoria froze. She sat close enough to Spencer that he could feel her tension. He quickly answered for her. "Because she only found out this evening earlier when Dr. Hollis examined her."

Mrs. Redmond and Victoria turned to him, both vying to be the first to say, "She did?" "I did?" Then, Victoria apparently caught on and turned her face up to her mother's. "Yes, I did. I didn't know until then. And Dr. Hollis said I was to rest, and then we didn't see you the remainder of the evening."

"But you did. I came back up with him, following supper."

Victoria stared blankly at her mother and nudged Spencer, who chanted: "We were going to tell you at breakfast today. We asked Dr. Hollis not to tell you. We wanted it to be a surprise."

"Oh, a surprise to announce at the barbecue, too. How nice," Mrs. Redmond said, sounding mollified. "But how did Edward know? He just said you didn't want it known."

Everyone turned to Edward, whose gaze darted from one to the other of the crowd. "Because I came up to their sitting room last evening the moment I arrived here from Savannah, remember?"

Mrs. Redmond considered Edward and, apparently, his explanation. She turned to her daughter. "You told him first and not me?"

"Oh, Mama, please—"

"I told my cousin, Mrs. Redmond," Spencer cut in, "quite separately from Victoria. She didn't know, until now, that Edward knew."

That apparently satisfied his mother-in-law because, looking very pleased, Mrs. Redmond straightened up and turned to her husband. "Did you hear that, Isaac? We are going to be grandparents. Come hug your daughter and tell her how much you love her."

"First, Mr. Redmond, if you would, please," Spencer quickly called out, "put that gun down." He had no wish to be blasted to kingdom come. And with him thus bound, it could hardly be sport for Mr. Redmond, at any rate.

Mr. Redmond dutifully handed the shotgun off to his son and came forward, speaking to his wife. "My love, don't you think we should first see to disentangling our son-in-law from Neville? I can't think either of them is enjoying their present arrangement." The tall, elegant, and gray-haired man, a titan of industry, stopped next to Spencer and Neville and stood there, frowning down at them as he scratched his head, which resulted in his hair standing up in gray spikes. "We might have to cut y'all apart."

Alarm screamed through Spencer. "Cut us apart . . . how?"

"What? Oh. I, of course, mean the netting . . . cut it apart. Not you and Neville. We'll cut the netting away from you since I don't think either of you would benefit from us rolling you over and over to unwind you. But, I swear, I never in all my life saw the likes of this pickle."

"I assure you, Mr. Redmond," Spencer said from the floor, "I have never in all my life been in the likes of such a pickle."

And he meant everything that had happened to him since he'd married the man's daughter.

Several hours later, on what turned out to be a pleasantly cool and sunny morning, Spencer stood slightly behind his cousin at the end of the rickety dock behind River's End. Bathed, dressed, and breakfasted, they had been excused from the house because it was being taken apart, or so it seemed, from top to bottom as Mrs. Redmond supervised the maids' cleaning and the cooks' cooking for this afternoon's infamous barbecue. The two Redmond men were on the far side of the large plantation home overseeing the roasting of the meat. And Victoria remained in bed, attended by Rosanna, and suffering from her morning sickness and resting up for the afternoon's festivities.

On the walk out here, with Neville benignly padding along beside them, Edward had, like a little boy, collected a tidy pile of smooth stones, which now resided in a stony pyramid on the dock. Employed in skipping them, one at a time, across the swamp's placid surface, he flung one and watched it skip only once before sinking. "Damn. I say, we were practically pushed outside just now, weren't we? Rather rude."

Spencer tucked his thumbs in his dark trousers' waist-band. "I didn't know you had a wish to remain inside and help Mrs. Redmond supervise the cleaning and the cooking."

Hands clamped to his slim waist, and attired in a shirt, vest, and long trousers, Edward pivoted around to show Spencer his devilish smile. "She is a lovely creature, isn't she?"

"I will personally take you apart if you make one overture to the woman."

Fighting a smirk, Edward shrugged. "You made the same threat to me last night when I told Victoria that you love her. And nothing has happened to me as yet."

"'As yet,' Edward, are the words you should concentrate on."

He grinned outright. "You do, though, don't you? Love Victoria, I mean."

"That is between my wife and me."

"You do," he chirped with supreme confidence. "And now everyone knows about the baby. That changes things, wouldn't you say?"

"I would not. But perhaps, Edward, with you apparently having nothing more to occupy you than sticking your nose in my business, you should offer your services to the men working on the other side of the house."

Edward wrinkled his nose. "Hardly. Mr. Redmond and Jefferson and their men are placing on spits those bloody carcasses for the barbecue. Do you really see me participating?"

"No. But it is a much safer pursuit than lusting after Mrs. Redmond or worrying my life. And a much more grown-up pursuit than skipping stones across the water."

"This from a man employed in merely watching me do so. You, sir, poke fun at my bit of sport because I am better at it than you are. We both know the truth of that."

"You break your mother's heart with your terrible penchant for lying, Edward."

"I do not. But speaking of grown-up pursuits, Spence, old

man, you looked quite cozy earlier this morning lying there on the floor with that dog on top of you. Though I wasn't surprised. I've known you, in your younger, more randy days, to wake up with far worse in your bedroom."

"Shut up, Edward." Still infused with a satisfaction deep inside born of having held his wife's sweet, warm body next to his for the remainder of the night, no matter what his lingering doubts might be, Spencer refused to be baited.

And yet, Edward insisted on trying. "Are you aware that is all you ever say to me? 'Shut up, Edward.'"

Spencer shrugged. "And are you aware that you never do?"

With a grunting chuckle, Edward bent over to retrieve another stone from the pile he'd laid on the dock's woodplanked deck. Neville sat hard up against the stash. "Pardon me, Neville, if you don't mind, old boy."

Ignoring Edward, the bloodhound sat with his attention focused on the leading edge of the swamp, no more than twenty yards away from the dock's end and across a green and glassy brackish stand of water.

Spencer turned his attention there, too, with a natural sense of unease for being so close to a foreign and inhospitable environment. The swamp, from here, appeared benign enough, but Spencer was not taken in. Despite being fascinating for its overgrowth of tropical trees and plants, this place held danger locked within its confines as surely as he was standing there on the dock. No doubt, and farther back in that wild jungle of plants and water, it teemed with large and hungry reptiles lying in wait for the unwary. Feeling no compunction to explore, Spencer quickly assured himself he was absolutely content to remain right here.

He watched Edward bounce another stone across the water. "Good show, Edward. Four bounces. Your best yet. Yet I half fear you'll hit a bad-tempered resident of the swamp's waters which could, in one bite, swallow us and this dock whole."

Edward spared Spencer a glance and grinned. "Surely your friend Neville would warn us if he sensed a predator in the immediate area."

Spencer noted the dog's perked ears and sustained concentration on the swamp. No doubt, he ate things that came out of there, and that accounted for his breath. "Yes, he's been following me everywhere since his attack earlier today. Either he feels a need to make it up to me, or he still believes he should keep a wary eye on me. Either way, he's a rather disconcerting presence."

"I think he believes you'll steal the silver."

"And do what with it, exactly?"

"Damn!" Edward's next stone had sunk on its first plunk. He turned to Spencer. "My arm is getting tired."

"My assessment, as well."

Abandoning that activity, Edward moved on to the next. Bent over at the waist, his knees bent and his hands braced against his knees, he peered over the dock's edge. "What say you, Spence, old man? Should we take this fancy little boat out for a spin over these pristine waters?"

"Not on your life—or without significant weaponry. But what boat?"

"Come here. This one." He motioned for Spencer to join him. "Most interesting design. Like some sort of rowboat, only not."

Spencer joined his cousin. So did Neville, now curiously looking over the edge of the dock with them. Adopting Edward's pose, Spencer saw, tied to the dock, a hideously unseaworthy little craft that didn't look as if it could hold Victoria's slight weight, much less his and Edward's, without sinking. "How does one direct the thing? Wait." He pointed to a long pole stuck in the boat, its other end extending out of the craft. "Perhaps it's poled as are the gondolas in Venice."

"Oh, I see. Yes. But it certainly doesn't resemble a gondola, does it?"

"No. And this swamp, for all its water, doesn't resemble Venice, either."

Edward was quiet a moment, then . . . "Do you think you could live here, Spencer? I mean in America. Georgia. Savannah."

As surprised as he was amused at Edward's quietly stated question, Spencer replied: "Would you care to narrow that down to a specific street and house?"

Still bent over, as was Spencer, Edward arrowed a glance his cousin's way. "Shut up, Spencer. And I'm being serious. I mean it. Could you live here?"

Spencer straightened up, and Edward followed suit. "I assume you have a reason for asking?"

To Spencer's further surprise, Edward turned increasingly red, even to the tops of his ears. "Yes, I do."

"Oh. Aha. I see. Now, what was the young lady's name you paid the call on yesterday? I forgot to ask how your visit was received."

"Very well, thank you. Miss Lucinda Barrett and her mother were duly charmed."

"I see. To the point of you wishing to stay in America?" Spencer turned serious. "Edward, you fall in and out of love so easily—"

"No, this is different." Edward forged ahead, positively animated. "I promise you it is. Miss Barrett is the epitome of femininity. She is sweet and charming and blond and her eyes are blue and she is witty and educated and so very warm and her family was very welcoming—"

"You're a titled earl, Edward. Of course they were welcoming." Spencer hated like hell to sound the voice of elder reasonableness, but with Edward, one must.

Not that he appreciated it. "You think a title is all I have to offer a woman? You think it's the only reason she would encourage me?"

"Hardly, Edward. You know me better than that. I am simply advising caution—"

"Because of the way your marriage worked out? Is that what you're saying—"

Cutting off Edward's harsh, intemperate words was Spencer, who had hauled him up to his face. "Don't you ever speak of my marriage in that manner. The circumstances are not the same and I will not—"

Cutting Spencer off was Neville, who growled and barked and yipped . . . and growled again and whined. Spencer quickly released the ruffled Edward and pivoted around, expecting to see the dog menacing them. But instead, the dog faced the swamp. He was on his feet. His long body fairly quivered with excitement, as though he were preparing to jump off the dock, right into the water. Exchanging a quick glance with Edward, Spencer followed the dog's line of sight out to the swamp . . . and gasped in surprise.

Right at the swamp's edge, and standing quietly in a boat larger but of the same make as the one tied to the dock, was a young and muscled black man dressed in tattered clothes and a sweat-banded slouch hat that had seen better days. With his powerful legs spread to maintain his balance, he evinced an air of pride and wariness. In his hand, held like a staff, was a long pole, which he obviously used to propel his craft. He neither spoke nor raised a hand in greeting . . . he merely stared.

Their own near-altercation abandoned in light of this turn of events, Edward grabbed Spencer's arm in a viselike grip and whispered: "Good Lord, how long do you suppose he's been there? And where the devil did he come from?"

Though not whispering, Spencer kept his voice down and his attention on the man. "The interior of the swamp, obviously. I think he's been there a while, too. Perhaps just out of our sight. His appearance certainly explains Neville's fixed attention on the swamp. I had thought he smelled some sort of prey."

"What do you think he wants? The fellow in the boat, I mean."

Spencer looked into Edward's fear-rounded eyes. "I assure you I have no idea."

"Well, what do we do now?"

"I suggest we greet him and ask him what he wants."

"Do you think that's wise, Spencer?"

"And why, Edward, would it not be?"

"I'm not certain. Just a natural caution. Perhaps it's the suddenness of his appearance and his continued silence. Seems . . . ominous, not quite above board."

"I hardly think we need fear him. After all, there are two of us to his one. But should we become faint-hearted and turn tail and run, I believe we could make it to the house before he seized us."

"Now you're making sport of me."

"Yes, I am. The fellow has allowed us to see him, after all, and it is daylight. And he doesn't appear to be armed. Therefore, and again, I suggest we speak to him and see what he wants."

Edward urged Spencer ahead of him. "A grand idea. Go ahead."

"Do not shove me, Edward. The last thing I need to do is fall in this awful water." Thus ruffled and irritated, Spencer straightened his vest and hitched his pants. Seeing that Neville had sat down on his haunches and wagged his tail in a friendly manner as he stared fixedly at the young man, Spencer felt more confident as he raised a hand in greeting and called out, across the water: "Hallo, out in the boat. Is there something you need?"

"You that British duke what married Miss Victoria, ain't you?" The man's voice was higher pitched than Spencer would have expected for a man his size. He sounded younger than he looked, too.

Surprised to be so quickly identified, Spencer turned to Edward, who looked as stymied as he felt and who merely shrugged. Spencer faced the man again. "Yes, I am. How did you know that?"

"Miss Cicely done tole me. She knows everything."

"Well, I don't know Miss Cicely, but she was right about that. I am John Spencer Whitfield, the Tenth Duke of Moreland, the Right Honorable the Earl of Shandsbury, Marquis of— Oof!"

Edward had elbowed him. He now smiled brightly, intensely. "I don't think he cares for a recitation of your many titles, impressive though they are, Spence, old man. It could take hours."

Spence, old man, glared at his cousin before returning his attention to the black man in the boat, who called across the water: "Miss Cicely sent me to fetch you and Miss Victoria. You got to come right now with me to see her. Got somethin' y'all needs to see."

"Good Lord," Edward hissed, "the presumption of the man."

Spencer said nothing for a moment as he assessed the situation, looking from the young man to the swamp behind him and back to the man. "And this Miss Cicely, where does she live?"

The black man pointed behind himself . . . into the swamp.

"Spencer," Edward whispered, "I don't like the sound of this at all. It could be a trap."

"It could be worse than a trap, Edward," Spencer whispered back, though he never looked away from the figure standing in the small boat. "It could be the height of ridiculousness even to consider going with him, which I am not going to do and which Victoria *certainly* is not going to do." His every sense on alert now, and feeling a prickle of danger run down his spine, Spencer called out to the boat: "I'm sorry, but I don't know who you are and—"

"My name Jubal. Miss Victoria know me. She'll tell you."

"I'm sure she will. However . . . Jubal, Miss Victoria cannot be disturbed this morning. I thank you for your invitation to go with you and see Miss Cicely, but as there is a barbecue planned for today and my wife is expecting a baby—"

"I knew that, too."

This stopped Spencer. Until early this morning, no one but he and Victoria and Edward had known she was with child. So how did this man know? Then Spencer caught himself. Of course he hadn't known. He'd merely seconded what Spencer had already said, just as he hadn't known, until Spencer told him, that he, and not Edward, was the duke who'd married Victoria. Comforted by the forthrightness of logic, Spencer good-naturedly replied: "You knew? I see. Miss Cicely again, I take it? She told you?"

"Yes, suh. She know everything."

"As you've said. However, knowing of my wife's fragile condition as you do, you can understand how she—we—cannot go with you. I hardly think it would do her any good to subject herself to the dangers of a swamp."

"Hunh. She come out here all the time to see Miss Cicely. Now, you got to go git Miss Victoria. She'll know she got to come, if'n I say she do."

"Absolutely extraordinary, Spencer. Victoria out in that swamp? I don't believe it."

"I do."

"You do?" Apparent surprise stood Edward sharply at attention.

"Yes." Though he shriveled inside with fear to think of his wife traversing the waters of the swamp, Spencer believed Jubal when he said Victoria knew him and that she would heed Jubal's invitation, as it were, to go with him now. Spencer also hated like hell where this path led. Because Edward still stared at him, Spencer added: "It makes sense when one thinks about it, Edward. Victoria lived right here on the edge of this water all her life until a few months ago. And there is the boat tied to the dock."

"None of that means Victoria makes use of the boat."

"True. But factor in Victoria's stubborn will—and her

penchant for crossing bodies of water despite the dangers to herself and being told not to do so."

"Ah. Good points, all. But the mere *thought* of her out there, Spencer."

"I know." Spencer also knew what he had to do now, so he called out to Jubal: "I'll tell Victoria you're here—"

"Hello!" Edward grabbed his arm. "You can't be serious, Spencer! Only a moment ago you said it would be the height of ridiculousness—"

"I know what I said, but I've changed my opinion." He'd spoken quietly to Edward, but again Spencer raised his voice enough to stretch his words across the water. "I will tell Victoria you are here, but first you have to tell me why Miss Cicely sent you."

The young black man's changed posture radiated surprise. Spencer pressed his point. "I have every right to ask, Jubal. If you don't tell me, I won't tell Victoria you're here." He then played a hunch. "And that would leave you no choice except to come out of the swamp and up to River's End to ask for her yourself."

Jubal's eyes widened in an evident panic. "I cain't do that, suh. You got to tell her for me. I cain't come outta the swamp."

"Are you saying you *live* out there, man?" Edward all but shouted.

Jubal's expression closed as his chest expanded with apparent offense. "Ain't to my likin'. I got no choice. Lot of us ain't got no choice." He focused again on Spencer, this time issuing orders. "You go git Miss Victoria and tell her what I said. Tell her it's about my sister."

Spencer's breath left him in a rush. His gaze locked with Edward's. Dread claimed Spencer, slowing his pulse to a thumping beat he could actually feel. "Jubal, what's your sister's name?"

"Jenny. My sister named Jenny."

"Heaven help us," Edward said under his breath.

"This be 'bout her and her baby, Sofie. You and Miss Victoria got to come. Won't take but a little time, neither. You be back long before that barbecue starts."

And suddenly, Spencer knew he had to go. So did Victoria. "All right. Wait here for us."

His brown eyes rimmed with white, Edward grabbed Spencer's arm. "Are you mad? You can't go out there. Neither can Victoria." He lowered his voice and hissed fearfully: "This could be a trap."

"I'm aware of that. But Victoria will know this man, or she won't. That's why I asked him to wait. If she doesn't recognize him—"

"Is of no import, Spencer. He could be in on the scheme, or whatever it is, that involves Sofie, and even Victoria might not know it. Once you go traipsing off with him, you'll have no one to help you."

"I do not *traipse*, Edward. Nor do I intend to go unarmed."

"Oh, I see, one gun against how many men? We don't know how many, do we?"

"Or it could be exactly as this man Jubal has said. Him and his mother. I hardly think we'll be overrun with the enemy."

"Spencer, I hate to say this, but this Jubal fellow said there are a lot of . . . *them* living out there. I mean his kind. Now, while he might be an upstanding citizen, what we don't know is how all of . . . his fellows feel. And if they're living in that swamp, there's got to be a reason."

Spencer made certain his level gaze met his cousin's. "Perhaps the reason they are has nothing to do with them, Edward. Perhaps it has more to do with people like us. White people. That swamp may be the only place Jubal and his fellows feel safe."

Edward let go of Spencer's arm. "Certainly a wretched existence for them, no doubt. I'm sorry. I . . . just worry. And I would feel the same way if that swamp were inhabited by white people, or orange people, because we don't know who the enemy is."

"I thank you for your worry, but I don't feel it's warranted as I've reasoned this out. Remember, Jubal said Victoria goes out there all the time. She must feel safe with him, with them. And she must know this swamp. That gives us two edges, so I will defer to her on this matter. It's the best I can do."

"No, the best you can do is not go. But, since you're determined, Neville and I are going with you. I can add a gun to your arsenal, and Neville has all those teeth and a short temper."

"I thank you for your offer, but neither of you is going," Spencer assured him. "Four people—or, rather, three and a dog—are more likely to be missed than two would be. At any rate, I need you here to cover for us until we get back."

Edward raised his eyebrows. "And exactly where do I tell people you two are?"

"Oh, come now, Edward. You are a most inventive fellow. You'll think of something. It shouldn't be hard, given how chaotic the household is today. Cite our need for privacy as loving newlyweds. Say we went for a walk together. Or a carriage ride. That should do it. And then keep everyone from talking to each other."

"A carriage ride? And should someone question one of the grooms and he knows nothing of having brought around a carriage for you, a carriage still clearly visible in the inventory? What should I tell them then?"

"Obviously, Edward," Spencer said through gritted teeth, "the carriage ride was a bad suggestion. I will instead rely on your penchant toward . . . *inventiveness* to adequately confuse and keep off our trail anyone who should ask. I trust you can do so brilliantly since I expect to be hard pressed to come up with answers to the questions I'm likely to get regarding the tales you told to the lady callers in Savannah. I refer to my alleged infirmities. A tropical fever that left me covered in red spots, Edward?"

He suddenly looked ill. "You know about those stories, then?"

"Obviously I do or I would not bring—"

"Hey, over there!" Along with Edward, Spencer pivoted to face Jubal, who glanced around nervously. "You got to go git Miss Victoria and come with me now in that there jon-boat." He, of course, pointed to the flimsy piece of carved wood riding queasily atop the brackish water and tied to the dock.

Spencer's heart sank. He'd thought he and Victoria would go with Jubal in his larger, sturdier craft. "How are we supposed to do that, Jubal? Perhaps that . . . pretentious hollowed-out log would hold my wife's weight but not our combined weight. It will sink."

"It ain't sunk yet. I ride in it with Miss Victoria all the time. Tell her I'll wait just outta sight where cain't no one see me. Hurry, now. We ain't got much time."

CHAPTER 18

Seated in the stern of the jonboat, and clothed again in the same pants and shirt of Jefferson's she'd worn on her last trip into the swamp, Victoria openly enjoyed the sight of Spencer's backside as he poled the craft through the swamp. The poor man. He'd been shocked when she'd appeared in her masculine attire, yet she'd quickly quelled his protests with one question: *How would you fare, Your Grace, in that jonboat if you were attired in a dress?* With his protest silenced, though his lips remained compressed with disapproval, they'd quickly stolen down a back stairway and out of the chaotically busy house. From there, the two of them had hurriedly made their way along the fringes of the more civilized border of River's End down to the dock. And now, Victoria tried to see the swamp through Spencer's eyes. How terribly strange and frightening it all must be. Not that he would admit it, big, strong man that he was.

She wondered if he appreciated the wild beauty of the place. She thought not. He was too terrified of the very real possibility of being eaten by an alligator at any moment. But still, what was Spencer seeing? The determined rays of sunlight dappling the glittering greenery, the musty earth and the brownish water alike? The knobby cypress knees poking their conical heads up as if they must surface to breathe?

Buzzing and flitting insects of every size and appetite crazily circling the occupants of the jonboat and occasionally lighting on them? The tangled vines hanging down like so many ropy tentacles? Or the giant fronds of stunted palms dripping menacingly with a dew that slithered down their spines?

All around them, the swamp was alive with life. A bird called in a strange warbling voice. A shy snake of astonishing size slithered through the underbrush and disappeared inland. And an occasional bubble broke the water's calm surface as a fish gulped an unwary insect.

She loved it in here. Victoria sat, with her knees together, her hands clasped in her lap, and again settled her gaze on her husband's broad back as he followed Jubal's lead and poled through the murky waters and dripping air of the swamp. Sweat had plastered his shirt to his skin, making the fabric almost transparent where it clung to him. Such an inspiring sight the man was . . . his long and muscled legs encased in the black Hessians he wore, the pleasant masculine whole of him.

A small part of Victoria's smile resulted from Spencer's explanation for his ease with poling. Grinning rakishly at her, he'd cited merrily drunken incidents in Venice in his misspent youth. No doubt, he'd misspent it every chance that had come his way. In some ways, Victoria wished she'd known him when he was younger. But for the most part, she was happier to have him as the fine man he had become.

She marveled at her own happy mood, given the troublesome nature of their present mission. But she couldn't help it. Life was so different today. Her husband loved her, and she loved him. This knowledge made the world a brighter place, a friendlier place, even this swamp. Victoria saw its jeweled aspects now through new eyes and sensibilities. Had the swamp always been this lovely? This jade green, this blood red, this velvety brown? Why hadn't she noticed before the soft yellow of the sun's rays? Or the magnolia-white splotches of water-lily blooms? So very . . . alive.

Startling her was how alive she felt, too. How serene and secure. She had tarried in bed this morning until the sickness had passed, but she'd spent the time looking, with joy, down the years ahead of her and Spencer's life together. She had envisioned their children, happy and running in the fresh air at Wetherington's Point. She'd seen them pink-cheeked and chortling on sleigh rides through the winter snows in England. She could picture this scene thanks to her family's occasional winters in New York City. She knew firsthand that snow was cold and blindingly white, a muffling blanket. Lovely. The thought of snow brought her thoughts forward to the Christmas presents her and Spencer's children would tear open with happy delight under the indulgent eyes of their parents.

Victoria brought her thoughts forward to that most amazing of moments much earlier this morning when Spencer had simply reversed himself, when he'd said he would claim her child as his own, birthmark or no, despite everything he stood for, despite hundreds of years of birthmarked Whitfields, despite hundreds of years of blueblood purity and pride and honor—

Victoria's smile abruptly fled. She could not allow him to do that. Yes, he'd said he loved her, which had freed her to admit she loved him, too. And, certainly, she'd been thrilled to learn she would not be put aside, not cast adrift with a broken heart and in a frightening world alone with only her child and her allowance to sustain them both. But not once—not one selfish once—had she given the first thought to what Spencer's sudden decision would do to him. After all, what if this child was a boy and clearly Loyal's and was named the heir? Why, it would be a travesty, no matter how much she would love her child, to pass the duchy on to him.

Even worse, what if she and Spencer had a second child,

another boy, the rightful heir but one who could not inherit because he wasn't, publicly, the firstborn? How soon would it be before Spencer came to regret his decision? Dear God, what would that do to him every day of his life when he knew his duchy was going to Loyal's blood and not his own? And what would it do to her and Spencer every time they looked at her firstborn, or even each other? She knew the answer: It would tear their love apart. Victoria covered her face with her hands and shook her head. Only by exerting a strong effort of will did she not cry out and alert Spencer to her distress.

She should have made more than a token protest when he'd said it didn't matter whose child she carried. Of course it mattered—and in every way she could imagine. Spencer would soon realize that, if he hadn't already. *Why* had he said he would acknowledge this child, no matter what? And why hadn't *she* thought before now about why he might have? Victoria fisted her hand and gently conked herself in the head. *I am such an awful person. Just awful. I'm selfish and spoiled, that's what. All I saw was a neat solution being handed to me, and I took it.*

That he loved her enough to say what he had only made Victoria love him all the more. And that was exactly why she couldn't allow him to do this wonderfully noble thing he'd said he'd do. She rushed her thoughts into the future, to the day this child she carried was born. She pictured Spencer staring down at the child and trying to keep off his face the knowledge that it was not his and that it did, in the end, matter. It mattered to her, too, but for Spencer's sake.

She had to tell him they were right back where they'd started . . . to the not knowing, to the doubts, to the not being able to be together. Victoria's bright and sunny world she'd created only moments ago evaporated, along with the determined rays of sunshine as Spencer poled them smoothly under an especially dense canopy of cypress, pine, and oak, and into the miasma of the swamp's sulfurous air. She had to do what was necessary. She had, at the very least, to tell him that she would release him from his declaration, should her child turn out not to be his.

"It's not much farther to Miss Cicely's, Spencer," was her overture to speaking her heart and mind. Her breaking heart. Her protesting mind. With bittersweet pleasure, she gazed upon her silent husband's finely formed and masculine self. Suddenly, to her, he looked so . . . achingly fragile, almost transparent in his lightness.

Suddenly she doubted if this moment was the proper time for such a discussion. Maybe she should put it off until another day. No, that was the way of a coward. If she waited, she might lose her courage and never speak up. She had to do it now. Swallowing hard, gathering her courage, she spoke up again. "Spencer, did you hear what I just said? It's not far now."

"Um-hmm," he grunted, no doubt concentrating totally on his poling task and looking out for alligators. She'd explained the reptiles slept or lazed about during the day and hunted at night, but he was not to be mollified . . . especially after a particularly monstrous example had leered at their passage earlier on and then slid easily into the water as they passed.

"Spencer, I have something I have to say to you."

"Then say it."

So bittersweet, the realization was to her, that not two minutes ago, before her own painful realization of what she had to say and do, Victoria would have smiled indulgently at his rigid intensity. But right now she could not force her mouth to perform the happy task. "Spencer, I've made up my mind about something."

"And what would that be?"

"It's about us."

"Us? Everything has been decided between us."

"No, I'm afraid not."

"Victoria, although I have no idea to what you're referring, I must ask: Do you really think this is the time for this? More to the point, have you seen that blasted alligator anywhere?" He hadn't once glanced her way over his shoulder. The man was endearingly terrified.

"No. Quit worrying about him. He probably went in the other direction."

"I should like confirmation of that."

"I'm sorry, but they do not generally announce their intentions."

"The bloody monsters should be made to—by law, if necessary."

She loved him so much. The realization was blinding in its intensity. But now, she had to end it. What a cruel fate: to yearn for love, to be shown love, to win love . . . and then to destroy love willfully. How, she wondered, was what she intended to say now any different from the act of putting an early end to her baby's fragile life? She remembered those horrible moments all too well . . . the parlor at Wetherington's Point, her misunderstanding Spencer and thinking he meant for her to undergo an abortion. And now, here she was, in a sense, doing exactly that . . . ending love. "Spencer, I can't let you claim this baby if it's not yours."

"Madam, who or what I claim as mine is not up to you."

Victoria could only stare in exasperation as Spencer smoothly lifted the long, dripping pole from port and dipped it into the water on the starboard side of the jonboat, expertly seeking resistance, finding it, and moving them through the water. The easy play of his muscles, the vigorous flexing of them, was very affecting. Still, Victoria had to admit that this was not a sight she would ever have expected to see . . . the Tenth Duke of Moreland poling through a Georgia swamp. "Spencer, you must listen to me. You cannot claim this baby if it is not yours."

"And you must listen to me. I have said I would, and I will."

"No you will not."

"Victoria, do you see what I'm doing up here? And have you looked around? Do you actually see where we are?"

"I'm fully aware of where we are, Spencer, and it's the perfect place for this discussion since neither of us can stomp off angrily. I'm serious about not allowing you to claim this child if it's not yours. And don't you dare tell me to shut up, as you do Edward. I won't be shut up."

"I am fully and painfully aware of that, madam."

"However," she said with sober determination, "I will have my say. I have been thinking—"

"Dear God."

Behind his back, she made a face at him. "I have been *thinking* should this child I carry not be yours but be male and you claim him as yours, he will be your heir. I worry how you'd subsequently feel, should a second male child be born to us, the true heir who cannot then inherit. I ask myself what that knowledge will do to you." Hot, heartbreaking tears pricked at Victoria's eyes. "I could not bear knowing what it would do. And I can't allow you to live with such hurt. I won't."

"A very interesting argument, madam. And convincing. Put that noble way, I do see your point."

She hadn't expected this. She'd expected more pomposity and denials . . . had perhaps hoped for them. But they were not to be. "I beg your pardon?"

"I'm saying you are absolutely right, my dear. In fact, jolly good thinking. All right, then, I won't claim this child if it's not mine; and you will be free to live your life elsewhere in England, divorced from me. Will that make you happy?"

Of course, Spencer assured his thumping heart, he'd said that simply to get her to leave off the subject. It wasn't open to discussion—and especially not in this alien and harrowing environment. Good Lord, the place teemed with predators. It was like being dropped into the Roman Colosseum, in the fight of their life, and all his darling wife wished to do, as lions and tigers and gladiators rushed them, was talk about the state of their marriage. Unbelievable.

His back to an ominously silent Victoria, Spencer waited, half believing he'd be pushed, at any moment, over the bow of the jonboat and into the brackish water that, he just knew, teemed with ravenous reptilian life. Or . . . she could shoot him. Not that she was armed. But he was. He blatantly checked, though he still felt his pistol's reassuring weight at his hip, to see if it still resided in its holster. No sense giving an incensed woman a ready weapon.

"Your gun is still there, sir. I'm not going to shoot you." Very chilly voice, despite her dulcet Southern tones.

"You will imagine my relief, madam." His voice . . . droll, British, upper class. Teasing. Of course he didn't want—and would not permit—her to leave him under any circumstances . . . even if he had to cling, begging, to her skirts. However, he remained prepared to die hideously before he would admit that to her. Still, she deserved what he'd said. Did she not think him a grown man who knew his mind and his heart? He'd said he would accept her child as his, and so the matter was closed. He would not revisit it.

Just then, up ahead, Jubal signaled that they were to pole to the right. Spencer waved his understanding.

"Miss Cicely's cabin is around this bend."

Her chill tone of voice had Spencer's grin widening. The brackish water should be freezing more and more with every word she spoke. "Thank you, my dear. That is indeed good news."

He meant it, too, as he turned the boat in the direction indicated. Until now, they'd traversed an especially narrow tributary, one that had allowed overhanging vegetation to brush menacingly over one's face and neck. A starkly frightening experience. Spencer had been certain, though he'd refused to let on, with each touch of something against his skin that a snake or spider of fantastic proportions and evil intent had fallen on him. So it was with infinite relief that he now saw the widening pool of water ahead that afforded one a more open vista and assured more maneuverability should this be, as Edward had feared, a trap.

Spencer feared the same thing. He was far from oblivious to the possibility. Given the appallingly unwelcoming environment of this overgrown jungle, a dangerous stand of water such as this one was the perfect place to commit a murder and get away with it. One could simply claim the wildlife got the victim. Or perhaps the victim drowned. Or became lost and blundered into unforgiving quicksand or, again, a hungry reptile.

Or, worse, a nasty-tempered serpent, such as a water moccasin. On the way into the swamp, Victoria had explained these creatures to him, regaling him with tales of how the snakes sometimes slithered out of the water and into a boat—right into one's boots . . . just because they could.

The indignity of it all was hair-raising. Damn Edward and Victoria, anyway, for putting notions of murder and hostile wildlife into his mind. Between his cousin and his wife and their dire tales, Spencer pronounced himself absolutely jumpy. And then, to top it off, Victoria had renewed that nonsense about the child she carried. He believed he had settled that account at about four o'clock this morning. But even if he hadn't, this moment was hardly the appropriate one for a discussion of the laws of primogeniture, now was it?

More appropriate to the setting was how to describe what lay before him as the watery avenue opened and revealed not only Miss Cicely's cabin—he realized now he'd expected only the one—but an entire village of rough-hewn and elevated cabins, some at the water's edge, some farther back on apparent land but still raised on stilts to several feet above the water's surface and—even more incredulously—built into the sturdy lower branches of huge trees. Amazing. A network of piers and jetties and docks and catwalks and ladders seemed to connect each cabin with the others, much like streets and sidewalks. Even now, the dark-skinned and soberly staring denizens of all ages and sizes slowly emerged from various dwellings to watch the approach of the two jonboats.

Even more amazing than this unexpected village was the grottolike or cavelike feel of the place. To Spencer, it seemed they existed under an overturned woven basket. Despite glimmers of sunshine that broke through in thin rays and speckled the scene, the treetops had grown together in such a way that one could imagine a giant having actually woven the thick branches into a naturally protective embracing dome. He found himself wondering if this was the only such community in this swamp. Certainly it was the first one they'd come to, but that did not mean there weren't others situated down other meandering and watery offshoots.

"Victoria," Spencer said quietly over his shoulder as they glided ever nearer a long pier Jubal had tied up to and motioned them toward. "This is the most astonishing and unbelievable sight I've ever seen."

"Yes. It is, isn't it?" Her voice held a note of pride and sympathy. "They've done so well for themselves in many ways. But, still . . . the poor souls."

"Indeed. Why *are* they all out here? Even in London, in the poorest sections, I've never seen anything like this."

"True. They've banded together out here for protection, really, and to be among their own kind with no outside interference. For some of them, it was simply choice. No, that's not true. No other choices really existed, especially for those like Jubal."

"He said something earlier about that when we first met. He said this was his home but not by his choice or liking. What happened?"

"Oh, it was awful, Spencer. Awful. Three white men—drunk, trashy sorts—caught his sweet little wife alone on a country lane and raped and then killed her."

Anguish tore at Spencer's heart. "The bastards!"

"Yes. Callie. She'd never hurt a soul."

"What did Jubal do?" Spencer knew in his heart what he'd do if such a thing happened to his wife.

"He caught them, one at a time, at night and slit their throats."

Though he winced at the brutality, Spencer also nodded. His thinking had been along those same lines. "And now he's wanted for murder. That's why he was so nervous about being seen out of the swamp."

"Yes. He'd be lynched on sight. But he's safe in here. No sensible white man dares to venture in here. But those who have . . . haven't come out."

Though, on the one hand, this turnabout form of justice seemed entirely fair, alarm raised the hairs at the back of Spencer's neck. Despite being engaged in bringing the jonboat alongside the dock, where Jubal already waited for Spencer to toss him the line so he could secure the craft, he risked a quick glance over his shoulder at his wife. "A lovely story, Victoria, when here I am, one of the whitest men you'll ever see."

"Uninvited white men, I mean. If you're invited, and you were, then you should be fine." Her blue eyes glittered with humor.

He focused again on the task at hand but said: "You're quite enjoying this, aren't you, my dear?"

"I have no idea what you're talking about. But if I were you, I wouldn't stray too far from my side."

"Have I yet?"

"No. Oh, there's Miss Cicely!" Victoria abruptly stood in the boat and excitedly waved. "Miss Cicely, hello! It's so good to see you! How are you?"

The jonboat's response to her enthusiasm was to rock threateningly from side to side and frighten the life out of Spencer—for his pregnant wife's sake, of course—and have him insisting stridently: "Victoria, be careful. Sit down before you fall down."

Of course, she did neither. Instead, as Spencer threw the line to Jubal and he had no more than caught it, she scrambled past Spencer and crabbed up a ladder to the dock above. Spencer firmed his lips together in determination and followed after her. Above him, he heard the sounds of a happy reunion. From the babble of voices greeting his ears, he surmised that everyone was talking at once and laughing—until *he* pulled himself head and shoulders above the dock's planked deck. An immediate silence fell over the assemblage. Inhaling for courage, Spencer hauled himself up onto the precariously swaying dock, constructed seemingly of scrap pieces of wood and rusted nails.

From a few paces away, Victoria stood facing him, smiling hugely and sincerely, her hands clasped together in front of her. Behind her and to both sides ranged a veritable sea of dark faces that seemed to run the length of the pier. No one seemed inclined to greet him. Or kill him. Some seemed merely curious; others were shy; and, still others, defiant, even hostile. A few did smile at him, but no one spoke to him. Spencer settled his gaze on Victoria's face, intending to take his cues from her. She subtly darted her gaze to her right, to the older woman standing next to her.

Spencer followed suit, seeing a tall, slender, attractive woman of color with her black hair pulled back tightly from her face, perhaps secured at the nape of her neck. Sober of expression and possessing impossibly high cheekbones, her dark eyes radiated intelligence and inherent sensuality. Dressed in a clean skirt of homespun and a simple blouse with a drawstring neckline, she separated from the throng flanking her and walked with gliding grace toward Spencer. Here then, he knew, was Miss Cicely . . . who knew everything, according to her son. It suddenly struck Spencer what a loving tribute that was to his mother.

The woman stopped in front of him and quietly ran her assessing gaze up and down him, from his head to his boots and back again. Spencer had no choice but to submit, even when Miss Cicely slowly walked around him as if he were a prize bull and made little noises like *tsk-tsk* and *hmmm* and *um-hmm*. Neither appreciative nor demeaning, but sounds a doctor might make during a patient's examination. Frowning, Spencer caught Victoria's attention. She winked at him and nodded reassuringly. Apparently, Spencer surmised, this was some test he must pass.

When Miss Cicely once again stood in front of him, she settled her hands at her waist, raised her head and looked him in the eye. "I know now whose baby my Victoria got growing in her belly and whether it be a boy baby or a girl baby."

Victoria's gasp arrowed Spencer's attention her way. "Why, Miss Cicely," she said, in a pout, "I asked you that when I was out here before. And you said you didn't know."

In one fluid movement that made her skirt sway, the woman turned to Victoria. "That's right, baby, and that's because I didn't know." Her voice and mannerisms softened considerably, revealing the depth of her caring for Victoria. Reason enough to like her, Spencer believed. "Sometimes it takes a while for 'the sight' to come to me. And sometimes it don't come at all, you know that. And sometimes I got to see the man before I know. That's just how it works."

Spencer looked on with cynicism coloring his reactions. Miss Cicely could tell who the father was and the sex of the child just by looking at the man? Why, if she had any degree of accuracy, she could make a fortune among the peers in London. Still, he found all this rather fantastic. But not for all the diamonds in the crown jewels would he voice that opinion out loud in this place.

"Well, child?" Miss Cicely questioned Victoria. "You want to know?"

Looking bereft, Victoria covered her face with her hands and spoke in a muffled voice through them. "Not if it's going to be an answer I don't want to hear."

"The truth is the truth, child. Got to face it." Chuckling,

clearly teasing, Miss Cicely shrugged her shoulders. "But it don't make me no never-mind. I won't tell you, if that's how you feel."

Spencer watched silently, trying to decide if he wanted to know the answer. No one had asked him. Victoria quickly pulled her hands away from her face and darted her anxious gaze between him and Miss Cicely. "No. You have to tell us, Miss Cicely. You just have to. You're right: it's best I—we—know."

"Hmm," the older woman said. She pivoted around to face Spencer. "You want to know? Both of you got to want to know."

Startled that Miss Cicely seemed to have picked up on his thoughts—pure coincidence, he assured himself—he found he did want to know. Whether or not he would believe her was another thing. But even if he hadn't wanted to know and had said as much, he feared Victoria would later kill him in his sleep. Put that way, what choice did he have? Spencer assumed a formal stance and bowed politely in respect. "I and my wife would be honored, Miss Cicely, if you would give us the benefit of your knowledge."

Holding her skirts out, the stately woman returned his gesture with a curtsy that was as good as any Spencer had seen at court. "As you wish." Relinquishing her pose, she straightened up and said: "The baby she carries in her belly is yours"—over his own gasp, Spencer heard Victoria's—"and it's a boy baby."

With that startling—stunning—announcement, Miss Cicely turned her back on him and walked regally back toward an astonished Victoria and the parting crowd. Victoria grabbed Miss Cicely and hugged her, kissing the woman's cheek enthusiastically. "Oh, thank you, thank you. I've been so worried and scared."

Miss Cicely pulled back and shook a finger in Victoria's face. "I know you have. But you ain't got no call to be thankin' me. I didn't make it so. I just told you what I see.

But, listen here, child, don't you go misbehavin' no more in ways where you got to worry, you hear me?"

Instantly contrite—to Spencer's utter shock—Victoria looked down at her lace-up boots. "Yes, ma'am. I won't. I'm . . . married and . . . happy."

Spencer's chest swelled with emotion to hear Victoria acknowledge her feelings out loud. He watched as, with a gesture of great affection, Miss Cicely smoothed Victoria's baby curls away from her temple. "I know you're happy, child. You got reason to be. This here baby is a good strong boy. Like his daddy. And don't you worry none about losin' your babies like your mama done. I don't see none of that for you."

Victoria's wonderfully blue eyes widened. "How did you know I was worrying about that? I never said—"

"What you doin' askin' me that?" Looking vexed, Miss Cicely clamped her hands to her waist. "I know what you thinkin' before you do, most of the time. Now, go on over there and hug your man."

Victoria shyly gazed at Spencer from under cover of her long and thick eyelashes. His heart full, he smiled back as she started toward him. But Spencer still had his doubts, which he would keep private. He tried to convince himself Miss Cicely was simply guessing. Or telling them what she had to know they wanted to hear. She didn't really know everything. She couldn't. No one would know until the baby was born and—

"Hold on right there, child." Miss Cicely raised a hand that stopped Victoria, whose eyes widened with apprehension. Spencer tensed and looked around, ready to reach for his gun, if need be. "What's that I hear?" Miss Cicely cocked her head as if listening for some sound only she could hear. Suddenly, she pivoted to face Spencer. "You doubting me right now in your head. But you mark my words," Miss Cicely said to Spencer, shaking a finger at him, "this baby boy is yours. In my mind's eye, I saw its little pecker. A big strong boy. Got the black hair and eyes of his daddy."

Completely amazed, yet still skeptical, Spencer suddenly realized the perfect test that would satisfy him. "Miss Cicely, you must understand how . . . startling your, uh, gift is to me. Can you just please tell me how you *know* the child is mine? I mean, besides the color of his hair and eyes."

Hearing himself speak of the child Victoria carried did something warm and strange to Spencer's heart. He was going to be a father. The unborn child now had an identity. A burst of fatherly love and joy nearly shook Spencer in his boots, but he did his best not to show it. It simply was not done to display emotion in public.

But apparently he was transparent to Miss Cicely, who smiled broadly and nodded knowingly at him. Spencer felt certain he'd fallen into her trap more so than she had his. "Land sakes, you talking about that mark, ain't you?"

Shocked, his jaw all but dropping open, Spencer sought Victoria's gaze. She'd said earlier she'd already asked Miss Cicely about the child and who the father was. No doubt, she'd told Miss Cicely then, too, about the birthmark it must have to be his. There was no other explanation.

"I never, ever told her about the birthmark, Spencer, I swear it on my grandmother's grave."

He arched an eyebrow. "The same grandmother's grave you swore on a few nights ago when you said you'd stay seated in that chair and yet did not?"

Her eyes widened, and she lowered her gaze to watch herself pluck nervously at her brother's shirt. "All right, perhaps my other grandmother, whom I love more."

"Whom you *love* more? Not *loved*? She hasn't passed on, I take it?"

"Oh, no, she's very much alive. You'll meet her today at the barbecue. So I will swear to you, on my grandmother's *heart,* that I didn't tell Miss Cicely, Spencer. I didn't."

"No, she didn't. She don't need to," Miss Cicely assured

Spencer—and then rocked him further by adding: "You ain't told her where the mark shows up on a baby, have you? You ain't told her why she cain't see it on you."

Dammit all to hell, Victoria could have told Miss Cicely all of this, but Spencer would not, in this place, expose the woman. "No, I haven't," he admitted.

Miss Cicely grinned like a contented cat. "It's on the head. The baby's scalp. Right about heah." She pointed to just behind her left ear. "It's red, and it look like the shape of England. It show through a new baby's thin hair, and that's how you know. But on a man like you, your hair covers it, keeps it safe."

An intense waiting silence permeated the crowd. Even the loudly buzzing insects all around them stopped as if they too awaited his verdict. The air of expectancy billowed and thickened . . . "Spencer?" The plaintive voice was Victoria's.

With what she'd said only minutes ago as they were pol-ing their way here uppermost in his thoughts, Spencer set-tled his gaze on his wife. "She's right."

Triumphant, Miss Cicely smiled broadly and turned to the crowd, raising her hands like a preacher exhorting heaven. In the next second, a great cry and laughing burst of joy claimed the crowd. Pats on the back and hugging and dancing ensued. At the front of the crowd, her hands over her mouth, her blue eyes dancing joyously, Victoria held Spencer's gaze.

Just then, Jubal, who Spencer realized had been standing quietly behind him after securing the jonboat, strutted past him, following his mother. "I tole you she know everything."

"And you were right," Spencer agreed readily.

In the next instant, and catching him off guard, Spencer's arms were full of his happily shrieking wife. Given her running momentum, the impact of her slight body with his more solid one staggered him back a few heart-stopping, stumbling steps. Exactly where was the end of the damned dock in relation to where he stood with his arms full of excited woman? Not that it seemed to matter to Victoria as she climbed right up him and wrapped her arms around his neck and her legs around his middle. She apparently intended to kiss him senseless, right in front of the appreciative crowd. Trying to hold on to her, or pull her away, for that matter, was like trying to corral a cat. She was everywhere.

"I told you, Spencer," Victoria cried, kissing his neck and his jaw and his chin. "I told you this baby was yours—"

"You did nothing of the sort," he accused good-naturedly. "Only a few minutes ago—really, Victoria, move your hand; we are being watched—you gave me that—I said stop that—noble speech about how you couldn't allow me to claim—now, I really must insist—"

"Victoria." The single word—her name spoken as a command coming out of the mouth of Miss Cicely—worked like a charm. Victoria froze, her blue eyes wide and only inches away from Spencer's face. He looked around his wife to the older black woman. "This child," Miss Cicely was saying as she poked a brown finger at her own chest, "didn't raise you to act like some no-account white trash. You git down off that man and git him and yo'self on over heah. We got some serious talkin' to do now. Got something to show you that you need to see."

"Yes, ma'am." Instantly obedient again, still much to Spencer's surprise, Victoria slid down him as he loosened his grip enough to allow her to do so and yet still support her. Once she stood on her own two feet and at his side, she soberly adjusted her brother's shirt and pants as though she were garbed in a ball gown of the finest silk.

Amused and amazed, Spencer affectionately touched his finger to the tip of his wife's nose. "I really must have Miss Cicely teach me that trick, the one that gets you to behave."

With a playful, endearing lift of her chin, Victoria wrinkled her nose at him and said, sweetly, "Shut up, Spencer."

With that, and accompanied by his chuckle, she strutted,

much like Jubal just had, after Miss Cicely. Spencer happily fell in step behind her, feasting his eyes on her sweetly swaying bottom as she sashayed through the parted crowd, which protectively, it seemed, closed in behind them.

CHAPTER 19

That sunny and pleasantly cool afternoon, the gala event at River's End unfolded beautifully and without a hitch. Attired in a new gown of gray silk with lace trim and a modest hoop skirt . . . with a generous waistline . . . Victoria stood with Spencer in the shade of her favorite big oak, a tree she'd spent many a happy hour in her childhood playing under or climbing on—sometimes, to her mother's horror, all the way to the top. In one hand, Victoria held a plate of the best barbecue River's End had to offer. But it was possible only to pick at the food as she needed a free hand to offer in greeting to the staggering number of their well-wishers—all while also conducting a whispered argument with her husband, who was just then holding forth in a hissing whisper.

"We were lucky that our little outing into the swamp this morning went undetected, Victoria. We are also lucky to have made it out alive, given the reptilian terrors lurking about, and even with Jubal's help. So I see no reason to tempt fate again today by having my wife—forgive my indelicacy, but my *pregnant* wife—become a pawn in a madman's game."

"Do you think I wish to be a pawn? I was not given a choice, Spencer."

"I understand that. But I will go in your stead."

"No you will not. You don't know the city like I do, where he lives or—"

"You will draw me a map, and I will go myself."

"Draw you a map? And how would I explain that to these hundred or so people here?"

"I did not say you must gather a crowd around you and make an announcement of our intentions. We could retire to some discreet place for such an activity. But, really, Victoria, as a duchess, you must get past this need to explain yourself to people. You command, and they accept and obey."

"Not here, Spencer. These people have known me all my life. They're not about to let me get away with sticking my nose in the air now."

"Be that as it may, you are a duchess, and they will treat you accordingly, or they will answer to me."

Though she secretly adored her husband for his stance regarding her, Victoria still felt on the verge of screaming her frustration with this arrogant peer of a man. If she had any gumption at all, she told herself, she would politely ask him to hold her plate while she shook the fool out of him. She knew, however, that all she would succeed in doing, given the difference in their sizes, would be to rattle her own eyeballs and teeth. "I swear to you, Spencer, you are the most maddening man I ever—"

"*I* am maddening, madam? *I* am?"

"Yes, you are. I promise you I do not know how much longer I can stand here. I want to toss this plate aside and run for the house and change my clothes and get on a horse—"

"The madness continues." Spencer sounded so long-suffering. "Get on a horse, Victoria? You? In your condition? No. Out of the question, madam."

When he called her "madam," Victoria knew, his mind was closed. "I have been riding since I got here, Spencer."

"You what?" He was no longer whispering. "I haven't seen you ride—"

"Shh. Lower your voice. People will think we're having a disagreement."

"We *are* having a disagreement, Victoria."

"We are not. Spencer, for heaven's sake, be careful with your plate. And you, sir, have not seen me ride because you've been here only a week, during which time my every free moment has been spent nursing you."

"Only because you or others insist on bashing me over the head with heavy objects. And also because your dog attacked me."

She ignored that. It wasn't really relevant right now. "Before you arrived, I had gone out riding with my father and brother. It's one of my favorite pastimes, so I could hardly tell them no when they asked me to go, now could I?"

"You risked your health and our child by riding a horse— a creature that could throw you and injure you?"

Offended, Victoria stood taller. "Our horses don't throw people. They're very well behaved. Besides, Miss Cicely said it wouldn't hurt the baby."

Spencer stared at her. "Well, then, there's the final authority for us."

"Don't you dare say anything about her, Spencer. She'll know if you do. You, of all people, after this morning, ought to be aware of her gifts. If she says I won't lose it, I won't lose it. And furthermore, I don't wish to speak with you anymore right now."

"Fine by me," Spencer griped, stabbing his fork into a hunk of shredded pork and poking it into his mouth. As he chewed—Victoria saw the angry flexing of his jaw—he stared off over the grounds and ignored her.

It was just as well. Angry beyond belief herself, Victoria somehow still managed to smile radiantly and nod her head politely as various aunts, uncles, cousins, her friends and her parents' friends—all well-heeled guests from among Savannah society's elite ranks—strolled by and sent further congratulations her and Spencer's way. All he did was glare and chew.

Earlier, her father had offered the formal toasts and announcements—as much as daring anyone present to have an ill word to say about his daughter or the scandal that had sent her across an ocean. Certainly, she had returned in triumph, the wife of a duke and a mother-to-be. She and Spencer had decided not to tell anyone yet the sex of the baby. How would they explain how they knew that? At any rate, Victoria was once again accepted into the circle of family and friends—although one part of her still wanted to tell everyone present that she hadn't given one whit for what they'd thought of her before. But that sentiment, she knew, was a sleeping dog best left undisturbed.

And so the afternoon had worn on until now. While the guests relaxed and visited and ate, they strolled the grounds and renewed friendships or just chatted and gossiped. All around, exuberant children ran to and fro, their happy, or unhappy, shrieks punctuating the adult conversations.

"Perhaps I spoke hastily," Spencer blurted into the angry silence between him and Victoria. "I have the utmost respect for Miss Cicely's abilities"—he said this loudly, as if he believed his conciliatory words would carry on the air all the way to Miss Cicely, who would then not curse him—"and I can readily see that you are in excellent health, Victoria. But, call me a fool for wishing to keep you thus. Along those lines—Oh, hello, there," Spencer said through the gritted teeth of his smile as he bowed to an elderly, cherubic, white-haired Southern matriarch who set about regaling him with her dislike of the British, all while offering her congratulations on his and Victoria's marriage and their coming happy event.

As she was hustled away by her embarrassed daughter, the woman's parting shot was what a handful Victoria had always been for her parents. Spencer agreed heartily with her and turned to Victoria, who, incensed, watched the old horse leave. "My point, Victoria, is we are the guests of honor and the focus of unrelenting attention. Given that, how the devil are we going to get away without our absence being noticed?"

A sharp hopeful feeling had Victoria looking at her husband. "What are you saying?"

"I'm saying I know you well enough to know there is no way I can stop you. The best I can hope to do is arm myself, choose a faster horse, and get there before you."

He was going to help her. Relieved, Victoria smiled broadly. "You cannot arrive ahead of me, faster horse or no. You don't know where you're going."

Spencer smiled into her eyes, showing her quite plainly the angry lights still remained there. "Dammit it all to hell, Victoria, you will tell me—"

"Oh, my word, there they are! I've been looking for them."

Obviously confused by her quick—and intentional—change of subject, Spencer looked around. "For whom? Where?"

"Mr. and Mrs. John Howell. His wife, Gwen, is my cousin. They are such wonderful people. Very prominent and gracious. I want you to meet them. They're over there on those benches with my great-aunt, Mrs. Helen Clifton—an absolute dear of a woman who could run the world, given one second's head start. Oh, and there's her brother, Mr. Bailey Carpenter, with her. You see him—that sweet-faced little gentleman with the white hair. Why, you'd think he was the mayor, so many people know and love him. I'll just go get them."

Spencer gripped her elbow and pulled her back to him. "No you won't, Victoria. Don't think I don't know what you're up to. The moment you're not at my side, you'd be gone to Savannah without me in half a flash. Don't play the innocent. You know, as well as I do, that I met the Howells and your great-aunt and -uncle earlier, just after your father's grand announcement. They came through what I believe was a receiving line as you and I and Edward stood next to your parents and brother."

Darn him. He'd learned her all too well and all too fast. "Oh, that's right," she said in her best self-effacing Southern-belle style. "Well, they're certainly worth a second conversation. And will you just look at all this, Spencer? I mean this gathering. It's perfect. My mother and father have outdone themselves." She cast her satisfied gaze over the assemblage. "Why, all of Savannah is here. Well, anyone who matters is, I mean to say."

"Yes, lovely. Victoria, look at me. What are you thinking?"

She dropped her pose and turned to her husband. Determination rushed her pulse. "I think we should go now. With all of Savannah out here today, they can't get in our way. And even better, this means *he* is alone in Savannah and will have nowhere to hide."

"If he's even in Savannah."

"Oh, he is, all right. Miss Cicely said he was. And I cannot help it; I want to go kill him, Spencer. I had no idea he was behind all this. None."

"I share your sentiment, my dear, regarding killing that son of a— Oh, how do you do? So nice to make your acquaintance. Red spots? Mine? Whatever do you mean? Oh, exactly—the Earl of Roxley told you of my infirmity. All cleared up now, thankfully. Some plant I brushed against, I suspect. You're very kind to inquire. Yes, we are quite happy with our news. We appreciate your stopping by." The moment the young couple was out of earshot, he turned to Victoria and took up where he'd left off. "If anyone should be riding to Savannah to confront this villain, it should be your brother—"

"But he can't, Spencer. He'd be shot on sight."

"What makes you think we won't be?"

"Because he doesn't know we know, or that we're even coming. So we have the element of surprise on our side."

"I disagree. He will know, the moment he sees us, that we know. Why else, on this day of all days, would we be in Savannah?"

"And that is exactly why Jeff can't go. I'd think you'd know that. You're the one who took him aside this morning and told him what had happened and that we knew and that he should go out to Miss Cicely's. He didn't deny anything, either— Why, Darlene Carpenter, it's been ages since I set eyes on you. Look at you! More beautiful than ever. Spencer, this is my cousin on my mother's side. You met her earlier. Oh, thank you, Darlene. We could not be more happy. Spencer's leg? No, it wasn't broken, only bruised. The Earl of Roxley spoke hastily that day. What? You're looking for Aunt Pauline? Why, I don't know. I think she's over there with Mama. Oh, yes, I see her now. Over there."

Alone again with her husband—as alone as anyone could be in the crush of people strolling by or standing nearby and chatting and laughing loudly—Victoria turned pleading eyes Spencer's way. "You heard what Miss Cicely said. We have to act now. He knows his game is up, but we can't just wait until *he* does something else. We have to act first. I, for one, am sick and tired of all this suspense and worrying. Every day, I fear there'll be another note on my pillow, or someone will take a shot at one of us. I just can't live with it anymore, Spencer. I want this resolved, I want my family safe, and I want to go home with you. I don't think that's asking a lot."

Spencer said nothing. He simply stared down at her. The warm and shining intensity radiating from his black eyes startled Victoria but in a pleasant way. "That was quite the noble speech, my dear," he finally said. "I find I am moved by it and your bravery. You are quite the most heroic—and foolhardy—woman I have ever met, and I will strive to be worthy of you in both regards. But I also find, my sweet wife, that if . . . something happened to you, it would be an ending I could not bear."

"Oh, Spencer. I couldn't bear it if it were you, either. I couldn't." Her heart melting with love for this man at her side, she set her plate on the bench behind her and hugged his arm impulsively, going so far as to rest her forehead against the muscled hardness of his biceps. The solidness of him, his very warmth, comforted her in ways she could not begin to describe. "What am I going to do, Spencer? Help me."

In the next moment, Spencer followed Victoria's example and set his plate down on the same bench. He then held her by her arms and stared down into her eyes. "Do you realize, Victoria, that is the first time you have ever asked me for my help? That is what I've been waiting for."

A bit taken aback, she cocked her head. "It is?"

Spencer chuckled. "Yes, it is—a declaration that you need me. Dare I hope, after holding me at arm's length all this while, you trust me now?"

"I have always trusted you, Spencer. I was afraid of you, yes, and feared you would keep me from doing what I had to do—I mean when I left England—but I always trusted you. At least, on other levels. You're a man of integrity, I know that. You have noble sensibilities. And you're very honorable—"

"Thank you for a wonderful litany of my virtues." His bright grin slowly faded. "But I am so sorry you were afraid of me. Edward says I can be a pompous ass, and he's right."

"But you had every right to be, Spencer. We were doing well . . . I mean you and I, at least reasonably well . . . until I had to tell you my ill-timed news. How else could you feel but angry and cautious?"

"You're very forgiving. And I am eternally grateful. But I cannot forgive myself for not considering, even once, what you must have been feeling that day or every day after. How scared and distraught you had to be. And how brave you were to tell me . . ." His voice trailed off; he looked up and away from her; exhaled; and then firmed his lips as if he'd come to some decision he wished to share with her. "Victoria, I just . . . I love you. And I never thought, in my whole life, that I would have anyone to whom I could say those words. But now I do . . . and it's you. You are such a gift in my life, one I have no intention of losing."

Victoria feared she was going to cry. She tried to raise a hand to her mouth, but with Spencer tenderly holding her arms, a chuckling sob escaped her first. He pulled her to his chest and held her in his embrace. Overcome, Victoria wrapped her arms around him and closed her eyes against the guests' indulgent smiles or shocked whispers coming their way. "I love you, too," she said. "Why are those the hardest words in the world to say?"

Spencer rested his chin atop her head. "I don't know." His voice vibrated in his chest and throughout her body. Victoria felt certain she'd never experienced anything this delicious or intimate . . . right here in broad daylight with all of Savannah looking on. Nothing could have been more inappropriate, but Victoria didn't give a fig about her breach of etiquette. Only Spencer mattered.

"Perhaps," he said into the cocoon of quiet that wrapped them softly in its folds, "they'll get easier to say if we say them more often to each other."

"I would like that . . . very much." She could have stayed like this, locked in the safe haven of his arms, for the rest of her life. But hers could prove to be a very short life if she didn't act soon. Today. Reluctant though she was to do so, Victoria pulled back and raised her gaze to her husband's. "I'm going to go after him, Spencer. I have to."

He stroked her arms and nodded. "I know."

"Go with me."

He chuckled. "I planned to do exactly that."

It suddenly hit her: This was real. They were finally going to act. Today. A fearful excitement coursed through Victoria's veins, making her shiver. "We'll take Edward, if we can pry him loose from Lucinda Barrett. That would be three of us, Spencer. Three against one. And it will be easier to slip away than you think. For one thing, the stables are off a ways on the other side of the house. We'll leave from there and travel a back road that doesn't connect to the main route to Savannah until we're off River's End property."

Looking amazed, Spencer said: "My, but you've thought this through, haven't you?"

"Yes, I have." She rushed on with no apology. "I'll pretend to be suddenly taken ill. It's expected with women who are in my condition. Everyone will sympathize. And you, playing the concerned and devoted husband, can carry me—"

"I daresay I am, in truth, a concerned and devoted husband—"

"Of course you are." Patting his chest . . . his wonderfully broad and muscular chest, Victoria smiled at his bruised feelings. "I'm simply saying how it will appear to everyone if you carry me to my room and then stay with me."

"It is *our* room, madam. But I see now what you mean. If you're ill, no one will want to be present for that and will understand your need to rest." Frowning, he pointed at Victoria. "But Edward. Explain to me how we will make off with him without raising suspicion."

"He can make up his own tale. He's wonderful at that, as you well know."

"Yes, don't I? I cannot count the number of people who have asked me about my red spots or my broken leg, which seems to be perfectly mended in only a matter of days. We need also to consider your mother. She will quite fuss if she thinks you ill. I doubt she'll leave your side."

"Maybe not at first. However, we can tell Jefferson what we're doing."

"We can. But he'll want to come, given everything that has been done against him."

Heartfelt sympathy for her brother coursed through Victoria. "And I wouldn't blame him a bit. But we'll tell him he can best serve his own interests by staying here—he's already been missed once today—to reassure Mama. She adores him and will do whatever he says. But should Mama linger in our bedroom, you can always order her out."

"Well, that should certainly solidify our relationship admirably, me ordering her out of her own house."

"Don't be silly. She'll go willingly. Mama is only too happy being the hostess. With Jeff's encouragement, she'll return quickly to her scene of triumph, God love her. She'll be so proud of my wonderful and *titled* husband who insists on tending me himself. She won't miss the opportunity to tell all her friends, either, how the *titled* duke dotes on his wife, and isn't it so sad that *their* daughters don't have such wonderful husbands with *titles*."

Spencer's frown veed his brows done right over his nose. "Dear God, mothers can be brutal. Maybe we ought to just send yours to Savannah in our stead."

"Spencer, even in a time of war, we did not allow General Sherman to level our fair city. We're not about to allow Mama to do so now."

"You make a good point." Firming his lips together, obviously in thought, Spencer said: "On the whole, though, your plan might work."

A bolt of excitement, shot through with fear for the danger they would face, raced through Victoria, propelling her even closer to her husband. She rested her palms on his coat's lapels. "It *will* work. Rosanna will keep everyone out and won't tell a soul if we slip away. She's as good a guardian as is Neville."

"That's true. So is Hornsby. I could discreetly send him around to the stables to have three horses readied." Spencer rubbed his chin and narrowed his eyes . . . clearly putting a plan together. Now that he agreed with her desire to act today, in good wifely form Victoria waited quietly and expectantly, allowing him to come up with the rest of the plan, which she would amend or veto if it didn't meet with her approval, of course. "And Mr. Milton, surprisingly enough, is quite the attraction today. I could instruct him to divert anyone who proves curious. No doubt there will be—"

"Excuse me, Your Lordship and Your Ladyship, but can I take these here plates for you?"

Along with Spencer, who cursed softly, Victoria jerked her attention to the girl standing behind her and next to the thick tree trunk. Tillie. She executed a rough curtsy. How long had the stringy-haired girl been standing there? How much had she heard? She'd probably been standing just out of sight on the other side of the tree and eavesdropping . . . for all the good it would do her. Her freedom of movement would very soon be restricted.

"Yes, Tillie, take the plates," Victoria said brusquely, not even pretending to be polite.

"Yes, ma'am. I'm just doin' my job, is all." With a sullen, sidelong glance her and Spencer's way, the maid curtsied again, picked the plates up and quickly walked away.

"That damned girl was everywhere," Spencer fussed. "Always in the way. I cannot tell you how many times I very nearly tripped over her."

Victoria watched, along with Spencer, the maid hurrying over to a knot of people, one of whom was Jefferson. He'd returned from Miss Cicely's just in time for the start of the barbecue and had explained his absence as having had to pay a quick call on a business acquaintance who hadn't been available until now. Not exactly ingenious, but an excuse their harried father, in charge of the men barbecuing the meat and the others setting up tables, had accepted distractedly.

"You weren't the only one tripping over her," Victoria said. "Rosanna told me numerous times she found the girl in places she shouldn't be and nosing around, but with no real reason for being there. I should have suspected her from the outset."

"I don't know how you could. We didn't know until this

morning that she's been, in effect, a spy, recounting our every move to our villain."

"Ooh, I'd like to just tie her up out in the swamp and leave her there, she makes me so angry."

"Suitably gruesome, my dear. I suspect she'd have a quick conversion if we did. But never mind her. She can do no more harm now. We'll have the law deal with her later."

Victoria nodded her agreement, but her mind was racing with the details of the plan she meant to set into motion. The chips would simply have to fall where they may . . . on the innocent and guilty alike. As much as she hated knowing that, she also knew there was a greater good here to be served than her own feelings, or even those of her family. She must come to terms with that, as much as she hated being the one on whom this responsibility had been thrust. But there was no way out now. She'd come back to Georgia to do this. And now, it was time to act.

Though many emotions roiled inside her, all of them tempered with regret and resignation, Victoria smiled up at her husband. "Spencer, stand ready to catch me, sir. I intend to swoon."

Grim, determined, and half scared out of her mind now that they had left River's End behind them in a clean getaway, Victoria's heart pounded with each beat of her horse's galloping hooves over the sandy road that roughly paralleled the southeasterly flow of the Savannah River. She realized now that she would never have had the courage for the coming confrontation in the city that shared its name with the river if Spencer, mounted on her father's favorite black gelding, hadn't been by her side as he was now. He was armed, as was Edward, who rode on her other side and made a slender brown-haired figure atop a sturdy roan. Victoria, no fool herself, had her brother's pistol tucked into the waistband of her britches, also Jefferson's—and rode his big, rangy dapple-gray, as well.

Jefferson. Victoria firmed her lips as she recalled what had been revealed to her and Spencer this morning. She'd been so relieved to learn her brother was not a heartless villain. Neither was he weak-willed or uncaring. Or even callous. In truth, his coolness and seeming meanness toward her had been a sincere effort on his part to get her to leave River's End and go back to England where she would be safe. What was more, had he succeeded in getting her to leave, his own life, and he knew this, would have been forfeit. Poor Jeff. A tale of greed and twisted love had held him paralyzed—and all in her name.

She knew now who had been lurking in the dark that night when she and Jeff met on the dock. And she knew why. The evil, monstrous man, to use Jeff so and to trade on his friendship and confidences as he had. How could anyone be so heartless? But what about her part in this? She'd been just as blind. Wracked now with guilt for her own silly innocence and crusading spirit, she condemned herself for thinking she could simply sail into town and play the heroine by rescuing them all with the strength of her will alone. How stupid. She had played unwittingly into the hands of the awful man she intended to confront today—and placed all their lives in greater danger.

Yes, all their lives. Even her mother's and father's lives. How horrible. And true. Should she and Spencer and Edward fail today, she and everyone she loved could conceivably then be killed in a violent spree the likes of which Savannah had never seen. But even should they succeed, the truth that her parents would have to learn of their son's duplicity could very well kill their spirits and split her family apart. What Victoria had to face was there was no possibility of a clean win here. The most awful truth was it was all for love, too. She exhaled sharply, feeling suddenly depleted of strength . . . and maybe her will for this coming battle.

No. Immediately she steeled her spine, telling herself she must think of her loved ones and not herself—

"Wait! Hold up! Stop! Stop right here!"

Terrified, Victoria looked over at her husband. Already he was reining in and signaling her and Edward to do the same, which they did. Victoria's excited horse sidestepped and whinnied and arched his neck. Spencer immediately grabbed its reins and held on, speaking softly, soothingly to the dapple-gray. Under other circumstances Victoria would have been highly indignant and told him to unhand her horse. In this instance, however, she wanted only to know one thing. "What is it, Spencer? What's wrong?"

He looked at her but cocked his head as if listening for something. "You don't hear that?"

"Hear what?" Edward asked before she could.

"That." Releasing her reins, his brow lowered with obvious perturbation, Spencer twisted in his saddle until he peered toward the heavily forested and winding road behind them.

Victoria gave the road her attention, too, seeing nothing but the expected sight. Loblolly pines and oaks and overgrown tropical vegetation, their broad leaves dusted with dried mud from the roadway and slouching over the rutted pathway to hide every curve but the last one they'd just rounded. Victoria strained her attention and her hearing . . . and suddenly heard a bloodhound's excited baying growing louder and louder. Relief swept through her, slumping her in her saddle. "You scared the life out of me, Spencer. That's just Neville."

"I am aware it is just Neville. And who is he bringing with him, do you suppose?"

"He could simply be out hunting." Victoria noted her husband's raised eyebrow that put the lie to her statement. "You're right," she conceded. "He's not simply out hunting. He's discovered I'm gone, and he's coming to join us. But I don't think he's bringing anyone with him. For one thing, we'd hear their horses, which we don't. And I hardly think anyone at River's End today is likely to take after a baying hound who does his own hunting all the time anyway."

Not looking the least bit convinced, Spencer pushed the narrow brim of his black-felt bowler hat up. "I hope you're right, or we're about to have company and no believable explanation to offer for our presence out here. Especially given Edward's ridiculous story that he must repair to his bedroom for his daily hours of prayer and meditation."

"Miss Lucinda Barrett is a devout Christian woman," Edward said primly, "and I thought only to impress her with my devotion."

"God save us all," Spencer muttered before turning again to his wife. "And you and I, my dear wife, are supposed to be sequestered in our bedroom with you in a swoon brought on by your delicate condition. And yet, here we are, the three of us—armed, on the road to Savannah and with my wife garbed as a man."

Victoria raised her chin a stubborn notch. "It is the same as with the jonboat, Spencer. I could hardly ride or be ready for whatever might happen next while dressed in a silk gown. And I'm telling you, Neville will be alone." She hoped. "In fact, we should have thought to bring him along in the first place. With his tracking skills, he could be very useful to us today."

"I am well aware of the tracking skills of bloodhounds, Victoria," Spencer said right down the end of his aristocratic nose. "We have them in England, as well."

"Not as good as Neville."

"Every bit as good as Neville."

Edward's throat-clearing noise garnered for him Victoria's and Spencer's angry attention. He raised his hands, reins and all, as if he were being robbed. "That was not meant for attention. I had a tickle in my throat. Believe me, I have heard 'Shut up, Edward' enough in the past several days to last me a—"

"Shut up, Edward." Spencer said it right along with Victoria. Sighing, Edward retreated back into his posture atop his horse and looked everywhere but at the bickering couple.

"Well, what do we do with the dog?" Spencer wanted to know, still sounding testy. "He won't go home if sent, will he?" Victoria shook her head no. "And he can't run all the way to Savannah"—Spencer's brow furrowed, apparently with his next thought, which he voiced—"Can he?" Victoria shook her head no. "I thought not . . . even for a Southern bloodhound."

That last comment he had muttered under his breath, but not quite far enough under his breath.

"I heard that," Victoria sharply let him know.

"And here we go," Edward said fatalistically, quickly adding, "Never mind. I am shutting up. But first, may I just say that we make one devil of a frightening posse, stopped in our tracks by the baying of one hound. No doubt, the mere sight of us will strike terror into the villain's heart."

Just then, and perhaps saving them all three from themselves and the others' sharp retorts, Neville came bounding around the last bend in the road and into plain view. Though he ran like all the demons of hell were after him, he was blessedly alone. His long ears flapped in a breeze his galloping gait produced and his tongue hung out one side of his mouth. Victoria chuckled. "Hold a tight rein on your horses, gentlemen."

"What?" they both asked. "Why?"

"This is why." Tightening her grip on her own horse, Victoria stuck two fingers in her mouth and whistled a sharp, piercing blast that had Spencer's horse rearing—and Spencer cursing; and Edward's horse bucking furiously all over the roadway—and Edward screaming wildly. Victoria's dapple-gray mount, an old hand at this trick of Jefferson and Victoria's, had merely stiffened his knees and stood stock-still.

"Come here, boy!" Victoria cried out to Neville as she scooted off the back of the saddle cinched to her horse and hit her thigh encouragingly. "Up you go. You can do it."

Neville stopped by the horse's side and whined up at Victoria. She again signaled him to make the attempt. The dog bunched his muscles and, with a great leap, landed squarely in the middle of the saddle, nimbly keeping his feet under him. Holding on to him, steadying him, Victoria laughed out loud and Neville bayed his happiness. Spencer and Edward, though they were again in control of their mounts, were not amused.

Victoria innocently looked from one to the other of the men. "Jefferson taught him. We do this all the time."

"Apparently." Spencer's complexion was suffused with the red of anger, yet the two little lines bracketing his mouth were white. "You cannot ride like that with that dog all the way to Savannah."

Victoria scooted forward until she'd edged back into the saddle, which she now shared with Neville. The bloodhound hunkered down across her thighs, settling sideways to her. Victoria grinned at her husband. "Yes I can. I've done it before."

When he didn't return her grin and only continued to look grim, she added: "I can, and I will, Spencer—unless you wish to put him on your horse with you. If you don't and I make him get down, he will attempt to run all the way to Savannah with us and it will be too much for him and his brave heart will burst and he will die. Are you prepared to live with me, should that happen to him because you chose to be hard-hearted and hard-headed, sir?"

An intense quiet followed her brisk laying out of the situation for her husband. Not too many sounds dared invade the silence between them. The occasional chirp of a bird. The twig-snapping sound of some small animal scurrying away through the underbrush fringing the roadside. From Victoria's right, with Spencer being on her left, she heard what she believed were the muffled sounds of a laugh quickly covered by a cough.

At last, Spencer resettled his hat low on his brow and exhaled. Looking terribly serious and in charge, he said: "Let's ride for Savannah."

As he urged his mount into a gallop and shot ahead of his wife and his cousin, leaving only a dusty trail in his wake, Victoria exchanged a look and a grin with Edward, who shook his head and chuckled. "I bow to you, madam," he said nobly. "In you, my cousin has met his match."

CHAPTER 20

Spencer's frustration only increased once they made it to Savannah. The residential streets in the better parts of the town, though sunny and stately as always, were now also eerily quiet. The skin-prickling feel was that of a city suddenly abandoned in the face of an overwhelming danger. As he, along with Victoria, Neville, and Edward, had ridden around the many squares and made the many turns that had taken them to Chippewa Square, the only sound had been their horses' hooves striking the cobbles on those streets paved with them. Only on the outskirts of Savannah had the mounted party passed any signs of human life, and that had been a desultory showing. A few tradesmen lazily loading their wagons; a fishmonger dispiritedly leaning against his cart; and three women of color ambling slowly along with young, dark children in tow.

The carriage trade these people depended on for their livelihoods were not at home today. They were all at River's End. Rather ironic, Spencer had concluded, since they, the honorees, had hared off to Savannah.

And now, here they all were in the quiet and tastefully decorated front parlor of a brick Italianate residence on Bull Street and facing Chippewa Square. "This is ridiculous," Spencer said to Victoria and Edward. "Look at us. We are casting about as if we expect a clue to a villain's where-abouts to jump out at us from behind a chair."

"Hopefully, not this one," Victoria said, looking to both sides of and then behind the overstuffed chair she sat on. Neville, crouching like a bored Sphinx beside her chair, frowned at his mistress's antics.

"What I find most disturbing," Edward said, "is this beautiful house has not the first appearance of . . . evil or a rottenness of spirit."

"You will have to explain your meaning, Edward, as it has defeated me."

Settling his gaze on Spencer, Edward explained: "I mean I half expected, given the man's criminal bent of mind, that his home would reflect his miscreant's mentality. A darkened cave of a house with slovenliness and rats running rampant in every room. A dungeon, maybe. Anything but this beautiful, airy, and sunny place that hides a secret. Rather frightening. I wonder if we removed the walls, would we find his true foul-smelling and cobwebbed lair?"

Spencer stared at Edward. "My dear earl, you have missed your calling. You must immediately pen a horrifically hair-raising novel for the enjoyment of the masses."

Edward nodded his agreement. "I have thought of doing just that."

"Lovely for you. In the meantime, could we permit our attention to linger where it is needed? We must face the truth. Except for his servants, we are the only ones present. The man is not here."

"Did you really expect him to be, old man? Perhaps awaiting us with refreshments and a musicale for our enjoyment?"

"I know it's hard, but don't be ridiculous, Edward."

Looking around, frowning, Edward absently hit his bowler hat against his thigh, producing a soft whump-whump of sound. "I feel like such an intruder."

"That's because we are." Spencer crossed his arms over his chest. "I don't quite know how to proceed from here.

We've done what we can by searching the house and the grounds and questioning his staff—"

"We did far more than question them. We imprisoned them in a room on the top floor." Edward made a face. "I didn't really like doing that."

"Neither did I," Spencer admitted. "But there's no sense in allowing them the run of the place and giving one or more of them the opportunity to abscond without our knowing it and go warn the man, if they indeed know where he is and simply won't tell us. Even if they don't, they're safest where they are for the moment. Hopefully, this will soon be over and we can free them, no harm done."

"Except to their pride. And won't they have a tale to tell then," Victoria said.

Spencer smiled. "Hopefully, a tale of our heroism."

She returned his smile, but he could see the fear in her eyes. "Such a tale with *my* name attached? Hmmm. A new sort of gossip and scandal to embarrass my family. How fresh."

"Yes. Heroism," Edward cut in, clearly impressed with himself. "That should put me in good stead with Miss Lucinda Barrett."

"First we must live through the day, Edward," Spencer reminded him.

"Yes, there is that." But the faraway look in his eyes told Spencer his cousin was already seeing his name in banner headlines.

"Be all that as it may," Spencer said loudly, clamping his hands to his waist and dividing his attention between his cousin and his wife. "Where is the man? We know his absence here has nothing to do with running from us, as he isn't aware, as far as we know, that we are on to him."

"But he easily could divine as much, Spencer," Edward said, for once serious. "After all, these events began last night. Plenty of time for his henchmen to inform him. And plenty of time for him to realize Miss Cicely now has no reason to remain silent. Surely, he will intuit exactly who she would first inform—and why."

Spencer rubbed his knuckles across his chin as he thought out loud. "Yes, of course. And Miss Cicely did tell us he would be here. Her gift for the sight aside, I have to agree with her. With his game being up, he can now only hope to cover his trail, first by destroying any incriminating papers he would have stored here, and then by leaving town quickly. As his personal belongings are still here and his study is not torn apart, as one would expect if he'd been in a panic to do that—and because he *has* had since last night as you said, Edward—then I am afraid we must assume he intends to confront us."

"Oh, my God, Spencer." Victoria rigidly gripped her chair's armrests. "Jefferson. He'll seek out my brother first."

Spencer went to her and squatted in front of her, covering her hands with his. "No, my dear, no. Think. He could get nowhere close to your brother today without first being detected. There's not a soul in attendance today who does not know Loyal Atherton should not be at River's End. Besides, my love, you know it's not your brother he wants. It's you."

"But that's just it, Spencer. He doesn't know I'm here. He thinks I'm there. At River's End. Don't forget he knows every back road to the plantation that I do. And we got cleanly away. He could just as easily, and undetected, sneak in using those same routes. Why, he could already be lying in wait out there and could have been since last night after he found out—"

"Victoria, my love, calm down. If what you're saying were true, he would have acted last night. Maybe in the middle of the night. But he didn't. I believe he didn't know how his plot was foiled until sometime today, if even yet. Really, can you imagine his henchmen were all that eager to report to him their failure without first making their own search? Only when it proved fruitless, as we know it did, would they tell him—"

"But his own servants said he hadn't had any visitors today."

"Of course he didn't. Do you really think, my dear, given servants' gossip, he has his nefarious meetings in his home with these ruffians? All we know, from questioning his staff, is he's been gone since mid-morning and he left in a hired carriage. Now, we have no way of knowing how his henchmen contact him or at what intervals—"

"Pirates House!"

"I beg your pardon?"

"A rough saloon and meeting house close to the river. It would be ideal. He could be there."

Spencer rose to his feet. "Hmm. My first inclination is to rush there to catch him, the bastard. But I daresay we'd have to fight the entire place to get to him. I don't like those odds."

"It's clear thinking like that, Spencer, old man, that makes you a valuable member of Parliament."

"Thank you, Edward." Spencer narrowed his eyes at his cousin and then focused on his wife. "I believe we have no choice but to wait for him to come to us here. This is the man's home. He will eventually return here." He smiled. "Besides, Miss Cicely said he would be here."

"So we will wait," Victoria said. "I can't say, though, that I'm anxious to see him. Although I would like the opportunity to slap his face for the way he accosted me in my own parlor."

Her bringing that day up suddenly brought to Spencer's mind a question he'd meant to ask her before now. "Victoria, on that day, what did he want? I mean I know he"—Spencer's temper flared, making him grit his teeth and swallow hard—"kissed you, but in the interim, with everything else that's happened, I never thought to ask."

If it were possible, she suddenly seemed even smaller than she was. She would barely look him in the eye. Spencer again went to her and squatted down in front of her, his knees spread to either side of her legs. He took her hands in his and held them. "I love you, Victoria. And I know you love me. I want you also to know that I don't blame you for any of this. I truly don't. You were an innocent, my sweet. But I just wonder what the man intended to accomplish by calling on you that day. Truly. It could be important."

Her expression softening, she stroked his cheek. Behind him, Spencer could hear Edward sniff and clear his throat. No doubt, the younger man was uncomfortable in the extreme with what should be a very private, domestic moment. "You are the most wonderful of men, Spencer," his very beautiful wife said. "And the most forgiving. I am such a lucky woman."

Spencer captured her hand and kissed her palm. "There is nothing to forgive. And it is I who am lucky. That a woman such as you could ever love me—"

"Oh, I say, I will absolutely swoon if you keep on in this vein. For heaven's sake, you're already married. And yes, I know: 'Shut up, Edward.' But I won't. Our villain could come home at any moment, as we have all agreed, and there our horses are—tethered right out front on the street. I daresay that three such large specimens of horseflesh would be a dead giveaway as to the man's having company he will not be amused, to put it mildly, to see."

Still clasping Victoria's hands in his, Spencer pivoted around and stared up at his cousin. "Are you quite done, Lord Roxley?"

Edward pursed his lips and looked stubborn. "I believe I am, Your Grace."

Eyeing his cousin with what he hoped was a clear threat in his narrowed eyes, Spencer said, "Good. Then why don't you go move the horses around back where they're not so obvious?"

"And if our villain returns through the alley—and there I am out there with the horses? What do I do then?"

"Clearly, you shoot him," Spencer said seriously before returning his attention to his wife.

But Edward apparently wasn't done. "And if I shoot him and kill him, will you vouch for me with the police?"

Spencer exhaled, smiled at Victoria, whose eyes had rounded—her most usual expression when he and Edward got into it—and again gave Edward his attention. "No, I will not. I will allow you to rot here in jail, and I will tell your mother you were lost at sea on our voyage home, much to the relief of many an anxious husband in England. Does that answer your question?"

"Quite admirably, yes."

"Good. Then please go see to the horses and be careful, will you? I've no heart for a gun battle in the streets of Savannah to defend your person."

His expression pinching into a sour snit, Edward stuffed his hat down on his head, pivoted sharply on his heel, and wordlessly marched out of the room. He slammed the parlor door behind him, stalked loudly down the short hall, jerked open the front door and then, going by the sounds and the dictates of logic, stepped out and slammed it behind him.

Spencer showed his long-suffering expression to his wife. "The silly fool gave not one thought to Loyal Atherton's possibly being right out front, did he?"

Victoria grinned. "You love him dearly, don't you?"

"Oh, quite so, but I must never let him know. I'm the only person in the world he's afraid of and so will mind. Now, my dear, what were you going to tell me about what our absent host had to say on the day he came to call?"

The mirth bled slowly from Victoria's expression. As he waited for her to speak of something he knew would be hard for her, he raked his loving gaze over her delicate features. She was incredibly beautiful with her wonderfully pale skin and high forehead and her rounded chin. Like a porcelain doll. Her unruly deep auburn hair cascaded in waves around her face and shoulders, emphasizing her large blue eyes and the shadow of the hollows under her cheekbones. Her pink lips, so very kissable, were just then thinned into an anxious line.

She lowered her gaze to where Neville crouched. "He said he'd just known I'd come back to him, I remember that."

"He'd *known*? He didn't mean literally, I presume. Unless he too has the Sight."

She managed a fleeting smile. "No, of course not. But I believe he was counting on the letter, which did work in getting me back here."

"Yes, it did." Spencer's heart nearly leaped right out of his chest with fear for her. Dear God, she'd been so dangerously vulnerable until he'd arrived here. He thanked the heavens that she'd been at River's End where the man was not welcome and therefore could not have easily got to her himself.

Victoria's expression crumpled as she leaned forward to rest her forehead on Spencer's shoulder. "I was such a fool, Spencer. How could I have—"

"Shh. Don't." He put his arms around her and held her, feeling her shoulders shake as she quietly cried. Intense anger shot through Spencer for the man who could have hurt her so badly, who used her so terribly and then hadn't stood by her—*But wait. Had he wanted to stand by her? And had he been prevented from doing so?* Spencer remembered wondering that before, but he hadn't asked her, fearing, as he had, her answer. But now he knew she loved him and so had nothing to fear from this other man. At least, not where his wife's feelings were concerned.

Shot through with urgency, Spencer eased Victoria back, holding her by her arms. Her tear-stained and reddened face, with damp tendrils of hair clinging to her skin, nearly tore Spencer's heart loose from its moorings. He helped her wipe away her tears and the hair from her face. "Victoria, could it be that Loyal Atherton fancies he loves you? What I mean is once you were, uh, *compromised,* did he state his wish to do the honorable thing and offer you marriage?"

"Yes, he did."

"I see. Then, why did that not happen? No one more than me is happy that it did not, but it seems such a neat solution—and much less scandalous than your being dragged off to England. Thank God you were, because now you're mine. But why didn't your parents go that easier route?"

Looking suddenly shy, she absently tugged yet another strand of hair behind her ear. "By all rights, it should have happened that way. Loyal was a dear friend of Jefferson's until . . . *that* happened to me. He was also a welcome guest at River's End and almost a part of our family."

"Was he courting you?"

"I suppose. But I was never serious about him, Spencer, not as he was about me. I wasn't casual, by any means, but I wasn't thinking marriage, that's for certain. But then *that* happened . . . I mean the . . ."

The catch in her voice had Spencer squeezing her hand reassuringly. "It's all right. I know what you mean."

She inhaled deeply and exhaled softly. "I don't think you do. Not entirely. You see, being with him . . . like that . . . was not something I wanted, Spencer. I want you to know that. He was a houseguest at that time and came into my room at night and . . . as much as seduced and coerced me into the act. It happened before I knew it was, really. He wasn't brutal, but neither would he take no for an answer. I was quite overpowered."

"The bastard!" This story was one of the hardest things Spencer had ever had to listen to—not for his sake, but for hers. "Where was Neville? He damned near killed me when I as much as threw you on the bed—quite mistakenly, too."

The dog, apparently upon hearing his name, sat up alertly and woofed at Spencer. Victoria reached over and rubbed the bloodhound's ears. "He was out hunting."

"Of course. Did your father know that? About the attack, I mean?"

She gave her head a vehement shake. "Dear God, no. I couldn't even scream; I was so shocked . . . during. But afterward, I was afraid to tell Daddy. I was afraid he would kill Loyal and go to prison for it. I couldn't have stood that."

Spencer stared into her guileless, innocent blue eyes. She had already borne so much, and he had significantly added to her load in the past few months. Why, he was no better than Loyal Atherton and in more ways than he cared to admit. "And so, instead, you poor girl, you bore in silence the knowledge of this unwanted attack on your person."

She wouldn't look at him. "You make me sound so noble."

He tipped her chin up until she was forced to look into his eyes. "You were. You still are. But, tell me, Victoria, why wouldn't your father simply allow the marriage with him— But hold on. You said you didn't tell your father what happened to you. Who did?"

"Loyal, of course. He was the only other one who knew. The very next morning, he went to my father and said that we had . . . consummated our relationship."

"The very next—? That you—? The *bastard*!" A surge of shock and outrage had Spencer on his feet before he even realized it. Neville came to his feet and growled low in his throat. "Oh, shut up, Neville. I wouldn't hurt her for anything in the world, and well you know it. Now, sit down." When the dog did, Spencer blinked and met his wife's wide-eyed gaze. "Amazing. But still, Victoria, I don't understand. If Loyal Atherton was a friend of the family, why wouldn't your father simply allow him to marry you?"

A ghost of a smile appeared on Victoria's lips. "He was willing that I should. He even demanded it. But I refused. I said I would run away and live in the swamp with Miss Cicely before I'd marry Loyal Atherton."

Completely taken aback—and just as surprised that he

would be, knowing his wife's spirit—Spencer chuckled. "I should have known. But perhaps it works differently in America than it does England. You could simply refuse and your father would allow that?"

"Oh, there was nothing simple about it. Over the next few days, there were many scenes and harsh words and tears and fights and threats to lock me in my room until I consented."

"I say. Did he ever actually lock you in your room?" Once again, Spencer found reason to chastise himself. Like her father, he too had attempted to lock her away until she cooperated. He began to be concerned for the entire male species' brutish tendencies. It was a wonder any woman anywhere had anything to do with any man anywhere at any time, he mused.

"Yes, he locked me in once," Victoria was saying. "That was following a particularly bad fight after he found out that Loyal had told everyone in Savannah that I had invited him into my bed and then refused him marriage."

Spencer fisted his hands at his waist. "I must say it again—the *bastard*! But did he—I mean your father—let you out when he calmed down?"

"No. Sometimes Daddy doesn't calm down for days. I couldn't risk that, so I climbed out the window and down the oak tree that grows outside my bedroom window."

Horrified, Spencer stared at her. "If any of our children takes after you, Victoria, I shall have no recourse except to drown myself."

"Understood." She, too, wore a very serious expression.

Spencer fought a grin. "But what did you do once you had reached the ground? Did you run away to Miss Cicely?"

"No, silly. She would have sent me right back to River's End. Instead, I went around front and knocked on the door, just to let Daddy know I could get out if I chose to. You should have seen his face when he opened the door, one of the rare times that he ever did."

Spencer began to be very afraid for himself. "I shall hazard a guess here. That was when he conceived of his plan to bring you to England, wasn't it?"

Looking very prim and harmless, she said: "We left the very next day."

For long seconds, Spencer could only stare at her. But then he gave a great laughing whoop of joy that startled her and Neville. Spencer snatched his wife up from the chair, held her close and slowly swung around with her, much to the bloodhound's baying protest. Ignoring the dog, Spencer kissed his wife and laughed as he never had before in his life. She'd flung her arms around his neck and laughed and kissed him and cried out her happiness—

The sharp report of a gun being fired out in the quiet street startled a yelp out of Neville and stopped Spencer abruptly. He still held his wife to his chest and off her feet, but now he stared, horrified, into her frightened blue eyes as her beloved face filled his vision.

"Edward!" Spencer whispered, shock and fear robbing him of his strength. He had sent Edward out front to move the horses.

In an instant, Victoria was free of Spencer and on her feet. "Could that be Edward who fired his gun?"

"I am about to go find out. Stay here."

Victoria made as if to bolt for the door, but got no farther than one step before Spencer pulled her back. "No!" He grabbed her arm. "It could be a trick, a way to get us to stupidly step outside where we'd be—"

"But Edward could be hurt—"

"I am aware of that. But I must first think of you."

"Me?" Victoria tugged against her husband's hold on her. "I am not in danger. It's Edward who is. We have to help—"

"I am trying to do exactly that. Do you have your gun?" His voice brooked no argument.

Victoria stilled in his grip and frowned at him. "Yes, of course I do."

"Then draw it and keep it ready to use. Hold it like this." Releasing her, standing between her and the door across the room, he demonstrated by pulling his gun from its holster and holding it pointed toward the ceiling, his elbow bent. "Don't let anyone but me or Edward into this room—"

"I'm not going to be in this room." Victoria pulled her gun out of her waistband.

Spencer's eyebrows shot up, making him look like a parent whose child had sassed him. "Yes, you most certainly will be."

She watched him worriedly glance over to the windows that showed a framed view of the street outside. Already, in his mind, Victoria could tell, he had dismissed her and was several steps ahead in his thinking. And whatever he was envisioning, it did not include her. Stubborn to the end, she announced, loudly: "No, I will not be here, Spencer. I am going with you."

Tall, dark, muscular . . . armed and dangerous . . . he snapped his gaze back to hers and held it in a viselike glare. Clearly he hadn't expected a second round of disobedience. "I have already spoken, and I expect—"

Neville bayed, lending the sound an impatient tone. Spencer jerked around to face the dog. By sidestepping her husband, Victoria saw the bloodhound had his sensitive black nose pressed hard to the closed door's jamb. He whined and shook all over in clear impatience to get outside.

Spencer turned again to Victoria, showing her he looked cool and determined. He gripped her arm firmly as though to emphasize his point. "I am ordering you to stay here."

She yanked her arm from his grip. "And I am telling you I will *not*."

Spencer shoved a hand through his hair. "For God's sake, Victoria, I am trying to think of you and Edward. And you should be thinking of the baby, if you won't think of yourself."

"I always think of the baby. Have I hurt it yet? No. The

baby is perfectly fine. I'm also thinking of you—and Edward, whom we both care deeply about. So if you're going out there, John Spencer Whitfield, then I am going with you. What if you leave me here and rush out there alone and get yourself killed, and Edward is already wounded or worse? There will be no one left to defend me. Have you thought of that?"

"Madam, that is the most convoluted bit of thinking I have ever—"

"Is it? Well, then, for another thing—and I have told you this once already today—if you get killed, then I don't want to live, either. So there." She pursed her lips together stubbornly and stared, unblinking, at her husband.

Spencer gritted his teeth . . . no doubt to keep a shout of frustration in check. Then he said, very quietly: "All right, you win. Let's go. But you stay behind me."

"I intended to do just that. You make a much bigger target and a better shield than I do." Frowning in concentration, Victoria checked her weapon, wondering how the devil these things worked. She'd only fired one once or twice before and that was with Jefferson taking care of all the catches and hammers and whatnot. Victoria suddenly realized it was awfully quiet in the room. She glanced up to see Spencer, a dubious expression on his face, watching her actions with the weapon.

"Do you actually know how to use a gun, Victoria?"

"Of course I do." She held it up as he'd just shown her to do. "I'm ready. And don't you dare let anything happen to Neville. I've loved him a lot longer than I have you."

Spencer muttered something under his breath that Victoria judged not to be an endearment. Immediately, he drew his own weapon, turned, and crossed the room in no more than four or five bounding steps. Victoria was right on his heels. With Neville nosed against the jamb, he was first out in the hallway as Spencer wrenched open the parlor door that Edward had slammed behind him not more than five minutes ago. Victoria could hardly stand to think about the dear earl, so afraid was she of seeing his bleeding body on the ground outside. And poor Spencer, what he must be going through with the same thoughts.

Her heart in her throat, and herself right behind her husband, who was right behind Neville, they again bunched up at the closed front door. Cursing, Spencer steadily prodded, with a booted foot, at Neville, trying to get him behind him with Victoria. "Madam, hold on to your dog so I can get to the door!"

For once obedient, and more than a little frightened about what truly awaited them out in the street, Victoria grabbed Neville's scruff and hauled back on him. In the same second, Spencer ripped open the front door. As she had expected him to rush outside, she was already in motion, and her forward momentum was such that she and Neville collided with her husband's back as he stood immobile in the doorway. In the next second, Victoria realized what he'd done. He'd stopped cold to keep her and the dog behind him until he could see if they faced any immediate danger.

The man stupidly and bravely intended to take any bullets that might have been coming their way. Victoria's soul twisted itself into knots. "No, Spencer!" She let go of Neville and pounded helplessly on Spencer's back with her open palm. "Don't you dare—"

"It's all right, Victoria. Come on."

How could it be all right? They'd heard gunfire. In the second it took Victoria to think that, Spencer and Neville vacated the doorway and were gone, darting to their left across the abbreviated porch with its decorative wrought-iron railing. That way led to the steps down from the elevated main entrance to the sidewalk, Victoria knew—and Spencer was leaving her behind.

Waving her gun wildly, she took off after him, all but stumbling down the steps and holding on to the iron handrail. She achieved the sidewalk and squatted behind

Spencer, who was crouched behind the hedges that fronted
the steps. With Neville standing alertly in front of him,
Spencer raised his head only enough to be able to rove his
gaze over the street and the square across the way. After several seconds of this, he was apparently satisfied that they
were safe because he said: "Come on. Stay behind me and
keep your weapon ready. And try not to shoot me."

Victoria forswore comment as she inched out of their
cover and followed his careful stalking northward up the
street, looking in every direction at once, it seemed, until they
were about two houses away from the Atherton abode. There,
he stood in the middle of the street, looking both ways. Victoria surmised that oncoming traffic was not his concern, but
any sudden and sneaking movements were. But it was the
oddest thing: The street was quiet and empty. And no bleeding body littered the ground . . . thankfully, of course. "We
did hear a gun being fired, didn't we, Spencer?"

He turned slowly in a circle, looking, always looking.
"Yes."

"Where do you suppose Edward is?"

"God alone knows. But wherever he is, he will have
heard the shot, too, and will be taking precautions."

She felt so vulnerable, being out in the middle of the
street. "Shouldn't we go check on him, just to be sure?"

Now facing south, back toward the corner-situated Atherton house, Spencer directed a long-suffering look her way.
"*I* would love to go check on Edward, who is presumably
out back with the horses. However, with you insistently one
step behind me I am reluctant to investigate until I know
what is afoot. As there have been no other shots fired, the
one we heard could simply be someone . . . just shooting off
his gun."

"That doesn't seem likely, Spencer."

"I am aware of that, Victoria."

Given the irritated tone of his voice, Victoria decided a
wiser policy might be to help her husband survey their sur-

roundings. In doing so, she happened to look up and over to her right. Her attention arrested on the frightened faces of the Atherton servants on the third floor. All bunched around one closed and narrow window, their eyes rounded, they gesticulated wildly, as if trying to tell her something. "Spencer, look up there. Why are they doing that, all that gesturing?"

He directed his gaze to where she indicated. "No doubt, they believe we are leaving them locked up there and wish to remind us of their presence."

Victoria searched Spencer's face, wondering if he made more of their antics than he was saying. He'd do that, she knew, not to worry her. But he also wouldn't tell her that was what he was doing. So there was no sense in asking him. Just then, Neville crossed in front of them and trotted over to the parklike square on Victoria and Spencer's left. His tail wagged as he quickly nosed around the grassy areas and the beds of shrubs and flowers.

"Neville doesn't seem too concerned," Spencer said, sounding as if he meant to reassure himself as much as he did her.

"No, he doesn't," Victoria replied, just as absently. Indeed the dog merrily nosed every bush or tree trunk he passed. To Victoria's experienced eye, Neville looked more to be searching for an appropriate place to relieve himself than he did for the telling scent of a bad man. Sure enough, Neville hiked his leg against a carefully chosen tree. Exasperated, she turned to Spencer, opening her mouth to remark on the dog's—

"Stay where you are—I have you surrounded! Drop your weapons!"

CHAPTER 21

The startling warning had Victoria gasping her shock. Confused, alert, she tightened her grip on her gun and quickly looked to Spencer . . . who, strangely, looked more perturbed and disgusted than he did alert to danger. At first, Victoria could make no sense of this. But then, her mind finally identified the voice, and she could have cried in relief.

Spencer ran a hand over his eyes. Looking very bleak, he said, quietly, to her: "The man is an idiot. I ought to shoot him myself."

"Don't you dare! That's Edward around the corner of the house, isn't it?"

"Of course it's Edward. Do you know any other idiots?" Spencer pointed at her. "Do not feel compelled to answer that." He followed this by calling out to his cousin: "Edward, you fool, it's us. Victoria and me."

"I heard a gun being fired," he called back from his hiding place, obviously around the far corner of the Atherton house.

Again, Spencer muttered something no doubt unflattering under his breath. "We heard a gun being fired, too," he called out. "Why do you think we're out here?"

"You came rushing out to the middle of the street, after hearing a gun being fired? That doesn't seem too brilliant."

"We did not simply rush outside, Edward," Spencer was saying. "And, apparently, whoever fired a gun did so in no relation to us because there appears to be no danger out here now except for that which *you* pose. Furthermore, since you mentioned being less than brilliant, Your Lordship, I feel compelled to point out that you cannot, by yourself, surround three people—"

"Two people and a dog," Victoria corrected . . . without thinking.

Spencer darted his exasperated gaze her way but said nothing to her as he continued his harangue of his cousin. "Unless you have enlisted the horses on your side and have armed them and conveyed your intentions to them somehow and spread them out around us, you alone cannot have us surrounded, Edward."

To Victoria's ear, Spencer sounded like an angry little boy who has been forced, yet again, to stop the game in progress and explain, once more, the simple rules to a particularly dull playmate. With Spencer, she waited for Edward's reply. He always had one. But this time . . . nothing. She looked to Spencer, who quirked his lips together in a clear sign of impatience.

"Edward?" Spencer's sharp bark of sound was met with continued silence. Victoria heard the metallic clicking that she recognized as that of a gun being cocked . . . and it was Spencer doing so. A sudden resurgence of fear tightened her chest and her grip on her gun.

Just then, Neville passed into her line of vision as he padded back across the street. His business in the square apparently conducted, the bloodhound stopped on the sidewalk in front of the Atherton house. His great head was cocked to one side in curiosity as he stared approximately where Edward would make an appearance, if he actually did. As the dog's tail stopped wagging and he gave an impression of heightened wariness, something fearful quickened inside Victoria.

"Edward?" Spencer called out again, his tone exploratory. He waited another second or two and then added, "Come out this instant before I feel compelled to come over there and thrash the daylights out of you."

And still, nothing happened. Victoria spared Neville another glance. He stood stock-still, every muscle tensed, his head up and alert. Victoria moved closer to Spencer and clutched at his sleeve. "Spencer," she all but whispered, "look at Neville."

Though Spencer never looked away from the far corner of the Atherton house across the way, he said: "I see him. Get behind me." He darted his gaze to her. "And don't argue."

"But Neville, Spencer," she whimpered, frightened for them all.

"He's a smart dog. A fighter. He can take care of himself. Now, do it, Victoria. Get behind me. And try not to shoot me in the back with that gun you're dangling about."

Minding her weapon, Victoria did as ordered and positioned herself behind her husband . . . but she did peek around his solid bulk. Several quiet seconds ticked off the clock. Nothing happened. Then, one second he wasn't there, and the next he was. Edward appeared from around the side of the house, weaponless, his hands in the air. "Oh, Spencer, I don't like how this looks," Victoria whispered.

"I don't, either," Spencer drawled, his attention still fixed on his cousin. "Victoria, quickly now, get away from me and go to the square. Hurry. Get behind a tree and stay there until . . . it's all over and I tell you to come out."

Fearful heartache gripped her. "No, I will not, Spencer. I won't leave you. I won't. Whatever happens, we'll face it together."

"This is no time for silly bravery, Victoria. Now, go."

"You're the one being brave and silly, making yourself a target like this. Don't think I don't know what you're doing. I won't go unless you go with me."

Spencer made a sound of disgust. "I cannot run and hide.

It's too late for that. Whoever is responsible—and I think we both know who is—for Edward being unarmed and with his hands up has already seen us, or he wouldn't have a need to present Edward as his hostage. I am in a stronger position to remain standing here where he can clearly see me and so may not feel a need to do something dramatic and fatal, like shoot Edward, to get me to show my—"

He'd cut off his own words and inhaled sharply. "Look who's decided to join Edward. Just as we feared."

Victoria directed her gaze southward to the Atherton house and saw, standing close behind Edward, a tall, brown-haired man.

"Oh, *no*," she said on her exhalation. Though she wasn't the least bit surprised, though they'd been expecting him all along, she was still shocked. Here then was the showdown. It just didn't seem real, not here in the quiet, elegant streets of Savannah, surrounded by tall oaks and neat beds of flowers. "Loyal Atherton. As sure as I'm alive, he's got a gun on Edward."

"Yes, he does."

From the angle of Edward's bent head, it was obvious to Victoria that Loyal was talking to him. Apparently, the heartless villain thought his appearance and the gun he held to Edward's back was sufficient to keep her and Spencer in place for the moment. And he was right—it was. "What is Edward doing?"

"If I know him, he's trying to talk the *honorable*"—this said very sarcastically—"Mr. Atherton out of killing him and me. I don't think he's going to be able to do so, not at this late date."

Though despair filled her, making her want to lie down in the middle of the street and curl up in a tiny, whimpering ball, Victoria stood strong. "Sometimes I wish Miss Cicely was wrong, Spencer. She said he would be here. He was the one who fired that gun, wasn't he?"

"Yes. He was shooting at us is my guess. And I suspect—

belatedly, stupidly—that there's a brick on the Atherton house, one right next to the parlor window, with a chunk shot out of it. He saw us inside, embracing, became enraged and fired his gun; then heard Edward coming, ran off around the near corner of his house and circled around behind him. It's the only thing that makes sense. However, if the man is a poor enough marksman to miss a target the size of that plate-glass window, then there is hope for us all."

What he didn't say, but what Victoria realized, was there was hope for her and Spencer, standing so far away, but not for Edward, who stood mere inches from Loyal. "I hate this, Spencer, that it would come to this. All this time I thought it had to do with Jefferson—"

"It does. But Mr. Atherton has needed you for his scheme to work. And now, with you married, it's all fallen apart . . . unless he can eliminate me—and Edward, an inconvenient witness—then concoct some story for the public and the law, and coerce you into marrying him."

"I would never—"

"I know that. But he's insane, remember. And that makes him very dangerous."

Victoria's next thought brought determination to her stance. She stood taller. What she intended to do next might be foolhardy, or much worse, but she had to make the attempt. "All right, then, it's me he wants." Gathering her courage, she stepped around Spencer's protective body. "I'll go to him. I'll talk to him, tell him about the baby and make him see— Ack!"

Spencer had pulled her to him. His nose was now mere inches from hers as he snarled: "Over my dead body, Victoria."

"That is exactly what I'm trying to avoid, Spencer," she hissed.

"Once he gets you, he'll have no qualms about killing me and Edward."

Though her knees went watery with fear, Victoria stuck to her determination to be the one to end this awful scene.

"But he has no qualms now. You said so yourself." She was very nearly in tears. "Let me go to him. Maybe I can reason with him—"

"You are going nowhere near that Atherton bastard! I will die first."

Victoria hit his arm hard with her fist. "You big, idiot man, I will not just stand here and allow—"

"Stop it." His grip on her had tightened. "We have to see what Loyal Atherton wants, Victoria. We don't have a choice. We must be alert and smart—and look for a chance."

"What chance? He has Edward, as you said."

"But Edward is not without his tricks. He's eluded more than one angry man with a gun pointed at him. Usually it was an irate husband, granted. But, nevertheless, Edward is experienced. I think our other chance lies with Neville, whom our villain seems to be ignoring."

"Neville?" Victoria made a feint to turn to see. "Where is Neville—?"

"Don't look. Not yet." Spencer's tug on her arm gained him her attention. "Does Neville like Loyal Atherton?"

"No. Not since Loyal kicked him when Neville was no more than a half-grown puppy and made a mistake when Jeff and Loyal were hunting. Neville never got over it. We had to lock him up when Loyal visited. Neville would actually stalk him and try to bite him."

Looking grim, though satisfied, Spencer nodded. "That explains his behavior now." With a wag of his chin, he indicated the direction of the Atherton house. "Be very discreet, but look at your dog."

Victoria did, shifting her gaze from the two men across the street to Neville. He had vacated the street and was padding quietly up the steps to the porch of the Atherton house. He could, and in one great bound, Victoria reasoned, jump up onto the wide, flat top of the porch rail and, from there, launch himself onto Loyal—who was armed and hated the dog.

Victoria's heart nearly stopped beating . . . all this crazy bravery on the part of her men. If they all survived this, she intended to kill every one of them herself for putting her through this. Despair entered her heart, telling her she was the one who had set them on the path that led inexorably to being here at this moment and with no other choices facing them. The pain of that knowledge was almost more than she could bear. She had to do something to end this—

"Sorry, old man, for this," Edward suddenly called out to Spencer.

Spencer shoved Victoria behind him. "Here we go," he whispered to her. Victoria again poked her head around her husband's solid body, just enough to see. Spencer called out to his cousin: "No need to apologize. I'll take it out of your hide later, Your Lordship."

"I certainly hope you get the chance, Your Grace—Aww." Edward's abrupt sound of pain and awkward twist of his body came as Loyal evidently shoved the butt of his pistol into the earl's back.

"Shut up," Loyal growled at Edward, loud enough for his voice to carry. "I am done arguing with you, sir." He then focused on Spencer. "You will get rid of your weapon, Your Grace, or I'll use mine on the earl. Throw your gun over to the grass in the square. Do it now."

Spencer hesitated only a second before tossing his gun away, just as Loyal had ordered. Victoria's mind shrieked an instant protest for her now-unarmed husband. Reacting on daring instinct, yet terrified her suddenly nerveless and fumbling fingers would cause her to drop her gun to the street, Victoria stealthily poked it in the back of Spencer's waistband.

He inhaled sharply. "Victoria, what are you doing? You might need your gun—"

"No. Shhh. It's all right," she whispered back. "I have another one with me. It's stuck in my pants pocket."

Standing tall and brave, Spencer grunted a chuckle. "You

are a wonderfully cunning woman, Victoria Whitfield. And very frightening."

Smiling, overcome, she momentarily allowed herself the comfort of touching Spencer. Pressing her palm against his back and feeling his muscled warmth, she kissed him through his shirt. "I love you," she whispered, hoping against hope that Spencer did not have to find out that she had lied. She didn't have another weapon on her.

"Victoria! Come over here right now."

Loyal Atherton's shouted order thoroughly incensed Victoria. *How dare he?* "I will *not*. You can go straight to hell in a handbasket, Loyal Atherton."

Spencer inhaled sharply. "Are you certain it's wise to—"

"Hush," she whispered urgently. "Maybe I can fix this." She then said loudly: "Loyal, you put that gun down right now, you hear me? We know everything you've done, but nothing's happened yet that can't be forgiven. But if you shoot one of us, you can't take that back."

"But I'm not going to shoot *you,* Victoria. I love you and need you."

"You *what*?" Anger and outrage propelled Victoria around Spencer. She heard him gasp and felt him reach for her, but she surged forward, out of his reach. As she talked, she walked . . . slowly, threateningly, toward Loyal Atherton. "You don't *need* me, Loyal. What you need is for me to marry you so you'll have access to my daddy's money."

"What are you talking about, Victoria? That's not true." Loyal pulled Edward back a few steps with him.

"It is true. All those shady deals you got mixed up in— and involved my brother in—are losing money now. You're going to be exposed to all of Savannah and ruined. A lot of these fine people here are going to lose money, too, based on your schemes. Why, they'll tar and feather you, if they don't lynch you first."

"You're talking crazy, Victoria." Loyal sounded scared

and a little erratic. He couldn't seem to settle his gaze on her. Instead, he kept looking from Victoria to Edward and over his own shoulder. "That Englishman has turned your mind against me—"

"No he hasn't, Loyal. My mind was turned against you long before I ever knew my husband."

"Don't call him your husband!" Clearly agitated now, and still clutching the back of Edward's frock coat, Loyal pulled him back several more steps with him.

He was retreating from her, Victoria realized. Was he afraid of her? It could be, but though her heart raced with fear, too, Victoria knew she could not let it show on her face or in her voice. Right now the only weapon she had was her bravado. "But I have to call him my husband, Loyal, because he is. And I'm going to have his baby. You wouldn't shoot a pregnant woman, would you? Not one you need because of her daddy's money?"

While Loyal made strangled noises of shock or disbelief, Victoria chanced a darting look into Edward's brown eyes and saw equal measures of fear and admiration there. With no more than a quirk of her lips, she smilingly acknowledged his trust in her. Edward flicked his eyes to his right. What . . . ? Victoria tested the limits of her peripheral vision—and caught a glimpse of her husband close behind her. No wonder Loyal was retreating. But for how long would he? How long, or how far, would it take for him to remember he had the advantage in his grip? The Earl of Roxley.

"We'll get rid of these two now, Victoria," Loyal argued, indicating with nods of his head Spencer and Edward. "And when this baby comes, we'll get rid of it, too. I'll give you other babies. You won't even miss it."

Even as she heard Spencer's gasp and saw Edward's outraged expression, Victoria fought a scream of horror. Dear God, the lengths he would go to in order to get what he wanted! Victoria had all she could do not to drop to her knees and retch. Now that she was close enough to see the huge bruise on Loyal's jaw where Spencer had hit him days ago, Victoria wished she'd never stopped Spencer from pounding the life out of him.

"No, Loyal, you won't give me babies." Her voice was a snarl of contempt and disgust. "The idea alone of you ever touching me again makes my skin crawl."

"Don't say that, Victoria." Loyal's shout of emotional pain was somehow inhuman. His brown eyes appeared hollow and sunken into their sockets. But then, his expression hardened. "If you keep saying lies like that, Victoria, I'll shoot this man right here, right now, in the back of the head." He moved his gun to the back of Edward's head. "You know you love me. Don't lie!"

"No, don't!" Terrified, sweating, weak in her knees, Victoria held a placating hand out to Loyal. She'd gone too far. Quickly, she backtracked. "All right, Loyal, I won't lie. But you have to tell me the truth, too. Remember, I know how you need my money to cover your losses and your bad business deals."

Peering around Edward, who was shorter than he was, Loyal protested: "It's not just money, Victoria. I love you. I do."

She realized then that he probably did, in his own sick and twisted way. But just the thought of it made her want to die . . . or bathe. "Then why are you doing all of this, Loyal? Why? Think of the people you've hurt—"

"I haven't hurt anyone." For whatever reason, perhaps a tired arm, he lowered his gun from Edward's head, but only so far as his back.

"But you *have*." Victoria's voice choked on her emotion. "You hurt my brother, and he loved *you* like a brother. And Jenny . . . Oh, Loyal, how could you have made her write such a letter as you did? How could you take advantage of her and Jeff's pain like that? How?"

"So you found Jenny." It wasn't a question. Loyal's frown of distaste twisted his features into an ugly mask.

Victoria shook her head. "No. Jenny found her way home in the middle of the night, and Miss Cicely sent for me this morning. Jenny told me all about how you'd been holding her prisoner so my brother and Jenny's family wouldn't act against you. But Jenny escaped that sharecropper's cabin where you took her. We know all about Tillie's family being paid to hold her and keep their mouths shut. We also know how Tillie kept you informed of our comings and goings. She put the notes on my pillow, too. Oh, Loyal, my mother is going to be very hurt that her compassion for Tillie was so abused."

"Compassion? How much compassion would she have had for that colored child of Jeff's and Jenny's? That's right—he and Jenny are lovers. How's your lily-white mother going to feel about that?"

So close was she now to Loyal and Edward that Victoria had to stop walking or run up against them. Loyal could go no farther, either. One more step and he would be off the sidewalk and literally in the tall and woody shrubs that fronted his house. Victoria, despite her heightened emotions, was very much aware of Edward in front of her, Spencer at her back, and Neville, hidden off to her right. While Edward and Spencer might realize what she was doing, she knew the dog didn't—and he could jump at any moment. If he did, they'd better all be ready.

"I don't how she'll feel about that, Loyal. But I know about Sofie. And I know Jeff should never have confided in you all those years ago about her. But Jenny told me the truth: Sofie died from a high fever when she was an infant. I know now that my brother loves Jenny and that's why he's never married. He can't bring himself to abandon the one woman he does love. And you knew that. And you waited, all these years, to use that knowledge against him. How could you? You ought to be glad Jefferson isn't here right now because he'd tear your head off and feed it to my daddy's hogs."

"Ha. Jefferson's a coward. He's not going to do a thing. I could always make him do what I wanted."

"Jeff couldn't do anything, not with you holding Jenny and as good as blackmailing him."

"I never did. Jeff and I were going to be business partners, and I was going to be married to you. We had it all planned out. Your whole family wanted that at one time. I could have had the respect and standing in this city that I deserve—"

"But you do have that." The suspense of wondering when Neville would jump had Victoria on edge. There was no way she could call the dog off—and no way the dog could know that his jumping on his old enemy could get Edward, and maybe her and Spencer, killed.

"I don't have standing in Savannah," Loyal cried. "You know that. In this city, if your family didn't come over from England with Oglethorpe, you're a newcomer. An outsider. I was tolerated, but I was never accepted, not in the ways that mattered."

Though she knew he was right—Savannah was endearingly, maddeningly that way—she still asked, just stalling for time: "What ways are those, Loyal?"

"In the men's societies and the social circles and in the finest homes—"

"But you had access to all of those."

"Only because of your family's influence and insistence on my inclusion. But then you ruined everything when you wouldn't have me. And now I'm an outcast. The invitations don't come anymore. And I'm going to lose everything. Because of you."

"No, Loyal. You're going to lose everything because of *you*. Because of your own crookedness and weakness and illegal business deals. And the scandal you caused regarding me. The good people of Savannah will see you now for what you really are—a scoundrel. None of this is my fault. It's all yours."

Loyal had been getting more and more upset. Spittle flecked the corners of his mouth, and his eyes were wild with insanity . . . but then he calmed and stared at Victoria, his expression showing he'd suffered a revelation. "Yes it is. It is your fault. I should have thought of that. *You're* the one I should kill."

"You'd make a big mistake in killing her, Mr. Atherton," Spencer said, his voice a low growl of warning as he drew the man's attention his way.

"Brave words coming from an unarmed man," Loyal Atherton taunted, laughing crazily and shoving Edward forward a step as if to prove he knew he had the advantage.

"Not so unarmed as you'd think." Spencer pulled Victoria to him and backed up several steps. He needed space and distance . . . for accuracy. As he did, he reached behind him with his other hand, freed the pistol Victoria had stuck in his waistband—and pointed it at her head. Her gasp of shock accompanied Edward's and even Loyal Atherton's.

"Spencer, what are you doing!" she cried.

"My God, man!" Edward blurted, looking horrified. "Have you taken leave of your senses?"

Spencer ignored the cries of protest. He kept his attention riveted on Loyal Atherton, even as he cocked the pistol he held to his wife's head. Not even her shaking body and her whimpers of fear could distract him. "Release my cousin, Mr. Atherton, and I mean right now. I'm willing to trade Victoria for his life. You let him go, I'll give her over to you—"

"No, Spencer. Oh, God, no," Victoria cried. "What are you saying? Why are you doing this? I love you!"

"Shut up, Victoria." Spencer said it savagely and then continued his conversation with Loyal Atherton. "Once my cousin is free and you allow us to leave, Mr. Atherton, what happens thereafter—right here, between you and Jefferson Redmond or Mr. Redmond, or all of Savannah, for that matter—will be none of my concern."

"Spencer, what has got into you?" Edward's mouth pulled down with abject disappointment. "I would rather die at this man's hand than be any part of your heinous scheme. Have you no honor?"

"I'm trying to save your life, Edward. I'd think you'd be grateful."

"Grateful? If this man does turn me loose, I'll kill you myself. I swear I will."

Spencer's expression never changed. "You can try." He turned his attention back to Loyal Atherton.

The color had bled from the man's face, and his gaze darted from Victoria's ineffectually wriggling body in Spencer's grasp to Spencer himself. "You're bluffing. You wouldn't shoot her."

"I might. And where would that leave you? You still need her for your plan to work. I, however, no longer need her. I have her dowry. And I'm certain Mr. Redmond would be willing to settle another sizable one on her. If she marries you, Mr. Redmond is likely to cover your debts and hush a scandal up, if only for his daughter's sake. After all, he did just that for me."

Victoria wrenched ineffectually in his grasp. Her voice choked with tears. "My father never would! He'd kill you first, Loyal Atherton. I'll tell him the truth of what you did to me and how it really happened. And I promise you he'll come after you—"

"Shut up, Victoria." Spencer flexed the arm he had around her middle, effectively whooshing her air out and quieting her. She went limp, her feet stumbling over his. Spencer relaxed his grip but still held on to her tightly.

"Victoria's right," Loyal Atherton said, not loosening his

grip on Edward. "And how could I marry her, if she's married to you?"

Spencer felt a thrill race through him. The crazy bastard was listening to him. This just might work. In only moments, Edward could be freed, and this awful business concluded. "I will have our marriage annulled."

"Why would you do that? How could you?"

"Simple. You see—and this is why I'll be pleased to bargain her life for my cousin's—the baby she carries is yours, not mine." Spencer watched as Loyal Atherton's and Edward's mouths became perfect O's. He felt Victoria freeze in his grip. "She knew it when she married me. That makes our marriage a sham, so an annulment will be easy. And you forget . . . I am a duke, which means the matter can be expedited."

"If this is true, why did you accost me the other day? Why were you so jealous? You act now as if you don't care about her, but you certainly did that day."

"True," Spencer said smoothly, "but I was merely pretending to care about her until I had reasoned this situation out. I only hit you once, which was all I intended to do, and that only as a mere show. It would be expected because you were, after all, kissing my wife. But Victoria quickly came to *your* defense and hit *me* over my head with a flower vase. You sustained a bruised jaw, sir. But I fell victim to a concussion at her hands."

"I should have killed you," Victoria said quite clearly. Spencer ignored her, still watching Loyal Atherton . . . and waiting.

"When did you find out the baby was mine?" he asked.

"She has been pregnant since we've been married. Whose baby do you think it is? Certainly not mine."

Edward shook his head slowly and stared at Spencer as if he'd never seen him before. Spencer spared him but a glance looking past him to his captor, whose expression reflected his consideration of Spencer's details. "You said she hit you to come to my defense. Why would she do that when she wouldn't even have me? When she wouldn't marry me? Even a moment ago she said she hated me."

"And she may well. But if I won't have her and her baby is yours, I don't think her pride will stand in her way, do you? She'll marry you or raise a bastard."

"I'll raise a bastard," Victoria said, again quite clearly and unhelpfully. "But what I will *not* do is stand here another minute and listen to you. Personally, I hate you both, so *there*."

With that, she stomped down, apparently as hard as she could, on Spencer's arch and ground her heel against his bones. Bellowing, he jerked back. She whirled out of his grasp and gave a piercing whistle, followed by: "Sic 'im, boy. Get 'im, Neville! Now!"

In a flying leap that stretched his body out to its capacity, the dog, all teeth and snarls, jumped off the porch. In the next second, a gun fired, the dog yelped piteously, twisted in the air, and landed with a thud in a flowerbed. Victoria screamed and grabbed the gun out of Spencer's numb hand. "Victoria, no!" he shouted hoarsely.

He grabbed for her, but she was too quick for him as she whirled on Loyal Atherton and held the pistol in both hands, out in front of her and at shoulder height. "You son of a bitch! You killed my dog!"

Spencer overcame his shock enough to turn to Edward and Loyal. The two men were involved in a rousing bout of fisticuffs. Instant logic told Spencer that when Loyal had moved the gun away from Edward to shoot Neville, Edward had turned on the man and grabbed his gun hand, which he now held up, his arm stretched out, in an ineffectual pose. Hitting each other with their free hands, they turned around and around—and kept Victoria from getting off a clean shot. But she was trying. She kept circling them and looking. The expression on her face said no one had better interfere.

Spencer did the only thing he could do. He tackled Edward and Loyal, sending them all three flying out into the bruising street, which fortunately was not paved with cobblestones. They landed hard, grunting and struggling and teeth bared. Over and over they rolled, an intimate mass of three sweating, frantic bodies, all punching the other and trying for the gun and no one winning. It seemed to go on forever. Then, suddenly and somehow, Loyal Atherton broke away—and still had the gun. He staggered to his feet and stood looking down on Edward and Spencer there on the hard-packed dirt of the street. His gun was trained on them both . . . his finger was on the trigger.

"Loyal." It was just a single word, said almost quietly.

The man's head came up; he seemed to be listening.

"Turn around, Loyal. Like you said, I'm the one you should kill, not them. And you have to admit, this has been a long time coming between me and you."

Spencer scrambled to untangle himself from Edward. But his limbs seemed weighted with lead, his movements slow. He could not extricate himself. Fear seized him . . . there was nothing he could do in time to save her. Victoria was going to die, right here in front of him. Spencer bellowed "No!" as Loyal Atherton, his intentions plain on his scratched and reddened and snarling face, spun around to Victoria, his gun held at the ready.

Two shots rang out, unnaturally loud and echoing in the otherwise deserted streets of Savannah. Time stood still; Spencer's heart froze. Then, Loyal Atherton staggered back but still stood on his feet, his back to Spencer and Edward, who had grabbed Spencer's arm in terror. Suddenly, the man's bones seemed to melt as he did a slow spin, turning to face Spencer and Edward.

A bloom of bright red spread down his shirt from his shoulder . . . but there was also a neat, round bullet hole that marked the exact center of his forehead. He fell dead to the ground, his body bouncing once before it lay still, not two feet from Spencer and Edward. With him no longer blocking their view, Spencer, along with his cousin, jerked his attention to Victoria, who'd obviously fired twice to Loyal's none.

Staring back at them, she stood unwounded, the smoking gun in her hand, and said, quite calmly: "He shot my dog."

CHAPTER 22

It was a week later, the night before the duke and duchess's combined and now quite sizable entourage would travel into Savannah, first thing in the morning, from River's End and board a steamship on which Mr. Milton, at the duke's behest, had booked their passage back to England. The tedious packing had been done by Rosanna and Hornsby, with Victoria's and Spencer's help . . . until they'd been dismissed. The result of all the lady's maid's and the valet's labor was an incredible mound of traveling trunks and soft-sided bags downstairs to be loaded tomorrow morning onto the heavy dray wagons.

As the Redmonds could not be dissuaded—they would all three of them accompany the traveling party to the docks—every River's End carriage and driver had been pressed into service to transport them all. The slower drays, carrying the luggage, would leave earlier than the party itself, just to ensure no tardiness, which could cause them to miss the ship or have to leave their luggage behind. Absolutely unthinkable.

But that was tomorrow. Sweetly sated from their lovemaking, Victoria still had the rest of tonight alone with her husband . . . in bed. Following many days of his pleading, and her ignoring him, she had finally forgiven him for his shocking ploy—admittedly brilliant but hardly endearing—of offering her life to Loyal Atherton in exchange for Edward's. With the entire household's nerves on edge, finally, her father—dubbing Spencer "you poor bastard"—had taken the distraught man aside and held a closed-door discussion with him. Mr. Redmond, a man more senior in these matters, had evidently told Spencer to spend every penny he owned until his wife was happy.

He was also advised to grovel on his damned knees, if necessary, to appease her. Otherwise, he could expect many nights of sleeping alone and just as many days of a veritable living hell on earth. Victoria knew this was what had been told to her husband because her mother had passed her tactics on to her daughter in their discussions of how to behave as a wife.

So now, all was forgiven, and here the duke and duchess lay, naked, their limbs entwined and their bodies tangled in the covering sheet. Victoria lay on her side, her head resting against Spencer's shoulder, an arm and a leg thrown over his chest and his legs. She loved the contrast of their bodies; how his was so powerful yet gentle; how his muscles were so firm yet warm; and how the sprinkling of short black hairs on his chest narrowed in a funnel pattern down to his navel. Lying on his back, an arm wrapped around Victoria's shoulders, he gently rubbed her arm and made her feel safe and happy and loved. For some time now, they'd stared quietly out the opened windows across the way at the full moon silvering the earth below and shining a bright light into the bedroom.

"Have I said yet," Spencer said into the quiet, "how glad I was to return to River's End last week, on that fateful day, to find Jefferson had taken your parents aside and confided the entire truth to them? I cannot imagine us having returned here from Savannah, in the shape we were in, and having to sort all the details for them. Though I gladly would have done, had that been the case. Still, I was glad."

"Yes, you have said. Every night."

"I am tedious, aren't I?"

"No. Just glad. I was equally glad the barbecue was over and the guests were leaving."

"Thank heavens for that back road you knew which kept us out of the departing guests' sight. We would have had to explain to each and every carriageful what the devil we were doing out there and why you were in men's clothing."

"You didn't have to burn them."

"Yes I did. Are you certain you're ready to make the trip back to Wetherington's Point tomorrow, Victoria?"

He'd asked her this, too, maybe twenty times in the past week. She grinned, knowing he couldn't see her do so. "Do you mean am I packed; am I ready to leave my family; or am I feeling up to the trip?"

"All of those, I suppose."

"Well, let's see." She ticked her points off by tapping her fingernails against Spencer's chest. "I haven't had any sickness for the past three or four days, so hopefully that will hold. And what else? Oh, yes—I cannot wait to see old Fredericks again. I have missed your butler. But my family . . . I'm never ready to leave them, I suppose."

"They'll be coming to England next spring to see the baby."

Victoria's heart gave a happy little flutter. "I know. I'm so happy about that. I will still miss them, though."

"Of course you will. It's been a most difficult visit for you, if one could call it a visit. More like a mission. Nothing restful about it."

"No. And in so many ways it didn't end well, did it?"

"It ended as well as one could expect. Crises are seldom settled amicably, Victoria, and hardly ever without some daunting results."

"I know." She shied away from unbidden images of Loyal Atherton's bleeding body and settled her thoughts instead on her brother. "I wish there was something we could do for Jeff and Jenny."

Spencer restlessly shifted his position on the bed but still held her close against him. "If there was, I would do it in a heartbeat, Victoria. I wish, too, there was something we could do for Jubal, stuck like that for all his life in a swamp."

Moved by his compassion, she planted a kiss on the firm, warm skin of his chest. "I know you would, and I love you all the more for it. But there isn't anything to be done."

Spencer was quiet a moment, pensively so. "I suppose he'll continue to go out to the swamp to see her."

He meant Jeff, she knew. "He'll have to. She made the decision to stay there with her mother and brother."

"I suppose, like her brother, I can hardly blame her, given how she's fared outside it."

"I know. And it's ironic, isn't it, Spencer? That a swamp could become a haven."

"Terribly. Your parents did try, though."

"Yes." The heartache only deepened for Victoria. "I ache for that little baby, Spencer. Sweet little Sofie. Poor Mama and Daddy . . . they lost a grandchild they could never publicly claim but never had the chance to love, either. But the shock of it all for them, to learn of Jeff and Jenny's love."

"Quite the test of their beliefs and convictions, I'd said. For all of us, actually."

"True. Miss Cicely was never happy with it, either. She knew if their love was found out, Jenny would pay a much steeper price than would Jeff. But Jenny loves Jeff, just as my parents love Jenny, so what can they say or do but worry?"

"It's not exactly a just world we live in, is it?"

"No. And then, poor Mama to suggest that Jenny come to River's End to live. Only then did she realize the depth of Jefferson's torment. 'In what capacity?' he asked her. 'A maid? A cook?' Mama had not known how to answer. 'She is as much my wife as Victoria is Spencer's,' he'd shouted. 'To be acknowledged as anything less is insulting.' "

"Yes. That was quite the painful supper gathering."

"How I hurt for them both. For all of us, really." A shiver slipped over Victoria's skin. "So much hatred in the world. To be hated for whom you love . . . I just can't imagine a worse thing."

"Nor can I."

"Do you suppose there will ever come a time when it's any different?"

"It's hard to see how, or even when, isn't it? We just don't seem to learn—and I mean as a species considered as a whole. But rest assured, my dear, that if you were confined to a swamp, I would make the trek, too—despite my admitted fear of alligators and water moccasins."

Victoria raised her head to look at him. "You'd do that for me? Pole a jonboat again? Travel through all that murk and fog just to see me? Why, you warm my heart, Your Grace." She laid her head again on his chest. "Not as much as it would if you'd said you'd come live with me there. But, nevertheless, you warm my heart."

Victoria felt Spencer slump as much as was possible while already lying down. He coupled this with groaning in good husbandly form. "Well, damn me for a fool. My thoughtless remark is going to cost me, isn't it?"

She patted his stomach. "I'm afraid so."

"But you have everything already." He sounded completely vexed, but Victoria knew better. "I know you do because I've already bought it—and two new traveling trunks to carry it all."

"You really had no choice, my love."

"Your father made that very plain to me." He now sounded like a suitably scolded schoolboy. "He told me a smart husband is terrified of his wife's anger or displeasure and will do whatever it takes to make certain he incurs neither. But should he, he must pay for it."

Biting back a chuckle, Victoria nodded her agreement. "Daddy is such a wise man."

"Yes, he is. He also worries about you, Victoria."

Again she raised her head to look into her husband's face. "Me? Why?"

"Why do you think? You were forced to take a life. He worries how this will haunt you. So do I."

Bombarded by conflicting emotions, Victoria rested her cheek against Spencer's shoulder . . . and said nothing.

Spencer hugged her close and kissed her forehead tenderly. "Your quietness speaks very loudly, my love. The man was a snake and deserved his fate. I only wish it had not been delivered by you. Taking a life, no matter how despicable the person, is an awful guilt to live with. And no, I've never taken a life, but one doesn't have to do so to imagine how it must feel. But you must forgive yourself, Victoria. Had you not killed him, he would have killed all three of us. You did the only thing you could."

"My head knows that, Spencer, but it's harder for my heart to accept. It feels like a stain on my soul." Now that she was talking about it, the confession flowed. "Do you know what scares me the most, Spencer? I did it so cavalierly. It was so . . . easy. And I have no regrets. Shouldn't I? Is something wrong with me, do you suppose?"

He chuckled. "Nothing is wrong with you. I hardly think you're likely to take to a life of crime and murder, my dear. If you have no regrets, couldn't it be because you are convinced, deep in your heart, of the rightness of your actions? Think of all the ways Loyal Atherton harmed you and your family and Miss Cicely's, as well. He wasn't going to stop, Victoria. Instead, he had to be stopped. And if you will remember, you did give him a chance. You told him to put his gun down because he'd done nothing yet that couldn't be forgiven. Do you remember?"

"Yes." She was listening . . . and feeling better.

"Good. And do you remember that he did not take the

olive branch that you extended to him? He chose evil over forgiveness. The decision was his, and he left you no choice. In a way, that was the last indignity he suffered upon you. Don't let him win, Victoria. Put him from your heart and mind."

Feeling her emotions boiling to the surface, Victoria reached out to Spencer, smoothing her arm up his chest to wrap her hand around his neck. She could feel the steady throb of his pulse there and felt comforted for it. "My father is not the only wise man in this household. Nor is he the most loved."

"You melt my heart, Victoria. I love you." Spencer's voice rang with the sincerity of his declaration. "But one last word regarding your father. I have been pleased to learn that he and his business partners are going to be able to recoup most of the money lost to those bad investments that involved Jefferson."

"I hate Loyal Atherton for that, too."

Spencer patted her shoulder. "That's the spirit, my love. He was very deserving of your hatred. The man did shoot your dog."

Victoria's heart turned over. "Oh . . . poor Neville. I can hardly stand to talk about that awful moment." Thinking of the brave bloodhound, Victoria pulled away from Spencer and rolled over onto her other side. Then, peering over the side of the bed, she patted the mattress. "Come here, Neville. Come here, boy."

The dog, his chest bandaged all around and very much the pampered hero in the household, reclined on the rag rug beside the bed. True to form, he merely raised his head now, stared at Victoria tiredly, and flopped his head back down.

Tsking her opinion of that, Victoria returned to her original position in her husband's embrace. "You'd think a bloodhound making a first-class crossing to England, in our cabin, no less, would be more grateful."

Neville's going to England with them was one of the concessions Spencer had made. Victoria heard it in his sigh. "Perhaps once his wound heals—Dr. Hollis did a wonderful job on him, by the way—and Neville sees the English-bloodhound ladies, he'll perk up."

"I expect he'll enrich the bloodlines over there as well. And make much better trackers of those English dogs."

Spencer ran his hand down her side and pinched her bottom, eliciting a squawk out of her. "I have already lost that argument, madam. I refuse to have it again."

"Yes, Your Grace. But do you think Sven will like England?"

"Sven? Who the devil is Sven?"

"The cook from my father's house in Savannah."

"Oh, yes. The man who boils nothing. You of course realize you are starting a war with my cook."

"Maybe Mrs. Pike will take to him, and they'll fall in love."

"Oh, perish the thought. Have you *seen* her, Victoria? Mrs. Pike was old when your Oglethorpe was a boy."

"That's true. Then maybe Mrs. Kevins will fall in love with him."

"Who the devil is Mrs. Kevins?"

"You are hopeless. The housekeeper I hired for Wetherington's Point before I left."

"Oh, that's right. I believe Fredericks mentioned her. But what makes you think this Sven fellow will fall for her?"

"Have you *seen* Mrs. Kevins, Spencer? She's an attractive widow. Not that you are allowed to look at her."

Spencer's laugh rumbled pleasantly through his chest and vibrated against Victoria's ear and cheek. She hugged him closer to her. Sometimes she felt she could not be close enough to him even if she were to snuggle down inside his skin. "I am ready to go home, Spencer, and have you to myself. I'm ready to start our life together. Our new life."

"Yes, ours. Including our third little party."

"I'm so very excited about the baby, Spencer." She paused, hesitant to speak but deciding she should. "Do you . . . do you believe Miss Cicely, Spencer? I mean . . . what she said about the baby."

Spencer's hesitation had Victoria holding her breath. Finally, and with a lot less conviction than she would have liked, he said: "Yes, I believe her."

Victoria knew better. Her mouth suddenly felt dry and her heartbeat seemed too slow and ponderous. "There is no birthmark, is there?"

Spencer inhaled deeply and then exhaled slowly. "No."

Victoria lay still a moment, absorbing this. She realized she wasn't surprised by his answer. Without lifting her head, she angled her face up until she could look into Spencer's. "We can't tell Miss Cicely."

"Absolutely not."

"But the baby then, Spencer, we don't know—"

"We do, and it's mine. If you persist in arguing this point with me, I shall jump out the window over there and end my torment."

"Yes, Your Grace." Victoria smiled. "You know, I ought to pinch you hard over this. I ought to be very angry and throw things at you for tricking me and her like that."

"As you wish. Only, please don't aim for my head. I am already quite addled as it is. But, Victoria, did you tell her about the birthmark in one of your trips out there?"

"No, I didn't. I was as surprised as you were when she mentioned it."

"Hmm. Then I wonder how she knew to even mention it. Very strange."

"Why *did* you make up the story of the birthmark, Spencer? I suppose I can understand . . . but it seems so mean to me. Although you really had every right—"

"Victoria, allow me, darling. I don't know where it came from, the birthmark. It just came out of my mouth in anger. I suppose I wanted to see if in the face of such a definite way of knowing for certain who the father was or was not, you would recant your story and confess that you knew the baby was Loyal Atherton's. But you didn't. You didn't hesitate for a moment to say you still believed it might be mine. After that day, we didn't see each other again until I arrived here. And then, with Miss Cicely saying the baby was mine, I . . . came to believe. I don't know how else to state it. Except to say I believe it."

Though she was very moved by his loving testimony, Victoria wasn't quite finished with him. "Hmph, well, I began to suspect, you should know, when Edward didn't know about a Whitfield birthmark. As close as he is to you, he would have known."

"Yes, Edward. A veritable thorn in my side, as always. But, Victoria, can you forgive me for putting you through all that?"

She smoothed her hand across his chest, loving the feel of him. "I already have. We were different people then, Spencer. Only a matter of weeks, I know, but such . . . awful and wonderful weeks."

"They were. But they showed us how to make a marriage, didn't they? And all that is important to me now, Victoria, is I love you and the child you carry. He is mine as much as he is yours. Now, that said, we will not have this discussion again."

So very imperious he was—and absolutely astounding in his grace and nobility, two mantles he wore so easily. "Yes, Your Grace," Victoria said dutifully, her heart overflowing with love for this magnificent man. "And speaking of Edward and marriage, can you believe him with Lucinda Barrett?"

"Good Lord, could the man be more tedious? He sits and stares at the girl, a vacant expression on his face, and rubs her hand and even forgets to eat, unless made to do so."

"He's in love."

Spencer shook his head. "I never thought he would be. I

suppose it's just as well he's going to bring the girl along and present her to his mother. At least Miss Barrett's family is not accompanying us home. Still, I shudder to think what Edward will be like as a husband."

"He'll be wonderful. Lucinda will see to it."

"Having found myself in the clutches of a Savannah woman, a woman as beautiful as a magnolia blossom and as true as any oak that ever grew, I can attest to the fact that he will, indeed, be whipped into shape in short order."

Smiling wickedly, feeling the languid stirrings of desire deep inside her, Victoria slid her hand down her husband's chest, down his belly . . . lower . . . "Ah, you poor man. Has it been as bad as all that for you?"

A gasp and a husky chuckle accompanied Spencer's capturing her hand, which he raised to his lips and kissed. "I find your forwardness shocking, my dear duchess."

Victoria grinned seductively. "Do you, Your Grace?"

"Yes. Pleasantly so." With one swift, muscled movement, Spencer pulled Victoria's naked and willing body on top of him.

Feeling his growing, hardening response to her, trapped as it was between him and her, Victoria looked deep into Spencer's black and glittering eyes and responded instantly, heatedly. Holding herself up with her palms braced against his chest, she nipped his neck and jaw and chin with tiny biting kisses. "With that look on your face, Your Grace, you look just like a pirate, do you know that?"

"I should," he murmured, all the while rubbing and kneading her buttocks, lending to the act a deep hunger that spoke of pleasures to come. "My ancestors were reputed to be pirates."

Victoria pulled back, flinging her long hair over her shoulders with one graceful motion of her head. "Really? Pirates in your bloodlines? I am shocked. And quite . . . excited by that. Kiss me."

A wicked grin captured his mouth. "I am happy to oblige, madam."

Holding her to him, Spencer performed a neat flip and, in an instant, had her under him on the mattress, her long hair tangled in his arms and around her face. Chuckling, Spencer helped her move it to one side. Victoria adored the delicious weight of him atop her, and how his body fit so perfectly with hers, and how he always took such great care to be tender with her. Even now, he braced himself with his elbows on the bed and stared down into her face, his own suffused with an expression of deepening desire for her. "I love you, Victoria. Something . . . magical happened inside me when you came into your parents' parlor the day I arrived from England."

She gasped. "You felt that, too? Oh, Spencer, I was so afraid I was the only one. I saw you, and I *knew*. I just knew I was supposed to spend the rest of my life with you. I love you, John Spencer Whitfield."

Spencer lowered his head and claimed her mouth. The instant his mouth touched hers, a surge of stinging desire shot through Victoria, centering itself low in her belly, where it pulsed and throbbed. As Spencer's kiss deepened, as his tongue dueled with hers, Victoria squirmed against him, eager for him to claim her wholly. But Spencer held off entering her. He broke their kiss and slid down her willing body, kissing and suckling her skin as he went. Her swollen breasts, no longer sore and tender, ached for his attention, and he obliged, taking first one budded nipple into his mouth and then the other. His swirling kisses made her ache for him to kiss her elsewhere.

As always, he knew her thoughts, her secret desires . . . and lowered himself farther down her body until he was positioned between her legs. Victoria opened herself to him in a great act of trust . . . and invited him in. Almost reverently, Spencer bent his head to take her woman's place in his mouth, kissing her there with swirling lashes of his tongue until she cried out his name and felt so very hot all over, on fire inside with the rippling undulations of her satiation, unable to move . . . and then he pulled himself up and over her, finally, finally sliding himself inside her until he was completely sheathed in her love-slicked tightness.

"Oh, Spencer," she murmured, tossing her head from side to side. "Oh, please . . ."

"Whatever you want, my love." His whisper was guttural, possessive. "For all your life, Victoria . . . whatever you want."

She wrapped her arms and legs around him, arching her hips against him. She looked deep into his eyes. "Take me, Spencer. Make me yours."

"You have been mine since the first moment I laid eyes on you, Victoria. And I have been yours." And then, he began to move against her . . .

As her husband's passion seized her and lifted her to levels of joy she had never known existed, as his lovemaking removed from her heart and soul any awareness except of him, Victoria's last coherent thought, as the heat within her began again to build and build, was: Should she tell Spencer that Miss Cicely had also told her, privately, that Victoria carried not one baby . . . but two? And that this other baby was a girl child . . . one Victoria had promised her and Jenny and Jefferson she would name Sofie?